BROKEN LIKE YOU

LUNA PIERCE

playlist

WAIT FOR YOU - TOM WALKER & ZOE WEES

LET'S GO HOME TOGETHER - ELLA HENDERSON & TOM GRENNAN

ONE DAY - TATE MCRAE

US - JAMES BAY

TRAIN WRECK - JAMES ARTHUR

GLASS HEART - TOMMEE PROFITT & SAM TINNESZ

RICOCHET - STARSET

STARS - SIXX:A.M.

MIDNIGHT - COLDPLAY

ALWAYS IN MY HEAD - COLDPLAY

THE BEGINNING OF THE END - KLERGY & VALERIE BROUSSARD

DUSK TILL DAWN - MADILYN BAILEY

I FOUND YOU - HIPPIE SABOTAGE

TAG, YOU'RE IT - MELANIE MARTINEZ

FAKE - THE TECH THIEVES

ALL YOUR EXES - JULIA MICHAELS

THRONE - BRING ME THE HORIZON

WALKED THROUGH HELL - ANSON SEABRA

AS THE WORLD CAVES IN - SARAH COTHRAN

This is a work of fiction. Names, characters, places, and incidents either are the product of the author's imagination or are used fictitiously. Any resemblance to actual persons, living or dead, events, or locales is entirely coincidental.

Book Cover Design by Opulent Swag & Design
Proofing by Cruel Ink Editing
Proofing by Tiffany Hernandez
First Edition 2022
ISBN 978-1-957238-05-0 *(paperback)*
ASIN B0B234Z3MF *(ebook)*

"And when I felt like I was an old cardigan under someone's bed, you put me on and said I was your favorite." — Taylor Swift

PART I

1
CLAIRE

I never imagined the week leading to my freshman year of college would be spent shoving what minimal belongings I could into boxes to be shipped to my new home on the other side of the country. But here I am, doing exactly that. The plan was always to go to Turner University and live where I have my entire life: on the East Coast, at home with my dad.

I sigh and shove a book into the cardboard container.

Dad speaks up from his spot against the doorframe of my bedroom. "Those go in that one." He points across my messy space. "Here. Give it to me." He takes it from my hand and examines it. "H.P. Lovecraft? Haven't you read this a million times?"

I shrug. "It's my comfort item, don't judge me." Some girls have stuffed animals or blankets, but I have stories that weave their way into my soul and hold on tight.

"Fair enough." Dad tosses it in with the others and turns to face me. "Listen, kiddo. We don't have to go through with this. It's not too late to back out."

Biting my lip, I pull myself together and look him straight in his deep blue eyes. "Dad, you've been waiting on an opportunity like this your entire career. You're not going to blow it off because of me. I won't allow that. I'll be fine. Really."

Part of me would be lying if I said I wasn't upset about the massive change in my future, but it would be incredibly selfish of me to make my dad miss out on the professional opportunity of a lifetime because I couldn't accept the new cards I've been dealt. Especially when he's already given up so much to raise me by himself. It's time for him to spread his wings and do something for himself for a change. And although it sucks to have things change, I fully support him following through with this dream.

Sure, moving to the other side of the country, where I have zero friends and have never actually visited, is a bit of a challenge. But that's not the most difficult part to swallow—it's the having to move into my mom's condo and her offering to help with tuition for my first year of school.

To an outsider, this comes across like a totally normal thing. But, when your mother abandons you as a toddler to relocate thousands of miles away to become a flight attendant, and then proceeds to have nothing to do with you your entire life, you're not exactly jumping for joy when she volunteers to play the role of "parent."

A massive bright side is that her schedule is basically nonstop, so I probably won't have to actually interact with her much. Living in her house is one thing but having to stomach awkward small talk and pretend to not hate her guts to her face is another.

If anything, this will be like a year-long vacation where I can soak up some sun and work my ass off to get the scholarship I applied for. The one that will allow me to return to my hometown and finish out the rest of my higher education in the place where I intended.

"I'm going to run down to Charlie's and pick up our pizza.

You want me to grab you a milkshake?" Dad fumbles around in his pockets until he finds what he was looking for.

"Sure. Thanks, Dad." I scan the room, locating my backpack. I put my laptop inside and neatly wrap up a cell phone charger to go in the front compartment.

The steady thump of his footsteps trail down the steps and out of the house. It's not long before the door opens again. Only it can't be him, unless he forgot something.

"Claire," a voice calls out. "You up there?" Footsteps pound up the stairs and into my room.

I take a breath to steady my pounding heartbeat, the reaction I always have with Griffin, my boyfriend. You never know which version of him you'll get. I'm constantly crossing my fingers that it's the sweet and romantic one. Most of the time, especially lately, I'm wrong.

It wasn't always this way. In the beginning, Griffin was good to me. He was kind and thoughtful and even made me laugh. Over time, though, the niceness faded and now…now I can't wrap my head around how I got to be so *stuck*. I've clung to the idea that the good Griff would come back, that I was just dealing with a temporary version of him. And in a way, he does return. I see it in waves. Blips of good moments with him. But they're fleeting and becoming fewer and further between. I'm not sure how much longer I can hold out hope that it will ever stick.

"Hey, babe." Griffin comes closer, grabbing my hand and pulling me from the ground. He drags me in for a hug and leans in to kiss my cheek.

Immediately, I sense the shift in his mood.

"What? No warm greeting for your man? Isn't your flight in a few hours? This is how you want to say goodbye?" He runs his palms down my shoulders and onto my forearms, gripping them tightly.

Too tightly.

"Griff, stop. You know I'm just stressed out." I try to pull my arms away, but he doesn't let go. I glance up at his stone-cold gaze, his ashy blond hair cascading down his forehead. "You're hurting me." I tug again with no success. "Seriously, cut it out." Tears well in my eyes at the force of his fingers pressing into my skin.

"Come here," he says through his clenched jaw, jerking me against his body.

The front door slams shut and with it, Griffin seems to snap out of his trance. If it weren't for the intrusion, I'm not sure he would have let go. That thought alone sends a chill down my spine.

"Let's eat." A wicked smile snakes itself onto his face; a face that I once thought was beautiful.

I swallow down the familiar anxiety that comes with his presence.

It's not that I *want* to stay with him, to continue being this person he torments, but I'm also not stupid enough to think that breaking up with him will be an easy feat.

I'm hopeful that with a couple thousand miles between us, I'll find the courage to finally rip his claws out of me. I'm a silver-lining kind of girl, and maybe this will be the chance I need to get him out of my life for good.

Griffin snatches a light-gray sweatshirt off the chair by my desk and extends it toward me. "You look cold."

I blink at him in confusion but take it anyway. It's not until my arm is stretched out to grab it that I see the finger marks already appearing on my skin. Sure enough, that's going to bruise.

I pull the thing over my head and tug the sleeves down to my wrists. I glance in the mirror and free my long, mud-colored hair, only to secure it in a low ponytail.

Griffin raises his hand near my face, and I instinctually flinch.

He's never outright hit me, but I wouldn't put it past him. Not anymore.

He loops his finger under the scrunchie and yanks it out. "I like it better down."

I step off the plane and immediately take in the drastically warmer air. It's different than back home, much drier than that of the humid East Coast. I've never really been a fan of colder weather, so skipping a snowy winter is another perk of being out west.

In reality, this whole experience wouldn't be terrible if I had a semi-normal relationship with my mother and visited enough to be comfortable with the area. Being thrown into this on such short notice has been a shock to my system.

Life is full of the unexpected though, and if I intend on doing this whole *adult* thing, I have to be resilient.

I turn my phone off airplane mode and order myself a ride to my mom's place. Of course, she couldn't be bothered to rearrange her work schedule to welcome her estranged daughter to her home.

Countless texts pop across my screen, but I swipe them away to finish my task. They're all from Griffin anyway. Usually, I wouldn't dare ignore them, but the thousands of miles between us gives me a newfound courage that I am definitely embracing.

I lug my bags across the airport, my long-sleeved shirt making me stick out among all the shorts and tank tops most of the people are wearing. I stand patiently with the rest of the arrivals waiting for their rescue from this overly crowded area. Everyone seems antsy and ready to get the hell out of here. Me on the other hand, I'm equal parts excited and anxious for this next chapter of my life.

Once I'm tucked inside my transportation, I thumb the

notification screen down, scanning through the messages from Griffin and clicking on the one from Rosie.

Rosie: *You landed!! I'm totally a stalker BFF. I've been tracking your flight!*

Me: *Haha, yeah. I made it. Heading to Beth's house now.*

The three little dots appear immediately.

My driver clears her throat and makes eye contact with me in the rearview mirror.

"You just visiting, sweetheart?" Her voice is scratchy but otherwise comforting.

I nod. "Yeah... Well, sort of. I'm hoping it's short-term."

She raises an eyebrow as if questioning my answer and then switches lanes.

My phone buzzes in my hand.

Rosie: *She's not there though, right?*

I quickly type a reply.

Me: *Nope, she's gone for another week, I think.*

I return my attention to the real-life woman in the front seat. "It's sort of a long story."

She points toward the GPS device attached to the dash. "We've got time."

I smile and settle back into my seat. "I'm not sure where to start."

"So, it's one of those situations... I see." She merges the car onto the highway. "Well, unless you're one of those overpackers, your luggage is telling me you'll be here more than a weekend."

"More like a year." I pause and then add, "At best." I scan the dash to locate her name badge.

Greta mumbles an acknowledgment of my declaration.

I continue, making my own taxicab confession. "It wasn't supposed to be this way. I was going to go to college back home. But my dad got this amazing job opportunity. He's a journalist. A damn good one. And his company offered to send him to Africa for two years to live with locals and do this crazy in-depth report. He wasn't going to accept it—that's how he is. Self-sacrificing to a fault. But I couldn't let him pass on an experience like that because of me. Not when he's given up so much already." I take a breath and watch the cars whipping past us.

"Do I want to ask about your mother?" Greta glances at me, giving off the vibe that she's aware of that topic's rocky terrain.

I cross my arms over my chest. "That's why I'm *here*. She's been absent my entire life; by her own choice. But when my dad told her about the situation, she volunteered to cover my living expenses, and her job has some deal with the local university for tuition reimbursement. I won't have many out-of-pocket expenses, and considering I never wanted college to be this thing that sent me into huge debt right out the gate, it would have been foolish to turn it down. I verified all my credits will transfer completely, so it's not a terrible compromise. But I'm not thrilled to spend a year pretending things are peachy."

"Nobody said you had to." Greta shrugs. "You don't owe anyone anything they don't deserve. I'm not telling you to be mean to this woman, but letting her off easily, given what you've just shared, doesn't seem appropriate either."

"Yeah, you're probably right. It's weird, ya know? I've only seen this woman in photos. I mean, she's my mother, for Christ's sake. And here I am, at the age of eighteen, going to live in her house for the first time."

My cell buzzes, and I ignore it.

"Maybe treat her like a roommate. Considering that's kind of what she is. Be courteous and all that, but also have your boundaries." Greta looks back at me briefly. "That's my advice. You can take it or leave it. I'm just a random old lady. I only wish that someone would have told me at an earlier age that it's okay to not always let people get what they want. It would have saved me a lot of heartbreak. You matter, too. Don't forget that."

I let her words sink in. It's not that I didn't already know these things, but I've never actually had someone confront me this way. I'm usually the people-pleaser who compartmentalizes my own feelings to serve others. Things are easier that way, at least for everyone else.

"You can get that if you want." Greta holds her thumb and pinky fingers up to the side of her head to signal a phone.

My gaze falls onto the glowing screen. Two texts from Rosie and seven missed calls from Griffin.

Shit.

I steady myself and click on the photo of Griff. It barely gets through one ring when he answers.

"Claire, what the fuck? Why haven't you been answering me? You've had me worried. Your location shows you almost to your mom's house." His tone is harsh and callous.

One of the requirements to being with Griffin is him knowing my every move. At first, he played it off like he was simply worried about me and wanted to make sure I was okay, but over time, I realized it was one of the ways to keep me under his thumb.

"Sorry, Griff. My phone died. I had to charge it in the Uber. It just came back on." I lie my ass off and hope he believes it.

Greta doesn't bother correcting me, nor does she bat an eye at my false story.

"Right. And you expect me to buy that? The messages show delivered. The calls were ringing through. If it was dead, it would have gone straight to voicemail." Griffin exhales dramatically. "This is already going south, and you've been there a whopping five minutes. You're going to have to try harder, Claire."

I swallow and grit my teeth, unable to form a proper response.

Griffin doesn't bother to wait. "I have to go. The guys are here."

"Where are you going?" Not that I entirely care, but shifting the focus away from me and my many failures is a bonus I'll gladly take.

"Out," is all he says.

"Oh." The word barely leaves my mouth, and the line disconnects.

Cool, he hung up on me.

Greta breaks through the awkward silence. "You okay, sweetheart?"

"Yeah." I shove my phone into the side of my backpack and focus on the landscape around us.

We're in a city now and driving much slower than we were. We pass buildings of various sizes and shapes. Trees are randomly placed along the sidewalks to bring some natural color to this land of concrete.

Greta puts on her turn signal and brings the car to a slow crawl, parking in front of a gated structure.

I recall the passcode that was given to me to get into the complex. *Six–two–one–three*. I had to repeat it in my head for days on end to get it to stick. It's not that I have a terrible memory, but there was no easy way to get that sequence to remain unless I said it over and over and over again.

Greta opens her door and steps out.

I grab my stuff from the back seat and follow suit, meeting her at the now-open trunk. Once I have all my luggage, I pause, not quite ready to say goodbye to this wise woman. I never would have expected I'd get attached to someone quite so easily. Greta feels like a gift from the universe, my own real-life guardian angel.

She puts her hand on my shoulder. "You got this, kid."

I force a smile.

"My next statement is the most cliché thing ever, but…do what makes you happy. I'm serious. Life is too short to let people walk all over you." Greta closes the hatch and makes her way to the driver's side. "I believe in you."

And somehow, despite the words coming from a complete stranger, they spark something alive in me that had been dormant my entire existence.

It's not at all strange when I find myself wrapping my arms around this woman I only just met, hugging her in hopes that she understands how much our short time together means to me.

"Thank you," I tell her, the significance of my words deeper than she might know.

I sling my backpack over my shoulder, grab the handles of my bags, and head straight to the keypad. I punch in the numbers and the gate unlocks. It takes me a second to get the door open and maneuver my bags through, but I manage to make it work.

I'm adjusting my belongings and turning toward the courtyard when a body slams into mine. The strap slides down my arm, and I lose my backpack. My cell goes flying out of the pocket and lands face down on the stone pavers.

I make the briefest eye contact with my target. Dark green with full eyelashes. A black T-shirt hugging his broad shoulders. He's kind of tall, I think. From this angle, it's hard to tell.

"Fuck," he says and keeps on going.

He doesn't bother to say sorry. He doesn't stop and help pick up my stuff. He simply keeps going on his merry way, not giving a damn that he just ran into me. Not a care in the world other than himself and whatever he's in a rush to get to.

Great, the first person I meet my age is a complete asshole. This better not set the stage for how the next year is going to go.

At least with my brand-new outlook on life, I know with certainty that he's the type of guy I need to ignore.

2
JOHNNY

I nearly mowed that girl down, but don't have a second to spare if I'm going to meet Franklin on time. The old me would have stopped to make sure she was okay. I would have taken in her subtle beauty and helped her off the ground. I would have carried her bags to wherever she was going. I wouldn't have been a dick.

But I don't have the luxury of such things anymore.

I wasn't supposed to have *work*-related shit today, but when the phone rings, I have to answer. The consequences for not doing so far outweigh whatever the reasoning could be.

Most of the time I don't even know what will be asked of me. And even more often, I don't want to follow through with their demands. They've made it clear that if I don't, there will be a penalty.

The last time, the price was blood.

I won't let that happen again.

So, I do what they say. I run their errands. I do their bitch work. I comply and hope like hell that eventually there will be a means to this end. There has to be. I can't keep this up forever. Not if I want to live.

Josey checks his watch when I round the corner to the rundown alleyway where he's standing guard. "You have thirteen seconds to get in there."

I rush past him and burst into the back of a small diner.

Everyone except Franklin flinches at my abrupt arrival.

"Cutting it close, Johnny." His thick voice cuts through me. Franklin gently picks up the mug in front of him and leans back into his chair. He takes a swig of his steaming coffee while staring me dead in the eyes. "I have a package that needs to be delivered." He nods to one of the larger-than-life men standing in the dimly lit corner.

The guy steps forward and extends the package to me. It's a padded envelope the size of a sheet of paper, but it's stuffed full of something. For the slightest second, I almost ask, but I know better than to question Franklin and his operation. Shit like that never plays out well; if I've learned anything from the last six months, it's that. Don't question anything.

I take it from the man and he retreats to his dark corner. I try not to analyze the weight or density in an attempt to figure out the contents. At this point, I think it's better that I *don't* know what's inside. Regardless, I don't underestimate the value or risk associated with transporting it to wherever he asks of me. It's clearly illegal, otherwise, he'd ask someone else to do it.

Me, on the other hand—I'm expendable to him.

"Here's the address." Franklin shoves a smaller envelope with a piece of paper on top of it across the table. "And a little something for your time. You know the drill; you'll get the other half upon completion."

Franklin may be a ruthless criminal, but he's still a businessman. I might make significantly less than he pays his other cronies, but he still compensates me in some capacity. And luckily, it's enough to cover my expenses and then some, considering I haven't managed to keep a steady job because of this illicit side-gig.

It's not ideal, any of this, but I have to hope it will all pay off eventually.

I reach for the parcel, and Franklin snatches my hand. We lock eyes.

"Under different circumstances, kid, things might not be like this. I'd venture to say we might get along." He slowly tightens his hold as his tone hardens. "But I'm no fool. And you better not cross me. You understand?"

I nod my head in obedience. "Yes."

"Yes, what?"

"Sir. Yes, sir. I understand."

A devious grin spreads across his fat face and he releases me. "Great. Glad to hear it. Now, you have until midnight."

I take my leave without another word, already scanning the address and trying to map out how to get there without being detected. I'll need to circle back home to get my backpack and form a proper plan.

I shove the package in the waistband of my pants and cover it with my shirt and tuck the envelope into my back pocket, making sure it's hidden, too.

Josey greets me in the alley. "That went better than last time, I take it."

I slap his massive shoulder. "Yeah, I'd say so."

Josey has never really given me any reason to dislike him. If anything, he's been the only one to actually show me any kindness. The first time I got involved with Franklin, I got the shit kicked out of me and left in this very dodgy backstreet. Josey waited until everyone went inside and helped me off the ground, dusting the dirt and trash off me and helping me get reoriented.

I think he's always known that I didn't get into this line of work because of a drug addiction or gambling debt. I'd wager to say he pities me for getting involved with Franklin but understands what I'm doing it for. And with that, he doesn't shit on me like all the other guys do.

Don't get me wrong, I've seen Josey be a complete badass and knock the crap out of some dudes, but he's got this gentle giant kind of thing going on. He only seems to crack heads when it's absolutely necessary.

And from what I've heard, he was born into this line of work. He didn't really have a choice. Going against his obligations would be going against family, and to his bloodline, that's a deadly sin.

At least I have the possibility of getting out of this—if I can stay alive long enough.

I arrive back at the complex without catching anyone's attention. I blend in reasonably well. Most people are too occupied on their cell phones to even notice when I walk by them. It makes my job that much easier. I wear clothes that are inconspicuous and try to make it difficult to pick me out of a lineup. There is no shortage of brown-haired guys running around this area. I'm just another one of the many.

I punch my code into the keypad and head through the courtyard. Picnic tables sit empty the way they normally do. Between the number of flight attendants that live in this building and the rest of the working class, the recreational space isn't usually occupied.

I run up the stairs at a pace that allows me to be careful not to drop the package tucked into my jeans. I turn the corner toward my door and my eyes catch on an unfamiliar brunette walking into Beth's place.

As if sensing my presence, the girl looks over her shoulder at me.

It's the girl from earlier. Those same sky-blue eyes pierce

through me the way they did not too long ago. It stops me in my tracks, and I find myself dumbfounded at my inability to walk the extra two steps to my apartment. I want to speak up, to tell her that I'm sorry, that I'm not usually like that, but I can't.

I'm frozen in place.

She narrows her gaze at me and turns around, sort of slamming the door shut behind her, putting something solid between her and the douchebag that ran into her.

In reality, she's doing us both a favor. Her hating me right off the bat means there's no way I can tangle her up in this nightmare I'm living. I'm getting good at this whole bad-guy thing, and I'll continue to play that role as long as it advances me in this dangerous game.

3
CLAIRE

Being in someone else's house, especially when they aren't home, and for the first time, is strange.

I tiptoe around, careful not to bump into or disturb anything. It's like walking through a minefield of bookshelves and house plants.

My mother's place reminds me of one of those staged model homes that no one actually lives in. It feels…off. Back at my dad's, our place was lived in. There were coffee cup rings on the counter and dirty dishes in the sink. Clean laundry would sit in baskets until one of us finally decided to put it away. Empty pizza boxes would be waiting to get recycled, and there were always blankets on the couch waiting for someone to curl up under.

Here though, there's none of that *homey* stuff. Sure, it's nice —clean, even. But houses aren't supposed to make you feel unwelcome, and this one definitely gives off those vibes.

I open the door to my bedroom and take in the contents. A bed covered in dark-gray linen is tucked in the corner, and a basic white desk is situated on the opposing wall. A wide, six-drawer dresser is along the wall with the closet door. It's not a big space, but it's enough for what I need. It'll get me by until I can get the hell out of here.

She did have the decency to leave me a note, briefly covering the essentials. My room was down the hall, the second door on the right. A spare bathroom was first. Towels are in the closet at the far end. There was an envelope of cash for groceries and a list of some takeout options. A mention about almost everyone in the building being pretty nice and that there's a lady named Martha in 237 who seems friendly if I need anything.

She must have been referring to the jerk guy with the *almost*.

Not of a warm welcome. Only a "see you soon" scribbled at the end.

This woman feels more and more like a roommate by the minute. My Uber driver Greta hit the nail on the head with that one.

My stomach growls, so I abandon my confines in search of something to eat. I could easily order from one of the places suggested, but I need a bit of fresh air. I had attempted to leave not too long ago, but my plan was halted when my sights landed on that asshole who ran into me earlier.

Seeing him, it was like my brain fogged up and my body went into autopilot, sending me back through the front door.

His gaze had locked onto mine, and for a second, we had a stare-off.

Part of me thought he was going to say something. Apologize, maybe. Tell me that his grandma was dying, and he had to rush out and *that* was why he knocked me down and didn't bother saying a thing. Anything to justify his jerk behavior. But he didn't, he just stood there, like a complete dumbass, frozen in place.

He had his opportunity, and he chose to not use it. Or well, maybe his lack of apology *was* him using it. He's shown his true colors twice now, and I need to make sure I'm paying attention.

I grab my phone off the nightstand beside my bed and swipe

a couple of the twenties off the counter on my way out. With my hand on the doorknob, I inhale deeply and do my best to prepare myself for whatever comes next.

The warm air hits me immediately, reminding me that I must still look like a fool with long sleeves. It's dark enough that any of the marks would probably go unnoticed, but if I happen to walk into a well-lit place, the bruises Griffin left on my arms would be visible.

Today is Friday, so I have until Monday for them to fade, otherwise, I'll be attending my first day of college looking like a total drug user. I'll be nervous enough without my attire making me sweat bullets. The campus isn't too far from here, but even with the short walk, I'm bound to get overheated. Smelling of body odor wouldn't be a good first impression either.

When I made the decision to take my mom up on her offer of housing, Dad and I did a little recon on the area around her place. A five-minute walk to school meant I wouldn't need to rely on transportation, and that alone was a huge plus. Restaurants and coffee shops are a dime a dozen out here, so finding food shouldn't be a big deal either. There are museums, a park, and plenty to keep me occupied within walking distance while I'm stuck living here.

If everything wasn't right at my fingertips, I might have been more resistant to saying yes to this major change in life.

"You can do this," I tell myself. I poke my head out of my new home and hesitantly scan my surroundings.

The hallway is empty. Not a person in sight.

I seize the moment and leave, closing the door tightly behind me to ensure it latches all the way. The sun has fully set, and the night sky is illuminated not by stars but by electricity glowing from buildings and streetlights.

I make a beeline for the stairs and then straight to the gate to get out of the complex. Noticing a creeping sensation on my back, like someone watching me, I glance over my shoulder on my way out. That same guy is standing outside his unit, his hand on the door handle and his gaze glued to me.

He's changed his clothes. His shirt is a bit looser, and his jeans are darker. He's wearing a baseball cap pulled down, like he's trying to obscure his eyes. He looks like he's up to no good, and if I'm being honest with myself, it's kind of hot.

I shake my head to rid the thought and continue forward, refusing to waste another moment on him.

I go out onto the sidewalk, where I blend in with the passing crowd. No one seems to notice me, and for that I'm grateful. I don't want to make idle small talk or fake pleasantries. Maybe another time. Right now, I just want to get something to eat.

4
JOHNNY

My mind and my body are two separate entities.

My head is urging me to follow through with my plan—to deliver this package and get it out of my possession. But my body has me following this new girl out of the complex. I can't get the two to agree on anything, even when my mind tries to tell my body that there will be consequences if I don't get my job done in time.

Something visceral convinced my legs to move, to go after this girl who I don't know. It wasn't a *creepy stalker* kind of thing. But more of a *she just got here and might get lost* thing. A strange rush of protectiveness washed over me when I saw her leave the building and venture out into the world. I already got her to hate me, and that alone might be all the protection she needs, but what if something else happens? Why is my brain telling me it's my responsibility?

If I just confirm she makes it to wherever she's going, maybe that will be enough.

I keep a natural pace while maintaining some distance between us, walking in the complete opposite direction from where I should really be going. I glance down at my watch, verifying that my little detour won't set me back too much.

The girl's chocolate brown hair falls down her mid-back, gently swaying with each step she takes. Her arms are crossed over her chest like she might be cold. Or like she's using it as some kind of barrier from the outside world.

That train of thought makes my protective urges rise even more. I don't know her name, and yet I have an innate need to shield her from any danger.

What the fuck is wrong with me?

She pauses in front of Bram's, a small, late-night diner, and peers at the menu posted on the large glass window. Personally, the little shop is one of my favorites; home of the best blueberry old-fashioned donuts around.

I want to go to her and tell her, to offer my local opinion on the cuisine and recommend something for her to eat. But I don't. I can't. Even if I found the courage to open my mouth and speak to her, she already hates me, and I don't blame her one bit for that. I'm better off keeping my distance. We both are.

The girl turns to take a quick look behind her before moving inside. I take notice of her dark blue eyes and slightly rosy cheeks. She has a sort of delicate beauty about her that I can't quite seem to fully comprehend. Without really knowing how or why, I realize she's too good for this world.

With her decision to go into Bram's, I make my move, too.

I need to act fast if I'm going to get this done.

I turn on my heel and head back the way I came, cutting through an alley to try to recover my lost time. The package digs at my waistband, and I use the shadows of the alley as an opportunity to adjust it. I was going to bring my backpack, but that would only make me seem more suspicious if someone spotted me.

I continue along until the sound of laughter catches in my ears.

Drunken hilarity, actually. I've done this enough to pick up on certain things like that. And given the circumstances, I can't afford to risk one of the idiots picking a fight with me. I've had that happen once in the past, and it didn't fare well for either of us.

I creep out of the passage and go back to the main street, sighing at the extra time this will add to my journey. I check my watch again and do the math in my head. I'm going to be cutting it close—too close.

I weave my way down a path, shed a few minutes, only to get caught up and lose time again. A bead of sweat rolls down my spine. I pick up my pace in the most discreet way I can, but I'm running out of time. The only way I'm going to pull this off is if I step out of my safety zone.

I wait until there are minimal bystanders and break out into a jog, hoping like hell the package stays in place and no one notices the random dude in a hurry.

I round the corner and rush down the alley where I've made deliveries twice before.

The large door swings open when I arrive.

I glance down at my watch and wince at the same time when a dude bigger than Josey appears from the opening.

His fist meets my face a second later, causing everything to go black temporarily and my hat to go flying. "You're late."

By sixty seconds at most, I think to myself through the ringing in my head.

My watch had *just* ticked over to a minute past when I entered the area. But shit like that doesn't matter to these kinds of people. They live for the tiniest mistakes to fuel their incessant thirst for blood.

I wipe my nose on the back of my hand, a red stain left behind. It's not a first, and this surely won't be the last. Not while I'm tangled up in this mess with the Sharps. I made a stupid deal with them, and they're going to make sure I live up to my end of the bargain.

I blink up at the guy.

He reaches forward and grabs the collar of my shirt, pulling me toward him. His nasty breath reeks of cigarettes and cheap booze. "Do you have it or not, kid?"

Instinctually, my brain defaults to some smart-ass comment, but I know better than to razz someone like this, especially when he's already thrown a punch. Anything remotely out of line will be used as ammunition to fuel his twisted role of tough guy. Despite my best efforts, my expression still betrays me. I hate myself for the laugh that bubbles up and out of my chest. It's one of my worst traits and happens at the worst fucking times.

"Oh, I'll give you something to smile about." The guy tightens his grip, tugging me closer and then slamming me into the ground. He's beside me in an instant, his knee pressed against my forearm, holding me in place. He fumbles around my pockets, then my back, finally finding what he's looking for under my shirt. He rips the package from me and then stands abruptly, kicking me in the gut the moment he's on both feet again.

I groan and clutch at my stomach, spitting out the blood that ran down my nose and into my mouth.

He sizes up the weight of the delivery in his palm, clearly guessing whether or not it's all there. Tucking it up under his arm, he reaches into his jean pocket and pulls out an envelope, throwing it at me on the dirty ground. "Get out of here before you bleed all over my alley."

I snatch my payment and my hat while still on the filthy pavement, then use my scuffed-up hands to prop myself up and rise to my feet. I don't bother dusting myself off, not here at least, and not in front of him.

"Don't be late again." The guy punctuates his warning by hocking a wad of spit only inches away from my shoes and then goes inside, letting the door slam shut behind him.

I exhale and sag in relief that another job is done. I won't relax until I'm home, and even then, it's only a matter of time before Franklin has me doing more of his bitch work.

I need to be more careful. I shouldn't have followed that girl tonight. If I left her alone, I would have probably made it here on time. I wouldn't have been late, and this guy wouldn't have potentially broken my nose. But even then, nothing is certain. He could have still been on some rampage to kick my ass. I haven't been doing this shit long, but I've done it enough to know that unnecessary risks aren't worth taking.

I shouldn't bother myself with whether or not the girl is safe. It's not my responsibility to save everyone, especially when I can't save myself.

I rest my hand along the bridge of my nose and confirm my suspicions. I grip it firmly and snap it back into its normal place, hissing with the knife of pain that shoots through my head. I shove the envelope into my pocket and leave this place behind.

Once I'm away from the drop point, I use the bottom of my shirt to wipe as much of the blood off my face as possible. I don't want to draw attention to myself, but my resources are limited. I hit my hat against my thigh to knock the dirt off and tug it onto my head.

My cheek throbs and has me pretty certain that the impact of this guy's fist is going to leave a lasting impression. With the way he hit me, the impact spanned the side of my head, across to my nose. I'm honestly lucky though, otherwise, he might have knocked me out or done worse damage.

I start my second year of college in a few days, and I don't exactly want to skip the first week because I'm hospitalized by some criminal. It's bad enough that I'll probably have a black eye.

I keep my head tucked low and avoid direct eye contact on my way back to the complex, only catching looks from a few people and making decent time. I sigh with relief when I punch the numbers into the gate and hear the familiar unlocking sound.

Nearly dragging myself through the courtyard and up the stairs, I finally make it to my door. I fumble in my pocket to locate the key. I slide it in and go inside the empty space, heading straight into my dim bathroom and collapsing onto the cold tile floor next to the toilet.

Closing my eyes, I let the weight of my body shift horizontally onto the rug near the vanity.

I stay this way only for a little while before I force myself to get up, to turn the water on and let it steam up the room. To take a shower and rinse the filth off my body. I go through the motions, taking the envelope out of my pants and putting tonight's money with the rest of my stash. I do what I've programmed myself to do to get through these dark days. I compartmentalize this incredibly fucked-up life I'm living and focus on getting through another day. One that brings me closer to the end I'm trying to reach.

Once I'm sprawled out on top of my bed, my thoughts flit to the mystery girl, to whether or not she made it back safely. Or what she decided to order at Bram's, and if she enjoyed it. I wonder if she sat in the corner and people-watched or chose a stool at the front. Maybe she got takeout and didn't stay at all. It's possible she changed her mind and went somewhere else the moment I walked away.

I shouldn't let my attention wander to this complete stranger, but I do. It happens naturally and without effort.

And with that, I embrace the strange comfort it brings despite the war raging inside of me.

5

CLAIRE

Falling asleep in a different time zone, let alone a new place, is not a simple task. It should be, given the exhausting day I've had and the dose of sleep-aid I took. But, instead of nodding off, I toss and turn, my mind flitting in a million different directions.

I don't settle on one specific topic very long before my brain throws me to the next. I think of my dad, and what it must be like for him to uproot everything and move out of the country. I can relate, obviously, but only to an extent. I don't focus on my mom much. I've spent a lot of my childhood wracking my brain on how this woman operates and the reasoning for her abandoning me and Dad, but I can never quite make sense of it.

I think of Rosie and my friends back home, starting at Turner University next week without me. I shudder at the memory of Griffin, and the fading parting gift he left on my arms. Each mile between us continues to build the courage I need to finally rid him from my story. I even ponder about Greta, my guardian angel Uber driver, and what her life here must be like.

No matter where my imagination takes me, I keep creeping

back to the guy from my building. I don't know why it bothers me so badly that he was such a dick. I think part of me had hoped asshole guys were going to be a thing of my past, but apparently, I'm a magnet for them.

I roll to the edge of my bed and bring my legs down to rest my feet gently on the floor. I slide my feet into my cozy slippers and grab a sweater from my suitcase.

Not having received my boxes from back home, I'm forced to resort to a blank notebook instead of losing myself in fiction.

I quietly make my way out of my mom's place and travel down the hall. The stairs don't even creak under the weight of my body. I take residency in the corner of the empty courtyard at a small table. My spot is nearly hidden but still gives me enough light to see the pages awaiting my pen.

For being in a busy-ish area, there isn't much sound that travels into the complex. It's more of a muted chaos than anything else; it's just enough to know there's stuff going on outside of here, but not overpowering to where I can't think. Although, at times, I wish there was something to drown out my own thoughts.

I stay there for a little while, doodling and writing lines of poetry that pop up. I don't reflect on what comes out, I just let it happen. I give my soul free rein to do what it pleases without dissecting the meaning behind it.

I'm grateful for this tiny sanctuary in this hectic world.

I wasn't quite sure what to expect when I found out I'd be living in a building like this, but I've been pleasantly surprised. I halfway expected it to be busy and loud, with people coming to and from at all hours, but overall, it's fairly laid-back. Aside from the asshole who knocked me down, I haven't drawn the attention of anyone else living here. I've noticed the sound of the occasional door shutting, but that's pretty much it. People don't seem to frequent the courtyard other than to walk through to get to their units, and for that, I'm thankful.

That means this will be a great spot for studying, and reading, whenever my packages arrive from home.

An electronic clicking steals my train of thought, and my attention shifts to the gate near the front.

A shadowy figure appears from behind it and slowly comes forward.

At first glance, I assume the person is drunk, especially when I notice them clutching their side like they might hurl.

But when I hear the person hiss in pain, and the light finally illuminates them to show their blood-caked cheek, I realize he's not intoxicated, he's injured.

My heart pounds as I watch the guy who ran into me earlier stumble his way closer to the stairs.

I don't dare move. From where I'm sitting, he must not know that I'm here, and I'd rather keep it that way.

I hold my breath when he's only a few feet away.

He drags himself up the stairs, letting out a faint groan with each labored step.

Whatever hurt his side must have broken a rib.

Or more like *who,* not what.

The guy gets to his door, and I continue to watch. I shouldn't stare—it's creepy—but I can't help but wonder if he's going to make it in.

He leans against the doorframe and fumbles in his pocket.

A second passes where I think he's not going to find his key, but he does.

He disappears into his house and I'm left alone, my thoughts wilder than they were when I came out here.

I spend most of my weekend in and out of bed. My entire Saturday was filled with Chinese takeout and binge-watching Netflix. Friday, the day of my arrival, had been mentally draining enough that I quarantined myself to get a little R&R. I'm not sure how well it worked, considering my mind hasn't really slowed down much at all.

And now here I am, Sunday morning, going stir-crazy, ready to get the heck out of here.

I take a long shower, standing under the water for way longer than I should, before getting ready for the day. Since the weather is warm here, I leave my hair to air dry on its own. I throw on a white spaghetti-strapped crop-top and faded jeans, but when I scan my arms, I decide on layering it with a lightweight cardigan. The bruising has faded, but not enough to make me comfortable in exposing myself yet.

I check my phone for any new notifications and slide it into my pocket. Griffin hasn't said a word to me since he hung up on me, and for once, I'm not going to give him the satisfaction of following up. It's all a game to him, and right now, what he wants is for me to grovel. I'm done playing by his rules.

I have been done for quite some time.

Our relationship was pretty much over six months ago, but we've both been going through the motions. I caught him cheating on me with a girl from his work. I walked in to surprise him, and boy was it a shock to us all. The two of them were making out in the break room, hot and heavy. His hand was down the front of her pants and hers was tangled in his hair. Who knows how far they would have taken it if I hadn't thrown a wrench into their plan.

Completely mortified and shocked, I ran out of there and went straight home.

To my further surprise, Griffin left, too, and followed me to my house. He jumped out of his car and dropped to his knees, pleading with me to forgive him.

In hindsight, I have no fucking clue what made me believe him. Maybe it was the desire to get him off my lawn so the neighbors would stop staring, or maybe it was hoping that the good Griff would come back. Or that, perhaps there was a logical explanation for why his lips were on someone else's.

I was a fool though, because the Griffin I saw then was the Griffin that exists every single day. The little blips of good Griff that come and go are the hooks he sinks in to keep me around. They're fake, not real, just a tool he uses. And like magic, they work every single time.

Things were different after that, though. I could feel myself slipping further from his grasp. Growing a little colder toward him. I was building a tolerance to his bullshit. Don't get me wrong, I continued to fall for his tricks, but each time the cycle of good to bad finished, I grew more aware of what was happening.

Not only had he deceived me, but he also had everyone else fooled, too. Which continued to complicate the situation that much more.

Even my dad was under Griffin's spell. Despite my dad's selfless and caring heart, I managed to hide the things Griffin did to me from him. I didn't want to burden him with my teenage problems; he was handling enough on his own.

I open the front door and turn back to take a last look for anything I forgot. I have my keys, phone, some cash, and my I.D. in my pocket. I don't plan on going far, but the basics are covered if needed.

Tomorrow is the unofficial first day of school. Campus will be open, and teachers will be coming and going from their rooms, but no actual classes will be in session. Freshmen are supposed to use this time to get acquainted with where everything is and prepare for Tuesday. And according to the mailer they sent out, the university uses this day to set up booths for extra-curriculars, too.

Considering I haven't even seen the school in person yet, I'm going to use my time now to walk the few blocks and make sure

I have it mapped out correctly. I'd rather not have any major surprises tomorrow.

Heading down the stairs and into the courtyard, I catch sight of something I haven't seen before in this building.

A kid.

A boy with brown shaggy hair, leaning on his elbow, his face buried in a book. He's sitting at the table I was at last night, lost in whatever he's reading.

I guess I'm not the only one who uses the space after all.

I'm opening the gate to leave when I'm startled by a loud bellow from above.

"Billy, get your ass up here!" the man yells down at the young boy.

Billy slams his book shut and hustles upstairs.

I try not to be obvious as I watch the two of them go inside and shut the door.

The man raises his voice again, but it's too muffled for me to hear.

I leave the building and attempt to shake the icky feeling that interaction just gave me. It could have been completely harmless, but it seemed much deeper than surface-level harsh parenting.

My phone vibrates in my back pocket, and I nearly jump out of my own skin.

I pull it out to see Rosie's face across the screen. Gratefully, I accept the FaceTime call.

"Hey, you!" She beams. Her dirty blonde hair is in her usual beachy waves. Her backdrop tells me that she's sitting on her bed at her house.

"Hi, Rose." I hold the phone in close proximity to my body to avoid being one of those obnoxious public phone users. There aren't too many people around, but I still want to be considerate.

"Where are you? It's all muffled."

I show her a little bit of my surroundings. "I'm walking down to check the campus out. Want to come with me?"

"Yeah, of course." Rosie pauses, and even with the distance and technology between us, I can sense the dynamic is about to change. "I wanted to talk to you about something, but it can wait until later."

I bring the phone up toward my face so I can get a good look at her. I narrow my gaze. "What's going on?"

She shakes her head and tucks a strand of hair behind her ear, averting her eyes for a moment. "Nothing." She quickly changes the subject. "Oh, what's that?"

I turn to check out what would have been in the frame of my shot. "Bram's. It's a diner; it's really good, actually. Definitely going to be a regular place. Their coffee is spot on."

Rosie raises her eyebrows. "Wow, and that's coming from *the* java snob."

I roll my eyes. "Whatever."

"Don't act like you aren't. I know it. You know it. Everyone who knows you knows it." She fluffs a pillow and lays back against her headframe. "What's the weather there? Are you wearing a sweater? I thought it was eighty-something?"

I bite at my lip and come up with a lie. "It's a bit chilly in the shade."

"Right, sure it is." Rosie adjusts the phone to her other hand and rolls over on her side. "You're coming in bright and sunny on my end."

I flip the screen to the forward-facing camera, glancing both ways and then crossing the street. "There it is."

Up ahead is the small but pretty campus. From the map I've been trying to commit to memory, there is one main building with four smaller structures jutting out from each corner. Walkways line the space between them with some tree coverage and the occasional picnic table or bench. It's not as intimidating as I thought it would be, but maybe that's because it's empty.

Tomorrow, when students will be filing in to find their classes, it will probably be a completely different story.

"Did I tell you I got accepted into that writing class?" Rosie anxiously tries to hide her excitement.

"Brantley?" The small, hard to get into six-week class we both daydreamed about taking together. The one that would potentially evolve our written word and shape us into better writers. Something we planned on doing together. Although I'm disappointed I can't be there with Rosie, it's such a huge step and I'm so fucking happy for her.

"Yep." No longer able to hold it back, her cheeks turn up into a beautiful smile.

"Rose, that's amazing!"

Within an instant, her grin fades. "It would be better if you were there."

I sigh and nod. It sucks, but it's not the end of the world. There are worse things that could happen than me missing a creative opportunity. "Maybe next year, okay?"

6
JOHNNY

My head fucking aches.

And the throbbing in my side doesn't seem to want to let up.

I down another shot of cheap whiskey in an attempt to numb the pain.

At the time, I didn't think it was a big deal. I've been punched in the face too many times to count. But the lingering misery of this incident is lasting much longer than the rest.

I avoid glancing in the mirror while I fill the bath and climb in, the sting of the hot water a relief on my skin. I slip down the side until it's only my head above the steaming liquid, then close my eyes and breathe deeply.

A year ago, if you told me I'd be covered in bruises and running errands for a criminal underground, I'd laugh my ass off.

Mister aspiring artist turned into errand boy? No way.

Don't get me wrong, I've always had a rebellious streak about me, but nothing like what I've gotten myself into now.

I suck in a breath and fully submerge myself. I stay under and let the burning desire for fresh oxygen bring the rush of adrenaline that I so desperately need to my system. The need for air has me gasping once I break through the surface.

My chest heaves and I grin, ready to take on this day.

I dry off and dress quickly in a band tee and jeans. I slide my chain over my head and tuck it into my shirt. A glance at the clock has me shoving my wallet and phone into my back pockets and snatching my keys off the counter. I should be more prepared but showing up will have to be good enough.

I make it to the door but double back to take another shot. My senses and the pain dull slightly with the liquid warming its way down my chest.

I walk at a casual pace down the stairs and across the courtyard. Usually, I'd ruffle the hair on Billy's head and tease him about his book of choice, but he must already be at school for the day. At least, that's what I hope.

I go down the sidewalk, avoiding eye contact the way I normally do. I pop into Bram's and head straight to the counter where a cup already waits for me.

"Thanks, Bram." I fish for my wallet, but he holds his hand out to stop me.

"On the house today. Looks like you could use it." Bram stares at me both critically and concerned. "I know you told me not to ask questions, but Johnny, I think you've seen better days, kid."

His throaty, worn-out voice cuts through me. He's usually on my ass about taking care of myself, but the concern in his tone is the strongest it ever has been.

I've known this man for years. I've been coming to his shop since I was a kid. And with my cousin in and out of deployments overseas, Bram is the closest thing to family I have left around here.

"Do I need to be worried?" He bags up a donut and shoves it across to me.

I shake my head. I don't want to lie to him, but I have to.

"No. But I'm sure that's not going to stop you." I swipe the bag from the counter and hold it in the air between us. "Thanks for breakfast."

Bram cups his hand and drags it across the counter, scooping crumbs into his palm. "Good luck today."

I wave goodbye and leave, the bell of the door clanging on my way out.

"Ah, Johnny, thanks for joining us." Professor Brown looks up from her lesson plan when I come into the room. She straightens and checks her watch. "Ten minutes late. Not your worst, not your best." She points toward an empty chair. "Take a seat."

She seems more fazed by my tardiness than she does the condition of my busted face. The shock value must have worn off a dozen black eyes ago.

I move in the direction she motioned, only to stop dead in my tracks when I see who's in the spot next to it. My heart pounds a little harder, and I thank God for that extra shot of whiskey I swallowed before I left my house.

Brown speaks up. "Something wrong, Mr. Jones?"

The girl and I make eye contact but she quickly looks away to focus on the teacher. For a second, I'm captivated by the most enchanting blue I've ever seen.

I settle into the seat, taking a sip of my coffee and leaning back. I flit my gaze to the girl and let it wander down her profile.

"Pass this behind you, please." Brown hands the boy in the front row a packet which makes its way to me.

The girl keeps her attention ahead, not deigning to look my way.

The professor signals to the board. "You'll want to copy the adjustments to the syllabus."

Realizing how incredibly unprepared I am, I reach out and gently touch the girl's arm to get her attention. I whisper, "Do you have an extra pen?"

Her jaw tenses, but she doesn't move. "Yes."

"Can I borrow it?"

She exhales and turns to rummage through her backpack. "Here." She shoves the thing across the table at me.

"Thanks." I click the top and jot the stuff onto the paper.

She takes her hand and sort of dusts off the spot where I had touched her like she's trying to get rid of boy cooties.

The old me would have never given her this reaction.

I study the area my finger grazed her and recall the way it felt. I shouldn't care about the strange electricity that seemed to crackle at my touch, but I do.

I narrow my eyes when I notice something unusual. Her forearm appears to have makeup on it, and near where she rubbed my touch away, it reveals a purplish-green hue under it, sort of resembling a bruise.

The more I take it in, the more I realize that's exactly what it is.

People get hurt all the time—why would she feel obligated to cover it up?

My mind races at the implications. I fight to pay attention to Brown ramble on about course expectations and extra credit opportunities, when the only thing I'm concerned with is what happened to this seemingly very good girl.

The rest of the class goes by at both a rate too slow and too fast. I glance over at my seatmate every now and then, but she's completely focused on paying attention.

Class is finally dismissed, and students funnel out. I try to dawdle, but considering I don't have anything to pack up, I look like an idiot wasting time. And if I keep this up, Brown will catch me on the way out and lecture me about being late.

I slowly sneak out the door when the girl is almost done gathering her stuff. I lean against the wall outside of the room, and for no apparent reason, I wait for her. I have no clue what I'll say. I guess I could probably start with apologizing for being a dick, but she's probably past sorry at this point. And having her hate me is the best option for all of us.

So, what the hell am I doing?

There's just something about her that draws me in. She's beautiful, obviously, but it's not *only* that. There's this pureness to her. This mysterious light that shines through my darkness. This longing to know her, to be around her. Even if it's strictly platonic.

The people in the hall pass in a blur along with each antagonizing minute.

When I no longer hear chatter inside the room, I poke my head in to find it completely empty except for the teacher I need to avoid. My gaze falls on the door on the opposite wall. She must have gone out that way instead.

But did she do it because it was convenient, or was it to avoid me?

7
CLAIRE

It's everything I can do to keep my focus on the professor at the front of the class. I feel his stare burning through me but refuse to look in his direction.

Johnny's stare.

The guy who has been weird as hell to me lately has a name. And somehow, it's strangely fitting. Almost like I knew it without knowing it, if that makes sense.

It doesn't, not really.

Class finally ends, and when it does, he seems to be looking for ways to drag out his departure, which results in me taking my sweet time putting my stuff into my backpack. If he's waiting to get me alone, he's going to have to try a little harder. Professor Brown has office hours following our period, so he's shit out of luck.

Once he finally takes his leave, I count to thirty in my head, secure the zipper, and sling the bag over my shoulder.

That should be plenty of time for him to have gone, right?

I make my way to the front of the class slowly, but Brown stands from her desk.

"Ms. Cooper," she says to me. She shuffles a few papers

around and then pulls one out.

I approach her desk, grateful for the continued delay in my departure. “Yes?”

She smiles kindly, showing her incredibly white teeth. Professor Brown is probably in her late thirties or early forties. She’s well put together with her black dress suit and perfectly pinned back dark hair. The giant rock on her ring finger tells me that her partner is either seriously in debt or she doesn’t *have* to be a working woman and chooses to be anyway.

"Your advisor, Sid Martin, reached out about the scholarship you've applied for. He mentioned you were trying to find an extracurricular to better your chance of acceptance."

I nod. “Yeah, I spoke to him yesterday, and he said he’d look for some options.”

She holds out the page to me. “If you’re willing, I think you’d be a great fit for our tutoring program. I went over your transcript, and you meet all the requirements and then some. It offers flexible hours and will easily fit into your current course load.”

I take the signup form from her and briefly look it over.

Brown continues. “And if all goes well, I’d be willing to write a letter of recommendation to the scholarship committee.”

With that, my attention goes back to her. “Really? You’d do that?”

That could be the huge push I need to help me win this chance to return back to the east-coast. To my life.

“Absolutely.” Brown smiles again. “Your endorsements from your home school are beaming. You’d be doing me a favor, honestly. It’s been a while since I’ve had a bright pupil like you to help with our tutoring program.”

I can’t help the blush that covers my cheeks. “Thanks.”

“Is that a yes?” She raises her brows with hesitant excitement.

What do I have to lose? This seems like a no-brainer—a

perfect opportunity laid right in my hands for the taking. I'd be a fool to turn it down. Not only is English Literature my favorite subject, but it's also my best. Being a tutor should be a piece of cake, especially at the freshman level.

"Definitely." I grin back at her.

"Awesome!" Brown tries to contain her enthusiasm. "Okay, just fill that out and bring it to class on Wednesday."

"Will do." I go to leave, but a familiar scent catches my attention near the door. I stop abruptly and carefully poke my head out of the room to see Johnny leaning against the wall. I bite at my lip and ponder an escape route.

I guess I could just camp out in Brown's room during her office hours—tell her I want to get ahead on my reading for the class. She'd totally buy that, given she already thinks I'm an overachiever.

But then I'd have to skip math. And what if Johnny stays there anyway and continues to wait? I'd run into him either way.

Clearly, I'm being a self-centered fool. He couldn't possibly be out there to catch me when I leave, is he? Maybe he's killing time for a friend, anyone other than me.

That's when my gaze settles on my saving grace.

I point toward the door on the opposite wall. "Does that lead to the other side of the building?"

Brown looks up from her laptop. "Yep, you can use it if you want. Shaves a few minutes off walking around if that's where you need to go." She pauses and adds. "Which building are you going to next?"

"Clark Hall," I blurt out.

A total and complete lie. But if I told her the truth, she'd suggest I take the normal path, out the door and right by the person I'm trying to avoid.

"Yep. Take that one. It's not too far."

"Thank you, I appreciate it." I shuffle quickly to the door and leave without wasting any more time.

I let out a breath once I'm outside, the relief of avoiding another awkward situation settling through me.

"How was your day?" Rosie says through yet another one of our FaceTime calls. She's sitting at the desk in her room, a stack of books piled haphazardly next to her.

I think back to the hours that led us to this moment, and the nerves that riddled me until I was safely inside my home away from home. I was somehow successful at not running into Johnny again, but I'm not sure if that's a good or bad thing.

"Uneventful," I tell her. "I had English, Math, and Economics today."

"Gross." Rosie sighs dramatically. "I'm totally going to fail without you."

I roll my eyes and lay on my stomach on my bed, propping myself up with my elbows. "You'll be fine." I revert the conversation to the thing she keeps avoiding. "What were you going to tell me the other day?"

She hesitates. "Are you mentally prepared for upsetting news?"

This is what we do when we need to tell the other something big that could potentially throw us for a loop. Sometimes we hold off and wait until things settle down, other times we can handle whatever it is.

I can't imagine a better moment than now for the secret she's been keeping. Life has been weird, but I'm sure I can handle it.

"Okay so…" Rosie hasn't been this nervous in ages. She's usually the first to blurt out random stuff without any filter. She's brutally honest, and it's one of the things I love most about her. "I wanted you to at least get through your first day before I sprung this on you."

"I'm fine. My day was no big deal. Tell me already, please." Other than the awkwardness with Johnny, things haven't entirely sucked since my arrival. I managed to find a solid coffee source, and that alone is a huge plus.

"Griffin... He...Well..."

Without her finishing, I can already sense where this conversation is heading, and honestly, I'm not surprised at all.

"Brice saw him at Sara's on Friday..."

"With Shelby," I add when she doesn't continue. The girl from his work, from six months ago.

Her eyes perk up. "You knew?"

I exhale. "Not for sure, no. But I suspected it."

"What a dick. I'm so sorry, Claire."

I want to cuss, to tell my best friend how much of a douchebag Griffin is. To spend the next hour venting about how bad he treats me and all the terrible things I wish would happen to him—but I don't. Griffin has already stolen too much of me, and in this moment, I refuse to give him any more.

Instead of doing all that, I simply say, "Yeah, me too."

It's strange to hear that your long-distance boyfriend is cheating on you and to be nothing but numb about it. Maybe it's because I saw it coming. Or because deep down, I knew it was happening this whole time. Or maybe because I stopped having feelings for him a while ago. Everything combined leads to this empty pit in my stomach and a dull ache in my chest.

I use it as fuel to stoke the fire of my empowerment; to put him in my past once and for all.

"Do you want to talk about it?" Rosie offers.

I snap out of my trance and flip onto my back, holding the phone out in front of me to focus on my friend. "Nope." I force a smile. "Tell me about your first day."

She ignores my change of conversation. "I'm going to kick

his ass for you."

As appealing as the offer sounds, Rosie would never do such a thing. She's all bark with no bite. She might rip him a new one, but she wouldn't lay a hand on him. And with Griffin's temperamental nature, I wouldn't want her to. That's a risk I wouldn't take.

"How was your Intro to Accounting class?" I continue to shift our talk. If we're going to maintain our friendship with all these miles between us, I don't want our conversation to revolve around that douchebag.

I crack open a bottle of Beth's wine' my mother's wine. I don't know her well enough to know if she'll mind, but I don't really care either way. If she didn't want me drinking her booze, she should have made that clear.

And right now, if I'm going to do what I have my mind set out to do, I need a little liquid courage.

I down the first glass in a hurry, not wanting to spend any more time than I have to with the bitter, dry red. I've never been a fan of wine, but it's the only alcoholic thing in the house I could find.

I exhale, and it's like the potent fumes have me breathing fire.

Tingling courses through me and my chest burns, but my mind remains fully intact. I give it a few minutes until the fog creeps in.

I sit on the edge of the stiff leather couch in the living room and glance at my phone. The message screen glares back at me. Griffin's name at the top.

It shouldn't be this difficult.

I drink another glass and decide now is the time. I have to do this.

With shaking hands, I grip the device and thumb a text to him.

Me: *We need to talk.*

I pause, not quite ready to hit send. There are two thousand miles between us, what is the worst thing that could happen?

I hover over the button.

"You can do this, Claire," I reassure myself.

Without giving it another second, I push the little blue arrow to hurl the words into the universe.

Dots appear immediately and I hold my breath in anticipation of his response. This is the part that worries me most of all. How will Griffin react? He's like a ticking time bomb, a minefield I'm constantly trying to navigate to avoid a massive explosion.

He types, and then it disappears. Then it shows up again, only to go away.

My heart pounds harder each time.

What could he be saying that is taking him so long?

Finally, a text pops through.

Griffin: *Call you later.*

Three words took him over ten minutes to send? And with them, he offers me almost no insight into his mindset. Is he pissed? Is he fine? Why later? Why not right now? When exactly? In an hour? Four? Tomorrow?

I can't stay slightly buzzed all night waiting for him to call.

I shove a cork into the bottle of wine and put it in the fridge. There's no point in drinking anymore if he's not going to talk to me anytime soon.

It's already dark here and with the time zone difference, it's almost midnight there. Apparently, he has better things to do than talk to his girlfriend.

I snatch my keys and cash off the counter. If he's not ready to have a chat, then I'm going to sober up. A cup of Bram's coffee will do just the trick.

8
JOHNNY

No one has ever avoided me so well in my entire life.

And honestly, I have to give her some credit.

I mean, we live in the same building, and go to the same college, yet she's managed to evade me all damn day.

Still, I have no fucking clue what I'm going to say to her. But I'm hoping once I get in front of her, the words will come to me. They have to.

My phone buzzes in my pocket and I internally cringe at what it might possibly say. I slide it out and read the one-word text.

Unknown: *Now.*

I sigh and put it back in place. I grab my shit and leave, because when duty calls, you don't mess around, not in my line of work.

I rush down the stairs and glance over at the girl's door. I never saw her go inside, but I can't imagine she's anywhere else at this hour.

I make quick work of getting to the alley where Josey stands guard.

"Brace yourself, kid," he tells me when I approach. "You musta pissed someone off."

I'm not at all surprised. It seems I can't do anything right these days.

"Do you know what it's about?" I ask him.

Josey shakes his head, his expression softening. "They don't tell me shit."

I grip the handle and take a deep breath, preparing myself for what's to come.

Franklin looks up at me from his spot at the same table he's always at. He slowly reaches up to take the thick cigar from his mouth.

I stand in silence as he discards the ashes in the tray sitting next to his crystal glass filled with brown liquid.

"You were late," he finally says.

By one fucking minute, I think to myself. I don't dare say it out loud. Franklin doesn't give a shit about minor details like that. He only cares about punishment, and retribution for disappointing him.

I had thought the beating I took from the delivery thug was enough, but apparently, I was wrong.

"Do we need to renegotiate our terms, Johnny?" His words are laced with a threat.

"No," I spit out immediately. I take a step forward. "What can I do?"

He cocks his head to the side and grins. "Obedient little thing, aren't you?"

I hate the demeaning tone of his voice, but I'm clearly at an obvious disadvantage here, and the only thing I *can* do is whatever he asks of me.

Franklin nods toward the dude in the corner. "Another delivery. You have until top of the hour."

I glance at my watch and fight the urge to panic. "That's only like twenty minutes."

Franklin takes another drag of his cigar. "You're a resourceful kid. You'll figure it out."

I swallow down my nerves. "Where am I going?"

"The place off Fifth." He picks up his glass and holds it to his lips. "You'll receive payment upon completion."

That building is over ten blocks away. Easily a fifteen-minute walk. And that's if I don't draw any attention to myself or have anything hold me up on the way. Usually I stop at my house to regroup and come up with a plan, but this time, I'm going to have to go straight from here to there. I don't enjoy being so unprepared, but in times like this, I have no choice but to go along with what Franklin demands of me.

I shove the bulky package into the waistband of my jeans, revealing part of my torso in the process.

"That looks uncomfortable." Franklin points toward my bruised side.

"It's fine," I lie. In reality, each breath sends a spike of pain through me, but I don't let him know that. Weakness only fuels him more.

"Good." Franklin lowers his drink to the table. "The clock is ticking."

The smoke-filled air is replaced by a putrid odor upon entering the alley. They're both equally gross, but being out of Franklin's line of sight is something I'd favor any day.

Josey stays leaning against the brick building. "You're still in one piece. I take it things went well."

"Maybe." I run possible route options through my head, each of them taking me into areas busier than I'd prefer to be in with a potentially illegal package. I don't know whether there are drugs or weapons or fucking gummy bears in there, but whatever it is, I can't get caught with it.

Not if I want my plan to work. If I get caught, all of this will have been for nothing.

I decide on a route, taking off without another wasted

second. I glance at the time. I'm going to need a fucking miracle to pull this off.

I dip down the alley and pop into another, blending in with the darkness and praying like hell I don't run into any trouble.

This is clearly a test. An impossible challenge to show Franklin whether or not I'm going to be an asset or a liability—if I'm worth keeping around. He's constantly setting me up for failure in hopes I back out or decide I don't want to be a part of his twisted game anymore.

But instead of giving him what he wants, I run his stupid errands and take the beatings that come my way, surprising him each time with my perseverance.

I never imagined my life becoming what it is, but sometimes you don't have a choice. And in this situation, I couldn't continue to stand back and watch what was happening with a clear conscience. I had to do something.

A few minutes pass and I make decent time on getting closer to my destination. I avoid highly trafficked areas and dodge a few of the security cameras I'm aware of. I'm not a perfect criminal, but I do my best with what I can.

And so far, I haven't been caught.

I pause under a fire escape and study the street ahead. If I cross here and take the alley, I should be smooth sailing the rest of the way.

I step out into the light and blend in with a group of people waiting for the pedestrian sign to signal them. Most of the group cuts left, heading toward the bustling restaurant side of the street, and the rest go right, to the various apartment and condo buildings.

I duck into the darkness ahead and glance over my shoulder to verify no one saw me enter. When I turn, a fist meets my face, knocking me off my feet and onto the soggy ground.

I scramble to my knees, only to be kicked in the ribs and spun around and onto my back. I wince from the new impact to a not-so-old injury. I desperately blink to clear my vision and see my attacker.

Two blurred figures stand above me, their heads covered in ski masks. They're not too much bigger than me, but together, I don't stand a chance.

If I could only get to my feet, maybe I could outrun them. My little bit of a size difference might mean that I'm faster than them. I know these streets like the back of my hand, which might give me the advantage I need.

Another kick to my side knocks the wind out of me. I crawl away, gripping onto a dumpster to help steady me.

Neither says a word, they only continue to come after me.

One of them slams a foot into my back, throwing me head-first into the metal thing. Warm liquid flows down from my brow and stars appear in my vision.

The biggest of the two grips my shoulder and spins me around, slamming another punch across my face.

I put my arms up to block the incoming hits but it's no use. They both know what they're doing, and I'm no match.

The other person fumbles inside my pockets and pulls out the contents.

My wallet, my phone, my keys.

I'm being robbed.

Panic courses through me. I don't give a shit about my own stuff, but if these thieves take Franklin's property, I'm a dead man.

I try to wiggle free, but another punch lands on the side of my head, knocking me over and onto the ground. I lay there, unable to move, the entire world spinning and blackness trying to consume me.

I don't scream for help. That would bring on unwanted attention and risk me getting caught. I fight to stay alert, to stay awake. I cower in an attempt to conceal the precious cargo tucked under my shirt.

I'm thrown onto my back, my shoulders pinned to the ground while the other person pats my body. They stop on the package I'm frantically failing to hide, ripping it out in one solid motion.

A fear unlike anything I've known courses through me, but before I can fully process it, another blow comes my way, almost in slow motion this time, sending me spiraling into complete darkness.

It's not the idea of dying alone in this alley that scares me, or what I'll have to endure for losing one of Franklin's packages. It's the consequences to everyone else involved that frightens me. How can I possibly protect anyone if I can't even protect myself?

Blood pools in my mouth and trickles down my face. I don't bother opening my eyes. I couldn't if I tried. I lay here and wait for the ability to regain enough strength to stand and drag myself home. Only, minutes pass, and instead of getting up like I have any other time I've had the shit knocked out of me, I float in and out of consciousness.

A soft, concerned voice appears. "Johnny?"

If she's here, I must be dreaming. And for once, I don't want to wake up.

9
CLAIRE

The door rattles shut behind me and I stand for a second, sizing up where I'm going to take a seat. The wine I drank still gives my body a strange tingling sensation that I can't wait to get rid of.

"This spot is clean," a bright-eyed older man says from behind the counter. He pulls a menu from the stack near the register and places it down.

"Thanks." I slide onto the cushy stool and glance at the specials on the chalkboard behind him. "I'll have a cup of coffee. And a blueberry old-fashioned, if you have any."

He turns, grabbing a fresh mug and the steaming pot. He pours my drink and slides it across to me.

"Thank you." I look for his nametag, but unlike the other employees, he doesn't have one. "Do you happen to have any cinnamon?"

He pauses, blinking at me like I asked him something in a different language. "Sorry, I… yeah, of course." He reaches under the counter and pulls out a shaker and hands it to me.

I put a couple dashes into my cup and stir it in. I ignore this man's strange stare at my apparently weird combo. I can't be the only one that has ever come in here that takes my coffee this way.

"Here you go." He sets a plate down with the donut I asked for.

"Thanks."

"Mmhm." He clears the countertop a few seats to my right. "You just start at the university?"

I nod. "Yeah, today."

"Nice place. We get a lot of traffic from the school. I know a few students that go there." He refills the sugar packet holder and puts it back in place.

"I like it so far. I'm hoping to transfer out by next year though." I bite off a chunk of the blueberry goodness and chase it down with a swig of my coffee.

"Oh?" This seems to grab his attention. "How come?"

I wipe at my mouth with the napkin. "I had some...extenuating circumstances that brought me here. It wasn't supposed to be a permanent thing."

"I see."

"It's not that I don't like it here. It's nice, honestly. But I grew up on the East Coast. It's home, you know? I don't know anyone out here. My life is back there." Here I am having word vomit with a stranger again, what the hell is wrong with me?

"That's understandable." The old man adjusts his thick brimmed glasses. "Change can come when you least expect it. Sometimes it's for the better, other times it's not. Obviously, I don't know your story, but if experience has taught me anything, it's that sometimes the most unexpected shifts pay off in the best of ways."

I eat the last of the donut and soak in his words, letting the combo of substance and caffeine help sober me up. I reach for the bills in my pocket, counting out how much I owe.

He holds out his hand. "This one is on the house. Consider it a welcome gift."

"Are you sure?" I flit my gaze around. "Can you do that?"

He chuckles. "I hope so. I own the place."

Which explains why he doesn't have a name tag. I'm probably the only idiot who didn't know who he was. My cheeks redden with embarrassment.

He extends his hand across the counter. "Bram."

"Claire." I take his and give it a firm shake.

"Nice to meet you, Claire." He takes my empty plate and mug.

"You, too. Thanks again." I hop down from the stool and leave the little café.

I cross my arms over my chest, the evening breeze a little cooler than I anticipated. I walk past a couple storefronts when my phone buzzes in my pocket. I pull it out and duck into the closest alley, gathering my bearings to answer the call.

A faint groan catches my attention. I let my eyes adjust to the darkness and settle my gaze on a crumpled figure lying on the dirty ground. My heart leaps in my chest.

I click the ignore button on my cell and turn on its flashlight. I tiptoe closer, my heart pounding a little harder with each step.

Blood is pooled all around him. His face is swollen, his hair matted to his forehead. His wallet and phone are next to him, his keys on the other side. Was this a robbery gone wrong? Why would they have left his stuff? If anything, this looks to be a strangely personal attack.

I glance behind me and bite at my lip. I focus back on him. "Johnny," I whisper.

His lip twitches and he reels his arm closer to his side, tugging the black fabric up with it.

I gently lift the shirt a few inches further. Bruising covers his ribs, probably from the injury over the weekend. Whoever beat him up must have made it worse tonight.

"Johnny, I'm going to call for help."

Somehow, he moves, grabbing onto my arm and stopping

me from getting my phone. “Please. Don’t.” His voice is barely audible. “Please.”

His touch stings, but not in a bad way. In an electrically surprising way.

If I can’t get backup, I have to do something. I can’t just leave him here.

I don’t owe him anything, especially after the weird way he’s treated me since I arrived, but I couldn’t live with myself if I walked away and left him behind.

He deserves better than that.

And in a way, I’m shocked by the anger that rises within me at whoever did this to him.

I take a steadying breath, careful not to focus too much on the stench of the nearby trash. “Johnny, can you sit up?” I place my hands on his shoulders. “I’m going to help you.”

He groans lightly but doesn’t open his eyes. They both seem to be swollen completely shut anyway.

I lean over and grab his belongings, shoving them into his pockets. “Come on.” I have to strain to lift him off the ground and bring him to his feet.

His weight leans against me, and it’s everything I can do to keep him up.

I throw his arm over my shoulder and reposition to get the best angle. “Let’s get you home.”

We aren’t far at all. But dragging his beaten body makes it one hell of a trek to our complex.

His head hangs low, and to unsuspecting passersby, he probably just appears super drunk. One short older woman gasps and covers her mouth, stopping dead in her tracks.

I force a smile before continuing on and mumble, "He'll be fine."

Johnny coughs and spews blood onto the concrete near the entrance of our building.

“We’re almost there,” I tell him. I punch my code into the

access box and maneuver us around the gate. The courtyard is empty, and it makes me semi-glad; at least I won't be asked questions I don't know how to answer.

I nearly drop him when his legs buckle, which is fitting considering this is the exact spot he had knocked me down only a few days prior. I won't be a dick like him, though.

I pause at the stairs. Suddenly they seem to be an impossibly difficult feat. "I'll need your help on this." I readjust to get a better grip on him.

"Mmmhm," he slurs.

One by one, we conquer each step. It takes freaking forever, but I manage to bring his mass to his front door. It feels wrong to go into his place uninvited, but it's a better option than taking him to my mom's.

I lean Johnny against the frame and reach into my pocket, only to remember I stuck his keys into his. I fish them out quickly and shove the one that looks like mine into the lock. I turn the handle and nudge the door open.

I glide my hand along the wall where my light switch is located and flip his on. My eyes adjust and I notice the layout is pretty much the same as mine, only it's decorated differently. My mom's looks like a staged rental home, and his looks like a total bachelor pad.

A gaming controller sits on top of a pizza box on the dining room table. Two whiskey bottles on the counter. Chinese takeout boxes stacked on top of each other.

"We made it." I continue to half-drag his body into his house, unsure of which room is his. I go down the hallway and enter the only bedroom with the door that's actually open, hoping it's his. I take him into the attached bathroom and guide him into the tub. It requires coaxing, but I manage to safely get him in.

I sigh at the release of weight. My shoulder aches, but it's nothing compared to what he must be feeling. I could have plopped him into his bed, but he would have ruined his sheets the second his blood and dirt-covered body touched them.

My phone buzzes, but I ignore it. I don't have time to deal with *that* situation right now.

Johnny groans as his head settles against the edge of the tub.

I stand and study him over.

He has numerous gashes on his face, the biggest of them on his brow. His nose is a bit more crooked than I recall, a sign that it's probably broken. His lip is split, and he's pretty much covered in blood. His palm rests on his stomach, clearly guarding some broken ribs.

I open the cabinet in the bathroom, hoping for some kind of antiseptic to clean his wounds. I manage to find a bottle of rubbing alcohol but nothing else. I check the linen closet but have no luck there either.

I kneel next to the tub. "Johnny. I'll be right back."

He slowly moves his other arm and reaches out toward me. He fumbles with locating me but ends up finding my hand. He leaves his on top of mine and mumbles something I can't quite make out.

"I'll only be a few minutes. I promise." Despite whatever happened between us, my heart aches at seeing him this way.

I can hate him tomorrow, but tonight, he needs me.

I rush out of his place, careful not to lock myself out, and go into mine. I go straight to the first-aid kit I recall seeing under the kitchen sink and toss it onto the counter. I search the medicine cabinet and grab anything that might be of assistance: a giant box of Band-Aids and antibacterial ointment, along with a few of those butterfly strips that I'm hoping will allow him to avoid getting stitches.

This is all a long shot, and definitely no replacement for actual medical care, but I'll do what I can for him given the circumstances. If he decides to change his mind and go to the hospital, I'll gladly take him. In the meantime, though, I can't force him to go if he refuses. And based on his pleading, he definitely doesn't want to go.

I shove everything into a grocery sack and grab the kit on the way out. Earlier today I was ignoring him, now I'm busting into his house to treat his wounds.

I snatch the half-empty whiskey bottle off his counter and go back to him.

He groans at my arrival and reaches into the air.

"I'm here," I reassure him. Although, I'm not sure how well that will comfort him in a time like this. I'm a complete stranger. A nobody to him.

Still, the tenseness in his face seems to resolve.

I unscrew the lid and pour some of the brownish liquid into the cap. I hold it to his lips. "Here."

He parts his mouth and allows me to tip it in carefully. "More," he manages to say.

I give him another capful and set the bottle on the floor. I grab a washcloth from the closet and run it under warm water from the sink. I wring it out and drop to my knees next to the tub. As gently as possible, I go to work on cleaning him up.

I start at his forehead, wiping away the dried-up blood and dirt caked to his skin. I do what I can to lightly tend to the wounds without making them any worse. I uncover a freckle on his cheek that I thought was dirt, and a few more sprinkled around.

I try not to concentrate on being this near him, my face only inches from his. I brush the brown hair off his brow and smooth it to the side.

He stays silent while I do my work, I assume drifting in and out of consciousness. He winces when I get close to the cuts, but otherwise, he lets me take care of him.

"This is going to hurt," I warn him. I soak a cloth with rubbing alcohol and dab it into his brow.

He hisses but stays still.

I do the same to the other visible wounds that I can find and wait until I'm sure they won't keep bleeding to apply the butterfly strip to help close them up.

I've done this one other time before, when my dad decided bicycling was a good idea and ended up wrecking in our gravel driveway about three seconds after getting on his bike. He had busted his knee and bumped his head, and of course, refused to get medical attention.

Must be a guy thing.

Dad had me run down to the pharmacy and grab these strips to hold the skin in place so he wouldn't have to get stitches. It seemed to work for him, but it's been a while, and I can't remember exactly how deep the wounds were compared to Johnny's.

I do what I can to fix Johnny's face and then sit back on my heels, studying him over. He looks like crap, but there's a sort of tender beauty to him that's captivating.

He grimaces and tries to move.

"Shh, take it easy." I rest my hand on his shoulder to calm him.

He tries to pry his eyes open, but the swelling is too much.

"Hold on." I rush to the kitchen and open the freezer in search of anything that can be of use. I snatch a bag of peas, the perfect thing to mold to his face.

He's mumbling something when I come back, but I ignore him and put the frozen veggies on him.

"Shit," he gets out. His palm comes up to hold onto the bag but ends up landing on mine instead.

I weasel it away and steady my gaze on his semi-exposed midriff. "Hey, um, do you think you could get your shirt off so I can check your ribs?"

"Help me." He pivots at the waist and sits up a little.

I swallow and grip the bottom of his tee, carefully tugging it over his head.

We both seem to gasp, him from pain and me from the sight of him.

His entire side is one solid bruise, his muscles much more prominent with the contrasting color. There's an inch-long cut trailing the center of the discoloration and smaller patches of redness are all over his torso.

Someone must have kicked him over and over again.

"Is it that bad?" he mutters.

Without thinking, I trace my fingers along the purple splotches. "Who did this to you?"

He swallows hard, like it might be difficult for him to do. "I don't know."

"I need to clean this." I grab the cloth and repeat the same steps from earlier, this time trying extra hard not to apply any more pressure than necessary.

He's patient and much quieter than I think anyone else would be in this same situation. Another person would have wanted to go to the hospital and probably gotten some strong painkillers, but other than a few low groans, Johnny is handling this like a freaking champ.

I can't help but wonder what else he's suffered through on his own.

I grab the bottle and unscrew the cap, taking a fiery swig myself and handing it to him.

He clutches it gratefully and chugs a few gulps down. When he's finished, he holds the bottle to his chest like a child does a stuffed animal.

I only hope it helps ease his pain.

I sit with him for a little while, not sure whether or not, or when, I should leave him. I've done pretty much all I can do, and unless he wants to go to the hospital, there's nothing else that can be done other than letting his body heal on its own.

I have this strange pull to make sure he's okay, to not let him be alone, even though he's not my responsibility.

He dozes off in the tub, still cuddling the whiskey.

I go into his room and pull the pillow and blanket from his bed and bring them into the bathroom. Propping him up gently, I place the pillow behind his head. I cover him up and tuck him into his makeshift sleep spot. It's probably uncomfortable, but I can almost guarantee there's no way I can drag him from there and get him onto his mattress.

After everything he's been through tonight, he looks at peace with where he is, and I don't want to be the reason to disturb that.

I kneel next to him one last time and tuck a rogue piece of his coffee-colored hair away from his face. "You're going to be okay," I whisper to him.

He moves slightly, almost leaning into my touch.

I quietly step away in an attempt to let him rest. It's then that I glance down at myself and notice the blood and dirt covering me.

10
JOHNNY

I wake up in my bathtub, a thawed bag of peas and a bottle of whiskey at my side. I can barely see through the thin slits of my eyelids, but I imagine it's better than nothing at all.

Everything aches.

My head, my chest, my torso, even my fucking legs.

How did I get here?

The last thing I remember was...getting the shit kicked out of me. Instinctually, I bring my hand to my forehead and stumble upon a bandage of some sort. I kick away the blanket that I'm not really sure how I got and raise myself from my makeshift bed.

I glance in the mirror and take myself in. Yep, it looks as bad as it feels.

I don't have a shirt on, but that's not the surprising part. Instead of being covered in blood and left in that alley, I'm here, partially cleaned up and my wounds treated.

A piece of my hair falls onto my forehead and a memory assaults me immediately. The girl, the one who has been doing everything she can to avoid me, tucking the strand away.

That can't be real. I must be fucking losing it. There's no way in hell *that* girl came to my rescue. I'm dreaming, I have to be. Or maybe I'm dead. That would be much more plausible than a nameless angel showing me such kindness.

My vision swims with fog and lightheadedness kicks in. I stagger over to my bed and plop down on the edge. I probably have a concussion, but it's the least of my worries.

I spot something unfamiliar on my nightstand. A glass of water. One that I didn't put there myself. Next to it, on a napkin, two little pills. Some kind of over-the-counter pain reliever. I scoot over and examine the offering further.

Scrawled in black ink on the white material are the words *feel better.*

My heart skips a beat, and my doubts are erased.

She was here. She saved me.

But why? I've been a dick to her.

She could have called an ambulance; she could have left me there to rot.

I think to that moment last night of hearing her say my name. I had thought I was hallucinating. That some pain-induced part of me created her in my imagination.

I shake my head in disbelief, and it throbs in response.

I down the pills and take the napkin into my hand, not wanting to let it go out of fear that it'll disappear, and I'll be stuck with the truth that I made all of this up.

I'm the one who does the saving, not the other way around.

My phone buzzes in my pocket and startles me out of my stupor. I pull it out and sigh at the busted screen, only then recalling the people who attacked me throwing all my shit to the ground.

I feel at my other leg, and the bulge of my wallet is completely unexpected. And if I'm inside my house, that means my keys were recovered, too. Unless she broke in, but I find that incredibly unlikely.

Given the questionable events that have taken place, I shouldn't rule anything out just yet.

Through the cracked glass, I cringe at the number of missed calls and texts.

It's then that everything comes full force into perspective.

I lost a package. Franklin's package.

For the first time since I've dealt with him, I was unsuccessful at making a delivery.

Franklin made it clear that I was already on thin ice, and this fuck up will surely continue to seal my fate with him.

I should have known eventually I would mess up. I was never cut out for this line of work. But how was I supposed to turn it down when it was my only chance at doing the right thing?

Slowly, I go back to the bathroom, snatching the whiskey I had left behind. I spin the cap off, a memory of her tipping some of the liquid into my mouth pops into my head. I bring the spout to my lips and chug what's left of the nearly empty bottle.

With my pillow and blanket in hand, I drag myself to my bed. I unbutton and step out of my dirty pants and crawl under the covers, ignoring the shit on my phone and tuning out reality.

I'm already a dead man—what's the harm in resting before Franklin kills me?

11
CLAIRE

He hasn't come out of his house all day.

Granted, I had to leave and attend my classes, so I can't be entirely sure. But I've come back during all of my breaks and waited in the courtyard, just in case.

Worry sets in that I shouldn't have left him alone. What if something happened? What if his injuries were worse than I thought they were? What if he hit his head hard enough that when he went to sleep, he didn't wake up? Did I leave him for dead?

I want to knock, to check on him and make sure he's okay, but if he really is just resting and recovering, I don't want to bother him. I just wish he would fucking turn a light on or *something* to signal that he's still alive in there.

"Hi," a small voice says.

I turn my attention toward the sound and settle my gaze on the young boy I had seen reading in this very spot.

"Hey," I respond.

"You seem…lost?" He tilts his head to the side, and his brown eyes glisten from the sunlight.

I force a smile. "Lost in thought, maybe." I point to the book in his hand. "Is that any good?"

My question seems to cheer him up.

"Yeah. It's about this town that has all these alien abductions and this weird presence that won't leave. No one can figure out what's causing it."

For a second, it's like he forgets I'm a stranger. It makes me realize how I haven't seen him with any other kids. Only that grumpy man who yelled at him.

"Billy," I sort of blurt out when the name crosses my mind. "Right? I think I heard your dad calling for you the other day."

He frowns. "That's my uncle, not my dad."

"My mistake." The alarm on my phone goes off, alerting me that it's time to head to school for my last class of the day. I glance up to the second level to check for life one more time.

"Are you friends with Johnny?" Billy asks me.

"No." I pause and shift to him. "Are you?"

He shrugs. "Yeah, I guess so."

"Have you seen him today?" I need to leave, but maybe Billy has the answers I need to settle my raging worries.

"Nope."

One word deflates the balloon of hope I was briefly holding on to.

The two-minute snooze on my phone goes off. "I have to go. I'll see you later." I step away and toward the exit. "Enjoy your book," I call out to him.

He smiles innocently. "Thanks."

Usually, I'm a well-disciplined student. I pay attention and take the best notes and *always* come prepared.

Today though? I'm a hot mess.

I can't think straight, and every time I desperately attempt to focus on what my teacher is saying, my mind wanders to the blood-covered guy from last night. It's not exactly an ideal start to my freshman year of college.

Each second leading up to class being dismissed is more antagonizing than the last. It's like I'm rushing to be done so I can sit and wait for some kind of reprieve from thinking Johnny might be dead.

That I left him when he needed someone the most.

I walk to the complex faster than I ever have, cringing when I pass the alley where I found him.

My cell buzzes, and I glance at the notification from Griffin.

I've been ignoring his calls and texts, for obvious reasons. I haven't been in the right headspace to deal with *this* situation, let alone *that* one.

Griffin has managed to go from blowing me off, to cussing me out, to apologizing and begging me to answer him. It's a mindfuck, but it's totally Griffin's way. He's trying to get some kind of reaction out of me so he's flipping through the versions of himself to see which one I will respond to.

Little does he know, I'm dealing with something much more important than his many mood swings.

I have a missed FaceTime from Rosie, too, but she was easily pacified with a quick text telling her that I'm swamped with assignments already.

It's not totally a lie, all things considered.

I arrive at the gate for my complex, and an idea pops into my head.

If Johnny *isn't* dead, and he's just resting, he's probably hungry. Given the takeout containers throughout his kitchen and living room, I doubt he has much to eat at his place.

I turn on my heel and go to the one place I'm familiar with.

Bram waves from his spot behind the counter when I walk in. "Welcome back."

"Do you happen to sell soup?" I ask him, not totally versed on his menu yet.

He glances behind him briefly. "Yep. Chicken noodle and broccoli cheddar today."

I bite at my lip as I deliberate. "I'll have a cup of both." Better safe than sorry. "To go," I add. "And two BLTs."

He jots it all down on his order pad. "Any coffee?"

"Um, yeah. Large black and...uh..." I rack my brain. I know next to nothing about Johnny, what if he's a tea drinker instead? "Make that another, too. Cinnamon in one, please."

"Coming right up." He attaches the slip to a little metal clip thing and spins it to his cook.

"Thanks," I tell him and settle onto a stool to wait.

He punches buttons on his register. "That'll be seventeen even."

I pull out a twenty and slide it across the counter. "Don't worry about the change."

"Thanks." He smiles, but then shifts his attention to my incessantly bouncing knee. "You okay?"

What a loaded question. How do I begin to answer it?

I force myself to sit still. "Yeah. Just waiting on news for something." No big deal, it's only life or death. And here I am, thinking soup and sandwiches are going to somehow make things better.

"Ah, that does sound stressful." Bram pulls out two disposable coffee cups and fills them to the top. He places them carefully into a drink carrier. "I'm sort of in the same boat."

I open my mouth to ask him if he's okay, to focus on anything other than my own issues, but a bell dings and steals his attention.

"Order up," the guy in the kitchen says. He shoves the bags through the opening to Bram who puts them in front of me.

I open them up, taking one of the sandwiches out and putting it with the soup, leaving the other behind for me. I can't say I have much of an appetite, but I need to eat *something* today if I want to stay somewhat sane.

"Any crackers?" Bram reaches under the counter and pulls a few packets out.

I hold the bag toward him to let him drop them inside. "Thanks, Bram."

"No problem. Good luck with your thing."

"You, too." I lean against the door to exit, nodding a goodbye in the process.

I make quick work of getting to the complex, not wanting to waste another second. I push in the access code and let the gate clang shut behind me.

I suck in a breath and slowly shift my gaze to Johnny's place.

My heart nearly thumps out of my chest when I notice light coming from the window. It's not much, but it's the sign that I desperately needed.

I walk through the empty courtyard and up the stairs, recalling last night and how difficult it was to drag his nearly lifeless body upstairs.

I knock on his door, not really sure what to expect. What will I even say?

Here's some food because I'm a weirdo and thought you should eat, even though we've never really spoken and you're kind of an asshole, but for some unknown reason, I'm still worried about you.

I suddenly realize how foolish I'm being. I lay the bag of his stuff down and pull out one of the coffees and set it carefully on his threshold.

I rush to my own sanctuary, exhaling deeply once I'm tucked inside.

I've done my part. I cleaned him up, I made sure he wasn't dead, and I fed him. There's nothing more that I need to do. He can take it from here.

Plus, I have my own problems to deal with. One glance at my phone tells me that.

12
JOHNNY

I'm just getting out of the shower when I hear a knock at the door. For a split-second, my mind goes wild, assuming that it's Franklin or one of his goons, but if history tells me anything, it's that he doesn't make house calls.

Franklin has succeeded for as long as he has in his industry because he keeps his hands clean. He hires other people to do his dirty work and uses his various business ventures, like the rundown diner I meet him at, to covertly operate. He's a wise man, and never makes mistakes. Showing his face at my complex or sending someone here to do it for him would pose too many risks.

The moment I step foot out of here, though—that's when I really need to worry. He's not going to let it slide that I lost a delivery. There will be a price to pay, and I'm not sure I'm ready to find out what it is.

Hurriedly, I dry myself off, careful not to agitate my many bumps and bruises. I wipe away the steam from the mirror, relieved to see the swelling in my face going down. I still look like I was stung by a bee, but I can open my eyes almost all the way, and that alone is a huge plus. They're bright green against the redness of the busted blood vessels.

The knock could have been Billy, coming to ask me to borrow something or ask for help on his homework.

I throw on a clean T-shirt and jeans, not bothering to slide any underwear on first. It was enough that I got up to take a shower, what more could the world ask from me in this condition?

I peek through the blinds covering the window, but no one is there. Slowly, I crack open the door and peer out. Not a soul in sight. My gaze trails down to the ground where a takeout bag and a cup sit.

Bram isn't really a home-delivery type person, and I've never told him the access code to get in, so unless he followed someone into the complex, it couldn't have been him. Plus, he probably would have banged on my door until I answered, not dropped off food and left.

I've severed ties with pretty much all of my friends since I started this new business venture, mostly to protect them. They all hate my guts now, meaning it couldn't have been one of them. Plus, they weren't really the type of friends that would drop in to check on me, let alone leave me food out of nowhere.

The only other explanation seems highly unlikely, too.

My stomach growls, telling me that I need to eat something to soak up the random booze I've been nursing all day for the pain.

I reluctantly grab the offering and go inside, dropping the food on the counter and opening the bag. Instantly, I'm greeted with a heavenly aroma. I must be hungrier than I thought if food smells *this* good.

I pop the lid off the cup and sniff at the contents. If I didn't know better, I'd assume this was my regular order, but if Bram didn't deliver it, there's no way someone could have guessed such a random combination. I take a sip to test my theory, swallowing down the cinnamon warmth.

How the hell did she know how I take my coffee?

I don't go to class all week. It's not that I don't care about my education, I'm just not really prepared to handle this Franklin situation quite yet. Not to mention, I don't want to answer questions about why my face is fucked up.

I spend most of the time sleeping, staring at the ceiling, and wondering how the fuck I'm going to get myself out of this mess. I barely have an appetite, but I end up forcing down a frozen meal or a bowl of cereal here or there.

I even fill my time doing something I shouldn't—watching out the window for her.

Her routine has become a bit predictable. She leaves her place and lingers around the courtyard for a little while before heading to what I assume is her first class of the day. Between courses, she returns to study at the corner table, tucked away from everything else. Once she's in for the evening, she bounces between staying inside and at her chosen courtyard hideaway.

Part of me wishes that I were invisible, making it possible to be near her. To give her company and let her know that she's not alone. She seems sad, like something is bothering her, besides the obvious asshole that lives in her building. I long to bring her a moment of peace. Which is entirely strange considering I still don't know her name.

Maybe those types of formalities don't matter in the grand scheme of things. Maybe you can be drawn to someone without really knowing them.

A door opens down the hall in the direction of her place and I freeze, still stealthily peering from inside my house.

She appears in my line of sight, and I swear it's like my heart is going to pound out of my chest and leap through the door at her.

I hold my breath, desperate not to alert her to my watchfulness.

The stunning girl pauses right outside.

I study the rise and fall of her shoulders with each bit of air that enters her lungs. Her V-neck charcoal gray tee and dark denim skinny jeans hug her body in the best way. Her chocolate brown hair is tied off to the left side in a low ponytail.

She raises her fist to my door, but nothing happens. Her hand lingers in the air and stays there.

I could move—I could rush to open it, to finally greet her properly and say something to redeem myself for being such a shitty person, but I don't do anything. I stand there, completely and utterly mesmerized by her beauty and the fact that such a being simply exists.

Slowly, she lowers her arm to her side and walks away, disappearing from my vision and taking a piece of me with her.

"It's better this way," I tell myself.

It's a reality that I have to force if I'm going to protect her from me and my world. I'm already messing up left and right, I can't afford to bring her down with me.

Even being her friend is a risk I'm not willing to take.

I can't. I won't.

And I will keep reminding myself that until I'm blue in the face.

I will be the bad guy if it means sheltering her from harm's way.

A phone rings, but it's not mine. I drag my attention back through the blinds.

She's still out there, standing against the railing of the stairs. She holds the device in her hand, her body tense as she studies it over.

I crack the window open to get a better vantage point.

"Hello," she says, a hint of something I can't quite pick up in her tone. Annoyance, maybe?

A loud voice vibrates through the other end but I can't quite make it out.

She shifts her weight. "Now's not a good time."

The person manages to get even noisier.

"I know I said I wanted to talk, but I've been busy. I don't want to get into it right now." She's much calmer than the other person.

The person must yell at her for a solid minute before taking a breath.

She wipes at her cheek, and it's everything I can do to stand here and watch this unfold. She doesn't deserve to be treated like this. No one does. But if I intervene, she might not continue to see me as the bad guy, and I can't let that happen. Still, it pains me to hear someone mistreat her. Like my heart is being ripped open alongside hers.

I can't imagine she, the girl who hauled a complete stranger from a dingy alley and brought them soup the next day, would ever warrant this type of behavior from anyone.

I raise my hand to the cold glass.

"Why are you this way?" she asks the pissed-off person.

There is no response. Radio silence. Which could only mean one thing.

They hung up on her.

The coward got called out on their shitty behavior and that's how they react? What a fucking loser.

She presses the button on the side of the phone and slides it into her back pocket. She rubs her hands across her face to wipe away the tears and does something I don't expect; she glances toward my unit.

I nearly trip and fall backward to avoid her catching me. I wince as I bang my side against the table and curse under my breath.

My own cell vibrates, a reminder that I can't hide from my problems forever. If I want to get my mind off this girl, I should focus on cleaning up the mess I've created.

I take the thing and do my best to navigate the busted screen. I'll need to get a replacement, but it'll have to be another day.

I click the last text that came through.

Unknown: *!!!*

I scroll down to Josey's number and type a response.

Me: *Tell B I'll be right there.*

Dots appear and my stomach tightens along with them.

Josey: *K*

I guess it could have been worse. I think if Franklin was going to off me, Josey would give me a little bit of a warning. He's the only one who's shown me kindness, and I'd like to assume he wouldn't let me walk into a complete death trap.

I snatch my keys off the counter and shove them in my pocket, along with my wallet and broken phone.

I leave my place in a hurry, not wanting to draw any attention from...well...her. I'd rather Billy not see me this way, but more so, I'd rather face Franklin than continue to put up the false asshole front to keep this girl hating me.

She clearly has enough douchebags in her life; I hate that I have to be another. Maybe one of these days I'll be able to explain to her why I am the way I am, and if the stars happen to align, maybe she'll forgive me.

I doubt I'll live long enough to tell the story, though, not after Franklin is done with me. I knew going into business with him would be the death of me, but I had to be the one to step up and put a stop to what was happening.

You can't save everyone, a little voice in my head calls out.

"Watch me try," I tell it.

I manage to make it to the alley behind Franklin's diner without getting the shit knocked out of me again. I kept my head down and avoided eye contact with people that passed me by. It was dark enough that no one seemed overly concerned about my busted face, or maybe they were focused on themselves instead of being concerned with random people on the street.

"Ouch," Josey says when I approach. "Your modeling career is definitely a thing of the past." He holds out a lit cigarette toward me.

"Funny. You should see the other guy." I take a drag and pass it back. I'm not a smoker, but right now, I'll take anything to settle the nerves of what's about to go down.

"Yeah?" Josey's brows perk up.

I let out a chuckle. "No. There were two of them. Completely caught me off guard. I didn't stand a chance."

"Damn, J. You really ought to strap up." He raises his shirt to expose a gun tucked into his waistband.

"Boss would never let me have one." Not that I really have the desire to anyway. What would I have done? Would I have shot two people? What would I have told the cops? That they were trying to steal my illegal contraband? I need to avoid that kind of attention if I'm going to succeed at my master plan. I can't have the authorities looking my way if any of this is going to work.

Josey shrugs and tosses his cigarette to the ground, stomping it out and lighting another one. "You're going to end up dead."

I place my hand on the door's latch and glance at him over my shoulder. "One way or another."

The stench of cigars and Franklin's overpowering cologne attacks me upon entering the close quarters. Stares melt into me and I clench my already tight jaw even more.

"Johnny..." Franklin begins. "Have a seat." His cool tone sends a chill down my spine. He flicks his wrist. "Everyone out."

They do what he says, some of them funneling through the front, some the rear. I claim the chair across from him, keeping my gaze trained on anything but him, and wait for him to continue.

"Listen, we all make mistakes. I get that. I'm not an unreasonable man. I understand why you're here, the sacrifice you made. But in my line of business, there is minimal room for error. And Johnny, you've exceeded the limit."

I bite at my cheek to avoid giving him any type of response.

"I can't afford slip-ups like this. You're well aware of that." His hand moves forward, grasping onto a glass sitting on the table. He drains the golden contents into his mouth and puts it down.

I don't mean to, but my gaze follows his movement and meets his glare.

"I'm going to give you an opportunity I don't offer often. Let's call it... redemption. You have two weeks to retrieve my lost package. Do so and all will be forgiven, and we go back to doing business as usual. Failure will result in renegotiating our terms." His dark eyes bore into me. "We both know what that entails." His last statement pierces through my soul in the very manner he means it to.

Everything I've done up until this point will have been for nothing if I don't make things right.

I have to find that package if it's the last thing I do.

13
CLAIRE

Johnny finally came out of his house. And the fact that I know this has me feeling like a total stalker. Over the last few days, I've managed to keep a close eye on his house, waiting for some *actual* sign of life, not just a light flipping on and off or food disappearing from his doorway.

My heart nearly thumped out of my chest when I glanced out my window and spotted him jogging down the stairs and rushing through the courtyard of our complex.

He was very much alive, and that alone made me relieved and pissed all at the same time.

Obviously, I don't want him to die, but he could have said something to me—*anything* at all—after I nursed him back to life.

Maybe I'm asking too much. It's not like Johnny requested my services. I offered them willingly. And just as I didn't owe him anything, he doesn't either. I shouldn't be upset with him for my own expectations of how I think he should react.

When I dropped food off the other day, I told myself he was no longer my problem. That I had done everything I could do for him, and I would focus on my own troubles. Why can't I stick to that? Why does he keep invading my thoughts with worries of whether or not he's okay?

It's infuriating, really. And I need to make it stop.

My phone buzzes, and I'm grateful when I notice that it's not Griffin. He gave me an earful earlier, and I'm not too thrilled to go through that again. Talking to Griffin is like playing a twisted game of Russian roulette, only instead of a bullet, it's gambling on which personality you're going to get, and all of them are pretty crappy options. Even the nice version of him sucks because it's short-lived, only to be replaced with a hateful one after he sinks his hooks into his victims.

I focus my gaze on the screen at the text from the girl in my English Lit class. We exchanged numbers this morning when she invited me to go out with her and a group of her friends tonight. Apparently, there's a few bars downtown that don't check for I.D. and serve college students. It's not my usual idea of fun, but considering it's the first decent friend I've made since I've been here, I embrace the opportunity at a normal life.

Cora: *Pick you up at ten?*

Me: *Sounds good, see you later!*

I push another button and dial Rosie. If I'm going to go out and socialize with people my age, I need help picking out something to wear. We might be two thousand miles apart, but she's still my best friend and my go-to for stuff like this.

"Shots, shots, shots!" Cora cheers the second we walk into the bar.

The music is loud, and the place is crowded, but I'm determined to have a good time. I need this. Life has been so chaotic lately between Griffin and the move and...Johnny...that I need something to take my mind away from things for a little while.

"Go find a table, I'll get the first round." Cora shoves me and two of her friends into the mass of people and makes her way to the bar. She disappears almost instantly, blending in with everyone else trying to get the bartender's attention.

One of the girls, Steff, grabs onto my hand and drags me through the horde to an empty spot near a couple pool tables.

I'm grateful for the can-do attitude she shares with Cora because I'm pretty lost.

The other friend trails behind, scoping the place out on her way.

"Earth to June," Steff calls out to her.

"Sorry." June does a final glance and approaches our area. "Just wanted to make sure Andrew isn't here. I don't really feel like dealing with *that* tonight."

"Are you two still on the outs?" Steff cranes her neck to look toward the bar.

"Permanently." June pulls out her phone.

"Good." Steff takes a seat on one of the stools lining our table. "I never did like him."

June lets out a laugh. "Me either."

"Oh, whatever, you were crazy about him." Steff reaches over and gently shoves June's shoulder.

"Crazy about getting him into bed…and he lasted all of three seconds." She rolls her eyes and sighs. "He's a thing of the past now." June turns her screen around to show us both a picture of a reasonably attractive guy. "He's been replaced. What do you think?"

Cora comes over with a huge smile on her beautiful face and four tall shot glasses squeezed between her hands. "Doubles!"

I grab mine and wait for the rest of the girls to get theirs.

"To us," Cora toasts.

"To us," the rest of us cheer over the noise of the booming bar.

I down the liquid without thinking twice. It's smooth at first, but then warms its way down my chest. That was definitely tequila.

Cora motions to the newly freed-up pool table. "You any good?"

I shake my head. "Not really."

She breaks out in a huge smile and grabs my arm, dragging me over to it. "Me either."

It's not long before we're all laughing and cheering each other on at how badly we collectively suck. According to Cora, June is a pool-shark, but she'd rather spectate than join us. She definitely gives off *look at me wrong and I'll stab you* vibes, which is the polar opposite of Cora and Steff. I welcome each of their personalities all the same, even the roughness of June's.

Forever comes and we still haven't finished a single game, none of us able to pocket any of the balls between our natural lack of talent and the booze that courses through our veins.

June and Steff both buy a round of drinks, more doubles from the former and something called a Washington Apple from the latter.

My head swims with fuzz, and for once, I feel freaking great.

It's my turn to buy next, but I urge the girls that we need to pace ourselves.

My phone goes off in my pocket and I pull it out, Griffin's stupid face on the screen.

"Nooo, don't answer it." Cora tries to reach and stop me to no success.

I laugh and swat away her arm.

Liquid courage has me pushing the green button and connecting the call.

"Hello!" I shout through the receiver.

"Where are you?"

"Out," I say, with a matter-of-fact tone.

"No shit, Claire. Are you at a fucking bar?" Griffin sounds pissed, but it doesn't affect me the way it normally does.

Yay, booze!

"Yes, Griff, I am. Where are you?"

Steff cups her hands around her mouth and loud whispers, "Who's Griff?"

"Who the fuck is that?" Griffin's tone shifts to further emphasize how *not* okay he is with all of this.

"What do you want? I'm busy." My voice slurs no matter how much I try to make it normal.

"You're fucking drunk? Are you there with a guy? You're there a goddamn week and you're already cheating on me? You're nothing but a slut, Claire. A dirty, ungrateful little bitch. You're lucky I—"

Rage builds inside of me and I snap. "Shut the fuck up, Griffin. I'm lucky—what? That you didn't give me an STD from that girl you fucked at your work? What's her name, Shelby? Where were *you* last weekend? Huh?" I pause but go right back to it, not ready for him to take over the conversation the way he always does. "I'm done, Griffin. Fucking done. You and me, we're over."

I hang up the phone like he's done to me so many times before.

All three of my new friends stand there wide-eyed, completely silent.

"Holy shit," Cora finally mutters. "That was..." She looks around to the other two girls, "Badass."

"Who do I need to hurt?" June's glare bores through me. She's ready to pounce and I adore how willing she is to defend my honor.

My body trembles with equal parts fear and adrenaline. I've never taken such a tone to Griffin before. He's always the one dominating our conversations and doing his best to make me feel small. There's something incredibly empowering about giving him a tiny taste of his own medicine.

The mixture of emotions is sobering, too. Despite the

copious amount of alcohol running through my veins, everything has become crystal clear.

"My turn," I say through a grin. I leave them behind and head through a swarm of people toward the bar to get our next round.

Three hours later, I'm quite literally falling off the pool table after Cora and Steff insisted that we dance on top of it.

Gentle but firm hands appear under my arms and lift me from the ground.

I open my blurry eyes and settle my sights on a beautifully broken man.

"Get the fuck off her," Cora snaps and shoves the guy.

I swallow and blink, a pathetic attempt to stop the room from spinning out of control. Like I'm stuck in a low gravity situation, I pivot my head slowly around to piece together what's happening. I must be really out of it if I'm hallucinating him.

"I'm trying to help." He holds his palms up and out in front of him. "Why'd you let her get this drunk?"

Cora grips my shoulder and spins me toward her too fast. "Do you know this guy?"

I stumble and frantically fail at regaining my footing. I close my eyes and brace for impact on the floor, but it never comes. Instead, I'm caught by him again. I squint up at his bruised and busted face, noticing one of the freckles I had tried to wash away.

"What's her name then, if you know her so well?" Cora pulls at me to break me away from him.

He parts his mouth, but nothing comes out.

"Johnny," I whisper while raising my hand to his cheek to verify that he's real.

He shifts his attention to me, his emerald eyes piercing through my soul. Is it the alcohol, or is he really this intense up close? It was one thing when he was in and out of consciousness from being beaten, it's totally another while he's fully alert.

"It's me," he assures me tenderly.

"Oh." Cora blurts out. "Well, okay."

Johnny turns back to the boss girl of our group. "I think she's had enough for tonight." He glances down at me. "Can you stand?"

I tilt my head. "I'm not already?"

He helps me onto solid ground, putting his arm around my torso to stabilize me. His fingers graze an exposed piece of my side, and my knees quite literally go weak.

"Come on, I'm taking you home."

14
JOHNNY

I should be doing a million other things than what I'm doing right now, but here I am, avoiding all of them and doing this instead.

Franklin gave me an opportunity to redeem myself, so that's what I'm going to do.

Only, a short while into my detective work, I spot her through a window, laughing and smiling and having fun.

I don't know why I was able to zero in on her in a room full of people, and I sure as shit couldn't help the magnetic pull she has on me, dragging me into that packed bar.

I claim a seat near the door, ordering a whiskey neat and keeping my distance from her in case I'm spotted. I just have to make sure she's okay, that she truly is having a good time, that she's safe.

She downs drink after drink, enough that I grow worried. Something feels off, like she's masking some emotion with the endless shots.

I can't leave, not yet, not until I know for sure.

The girl with bright blonde hair grabs her arm and tugs her onto the pool table.

I cringe when her light-lilac shirt slides up a little, exposing part of her side. Something primal kicks in and nearly has me jumping from my seat to toss my denim jacket around her and shield her from all of the prying eyes.

But the fabric goes down and I stay put, not making a scene in front of everyone.

If she wants to dance, she can dance.

I try not to be another one of the many looking her way, but each time she sways to the edge of the table, I find myself inching closer in her direction.

I pay my bill and down the rest of my drink, somehow sensing the finale coming soon. I shouldn't intrude. I should let her carry on and do what she wants. But something inside of me won't allow me to stand back and watch it unfold.

She does exactly what I think she's going to do—she falls, and thankfully, I time everything just right to catch her in my arms.

I bring her to her feet and the blonde girl shoves me.

"Get the fuck off her," she spits.

I calm myself, not wanting to react negatively to her friend. I'm sure this comes across like I'm some random weirdo trying to cop a feel, when in reality, I'm desperately working to make sure that *doesn't* happen.

"I'm trying to help." I extend my hands to show them that I'm not a threat. "Why'd you let her get this drunk?"

The blonde grabs her from my arms and moves her quickly —too quickly. "Do you know this guy?"

I move on instinct, catching her when she's about to fall again. It takes everything I have to not scoop her up and take her away from here immediately.

"What's her name then, if you know her so well?" Her friend tries to break her away from me again.

After all this time, all that we've been through, I still don't know her fucking name. How is that even possible?

"Johnny." Her voice is just a whisper. Her hand cups my cheek, and I'm reminded of a few nights ago when she did the same thing moments prior to me passing out in a pain-induced stupor.

I stare into her ocean blue eyes, eager for her to know I'm here. "It's me."

The friend blurts something out, but I don't hear her, not when I'm focused on the helpless creature in my arms.

"I think she's had enough for tonight." I hold onto her so she doesn't fall. "Can you stand?"

"I'm not already?"

I help her stand, giving her my arm to stabilize her. I ignore the shock of electricity coursing through my fingers as they graze across her bare skin.

"Come on, I'm taking you home." I move her through the crowd and toward the door, not caring to continue the mind-numbing conversation with her friend while the other two girls stood back and gawked.

They've all had more than enough to drink tonight, but her friends seem to be a bit more experienced in this department.

"Ay, Johnny!" The bartender catches my attention on the way out. He points to the sloppy girl in my arms. "She hasn't paid her tab."

I reach into my pocket, fishing a hundred out and slapping it onto the counter. "Does that cover it?"

He slides it across and holds it up to the light. "Yep."

I continue to navigate us through the crowd and out into the brisk night. It's refreshing to get away from the thick atmosphere of that bar.

I glance down at the girl at my side. "You okay?"

She's not heavy by any means, which makes me wonder how the hell she managed to drag my ass out of that alley and into my place.

"Mmm," she mumbles. "I can w-walk." She pulls herself from my assistance.

I hold out my arms in case she falls again. I don't want to encroach, but I'd like to be there if she needs me. "I can help."

"Y-you can't...help...me." She walks a few feet and stops, perking up and glancing around. "Where are we?" She blinks stiffly.

I point in the direction of our complex. "We're this way."

"Right." She takes off the opposite way.

I steady her by the shoulders and spin her around toward the proper route.

"Yes, that's what I meant." She giggles. "I was...testing you." She reaches out, weaving her hand around mine, our fingers interlocking, and pulling me with her. "Come on."

My breath hitches, and I stare like an idiot at the joined connection. I have to force myself to move, otherwise I'd stand there totally flabbergasted by the ease of our hands fitting together.

We walk a little until we're about to pass a food cart.

"I'm starvingggg," she emphasizes while holding onto her stomach.

Getting something in there to soak up some of that booze is probably a good idea, and considering how adorable she is, I can't exactly refuse her.

I buy her a slice of pizza and her eyes light up like I gave her the moon. Her reaction warms my heart in a way I sort of wish I could shut off.

She walks slowly and manages to devour it within minutes. She balls up the wrapper and turns, looking for a trash can.

My gaze falls to the red splotch of sauce on her chin. Everything turns to slow motion, and without thinking, I reach up and swipe it away with my thumb. Another one of the things I've done tonight that I clearly shouldn't have.

Her eyes meet mine, and she seems just as surprised as I am by the entire interaction. Her breath is steady and even.

We stay that way for a long second, peering at each other.

Finally, she grins and grabs onto my hand, pulling us in the direction of our complex.

I take her garbage and toss it into a dumpster that we pass.

I don't say another word on the trek to our building, and thankfully, she doesn't either. There are so many things I should tell her, but now isn't the time. I don't know if there ever will be. An apology would potentially repair things between us, and if that happens, I lose the advantage I have of her hating me. The one that helps keep her safe.

All I have to do is get her home. Get her into her house, and the rest will be history. She's drunk enough that she'll probably forget all of this happened and assume one of her friends walked her back. She won't remember holding my hand or touching my face, or the many times I caught her when she was falling.

I'll be able to walk away and pretend nothing happened. I'll live with the secret memory of her skin on my fingertips and the strange sensation in my chest when she's around.

I'll cherish it but tuck it away, like a photograph from a long-ago era.

We arrive at the gate outside our complex, and she breaks the connection between us. The absence of her touch stays with me long after it should.

She pokes the access box, and it beeps loudly, blinking red. She sighs and repeats the same process two more times.

"Here." I enter my code and the latch unlocks, granting us entry.

She stumbles walking through the courtyard, bumping into a potted plant and seeming highly offended that it had the nerve to be in her way.

I stifle a laugh at how completely adorable she is when she's drunk. Or maybe it's not the alcohol and just her that brings a smile to my face. I shake the thought away and focus on the last few steps to get her settled in for the night.

We pause at her door, and she shoves her hands into her pockets.

"Uh..." She reaches behind her, pulling out her cell phone but nothing else. She giggles and leans against her door, a mixture of exhaustion and intoxication settling heavily over her.

"Where're your keys?" I ask her.

She bites at her lip and averts her gaze, like she's trying to recall a memory.

I force myself to look away from her mouth.

She shrugs. "Where's yours?" Without warning, she shoves her hand into the pocket of my jeans and tugs the chain out. She holds them out between us and rattles them. "Finders keepers."

It's everything I can do to not let my jaw drop to the floor. She's a fireball when she's been drinking.

She strolls over to my door and slides the correct key into the lock, turning the handle and going inside.

I follow after her. "Hey, wait, what are you doing?"

She doesn't bother turning on the light; she just goes straight past the kitchen, and down the hallway, like she's already memorized where to go. She's about to step into my room when she strips her shirt over her head and tosses it onto the floor.

"Whoa!" I turn my head and throw my arm up to cover my face.

What the hell is she doing?

I carefully make my way down the hall and peek into the room. "Dude."

My heart thuds loudly and I shield my eyes again while she unbuttons her skin-tight jeans and steps out of them.

"Johnnyyy..."

I don't even know her name, and she's undressed and

sprawled out on my bed. Thank God I decided to wash my sheets after I bled all over them.

I backtrack to the laundry room and pull the blanket out of the dryer. I clutch it in my hand and keep my eyes sealed shut on my way to where she is. I toss it onto where I think the bed is and squint to confirm she's covered.

She sighs and nuzzles into the pillow. "This is nice," she murmurs.

I approach cautiously, leaning down to bring the comforter over her exposed shoulder.

Her eyes open slowly, and for a second, I worry how she'll react to seeing me here in front of her.

She reaches toward me. "Are you real?" Her hand grips onto mine.

I kneel there, next to the bed, wondering the same about her. "Yeah." I study the way our skin touches, not wanting to forget a single detail. "Can I ask you something?"

Part of me is hesitant to have the answer, that if I finally know, maybe she'll vanish before my eyes, never to be seen or heard from again. Disappearing quicker than she appeared. Leaving a bigger void than the one she created when she suddenly showed up in my life.

If I solve the mystery, will I lose her?

"Anything," she whispers.

I swallow the lump in my throat. If I'm going to do this, what better time than now? At least, if she evaporates into thin air, I'll be with her when it happens.

We'll have been together.

"What's your name?" Each word is more difficult than the last to get out. I hold my breath, afraid of the unknown. The irrational possibility that she's just a figment of my twisted imagination.

Her lips part slowly. "Claire."

And with that one syllable, a new life is awakened within me.

"Claire." I let it roll off my tongue, testing the name out.

It's beautiful and angelic, like her, and I'm not at all surprised with how familiar it feels.

Moments pass and she stays, disproving my foolish fears.

She struggles to keep her eyes open, and once they close, she becomes even more delicate than before. There's a saying about not plucking a beautiful flower, because when you do, it will wither and die. Well, Claire is a rare flower that should never be picked. Not a soul could ever be worthy of what she has to offer. She is a gift from the universe that should not be disturbed or tainted by this cruel world.

It pains me to know that there's no way I can have her in my life. Not if I intend on putting her safety first. The best thing I could ever do for her is to push her away, not allow what's going on with me to corrupt her in the same manner it's doing to me.

At the very least, I owe her that.

I pull my hand away from hers, despite fighting the desire to keep it there for as long as possible.

Her dark brown eyebrow raises, and she extends her arm into the space between us. "Stay."

My heart constricts, but I remind myself that she's drunk. She probably doesn't know what she's saying. Maybe she thinks I'm someone else. Anyone other than me. I have done nothing to deserve the privilege of staying here with her.

"Johnny…" She adjusts her head on my pillow and exhales deeply.

If tomorrow comes and I have to say goodbye, at the very minimum, I can give myself the night.

I tuck a strand of her long hair behind her ear and glance over to the recliner in the corner of my room. I quietly grab a blanket from the linen closet and settle into my makeshift bed.

It's not far, but it still doesn't seem close enough. I'll be able to keep an eye on her in case she needs anything. Or I tell myself that to excuse my decision of sleeping in here instead of on the couch in the living room.

I stay in that old chair for hours, praying for sleep to finally take me. But it never comes. I watch her steady in and out breaths to reassure myself that she's okay and contemplate what the fuck I'm going to do about the Franklin situation. I can't seem to shut my mind off and get any of the rest I desperately need.

I'm never going to heal from all of these injuries if I can't doze off for even a minute.

Claire rolls over and flops her arm against the bed. Her face is strained, and her leg twitches under the blanket. She mumbles something but I can't make it out.

I raise my head and take a better look.

"Stop," she urges.

She's having a nightmare.

My first instinct is to wake her up, but if I learned anything from the night terrors my cousin has when he's home from his deployment, it's that you should avoid disturbing someone during an episode. It can cause them to be confused and disoriented, and often does more harm than good.

It's for the best, but it doesn't make it any easier to sit back and watch.

"Get off me." She grips at the sheet and moves her head.

Something is trying to get to her in her dream, and I wish like hell I could be there to save her.

She turns the other way. "Please, Griff, you're hurting me."

Not *something,* but *someone.*

A metaphorical knife cuts through my chest at the plea that leaves her mouth.

Even in her imagination, how could anyone ever hurt her?

I hop out of the chair and rush to the side of the bed. If this goes any further, I have to wake her up. I can't allow anyone to lay a hand on her. Real or not.

"I said *stop*." She flails one last time and then the tension in her body relaxes.

I let out a sobering breath and sink against the mattress. I close my eyes and lean my head back. A second later, a warm hand lands on my shoulder.

I glance over and see that her eyes are closed, telling me that she probably didn't do it on purpose. In the words of Bob Ross, "It's a happy little accident."

15
CLAIRE

The aroma of coffee greets me when I wake. My head throbs, and I can think of nothing better than an oil-drum sized cup of coffee. Only, I live alone, and there's no reason that smell should be wafting into my room.

Without opening my eyes, I feel around the bed I'm in, noticing these sheets feel nothing like mine.

A familiar scent lingers, and I realize I'm not at my place at all.

I pry open my eyes and take in my surroundings, confirming my suspicions.

Shit, shit, shit.

I sit up abruptly and the blanket falls down, revealing my barely clothed body.

Panic intensifies my already aching skull. "No, oh God, no."

I spot my pants a few feet from the foot of the bed in a pile on the floor. I crane my neck to glance down the hall before committing to getting up. When I don't see anyone, I jump out of Johnny's bed, hugging the comforter around my chest and making a beeline toward my bottoms.

What was I thinking? What was *he* thinking?

I'm stepping into them when the sound of footsteps approaches.

"Oh, crap," his voice calls out. "Sorry." He immediately covers his eyes.

Not exactly the reaction I'd expect after having slept with someone. I guess chivalry isn't dead?

He holds a cup in my direction. "Here, uh, do you want this?"

"Where's my shirt?"

Still concealed, he points behind him. "You dropped it in the hall."

I rush around him and snatch it up, throwing it over my head and relaxing a tiny bit once I'm not almost naked.

"You decent?" He keeps his hand up to block his vision.

I fold my arms across myself. "Yeah."

Johnny turns and extends the drink again. "Coffee?" He has total bedhead, and his face is still swollen from the other night.

There's this strange urge to run my fingers through his hair, but I shove the desire away.

I glance from him to the cup, then back to him.

"I didn't poison it, if that's what you're wondering." He takes a sip and holds it out. "See."

I guess I'm sort of in shock. Johnny and I have been in this cat and mouse game of avoiding each other, so to have him so matter-of-factly offering me a drink is mind-blowing.

And honestly, this is the longest conversation we've had while both of us were conscious.

"Claire."

The way he says my name makes my heart skip a beat.

"Um, thanks." I take the mug from him, our hands grazing in the process. I ignore the things that stir in my chest. "Do you know where my phone is?"

"Best guess, it's somewhere in here." He pulls back the blanket, exposing the corner of my cell case. He grabs hold of it and gives it to me.

"And my keys?" I lift my shoulders a bit helplessly.

"Now that one, I can't help you with. You didn't have them when I obtained you."

I check my pockets again but they're not there. I must have lost them at some point last night. I'll have to retrace my steps. I tap the screen on my phone, but it doesn't light up.

"Charger?" Johnny seems to read my mind.

I bite at my lip. "Yeah."

He points out the door. "There's one in the kitchen."

I follow him out and down the hall. It's a strange sort of walk of shame not remembering what happened between us. "Thanks." I plug my phone in and wait for it to boot up. I stand there awkwardly wishing time would speed up a little.

He twists the tip of his sock-covered foot into the tile floor. "Claire, so—"

I cut him off. "Did we hook up last night?"

His eyes go wide, and he frantically shakes his head. "No, God no. Seriously?"

"Thank God." I bring my hand to my chest then narrow my eyes at him. "Wait, why is that such a bad thing?"

"You were stupid drunk. I'm not *that* bad of a guy." He seems offended by my questioning, like I should assume he wouldn't take advantage of some intoxicated girl.

He's an asshole, but apparently, he has some kind of moral code of conduct.

"Why were *you* so relieved?"

Is it really not that obvious? "Because I'm not really into having sex with random guys..."

"Right. Yeah. Makes sense."

I finally take a drink of the coffee he gave me. It's pretty decent for home-brewed, but I don't tell him that. It'd be even better with a little cinnamon.

"Listen, Claire." His serious tone pulls all of my attention. "I don't really know how to say this."

"Just say it." Instantly, a million things cross my mind. "Did I snore or something?"

"No." His emerald gaze meets mine. "You did have a nightmare though."

My cheeks redden with embarrassment. That's much worse.

"Oh." I take another drink while I try to come up with something else to say.

He breaks the uncomfortable silence I create. "We can't be friends."

His declaration strangely kicks me in the gut.

"What?" I set my cup on the counter and face him.

My phone buzzes, alerting me that it's charged enough to turn on. It continues to vibrate with the incoming text messages that were never delivered while it was shut off.

We both glance at it and then at each other.

"I'm sorry." Johnny's expression remains grave.

I unplug my cell and shove it into my pocket, not bothering to check the notifications. I look around and locate my shoes, sliding into them while Johnny's gaze follows me.

"Say something." He reaches out and grabs onto my wrist.

There's this soundless pleading with the way his stare bores into me. I don't bother trying to figure out what it means.

I pull my arm away. "I saved you, you saved me, we're even. That's it. There's nothing else to talk about."

"Claire, wait—"

I rush out of his place, shutting the door behind me and jogging down the stairs. I clench my jaw to distract myself from the overwhelming emotions pouring through me. I refuse to let something so stupid bother me.

Of course we aren't friends. He's made that clear from the very moment we crossed paths. But there's something about the finality of hearing it come from his lips that unexpectedly pulls the rug out from under me.

I leave the confines of the complex and go in the direction of the bar we were at last night. That's the last place I remember having them. I have a vague recollection of kicking them off the pool table during my dance number.

Yet another embarrassing moment to add to my growing list.

I squint to shield my eyes from the brightly shining sun and continue on my journey to freedom. I pass a closed-up food cart and a memory pops into my head.

I stop, bringing my hand to my chin. I had pizza sauce on my face, and he wiped it away. I sigh heavily. Could I have done anything else to make a fool of myself?

I keep walking, not bothering to sight-see any more on my trek to the bar.

The closed sign in the window sticks out like a sore thumb.

"Shit," I mutter.

I knock anyway. Maybe someone's inside. That's not totally unreasonable, right? Businesses have to clean and prepare their staff at some point.

The clanking of the door unlocking is heaven to my ears.

I step back and a petite woman greets me.

"Can I help you?" She scans me up and down.

"Um, hi. I think I lost my keys here last night. I was wondering if you could check the lost and found for me? Pretty please."

The lady pulls the door open to grant me access. "Sure. Come on in."

I follow her over to the dimly lit bar.

She goes behind the counter and pulls out a basket. "Have at it."

A wave of relief hits me when I spot mine sitting right on top of the mound. I snatch them off and hug them. "Thank you so much."

"Yep." She puts the container back in its place.

I let myself out and thank her again for helping me, feeling a crap ton better than I did when I went in there.

My throbbing head reminds me that I could really go for a cup of coffee. I detour past my building and into the one reliable thing I've found since I've been here.

Bram's.

His smile is the first thing I see when I go into the café. "Claire."

"Hey." I wave while maneuvering myself around a small group of people to claim a spot at the counter.

I should have probably gone home first, taken a proper shower, and prepared for being in public. But given how stupid I was last night, having breakfast with yesterday's clothes on is the least of my worries.

Bram pours me a cup of coffee without asking and sets the shaker of cinnamon next to it. "Hungry?"

"Famished." I glance at the board behind him. "I'll have the blueberry pancakes and an order of bacon."

He leans toward the opening leading to the kitchen. "Blue stack and a side of b."

"Thanks." I stir the contents of the mug and set the spoon aside, breathing in the delicious aroma. The first sip is hot, nearly melting my damn tastebuds off, but it's well worth it.

I pull the vibrating phone from my pocket and skim the notifications. The low battery signal alerts me, and I swipe it away.

Cora: *HELLO?!? ARE YOU ALIVE?*

Along with a bunch of other messages from her, Griffin, and Rosie.

Me: *Yeah, sorry, phone died. I'm good.*

Immediate dots appear on the screen.

Cora: *Jesus, Lord, I thought that guy kidnapped you!*

Me: *LOL. Pretty sure if he did, I'd be dead by now. Good lookin' out.*

Cora: *Hey now, he was pretty hot. I gave him the benefit of the doubt.*

Cora: *Plus, you were all **swoon** JOHNNY.*

Me: *I was not!*

Cora: *Totally, I mean, I don't blame you. He's got those bad boy vibes and all.*

Me: *Don't EVER let me drink that much again.*

Cora: *Same time tonight?*

Me: *I'm rolling my eyes right now, just so you know.*

Cora: *See you at ten.*

I click out of her message and onto Rosie's screen. There are a few in all caps, mentioning Griffin and a lot of exclamation points. I focus on the last one.

Rosie: *Are you okay? I'm freaking out. Text me back or better yet, ANSWER YOUR DAMN PHONE.*

Me: *Hey, I'm fine. Seriously. Went out with those friends I was telling you about and got a little wasted. Forgot to charge my cell when I got home.*

I leave out the part about being pretty much black-out drunk and waking up at a random guy's house.

Rosie: *Girl, you had me ready to book a flight and form a search party.*

Me: *Sorry!!! Love me still?*

Rosie: *Obvs.*

Dots form again so I wait for her to keep typing. They disappear but then come right back. The percent bar drops to one.

Rosie: *But hey, we saw Griffin again last night...*

The conversation I had with Griffin pops up in my memory. Shit. I finally stood up to him. And I was super intoxicated. Regardless, it doesn't make anything I said or did any less true. I'm actually grateful for the liquid courage.

Me: *It's fine. We broke up, let him do what he wants.*

Rosie: *YOU WHAT?!*

Rosie: *I mean, I'm happy for you, I think? Am I supposed to be happy? No wait, I'm sad. Are you sad? ARE YOU OKAY?*

Me: *Lol, I'm better than okay!*

Rosie: *Thank God!*

Me: *My phone's about to die again. I ran down the street to get breakfast. I'll get ahold of you in a little bit.*

Rosie: *Ugh, fine. But I'm holding you to it!*

The screen goes black at the same time Bram slides a plate in front of me. The timing couldn't have worked out any better.

"Here you go." He sets a napkin folded silverware set down, too.

"Thanks." I unwrap it and reach for the syrup.

I'm halfway through my pancakes when Bram comes over.

"You ever get that news you were waiting on?" He tops off my cup of coffee.

It takes me a second to recall what he's referring to. Finally, it dawns on me, so I nod, swallowing the bite in my mouth. "Yep."

"Hopefully it was what you were hoping for."

I shrug. "I mean, it could have been much worse." Johnny could have been dead, rotting away in his tub where I had left him. "What about you?"

"The same, actually." Bram's attention shifts to the ringing of the bell on the door, alerting him to a new customer. He grabs an empty to-go cup and fills it to the top with coffee and sprinkles cinnamon on top.

For a second, I think he's about to hand it to me, but he extends it across the counter to the person who just walked in.

"Thanks, Bram." His voice cuts through me.

I keep my eyes trained on my food, not bothering to turn and face him. After all, we aren't *friends*.

"Sure thing, Johnny. You hungry?" Bram points to the open spot next to me. "There's a seat here if you want to dine in."

Without looking, I sense Johnny's gaze fall on me.

"No," he says abruptly. "Thanks though. I have a thing. I'll take a donut to go."

I slowly reach for my mug, bringing it to my lips and giving myself something else to focus on other than this awkward interaction.

"Just one?" Bram strolls to the glass cabinet where his bakery items are stored. He snags a blueberry old-fashioned and plops it into a white bag stamped with his logo.

"Yeah."

Bram glances down at me. "Claire, this is Johnny. Johnny, this is Claire. You two go to the same school."

Out of the corner of my eye, I notice Johnny extend his arm like he's totally going along with Bram's introduction.

A few days ago, I would have been much more friendly. I would have attempted to make small talk with this good-looking guy. But Johnny has shown me time and time again that he wants nothing to do with me, other than to be an asshole.

I'd rather ignore him and pretend he doesn't exist, but since Bram is standing here, I have to do something.

I swivel the seat toward Johnny and shake his hand. My gaze trails up to his and our eyes lock, his still red and swollen from his beating the other night.

"Nice to meet you," he lies.

"You, too."

We stay that way for an awkward moment, clasped onto each other.

Another customer walks in and the chiming of the doorbell snaps us out of our trance.

Johnny fishes into his pocket and pulls out a twenty. "For hers, too." He turns and walks out without saying another word.

I watch him the whole time, completely confused by every single thing he does. He's so hot and cold, it's like I'll never figure him out.

I shake my head and go back to my food. When I glance up, Bram is grinning.

"Don't even think about it," I tell him.

He throws up his hands and laughs. "I've been known to be a pretty good matchmaker in my day."

"Nope, not with that one." I bite off a piece of the bacon.

"Ah, he's not so terrible, is he?"

"He's got bad boy written all over him." Not to mention, he's treated me mostly like shit since the second our paths crossed. I can't exactly tell Bram that, considering he thinks Johnny and I just met sixty seconds ago.

"That's a cover up. There's a lot more to him than what meets the eye." Bram seems genuine in his defense of Johnny. "I've known him since he was this tall." He holds his hand somewhere close to the floor where I can't see behind the counter.

Maybe Bram does have a different insight into him than I do, but that still doesn't excuse his behavior toward me. Plus, the whole, *we can't be friends* thing.

"You should give him a chance. Maybe consider it, at the very least." Bram grabs onto the towel from the counter and slings it over his shoulder. "He could use someone like you in his life."

His last statement sits with me long after he walks away to tend to the other customers.

What does he mean, someone like me?

16
JOHNNY

Bram's lucky he's old, otherwise, I would have punched him for forcing me and Claire together the way he did.

Sure, it was totally harmless in his eyes, but it couldn't have been any more awkward.

A year ago, I would have been grateful for the introduction. But considering I need to steer clear of Claire and do everything I can to make her see me as the bad guy, his meet-cute wasn't exactly ideal.

I lean against the brick building and study the place where I got my ass kicked a few nights ago. If I'm going to find this package, I have to focus on finding any kind of lead to help me figure out who robbed me.

My dried blood still coats the ground near the dumpster, and random trash is haphazardly strewn about. I close my eyes and try to remember anything I can.

I wince at the memory of a shoe slamming into my side. A fist striking my face and splitting my brow. A delicate voice saying my name.

I shake my head to rid the thought.

I can't let Claire saving me from my own stupidity be the one thing I focus on.

My phone dings, reminding me that the thieves didn't take it. They left my wallet and everything in it, too. The only thing they stole was Franklin's package.

Which means they knew I had it. They targeted me specifically because of it. They waited for me to come down this dark alley and used the opportunity to steal it from me. These people not only knew I was running a package, but they knew the route I was going to take.

I've been made.

All these months, I thought I was being careful, flying under the radar and blending in so no one knew what I was up to. My efforts have been for nothing if someone figured me out this easily.

I run my hand through my hair, tugging it out of my face. "Shit." I kick off from the wall and leave this piss-soaked alley behind. I need to think, and if I'm going to do it anywhere, it's not going to be here.

It doesn't take me long to get to the complex. The gate clangs shut behind me and a familiar smile greets me from the courtyard.

"Johnny!" Billy rushes over from his spot and wraps his arms around me.

I grit my teeth at the impact on my still sore ribs. "Hey, kid."

Billy tilts his head up at me. "You look like crap."

I nudge his shoulder. "Thanks, that's so sweet of you."

"You know what I mean." He rolls his eyes and lowers his voice. "What happened?"

"Nothing you need to worry about, little man." I ruffle his hair and point toward his stack of books. "What're you working on?"

"Math," he groans.

I follow him over and sit across from where he had been sitting. "Let me see."

Billy slides his scribbled-out homework over to me.

"Right here." I point at the paper. "You have to carry the one."

Billy's brown eyes light up. "Ohh. Duh."

The gate jangles shut, and when I glance over my shoulder, Claire appears.

She instantly averts her gaze and focuses on making her way through the courtyard and to her place. She does a better job than I do at looking away.

"You're the best, Johnny," Billy says with a happy smile. He finishes the problem and turns it for me to check.

"Yep, good job, Billy. Just remember that on your test and you'll be golden."

Billy sighs. "I hate math."

"Me, too."

A door creaks open. "Billy! Get your ass up here."

Anger rolls through me.

Billy jumps up and starts gathering his stuff. "I have to go, J."

"Hey." I gently grab his wrist and look him straight in the eyes. "Has he laid a hand on you?"

"No, not since I told you what was happening. He yells a lot still though."

I assess his answer and feel decently confident that he isn't lying. There are no obvious bruises on his skin, and unless his uncle is hitting him in places that are hidden by clothing, I think Billy is telling the truth.

"Okay." I let go of his arm. "You'll tell me if anything changes though, right?"

Billy nods. "Yeah." He shoves everything into his backpack and pauses. "Did the bad men do that?" He points at my still healing face.

"Don't worry about me, okay?"

"Too late." Billy rushes upstairs and disappears into the unit.

My stomach sinks at not knowing what goes on behind that door. There's only so much I can do to protect him out here, but in there, anything could happen.

I put my head in my hands, leaning onto my elbows on the table. Defeat is a strong word, but basically sums up my existence. It's like every time I figure a problem out, another one pops up and slams me back to reality.

I can't just sit back and do nothing. Someone has to do something.

And maybe I'm an idiot for thinking it has to be me, my fucking hero complex constantly on overdrive to save everyone.

Relentlessly putting others ahead of myself.

I was that kid once, though. The one that needed help. That could have used someone looking out for me. If someone like me would have stepped in, maybe things wouldn't have turned out the way they did. Maybe I wouldn't be so fucking broken. Maybe I wouldn't have to try, and fail, at saving everyone else.

My phone goes off again, snapping me out of my shitty mindset.

I pull it out and let the facial recognition do its thing. Through the cracked screen, there are two texts.

Josey: *You busy?*

Josey: *Could use your help at Washington.*

It doesn't come across like a direct order, meaning it's probably not a mandatory job Franklin is demanding of me. Josey has never done anything to make me dislike him, though, so if he's asking for assistance, I have no real reason not to give it to him.

Me: *Be there in 5.*

Josey: *Thanks.*

I take the main streets to the destination and manage to make it there in under four minutes. I turn into the alley and find Josey leaning against a fully blacked-out SUV.

"What's up?" I ask him.

He approaches and shakes my hand. "You got an hour? I need an extra body." He nods toward the vehicle where two people are already sitting in the back seat.

I can barely make them out through the deeply tinted windows. "Sure. What are we doing?"

Josey chuckles. "Right." He pushes a button on the key fob and the big thing starts up. "Hop in. You're riding shotgun."

I do what he says and slide into the front, trying not to make it too obvious when I check out the passengers. I don't recognize either one of them, which doesn't help my cluelessness at what I'm tagging along for.

The guy with the military short hair nods a silent hello but doesn't say anything else. The other, a smaller guy, just sits there and avoids eye contact.

We drive across town, about ten minutes away, and park at one of the empty buildings in the warehouse district near the entrance.

Josey cuts the ignition. "There you go."

The two men get out and go into the structure.

I'm left here still wondering what the heck is going on.

Once they're inside, Josey opens his mouth. "You busy tonight?"

I side-eye him. "Are you asking me on a date?"

Josey slams the back of his hand into my chest. "Don't make me shoot you."

I laugh. "Is it wrong to say you're not my type? You're not a bad-looking dude, I'm just into chicks."

"I hate you." Josey shakes his head. "No, you fucking idiot. I'm not coming onto you. I have a girlfriend." He exhales. "I thought maybe we could grab a beer at Whiskers. There was something I wanted to talk to you about. Didn't want to bring any attention to it, though, so I couldn't ask you over a text."

"Wait, this was just a cover up? You didn't actually need me right now?"

Josey folds his arms over his wide chest. "Been at this game *much* longer than you, kid. I can handle shit on my own."

"Oh." I process what he's saying. "Yeah, sure. What time?"

"Meet me there at ten. But listen, don't tell anyone about this. It's between you and me." His serious gaze burns into me.

If I didn't know better, I'd say they hired Josey to finish the job and off me. But Josey has never been that kind of person toward me, and if what he's saying is true, he's putting his neck on the line to tell me something he thinks I should know.

The two guys come out of the building and make their way to us.

"Do you understand?" Josey urges before we're interrupted.

"Yes." I swallow down the lump that forms in my throat. The unknown of what this could potentially mean.

My mind races on the way back into town. I try to settle it, but I can't. There are too many variables, and I don't know which one to focus on first. There's this stolen package and how the hell I'm going to locate and retrieve it, the overall situation with Franklin, Josey wanting to have a *talk* with me, and the person that keeps vying for my main attention—Claire. Not to mention the week of school I've missed and everything else going on in my life.

I told Claire we couldn't be friends. Why can't my own brain wrap itself around that concept? Why is she *still* in my head even though I keep pushing her away? Why do I have this desperate need to be around her despite knowing that's quite literally the worst thing I could possibly do?

Even if all of my other problems were fixed, it wouldn't erase the way I've treated her. Buying her breakfast and letting her crash at my place when she was wasted will never begin to excuse the shitty treatment I've dished out.

I can't imagine how fucking confusing I must be. One minute, I'm a total asshole, the next I'm catching her as she falls off a pool table. What the fuck is wrong with me? Why can't I just leave her alone?

We'd both be better off if I could figure out how to keep my distance once and for all.

I recall her cobalt blue eyes and the way they stared into mine on many different occasions. There's this weird connection. This pull to each other that's undeniable. Or maybe I'm fucking losing it and it's all in my head. Maybe I'm twisted and clinging to something that doesn't exist.

But if that's true, why does she look at me the way she does?

With curiosity. With longing. With desire.

Josey puts the SUV into park and turns off the ignition. "Thanks for your help, J."

I blink and take in our surroundings. We're stopped in the alley I met him in not too long ago.

The two random dudes get out and slam the doors behind them, disappearing into wherever they came from.

"You good?" Josey asks me.

I bob my head up and down. "Yeah. Catch you later."

17
CLAIRE

"Wow, I can't believe you finally did it," Rosie says through the speaker of my phone. "I mean, I'm glad. Griffin is a major tool, but I know you liked him. You've got that *always seeing the good in people even if it's not really there* thing going on."

"Yeah." I slump against the stiff couch in my mother's living room. "It was time. Had been for a while." I pause and shift the subject. "Have I told you how weird it is being here? Existing in someone else's house while they're not here?"

"Only once or fifty times." Rosie's reception cuts out a little. "Why don't you pretend you're at an Airbnb or something?"

"I guess…but eventually she's going to show up, which will make everything super awkward." And I'm not sure I can handle more weird stuff going on right now.

"Get your room situated so you don't have to leave it if you don't want to. You have your own bathroom, right?"

"Yep."

"See, there you go. Stock up on snacks and you'll be good. What about your dad, have you heard from him?"

"Only a few texts. He hasn't gotten his data plan sorted out yet for international stuff." I realize how one-sided this conversation is going. "Tell me about your weekend. Which party did you decide to go to? Where was it?"

She sighs like she's about to settle into a long-winded rant. "Well, Brice wanted to do one and I wanted to do the other, so we compromised and went to both. Let me tell you, I have never seen that many frat boys stuffed into a house in my entire life. I shit you not, I was one of the only girls there."

I let the sound of her voice lull and distract my mind from everything else that's going on. It's a Band-Aid, but I'm grateful for it, and for her.

I finish typing my English paper and submit it to the professor. I had intended to spend the rest of the weekend getting my homework completed, but come Saturday evening, I'm nearly done with all of my assignments.

Cora has sent me two messages, following up about going out tonight, but I've blown her off to study. Now though, my excuse doesn't seem as valid.

I order Chinese takeout and wait for it to arrive, clicking through the channels on the cable TV in hopes of finding something decent to watch. I settle on reruns of *The Office* and braid my still-damp hair in pigtails to kill more time.

The buzzer goes off and I ring the delivery guy into the complex. I grab a twenty and make my way to the door.

I open it and find a pimple-faced teenager holding my bag of food.

"Thanks, how much?"

The kid shakes his head. "Taken care of." He points down the hallway. "Tip, too."

I exhale and try to keep my composure. "Thank you." I force a smile, taking my dinner and leaving him behind.

How can Johnny think that feeding me will make me hate him any less? Is food his love language? Who does this? It's like the weirdest form of stalking. And I can't exactly stop him from doing it. What am I supposed to do, give the kid the money and tell him to go give Johnny a refund?

It makes no sense at all. He's an asshole. He clearly told me we couldn't be friends. Why is he randomly picking up the bill every chance he gets? Is it a peace offering? An olive branch of some sort?

Whatever it is, I wish he would stop. If he's not willing to use his damn words, I don't care to be bothered by him.

He's driving me insane with this back and forth. He needs to pick which side he's on and stick to it.

I toss the bag onto the dining room table and pull out a carton, diving straight into some lo mein to distract myself from the chaos that is my brain.

I'm only ten minutes in when my phone goes off. Then it vibrates three more times. I glance down and my stomach tightens.

Griffin.

I've been doing my best at not responding to him since our blow-up last night. I said everything that needed to be said, even if it was in an incredibly intoxicated state, and now I want to move on with my life.

Only with him, nothing is that simple.

Griffin: *Please Claire, talk to me.*

Griffin: *I'm lost without you.*

Griffin: *I'm scared. I need you.*

Griffin: *If you ever cared about me, about us, you'll call me.*

Griffin: *I'm begging you. I don't think I can go on without you.*

Griffin: *I won't stop until you answer. I just need to hear your voice, please.*

His face lights up my screen and the green and red buttons stare at me. Accept and ignore. Which one should I choose?

Maybe if I answer, he'll stop blowing up my phone?

Because the opposite has only resulted in him calling and texting me every few hours and continuing to beg me to reach out to him.

Against my better judgment, I accept the call.

"Hello?" I bite my lip and wait for which version of him that will show up.

"Claire, thank God." He's out of breath. "You had me worried. Are you okay?"

"Yes, Griffin. I'm fine." I maintain my composure.

"Good, I'm glad." The nice Griffin is here, but for how long? "We're going to get through this, okay? Together."

I shake my head to rid myself of his stupid words. Is he really this dumb? "Griffin, hold up."

He cuts me off. "I know you were drinking. You didn't mean what you said. It's okay. I know you're sorry."

Is he freaking serious right now?

Griffin continues in his cool and calm voice. "We all make mistakes. I forgive you."

It's everything I can do to not explode from every single thing he's implying.

"Look, Claire, you can make it up to me. How's that sound?"

I try and try and try to hold back the tidal wave of fury, but I can't.

"Have you lost your mind? I meant every single word I said to you last night. Especially the part about being done. I don't have to be drunk to acknowledge the truth. You're horrible to me. You have been for a long time. Do we have to even mention the *cheating*? You're a disgusting pig, Griffin."

He doesn't bother playing pretend anymore either. "Oh, and you're any better? Don't act like you aren't already fucking around. All those early mornings and late nights at some place called Bram's…is that where you're meeting him? Did you forget I can still see your location?"

"Meeting who? Are you listening to yourself right now? You're accusing me of sleeping around because I found decent coffee?"

"Don't lie to me. I knew the moment you told me you were going out west that you'd fuck the first guy who gave you any attention."

I stand from the couch. "I don't have to listen to this anymore. There's no point in trying to convince you of something you already have your mind made up over. And if that's the story you have to tell yourself to sleep better at night, knowing you're *still* messing around with Shelby, then so be it. I couldn't care less. Forget my number, forget I ever existed."

He starts to mouth off again, but I don't allow it to happen.

I disconnect the call and throw my phone onto the loveseat next to me. I grab a nearby pillow, holding it to my face to muffle the scream that leaves my body.

How can one person be so incredibly infuriating?

He managed to manipulate me into accepting a phone call, only to turn it around and make *me* the bad guy somehow. The craziest thing of all is he probably actually believes the things that he says.

I reach through the cushion and pull my cell back out. If there's any hope of going five minutes without losing my own mind, I can't stay cooped up in this condo all alone.

I flip through my text screen and find the person I'm looking for.

Me: *Text me an address.*

I need another night like last night to forget all about what's going on. Only this time, I plan to pace myself a bit better and not end up in a stranger's bed.

I get ready in a hurry, tossing on the first outfit I find in my closet, a black bodysuit and high-waisted ripped denim jeans. I lace up my all-white converse and glance in the mirror. I don't give much thought to my face, dabbing a little blush on my cheeks and a coat of mascara on my lashes. My braids are tousled from being on the couch and unless I want to re-do them, they're a lost cause.

I settle on grabbing the blow-dryer and applying some heat before pulling the braids out and running my fingers through my hair. Luckily, my hair ends up with a decent little wave and doesn't look too horrible.

With an application of Chapstick, I complete my ten-minute transformation.

It's not much longer until I have all of my necessary belongings and am making my way out of the condo. I latch the door shut behind me and check Cora's last message she sent me with the details. Tonight's bar is only a few blocks away.

I'm just about to reach the stairs when another unit opens. I pray like hell it's not him. I don't need to deal with *that* right now.

But the universe enjoys taunting me because that's the exact person who appears. White pocket tee and black jeans. Effortless and infuriating, just like him.

His wide emerald gaze meets mine. "Hey."

I shake my head. "Nope. Not happening." I continue on my path, making my way down the stairs and into the courtyard.

Johnny rushes to catch up. "What did I do now?"

"What didn't you do?" I mouth off.

"That's fair." He matches my pace. "Um. How was dinner?"

I stop suddenly, grabbing his arm and stopping him, too. I ignore the way his skin feels against mine. "Listen, buying me food is not going to win me over. If that's even what you're trying to do. I appreciate it, and I'm not ungrateful, so *thank you,* but seriously, cut it out. You don't owe me anything. We aren't friends, remember?"

His lips part and he hesitates for a second. "It's not that I don't want to be friends."

I roll my eyes and take off again. "Whatever."

He moves too, so I halt.

"I'm not lying," he continues.

"Don't follow me," I tell him.

"I'm not." He points toward the gate. "I was leaving, too."

Stupidity washes over me. "Oh. Right."

Johnny keeps his attention on me. With his voice quiet, like he's speaking to himself he says, "You look beautiful tonight."

I disregard the seriousness of his tone and the tingling in my chest that follows.

I don't allow how much he affected me to show. "Thanks."

We approach the gate at the same time, but he rushes forward to grab onto the handle and open it for me. He motions for me to go through ahead of him.

I head off in the direction of the address Cora sent me, but Johnny follows.

"My thing really is this way," he reassures.

We walk in silence for a minute until we come upon a group of rowdy people.

Johnny steps closer, placing his hand on my lower back to guide me through the throng. When the crowd gets too tight, he slides his fingers down my arm and latches them onto my hand, weaving me safely through.

My breath hitches at his touch, and for a second, I think I've gone into shock.

Together, we make it through, his grasp lingering once we've cleared the boisterous bunch.

He drops my hand. "Sorry."

I swallow and keep my mouth shut, words seeming to fail me at the moment. I cross my arms over my chest and eliminate the possibility of something like that happening again.

I hate that I didn't hate it.

That it felt natural. Like it was something we had done a million times before.

The illuminated sign up ahead signals that I'm near my destination.

Johnny trails by my side, not showing any indication that he'll be departing.

Was he lying? Is he actually following me? Is he really going somewhere in this direction, just maybe past where I'll be stopping?

"Did something happen?" He glances down at me.

"What?"

He keeps walking a few inches to my left. "You seem different. Tense?"

How is it possible that he's picking up on that kind of energy? Clearly, I'm edgy, but he doesn't need to know that.

"I'm not trying to pry." He meets my gaze again.

"Then don't," I snap at him. If he isn't trying to intrude, then why is he?

"You're right. I shouldn't have asked."

I notice the inflection in his tone. "Why does it matter?" I stop in front of the bar.

He points to the entrance, and I nod a confirmation.

"I'll let you know when I figure it out." He clutches the handle and tugs on the door, holding it open for me.

18
JOHNNY

Claire leaves my side to meet her friends, and I swear it's like a chunk of my fucking soul goes with her.

I hate it, the intense desire I have to be near her, if only to keep her safe and out of harm's reach. It's out of my control.

I'm the one she needs to be protected from.

The girl who shoved me last night stares directly at me from across the bar while talking to Claire. "Your boyfriend can join us."

"He's not my boyfriend." Claire shoots a glare my way.

"JJ!" Josey waves at me from his spot in the corner, hijacking my attention.

"Hey, man." I shake his hand and take the seat next to him. "Whiskey, neat," I tell the barkeep when he approaches.

"That your lady?" Josey tips his glass in the direction of Claire.

I shake my head. "No. Farthest thing from it, actually."

"Sure." He downs the contents of his drink and pushes it forward for a refill. "Why does she keep looking over here then?"

"Maybe she's got the hots for you." I take a sip and let the booze tingle its way into my body. Anything to distract me from turning toward her again.

Josey chuckles. "Doubtful. Five years ago, possibly. I'm an old man now."

"What are you, like twenty-six?"

"I'll be thirty in a few months."

"Damn. You're nearly a senior citizen." I gulp down the rest of my whiskey. "I know you didn't ask me to come here to have small talk." I tilt my head. "What's this about?"

"Listen, J, I feel for you. I really do. You've always pegged me as a decent dude. I understand why you're doing what you are, but I think you underestimate how dangerous this world is." Josey points to my face. "That shit, it's nothing compared to some of the stuff I've seen."

I scratch at my chin. "Is this an intervention or something? You think I'm unaware of what I signed up for? Are you trying to scare me straight?"

Josey swirls his finger around the rim of his glass. "No. Not at all. I get it. You're going to keep doing what you are. There's no backing out for you at this point, not while you're still figuring out a contingency plan. But I'm not the only one who sees that. And I'm not the person you need to be worried about."

A loud crash has everyone stunned for a brief second and a server curses about their dropped tray. Just as quick, the room resumes partying.

Josey continues. "Boss treats you like a toy. He won't stop until you're begging him for your life. And he'll stop at nothing to make damn sure that happens."

I face him. "This isn't news to me, Josey. I'm fucked. I'm in over my head, and I have no fucking clue how I'm going to get out of this alive. But you and I both know it's not about me. If it was, I wouldn't be tied up in this shit to begin with. I'd be out there." I motion toward the college crowd laughing and drinking and enjoying their Saturday night. "I wouldn't be failing all my classes, and I'd probably have some lame job at a coffee shop or something, and I'd sure as shit be chasing after that girl over there. I wouldn't have two black eyes and busted ribs. I'd be normal. I'd be boring. But that life is over. I left it behind the moment I volunteered to be his bitch because it was the only thing I could do at the time. And until I figure something else out, I have no other choice in the matter."

I raise my hand to get another round.

Josey keeps his voice low. "I don't want to see you end up dead, J."

"Me either." I peer over my shoulder and locate Claire, just to confirm she's still okay. If I can't protect myself, at least I can watch over her when I'm around.

"That package…you get any leads yet?"

"Not a damn thing." And if I don't find a lead soon, I really will be a dead man.

Josey shifts his focus around the crowded bar and leans in close. "I can trust you, right?" His dark brown eyes pierce through me with his serious tone.

"Yeah, of course." I'd never betray Josey, not in a million years.

"I could lose my head for this."

"I swear, man. What is it? Do you know what was in it?" Because I sure as shit don't, and the probability of locating something when I don't even know what it is seems impossible.

"I overheard some talk. I don't think I was supposed to, but it didn't stop me from listening anyway. Especially when I heard your name brought up."

"Jesus Christ, Josey, tell me already." The anticipation is going to give me a fucking heart attack.

He lowers his voice even more but maintains eye contact with me. "Sounds like it was an inside job."

Pieces of the puzzle start to slide into place, making more and more sense of what happened.

I was robbed. But the only thing that was taken was the package. Not my overpriced iPhone, not my wallet, or the hundreds of dollars I had on me. Not the rings on my hand or the chain around my neck. My keys were tossed to the side, and I got my ass kicked. If it was a true robbery, they would've have taken all my stuff, right? Or at least *some* of it...

No, they left it all behind. They knew where I was. They knew which path I'd be taking because Franklin gave me minimal time to get it there, which eliminated the precautions that I normally take.

He forced my hand, and I played right into his stupid fucking game. He knew exactly what would happen and planned it out to a T.

And that's why he acted composed and cool and gave me an opportunity to redeem myself. It was a losing battle, and I never stood a chance given the cards were stacked against me all along.

Franklin isn't dumb, and setting me up for failure like this is his way of making sure his hands are clean of me. He ends up looking like he gave me a chance, and I appear to be the failure everyone assumes I will be. It's a win-win in his book.

Only Franklin didn't consider one thing: Josey's loyalty and where it lies.

Josey might be a ruthless pawn in Franklin's twisted story, but he has a heart, and his eyes are open enough to see that I do, too.

Franklin may have gotten a lot of things right about me, but I'm going to do everything I can to prove him wrong going forward. He thinks I'll fold, that I'll cower and submit when I can't find the package. That couldn't be further from the truth.

I'll stop at nothing until I pry it from whoever beat it out of me.

"You good, kid?" Josey snaps his fingers in front of my face.

"Your veins are starting to bulge right there." He pokes the side of my head.

"Yeah." I blink back to reality. "Tell me everything else."

Josey opens his mouth but stops, reaches into his pocket, and pulls out his phone. The screen lights up and he exhales. "I've got to run."

Shit. No. This might be our only chance to talk about what happened. Josey is my first and only solid lead, I can't lose it without getting *something* else.

Josey unfolds a few bills from his money clip and sets them on the counter.

Anxiety bubbles up through me at the many questions that cross my mind.

"Do you have any idea who it was?" I ask him.

"No, but it was someone young. New recruits. I heard they were bragging about the beating they gave you. Cocky little shits." Josey glances around. "I don't need to remind you that this stays between us, right? If he knew I was helping you in any way—"

I hold up my hands. "I swear it, Josey. I won't say a word."

"Good." He turns to leave. "I don't want to see something bad happen to you, kid." Josey seems genuinely concerned about my well-being.

"Ay," I call out. "Thank you. Seriously."

Josey nods. "Don't make me regret it."

I sit for a while, my head in my hands, trying like hell to solve the puzzle that is my life.

The bartender keeps my glass filled, and for that I'm grateful.

I get decent service pretty much everywhere I frequent because I tip well. This place is no different. It's not that I flaunt my money, but growing up and not having much of it, I tend to give back when I can.

Even making the low wage that Franklin pays me, I still earn more than I would at any other job and have plenty left in my savings after I pay all the monthly expenses. My cousin covers half the bills with his housing allowance, but he's rarely around. I basically live alone aside from a rare couple of weeks out of the year that he pops in between deployments.

It's ideal though, considering I prefer solitude. Especially now that I'm wrapped up with what I am.

"So," a voice breaks through my train of thought. "What's your story?"

I turn to find that blonde from last night at my side. "I don't have one."

"Sure you do," she says plainly. "Everyone does." She attempts to get the bartender's attention, but the guy goes toward another patron.

I raise my hand to signal him.

He stops what he's doing and comes right over. "Top you off?"

I nod. "Yeah. And whatever she's having."

The girl raises her eyebrow. "Whatever?"

"Yep, that's what I said."

"Four shots of tequila. Doubles, please." She extends her hand to me. "I'm Cora."

"Johnny."

"Are you here with anyone?" Cora props her elbow on the bar and bats her long eyelashes. She's decently attractive in conventional ways, but not in a manner that captivates me.

"Nope." I scan the crowd until I spot the one person I can't get off my mind. It's like the whole place is a blur except for her.

My heart stutters when our eyes lock, and I have to force myself to look away.

"Shame." Cora grabs all of her shots between her fingers. "Thanks for these," she says over her shoulder while making her way through the people gathered near the bar.

Shit. One of those shots will be for Claire. And if Cora mentions I paid for them, Claire is going to be pissed. She literally *just* got done demanding that I stop buying her stuff. Whoops. I mean, technically I didn't know at the time. I was just trying to be nice to her friend. But wasn't I only doing that to look better in Claire's eyes?

I run my hand through my unruly hair to get it out of my face. I have to fucking stop caring what this girl thinks of me. I need to stick to being the bad guy, not the random dude who keeps doing good deeds for her.

"Focus," I tell myself. I let out a breath and take a swig of my drink.

The familiar burn is a welcomed distraction that I accept gratefully.

"Do you have a pen?" I ask a server that walks by.

He snatches one out of his pocket and tosses it to me, continuing on his path to deliver the deep-fried food on his tray.

I swipe the napkin from under my drink and make a list of names that come to mind.

Josey mentioned new recruits. Young ones.

I jot down every person fitting into that category that I've come across these past few weeks.

Brandon

Jackson

Black haired guy

Emo kid

Steven...and the other Steve

Eric

The one dude who smells like feet

It's not much, but it's a start. And if I cross-reference their stature to what I recall from the beating, maybe I can narrow down someone who might have been in on this and be one step closer to foiling Franklin's plan to eliminate me.

Earlier today, I thought finding the package might be a lost cause. It's still a long shot, but feels more possible, and I'll take every bit of hope I can get.

I empty the rest of my whiskey into my mouth and stand from the stool. I fish in my pocket for cash, tossing it onto the counter and pushing the chair in.

Those recognizable blue eyes latch onto mine from across the room.

She doesn't look mad—or happy. She appears more curious than anything.

A large part of me wants to stay, to hang back and verify that she'll be okay. That she won't drink too much and get herself into trouble the way she did last night. But I know that's wrong of me. It's too intrusive. It's not my place. And I can't keep putting myself into situations I don't belong. If she wants me to leave her alone, I need to respect that, even if it's super fucking difficult.

I need to do what's best for her, and that means walking away.

19
CLAIRE

I'm not really sure which is more annoying—Johnny being *everywhere* or Johnny being *nowhere*.

When he's around, he frustrates me. But when he's not, I can't seem to take my mind off of him. Especially considering the danger he surrounds himself with. It's no coincidence he stumbled in one night all beaten up, and then I found him in that alley nearly unconscious a few days later. He's gotten tangled up with something bad, and it's clearly a risk to his safety.

So, when he walks out of the bar Saturday night and I don't see him the rest of the weekend, naturally, I worry.

My mind runs wild with the endless potential scenarios that could have played out. The one that concerns me the most is him ending up dead in a ditch, never to be seen or heard from again. His John Doe body getting lost in the mess of other unsolved homicides.

It's not my responsibility to make sure he's okay, yet I can't help feeling like *someone* needs to be concerned about his well-being. I haven't noticed anyone else coming in or out of his house, meaning he probably lives alone. There was a bedroom door that was shut but it could have been an office or storage. Other than Johnny chatting with Bram, the kid in our building, or that random guy he met at the bar, he's been alone.

He's a loner.

What a sad life that must be for him.

Don't get me wrong, I'm learning that being alone can be great. It's freeing. Empowering, really. But with Johnny, it feels forced, like deep down it's not really what he wants. He does it out of necessity. He pushes everyone away.

Why would he do that?

I walk into class and half-expect to see him sitting in that same seat from last week. My heart drops when it's empty. I take its companion anyway.

What if something bad really did happen to him? Should I file a missing person's report? I didn't exactly go over to his place and knock on the door. He could be inside laying low for all I know. Maybe I'll check in with Bram and ask if Johnny has been in lately. There has to be some reasonable explanation for his absence.

Professor Brown clears her throat and pulls a stack of papers from her backpack. "Class. Let's begin." She glides to the front row and distributes them throughout. "Pass these back," she tells each of them.

The students do what they're asked while settling into their chosen seats.

"Group project time. If you read the syllabus, you already know this will account for thirty percent of your grade in this class." Her heels click against the floor.

A collective gasp floats around the room at the oblivious pupils hearing this for the first time.

"The assignment is simple, really. All of the details are listed on the packet you've been provided. Put in the work, get a passing grade. Slack and you fail. Both parties *must* participate. This will not be a one-sided effort. And trust me, I'll be able to tell." She leans against her desk, and continues, "Part of this whole college experience is to learn how to work together with others. Here is your opportunity."

The door creaks open and my breath hitches.

It's him. It's Johnny. In the flesh. Looking ragged but very freaking alive.

A figurative weight lifts from my shoulders and my body relaxes.

"Mr. Jones, have a seat." Her voice is laced with irritation.

His green eyes flicker in my direction and then settle on the open seat a few spots away. He slides into it and eases into the chair.

A tinge of disappointment courses through me, and I bite my lip to ground myself.

He's not dead, don't ask for anything else, Claire.

The professor keeps explaining the assignment. "I've decided to take things into my own hands and assign the partners for this project, basing it on a balanced skill level you two will share. I utilized those assessments you took on day one and matched you appropriately. I tried this last semester and it resulted in the highest success rate I've had for a course in all my years."

The class quiets down and anxious energy fills the room at the realization that the partnerships have already been decided.

"I'll go ahead and get started. When I call your name, please remain seated. Once I've gotten through the list, you may relocate with your partner and begin discussing your strategy. You're free to leave, but I'll be staying until the end of the session if anyone has any questions. I have office hours following this period, too." She glances around the room and latches onto a sheet of paper on her desk. "Okay, then."

I scan the backs of heads and sides of faces, wondering which of these strangers I'll be paired up with. The bubbly girl with the thick-rimmed glasses catches my eye. She always smiles at me when I walk by. Or the curly-headed boy who looks like he skipped a few years in high school to get here. Either of them would be fine with me.

I don't dare glance to my right, not in his direction. There's about a one in thirty chance we'll be stuck together, and I'm hoping like hell it's anyone but him.

"Brayden, Pamela. Brice and Jude. Ava and Sophia. Chloe, you're with Aria."

Every single name sends my pulse skyrocketing.

Professor Brown meets my gaze. "Claire," she hesitates, "and Johnny."

My heart thumps loudly, drowning out everything else she says. I must have heard her wrong, right? No way is she pairing me with him. *Anyone* but him. This has to be some kind of mistake.

The room seems to spin, and I have to plant my hands on the cold hard surface of the desk to bring myself closer to reality.

Bodies are up and moving around, most of them funneling out the door with their partners. A few stragglers post up in various corners and start their work together.

"Johnny," Brown says.

He stands in front of her at her desk.

"I'm not switching things around. Decision is final. Unless you have some incredible excuse, I won't make an exception." She lowers her voice, but I still hear her. "Honestly, you should be thanking me. She's the brightest one in this room."

"But—" Johnny tries to interject.

"There are no buts. Not after the crap you've pulled. This isn't going to be another repeat of last semester. You're setting yourself up for failure if you're going to just show up whenever you please." She motions to his healing face. "I get it. You have a life. A complicated one, it seems. But your education is important, and you need to take it seriously. If you're not going to, I'll do it for you."

I gather my belongings and walk over toward them. Each step thick and heavy like something's wrong with gravity.

"Ah, Miss Cooper. Speak of the devil." Brown waves me over. "I wanted to talk to you—both of you, actually."

Why does this sound like things are about to get somehow worse than they already are? Why is there a cloud of impending doom lingering over me at the tone of her voice?

"You did?" I cling my notebook to my chest, my fingers digging into the sides.

"Mmhm." She looks at each of us. "Johnny's been struggling a bit the last few months, and if he stands any chance of passing this class *the second time around,* he's going to need all hands on deck. That's where you come in, Claire. Johnny will be your tutoring assignment for the term."

My entire body seems to float away from me, and it's everything I can do to not pass out. She can't be serious. This has to be a dream—a nightmare.

Johnny opens his mouth to speak, but I cut him off.

"I—uh, Professor, I don't think that's a good idea," I finally say.

"Yeah, what she said," Johnny adds.

She snatches a paper off her desk. "I do. It shows here that you two live in the same area. I don't think there's a better match, honestly."

"But, I..." I don't know what to say.

"Claire." Her tone becomes more serious. "Need I remind you why you signed up for the program? If you're not willing to work within the requirements, you'll have to reconsider your position. And if I'm not mistaken, your alternatives are slim at this point." She takes a breath. "I'm not sure what's going on between you two, but unless there are extenuating circumstances that I'm unaware of, this decision is final."

"Okay," I whisper.

Another pair of students approach, ready for their turn to talk to the professor.

"Very well, let me know if you have any other questions." She turns her attention to the other people, leaving me and Johnny on our own.

I walk out of the room, not bothered with whether or not he follows. I need fresh air if I'm going to remain standing upright.

I spot an open picnic table in a grassy area between buildings and head straight to it, perching on the edge of the seat.

"Claire." Johnny's voice breaks through my daze.

"What?" I snap at him.

He lowers himself onto the bench. "Can we talk about this?"

I turn toward him, his stupid green eyes pleading with me to figure this out. I hate the effect he has on me, melting away every ounce of anger I want to harbor. Even if he's the one who often brings it on.

I clear my throat. "Listen, I know you don't like me, for whatever reason, and that's fine. But I can't drop the tutoring program, and you apparently need it. Obviously, we can't switch partners on the assignment, either. My grades are important to me, and I won't let you ruin that because you hate me."

Johnny stares at me intensely. "I don't hate you."

"It doesn't matter." I avoid the shockwave that rattles my core. "Let's just consider this a business transaction. We can agree to get along enough to get the required work done, right? Can you play pretend for a couple months? Once this class is over, you can go back to never talking to me again. Can you handle that, or am I asking too much?"

"Yeah," is all he says.

It's not going to be easy, and I'm not even sure if it's something *I* can manage. Johnny is a force that wrecks me every second he's around. But I can't allow my plan to be derailed because I can't figure out how to be near him. He's only human, and so am I. There's no reason I can't trick myself into thinking he's just a means to an end—a way for me to further my chances of getting that scholarship and getting the hell back home.

20
JOHNNY

How am I going to make this work?

I've been doing everything I can to avoid her, and now I'm quite literally being forced to be around her.

I'm going to ruin everything.

Each time I look at her, my hand twitches in its attempt to reach out to tuck her dark brown hair behind her ear. My gaze trails from her eyes down her delicate jawline, onto her perfectly plush lips. I don't allow myself to go any lower, her body is enough to make my heart pound out of my chest.

It's only a couple months.

I've done crazier things in my life, what's one more?

"Okay, then. We should make a schedule." She flips open her notebook and pulls out a pen. "Coordinate when we'll be meeting."

How can I possibly give her my availability when I have no fucking clue when Franklin will be requiring my services? He doesn't exactly give me much notice, and if I keep him waiting, there is always a punishment of some kind.

But what's the penalty with Claire? She already thinks I hate her, and I can only imagine she feels something similar toward me.

It's one thing to ignore her and treat her badly, but wrecking whatever plans she has with her education would be the nail in my coffin.

"I'm free whenever." The words that leave my mouth could both be the truth and a lie, but only time will tell which one it is.

She stops writing and glares at me. "Let's take this day by day then." Claire sighs and bites at her lip. "This evening? Six-ish? Are you free?"

My phone hasn't gone off all day, and as of right now, I don't foresee any issues with that time. Things are always subject to change, though. I had planned on doing some recon on my package location situation, but that can wait.

It's not the brightest idea to blow off this impossible quest Franklin has thrown at me, but I can forfeit sleep to do that later. I'll figure out a way to do everything, even if it spreads me super fucking thin.

"Yeah, that works."

She nods. "Okay. We'll meet in the courtyard, deal?"

For some stupid fucking reason, I extend my hand.

Even more surprising, she takes it into hers.

"Deal," I say while I battle the distracting, incredible softness of her skin against mine.

The rest of the day goes by in a blur, my mind shifting in and out of the many things I need to be doing. I have homework to complete and a package to find, but everything seems unimportant compared to this six o'clock study date.

Why am I nervous? Why do I care? She already hates me. And honestly, that's a good thing. Then maybe she won't start to feel the way I do about her, and we'll be able to maintain distance from each other outside of our obligations. She'll be safe that way. From me, my world, and whatever danger comes with being a part of my life.

I have self-control! Why am I struggling so fucking much with this?

It's just studying. Tutoring. Whatever you want to call it. She's doing a job. And together, we're completing an assignment that everyone else in the class has to finish.

"You all right, kid?" Bram nudges my shoulder.

I blink and take in the bright fluorescent lighting in his café. "Yeah."

"You going to order anything?" He stands there waiting for me to stop being such an idiot.

"Coffee, to go. And um…"

"Did you bump your head too hard last time?" He places his hands on the counter and stares at me.

"No, I mean maybe. I don't know." I run my fingers through my hair. "I've got this study thing with Claire." I let out a breath. "What does she usually get?"

A wide grin spreads across Bram's wrinkly old face. "I've got you covered."

Thankfully she comes in here enough that Bram probably has a decent grasp on the kind of stuff she likes. He's thorough that way, paying attention to what his regulars order.

He pulls two paper cups out and fills them to the top, putting a dash of cinnamon into each of them. He strolls over to the bakery area and grabs two blueberry old-fashioned donuts from the case.

"You're kidding me?" Bram must be playing a trick on me.

He shakes his head. "Nope. Trust me, I was just as shocked as you."

The memory of Bram's food showing up on my doorstep comes crashing in. It wasn't that she had guessed my order correctly, it was that she mixed up mine with hers. She probably had ordered for herself, too, and gotten mine plain, but swapped them on accident.

It shouldn't matter that we share such a very simple thing in common, but somehow, it makes me feel that much closer to this fascinating girl I can't seem to get out of my head.

It's hard to believe that she wasn't put in my path for some higher reason.

But it's all for nothing, because I can't pursue her. I can't entertain a reality where I selfishly go after something I truly want. I'd be risking too much, and that wouldn't be fair to her.

"On the house, I insist." Bram shoves the rolled-up takeout bag toward me. "She's a special one, don't mess it up."

"It's not like that. It's strictly professional."

"Then why are you nervous?" Bram's never been the type of guy to sugar-coat shit or beat around the bush.

He's the closest thing to family that I have, and I'm not sure I would have made it this far in life without him. He's aware I've gotten myself tangled into a dangerous mess, but he somehow still has faith that I'll find a way out of it. It kills me that I have to keep secrets from him, but the less he knows, the better. I wouldn't put it past him to storm over to Franklin's place of business and give him an earful. People like Franklin can't be reasoned with though, not the way Bram would expect, and attempting to do so would only put Bram's life in danger.

I keep him in the dark to protect him.

Right now, though, he can see straight through my smokescreen.

I roll my eyes and grab the coffees from the counter. "See you later, old man." I make my way toward the exit.

He calls out across the moderately busy crowd. "I want an invite to the wedding."

I keep walking, not entertaining his antics anymore.

Claire may be absolutely perfect in my eyes, but I'm a broken shell of a man, and I would never allow myself to ruin her with my tortured soul.

She deserves someone kind and thoughtful and chivalrous, someone who is there for her at all times, who treats her with every single ounce of respect and never lets her down. Someone who appreciates her beauty and handles her with the utmost admiration.

Not someone like me. Not an unreliable, hotheaded asshole. Not me.

I belong in hell, and she belongs in heaven.

I punch in the code to gain access to our complex and stroll across the courtyard, approaching her from behind.

She has her back to me, headphones covering her ears, completely lost in whatever she's writing down frantically onto her notebook. She's this piece of art that shouldn't be touched.

She's everything and I am nothing.

The moment expires when my shadow casts over her shoulder, distracting her from what she's doing.

She tugs the headphones down and quickly snaps her book shut. "Hey." Her gaze falls on the stuff in my hands.

I hold one of the cups out to her. "Here." I motion to the spot next to her. "Do you mind?"

"No, of course not." She pops the lid to let some of the heat from her coffee escape. "Is that...?" Claire stares at the floating specks in her drink.

A sudden rush of panic courses through me. Did Bram set me up? Did he give me the wrong order on purpose to make a fool of me? Was that his plan all along?

How would that make any sense? I'm being an irrational idiot.

"How'd you know?" She glances over at me.

"Bram." I plop the bag between us on the table. "I hope he got it right."

Claire opens the sack and peers inside. "You like these, too?"

"Mmhm."

"Interesting." She hesitates before pulling one out. "Thanks." She takes a bite and covers her mouth while she chews.

I stare like a fucking idiot and have to force myself to look away. How can someone make a normal function so attractive?

I distract myself with the other donut, focusing my attention on anything except how pretty she is up close. What the fuck is wrong with me? I'm a teenager all over again, smitten with this girl who's way too good for me.

"Have you had a chance to read the assignment requirements yet? I figure we should start there before we get into the whole tutoring thing." She fumbles through her backpack to pull out the packet our teacher had given us earlier.

"Uh."

"I'm not surprised. Here." She holds it out to me. "It's a three-part opinion piece. Basically, we read the text, then write a discussion paper on what we think the author meant, how we interpreted it, and then compare and contrast between the viewpoints. It's incredibly straightforward but will require you to actually pick up a book and put in a little effort."

A part of me takes offense to her last statement, but considering my track record, she's well within her rights to make these kinds of assumptions about me.

I've only shown up for two of the classes I have with her, and I was late both times. I'm not exactly setting a model student example.

Old Johnny would be disappointed in the new me.

But old me was the one who decided to sign me up for this fucking nightmare I'm currently living. He's not allowed to hold judgment based on the mess he got me roped into.

"That's fair."

"I've already read this book, so I'll be doing a re-read. Do you want to get yours done on your own or together?" Claire's bright blue eyes burn a hole through me.

Of course, I should do it alone, without her. Far, far, far away from where she is. Keeping as much distance as humanly possible between us. I should only be around her when it's absolutely necessary. When there is no other choice.

At least, that's what my brain is urging me to do.

But somehow, my mouth opens and something else entirely comes out. "Together works for me." The self-control I thought I had fails me completely.

"Okay." She slides the book across the table. "Here. It's a fairly quick one. You can go ahead and get started while I finish something else. Read the first three chapters and then we can discuss once you're done." She pauses. "Unless you're in a hurry."

I shake my head, reaching out to latch onto the book but accidentally landing on her hand instead. "Not at all."

Her phone buzzes on the table, and when I glance down, I settle my sights on a text message from Griffin. The same name from the nightmare she had in my bed, where she was begging him to leave her alone. The one I saw on her phone the next morning when she had charged it in my kitchen. Could that also be the person who was screaming at her over the phone not too long ago?

She pushes the button on the side and the screen turns black. Not even two seconds later, it lights up again. Three more alerts this time.

"You need to get that?" I ask her, trying to keep my voice calm.

It's clear this person isn't a welcomed part of her life with how she keeps blowing them off.

"No."

The device goes off again, this time a guy's face appears across the whole thing. He gave up on texting and is now calling her.

She hits the ignore button twice, but he keeps at it.

"I'll be right back." She hops up from the table and rushes a few feet away.

I shouldn't impose, but I can't help listening in on the conversation, at least the one side of it that I can make out.

"Griffin, you have to leave me alone. Seriously. This isn't healthy." She stands with her back to me, her shoulders tense and her entire body rigid.

How can one person have this effect on her over the phone?

"Suicide isn't something to joke about." She sounds annoyed. "The next time you mention it I'm calling the cops to do a welfare check on you."

I continue to watch her shift her weight back and forth nervously.

"Stop calling me. I'm trying to move on with my life here, you should do the same." She doesn't bother waiting for a response, she simply ends the call and flicks the button on the side to silence anything else that may come through.

Claire takes a steadying breath before turning toward me.

I shift my own attention to the book in my hand to avoid coming across like a total creep. "Everything okay?"

She forces a toothless smile. "Yep."

"Was that your boyfriend?" I shouldn't ask, but my mind and mouth seem to have a communication issue I'm struggling to deal with.

Claire's jaw tightens. "Ex."

I let out a puff of air I didn't realize I was holding. Why would it matter either way? She's out of my league regardless of her relationship status.

"Does he live around here?" I continue to probe where I obviously shouldn't. It's none of my business, but I'd like to know if some psycho is going to show up and cause trouble.

This guy doesn't seem to understand boundaries.

"No." She puts her phone face down on the table. "He's back home."

“Where’s that?” Why can’t I just shut up?

“East Coast.”

Oh. He’s really far away then. Which means she is, too.

“What brought you out here?” I have this strong overwhelming desire to know every single detail about her.

“Life changes.” She tilts her head to glance at me and then shifts back to the blank page in front of her. “Long story short, my dad got an unexpected new job, and I couldn’t continue to stay there...financial reasons. So now I'm here, living at my mom's, two thousand miles away from where I grew up, basically starting completely over."

“Wait, Beth is your mom?”

“By birth, yeah. I guess so.” She faces me again, but this time curiosity fills her features. “You know her?”

"Not well, but a decent amount. She's always been nice to me. Pretty sure she was already here when I moved in. And that was ten years ago. She and a few of the other residents are flight attendants. They come and go randomly, often leaving for weeks at a time."

She lets out a sort of sad laugh. “Wow, well, you officially have a better relationship with her than I do.”

“I’m sorry.” The two words slip out like everything else I can’t seem to keep contained. It’s one of the many apologies she deserves from me but the only one I’m willing to give her right now. There’s still the need to keep a wedge shoved between us to eliminate any danger I might pose.

“It’s fine.” She’s not very good at lying.

“When was the last time you saw her?”

Claire picks at the eraser on her pencil. “Eighteen years ago.”

“How old are you?” The math suddenly adds up in my head.

“Almost nineteen.” The tone of her voice sends a knife through my heart.

I'm not sure about her story, or why her mom made the

choice to leave her daughter behind, but I do understand the impact losing a mother can have on a person.

I want to tell her this, to share that I can comprehend a bit of what she's going through. But doing so would open up an injury that I've still never properly recovered from, and I'm not in a position to spiral out of control once I dive back down that rabbit hole.

"Anyway. Enough about me." She taps the book. "Read."

21
CLAIRE

Johnny must think I'm a freaking pathetic loser.

One minute, my lunatic ex-boyfriend is blowing up my phone, and the next I'm opening up about childhood trauma caused by my estranged mother.

I shouldn't care what he thinks, but I do.

I do too much, actually.

And I hate it.

For each question he asked me, I had to force myself not to confess everything to him. There's this instinctual pull, this need to declare my inner thoughts and feelings, and for him to do the same. It's like we're on some private wavelength with an invisible thread that ties us together.

Or I'm losing my mind. That's probably it. There's possibly *nothing* between us, and I'm detecting something that isn't there at all.

That would make much more sense than the alternative.

I take a drink of my cooling coffee and flip my phone over to check the time.

There are seven missed calls from Griffin, four voicemails, and twenty-two text messages.

"You sure everything is okay?" Johnny breaks through the silence. He rakes his fingers through his hair, completely distracting me from the current disaster taking over my cell.

"Yeah." I swallow and have to look away.

Even with the healing cuts and bruises on his face, he's still incredibly good-looking, with his long, dark lashes and piercingly green eyes. I didn't realize such a vibrant color like that existed until he walked—or well, bumped—into my life.

My cheeks flush and betray me.

"Hey." He reaches out and touches my shoulder gently. "You don't deserve to be treated that way."

"How do you know what I deserve?" My words come out much harsher than I intend.

I could be a terrible person. A selfish and cruel one who kicks puppies or something. I could have been cheating on Griffin or treating him poorly. I could have been abusing or taking advantage of him.

"Claire." Johnny tilts his head. "I'd be a fool if I didn't recognize what kind of person you are."

His declaration startles me. He says this but then treats me like I'm a nuisance to his life. His words and actions don't align, and he constantly contradicts everything. One minute we can't be friends. The next he's bringing me coffee and rescuing me from falling on my face at the bar. It's like he *wants* to be a good guy, but something stops him and turns him into the opposite.

What Bram told me at the diner suddenly floats into my head.

"That's a cover up. There's a lot more to him than what meets the eye."

Which is it? Is Johnny a wolf in sheep's clothing or a sheep in wolf's clothing?

I think deep down I already know the answer to that question, I'm just not willing to admit it until he does.

And if he's not going to confess, I won't play into his game.

I turn toward my stack of stuff. "I think we're good for the day. Why don't you finish those chapters, and we can discuss it later?" I shove everything inside my backpack and rise from the table.

"Um, yeah, sure." He shuffles to his feet. "I…I didn't mean to upset you."

"Listen." I struggle with my train of thought. "When I said pretend to get along for the sake of our assignments, I didn't mean you had to fake like you care. I get it. Really. We aren't friends. That's fine. I don't need your pity."

"Wait." Johnny reaches out to stop me when I try to pass him. "That's not what this is about, Claire. I get it, I've been an asshole to you, but that is not a reflection of who *you* are. That's on me. I don't want to be this way, I have to. But don't you dare doubt for a second that you deserve anything less than the best."

I rip my arm away and continue around him. "That's not for you to decide." I rush up the stairs and shove my key into the handle, unlocking it quickly and disappearing inside.

I lean against the cold door and slide to the floor.

A light knock sounds, but I don't respond to it.

"Claire…" He lets out a sigh. "I'm sorry."

That's the second time he's said that tonight. The first about my mom. I was surprised when I heard it leave his mouth, because up to that point, I wasn't sure if he was capable of apologizing. Now though, the two words mean so much more than they seem, like he's trying to cover all the moments in the past couple of weeks where he's been in the wrong, including the very first when we ran into each other.

His footsteps disappear down the hallway and I'm left alone with the mystery of what he meant.

How am I going to make this arrangement work if I can't even get through a single study session with him? I have to figure out a way to block out any and all feelings I have for him and leave things strictly platonic. Going into this evening, that was the plan, but I'm going to have to try a little harder than that if I'm going to pull off this tutoring thing and actually pass my English Lit class.

I *need* this. I also need that letter of recommendation from Professor Brown on my scholarship resume if I stand any chance of actually getting it. Griffin might be a huge pain in my ass, but there's so much more waiting on me back home. My friends, my hometown, everything I grew up around. I can't allow it to slip out of my grasp because of some guy.

Some enigmatic and frustratingly gorgeous guy.

I climb from the floor and drag myself over to the couch, plopping myself horizontal and covering my face with my arm.

I wake up to knocking at my door. I rub my eyes and check the time, realizing that I accidentally slept for an hour. There are more alerts from Griffin that I choose to ignore.

I peek through the blinds and spot Johnny standing there. I turn the handle and peer outside.

"Hey." He holds out a bag in front of him.

Whatever it is reminds me that I skipped dinner.

"You must be hungry, right?"

I narrow my gaze. "I told you to stop buying me food."

"Technically, I bought myself food. A lot of it. And I have enough to share, if you haven't already eaten. If you have, I'll..."

I sigh and prop the door open further. "Come in."

A shy smile creeps across his face. "You sure?"

"Yep. Better hurry before I change my mind."

"Were you sleeping?"

"Maybe." I move to the kitchen and search for the plates. I still haven't gotten used to where everything is in my mom's house. I stand on my tiptoes to reach them.

"Here." Johnny puts his hand on the small of my back and grabs them from the top shelf. He pauses for the briefest second to stare into my eyes before walking away. "I wasn't sure what you liked so I got a variety."

"I thought you said it wasn't for me."

"Wishful thinking." He winks at me, a new version of him showing through that I haven't met yet. Playful Johnny.

I don't hate it.

Although, it makes staying mad at him quite difficult.

He unfolds the Chinese takeout box. "Um, this one's orange chicken."

One for one so far.

"Spicy cashew." He sets another aside. "Beef lo mein."

Three for three.

"Fried rice." He takes out a small container. "I got white, too, just in case. And egg rolls."

"You got enough food to feed a small army." I reach for a box at random.

"Sometimes it's nice to have choices." He shrugs and grabs a fork.

I don't think he's referring to dinner, but I'm not going to pry and ruin this decent moment we're having. Things are clearly weird between us, and if we're able to get along, even for one meal, I'll gladly take it.

Whatever this is, something less than friends but more than enemies, it's worth having.

I slide an eggroll out of the plastic bag and put one on both of our plates. "You want a beer?" I go to the fridge and open it up. "Or there's tea, and water."

"Surprise me." He lifts both of our mounds of food and puts them on the bar.

I grab two beers and pop the tops, placing one in front of both of our spots. I climb into the stool next to him and pick my drink up again. "Cheers."

He grins. "What are we cheers-ing?"

"Our first meal together." And taking a break from hating each other. I don't say that one aloud though.

"Hopefully, not our last." He clinks his bottle against mine.

I push away the rampant thoughts that follow with his words. It's like every time he opens his mouth my mind runs wild with dissecting the hidden meaning behind everything he says.

"Thanks for dinner." I take a big bite of chicken.

He leans over and nudges me with his shoulder. "Thanks for joining me."

If I didn't know any better, I'd say he was flirting with me, but I do know better, and Johnny is incapable of such things. Especially given his track record of hot and cold. I'm evidently not his type or something. Still, though, his touch rattles my core and warms my chest in a way I wasn't expecting.

He keeps having this effect on me with pretty much everything he does.

I watch him out of the corner of my eye, taking a swig of his brew and simply existing like a normal guy his age. Only, Johnny is far from ordinary, and there is much more under the surface that has yet to be uncovered about him. He's a mystery waiting to be unraveled.

And for some unknown reason, I hope like hell I'm the person who gets the chance to figure him out.

22
JOHNNY

Putting Claire first makes more sense than me being another one of the bad things in her life. She already has enough to deal with between moving across the country, her psycho ex, and the situation with her mom, not to mention whatever else I don't know about. I've only been around her a little bit, but it's obvious she's suffering more than she should.

She puts up a good front, but if anyone took an extra second to really study her, they'd see all the torment she hides from the world.

And maybe it's not my place to try to save her, I can't be the reason things get worse for her. So, I'll stomach my pride and do what I can to make the forced arrangement Professor Brown pushed on us less painful. It's clear that Claire's education is important to her, and I won't stand in the way of that.

Plus, there might be the tiniest bit of selfishness involved. Being around Claire is like someone putting a defibrillator to my chest, bringing me back from a death I never thought I'd escape.

She's something I haven't had in a while... She's hope.

I shouldn't rely on it, because it's a fleeting feeling, but I will cling to every ounce of it while I can, like it's the only thing keeping me alive.

Given my situation, it might be the very thing that *does* keep me alive.

The clock is ticking on locating this package, and I haven't gotten any closer to figuring out who took it, let alone where it is. Luckily, Franklin hasn't been too demanding of my services lately, either because he doesn't trust I'll actually get them delivered, or because I'm about to meet my end. Both alternatives are bad news for me.

"What are you working on?" Claire approaches from the entrance of the courtyard. She must be finished with her classes for the day.

Her eyes sparkle and her ponytail bobs as she walks closer. There's something different about her. A newfound light that shines a little brighter.

Last night was a turning point for us. An olive branch that solidified into a common understanding, that we would get through this together, considering there were no other choices.

We're doing what we have to do, given the circumstances.

Granted, being forced to be together is equal parts a blessing and a curse.

"Um, nothing." I move my arm over to cover the page.

She narrows her gaze. "You are a terrible liar. What is it?"

"A school thing."

"Well, since I'm your tutor…" She pokes at my side to distract me.

I wince at my still sore rib and end up giving her the perfect opening.

Claire glides the paper out from under me. "I'm sorry, I forgot those take time to heal." She scans the document and props herself onto the picnic table. "I don't get it. It's just a bunch of names with random notes."

I scratch my head and think like hell, trying to come up with an explanation. "Mmhm."

She drops her goofy attitude and looks at it again, then at me. "Johnny," she lowers her voice. "Is this what I think it is?"

I swallow, the carefree atmosphere drifting away with the shift in her tone. "What do you think it is?"

There's absolutely no way that she has any idea what the scribbles mean.

"Is this a list of suspects?" She stares me deeply in the eyes.

How the fuck am I supposed to lie to her when she asked me such a direct question? We're five minutes into a truce and she's already dipping her toes into a world that she should stay far, far away from.

My mouth opens and betrays me. "Yes." I shouldn't, but I continue, "They took something from me, and I need to get it back."

What have I done? This isn't going to end well.

She slides off the top of the table and positions herself next to me, only a few inches away. Her jaw tenses as she holds the paper between us. She lowers her head to take in the names once more and then glances up at me through her lashes.

My heart pounds wildly, not having a clue what she's about to do or say next. Is she mad? Does she think I'm crazy? Is she going to take the list to the authorities? Is she going to tell me I'm being an idiot, or worse—decide we can't continue whatever this is that we're doing because I'm being reckless?

"I want to help." Her words are a shock to my system.

"What?" There's no hiding the surprise in my voice.

"You're going to let me help you."

"No, Claire, you don't—"

She cuts me off. "Two heads are better than one. If this is important to you, you'll need another set of eyes. This is too much for you to take on yourself. I'm willing, and I'm able. So, you don't have a choice."

"There's always a choice."

"Nope, you're stuck with me. Sorry, not sorry." She hands me the paper. "I'm not taking no as an answer. Consider it another one of our assignments."

There's something about the way she insists on volunteering that tells me this is about more than just helping me figure out an old-fashioned whodunit. There's a fierceness about her that I haven't seen before, a wild darkness brewing just on the brim, ready to explode through the surface.

I'd be lying if I said I didn't want to kiss her so fucking badly in this very moment.

But that would only complicate things that much more. And I'm already at a loss on how I'm going to manage the details of this investigation without telling her more than she needs to know. Like, the part about all of this being tied to a criminal underworld, and that the stolen package was probably drugs or something fucking illegal. And if I don't locate it by the Friday after next I'm almost certain I'm a dead man, or worse, Franklin will go back on the deal we made.

Punishing me is one thing, but I can't allow him to take out his wrath on someone else, especially an innocent person.

"You don't know what you're signing yourself up for," I tell her, although I'm not as convincing as I should be.

She reaches out and puts her hand on my shoulder. "We're in this together now."

Maybe it's the rush of dopamine from her touch, maybe I'm already dead and someone accidentally granted me access to heaven, but there's a sort of finality to her declaration that shoots a shock wave straight through my heart.

Claire blushes and turns to face away. "We have to prioritize though. We've got this, our project, and getting you caught up on your other assignments. We have a lot of work cut out for us if we're going to succeed at it all."

I can't help but just stare at her in total and utter awe.

All of a sudden, life doesn't seem so lonely. I've been by myself for so long that I never considered what it would be like with someone by my side. It's obviously temporary, since the tutoring is only for the duration of the course and there's a deadline on finding the package, but right now, I will embrace whatever time I get with her.

If I'm a dead man walking, I might as well live a little.

"Listen." Claire glances at me again. "I know something is going on...something you don't want to tell me. Or can't tell me? I promise though, this will all be easier if you do. Whatever it is. If you're worried I'm going to judge you, or tell someone, I won't. I swear. Your secret is safe with me."

Without really knowing how or why—I believe her, I trust her.

And that by itself terrifies the fuck out of me.

She brings her hand slowly toward my face. "You probably don't remember this, but when I found you, you asked me not to call for help. I wasn't sure if it was pride, or something else, and I don't really know why I listened, but I knew then that you had a secret, and I wasn't going to be the one to expose you. Not then and not now. Whatever it is, Johnny, you don't have to do it alone.

"You might not want my help. You might actually hate my guts like you sometimes pretend to. But that isn't going to stop me from offering."

I reach out and tuck her hair behind her ear, something that I'm constantly drawn to do but always stop myself from doing. "I don't hate you."

Her lips twitch as she fights back a smile, but her twinkling eyes really give it all away.

"Never think that." I run my thumb along the side of her cheek and down her jaw.

My phone buzzes on the table, but I can't force myself to look away.

It goes off again.

"You should get that," Claire suggests.

"I don't want to." I'd rather sit here and stare at her until my eyes fall out of my head. It's totally not a very romantic thought, but stuff like this doesn't often happen to me, and if I blink, I'm afraid it'll be gone forever.

Another vibration takes her completely out of the moment.

I sigh and flip the thing over. All texts from a blocked caller, telling me my services are needed.

"I have to go." I run my hand through my hair.

She nods. "Okay. Do you know when you'll be back?"

How do I answer that when I'm not even sure what is being asked of me? How do I not lie when I can't exactly tell her the truth?

"A few hours, hopefully. But, um, depending on the circumstances, I might have to stop back before going out again." I'm telling her more than I should. "It's complicated."

She grabs onto my hand and looks up at me. "Will you do me a favor?"

"Yeah, anything." Because how could I possibly say no to her?

"Be careful."

If only her request wasn't totally out of my control.

23
CLAIRE

I've been braver today than I have in a *very* long time. I've said and done things so out of character that I've honestly surprised myself.

Don't get me wrong, it's been freaking terrifying, but having those little breakthrough moments with Johnny, where I saw his walls start to come down, made it all totally freaking worth it.

He's hiding something. And if my intuition is right, it's big. Big and dangerous and probably illegal.

Some risks are worth taking, and with him, my gut is screaming at me to take this leap of faith. What do I have to lose, anyway?

I'm sitting on the couch in my mom's condo when a knock rattles the door. I jump up and rush over, holding my breath in anticipation for what's on the other side.

Part of me is scared of what condition Johnny will be in when he returns from whatever he's doing. He's been in a constant state of bumps and bruises since I met him, and I can only imagine that will continue while he's wrapped up with his *thing*. It's tough to stomach and not be able to do anything about it.

Revenge is bittersweet, and I'd be lying if I said that wasn't one of the main reasons I offered to help him figure out who it was that attacked him in the alley.

I'm not even sure what the hell I'd do, but the psycho who did that to him deserves to pay in *some* kind of way.

I open the door to find him standing there in the condition he was when he left me a couple hours ago, only he's wearing a different shirt. A black one. I quickly scan his face and arms for any sign of distress. I exhale and try to hide the relief that courses through me.

"Hey." He's failing miserably at hiding his grin.

"Hey."

"You ready to get back to work?" Johnny leans against the frame.

"Yeah. You want to come in?"

"Have you eaten?"

Is this where I admit that I've been sitting here frantically watching the seconds tick by on the clock while I waited for him to arrive back safely? "Nope."

"Grab your stuff."

I follow along without question, going back to the living room and shoving my notebooks into my bag. I slide my phone and keys in my pocket on the way out.

"Here, let me." He takes my backpack from me and slings it over his shoulder.

Did I just time travel to the seventh grade, where a boy is carrying my books for me?

"Uh, thanks." I find myself unsure of how to react to such a thoughtful gesture.

At least the errand he was sent out on didn't put him in a bad mood, or worse, damage his pretty face.

Questions rattle their way through my head at the missing hours between when I saw him last. I want the answers to all of them, but I don't think it's my place to ask.

I choose something basic. "Everything go okay?" A simple yes or no that doesn't give away anything too incriminating.

We stroll side by side down the stairs and across the empty courtyard.

He pauses to open the gate and glances down at me. "Surprisingly, yeah."

I assume from the reoccurring black eyes and busted lip that not being injured *is* a surprise.

"Good." I try not to pry anymore despite nearly bursting at the seams with the need to follow up.

Johnny places his hand on my lower back and leads me out of the complex.

The sun casts a beautiful orange and pink on the horizon, and the heat from the day has dissipated. The temperature is perfect for an evening stroll.

A few minutes later we arrive at a familiar spot. The door jingles, and the cheery old man greets us from across the diner.

Johnny scans the diner and grabs my hand, tugging me toward a booth in the corner.

That's twice now in a short period that I've had to ignore the way his touch affected me. For him, it seems casual and natural —for me, it's like fire igniting my soul.

"Is this okay?" He motions for me to take a seat.

"Mmhm." I slide across the cushy material.

He drops my backpack next to me and climbs to the opposite side.

Bram glides over with a shit-eating grin on his face. He swivels an empty chair from a nearby vacant table and straddles it. "What's going on you two?"

Johnny points to my bag. "Studying."

"Ah, I see," Bram drags out the last syllable.

"And we need to eat," Johnny adds.

"Sure. Obviously." Bram bobs his head up and down. He

straightens up and grabs his notepad and pencil. "Well then, do you know what you want, or do you want a minute?"

I glance over at Johnny, letting the simple question from Bram settle into my head. Clearly, he was referring to something completely different, but I can't help the way my thoughts wander to this beautifully broken boy sitting across from me.

We're just two damaged souls who stumbled into each other unexpectedly.

And maybe that's all we ever will be, paths that were temporarily crossed.

Johnny meets my gaze, almost like he's thinking the exact same thing. "You ready or do you need time?"

I've never been so certainly uncertain about something in my life. I force myself to look away from Johnny and focus on Bram. "Stack of blue with a side of b. And a coffee, please."

Bram's eyes twinkle while he jots down my order. "Keep it up and I'll be offering you a job."

"Are you hiring?" I let out a laugh, although I'm partially serious. I could use the extra cash to save for the move back home. I've seen a few wanted signs going to and from school, but nothing jumped out at me to apply.

Bram tilts his head. "Are you looking?"

I shrug and nod. "Yeah, kind of."

"Congratulations." Bram extends his hand. "You got the job."

I look to Johnny. "Is he messing with me?"

Johnny leans back and throws his arm across the top of the booth. "Nope."

"Thanks." I give Bram a firm shake, completely in disbelief at the turn of events.

A small pit forms in my stomach, reminding me that good things don't last. At some point, the other shoe will eventually drop. For now, though, I will ride the wave of decentness that comes my way.

"No, thank you." Bram lets go and turns to Johnny. "And for you?"

"I'll have the same, minus the job."

Bram chuckles. "You sure? You'd look snazzy in a hair net."

Johnny rolls his eyes and repositions in his seat.

The dynamic between the two of them is something like a father and son. It's adorable to watch play out, especially when Bram manages to slightly embarrass Johnny. Another one of the many layers of Johnny Jones that not everyone gets to witness.

"I'm glad you got breakfast." Johnny glances across the diner and then back at me. "I figured you'd think I was a weirdo for ordering it this late."

"Are you kidding me? I could eat it for every meal."

"Same."

We lock eyes and my heart stutters at the intensity of it.

Bram plants our mugs on the table and fills each one with steaming coffee. He slides a cinnamon shaker between us and walks away without another word.

"So," I finally say. "We should get to work."

"Yeah, of course." He snaps out of his trance.

"Have you done *any* of your assignments yet?" I bite my lip and wait for the answer I already know is coming.

"I—uh...no."

"Okay. We can catch up. No big deal." I exhale. "Are you behind in all of your classes?"

Johnny scratches his head and averts his gaze. "I've been a little preoccupied."

"I know. I understand. But I can't help you if I don't see the big picture."

"Claire, Brown only put you up to tutoring me in English. You don't have to worry about the rest." He pauses. "I'm sort of a lost cause."

Without thinking, I reach across the table and latch onto his hand. "Hey, don't say that. We'll figure it out. *All* of it."

It suddenly dawns on me that Johnny probably hasn't ever had someone in his corner. Someone pulling a little bit of the heavy weight he carries around with him daily. Someone looking out for him and caring about his well-being.

He glances down at our interwoven fingers. "That's not your burden to carry."

"What are friends for?"

"After everything I've done to you?" Johnny shifts his attention back to me.

I raise my shoulders. "Meh. Water under the bridge."

Sure, Johnny has been a royal jerk at times, but deep down, I think his intentions were always for the best. If anything, the last twenty-four hours have proven that there's good in him. He's got a hell of a lot more going on than most people our age, and without even knowing the whole story, I'd say he's handling things pretty well.

"But," I continue, "if we're going to do this, you have to work with me."

Bram approaches with an armful of plates. "Here we go, kids."

We break our moment to give Bram room to lay the food on the table. There's a lingering absence where Johnny's skin was touching mine, and I can't help but wonder if he feels that, too.

It's pretty obvious that Johnny doesn't actually hate me like I had once thought. But aside from being his friend, I'm not sure how he views me. Maybe I'm exaggerating the sparks between us—the natural pull to each other that we seem to have. It could be one-sided, and I may be imagining it entirely.

One thing is sure, though—I have never wanted to be a part of someone's life so badly, no matter how big or small that role might be.

24
JOHNNY

We develop a routine without really planning it.

Between classes, gravity seems to pull us together. After school, Claire works for a few hours training at Bram's while I study in the corner or turn into Franklin's bitch boy. And when she's done, we eat some kind of takeout dinner while we catch up on assignments.

She's a fucking superhero, managing to get me nearly caught up in the few days we've spent with each other, all while staying on top of her own stuff, and her new job as a waitress.

I click the screen on my phone, the word *Friday* glaring back at me.

I officially have one week to locate this package, and I haven't made any more progress on it since I got the lead from Josey. I haven't mentioned the time constraint to Claire, because then I'd have to come up with some excuse to explain the severity of the situation. And so far, I've managed to keep her distracted with homework to take her mind off my colossal problem.

It's not ideal, given I'll probably be executed in seven days, but it's worth it to spend a little more time with her.

"What are you thinking about?" Claire tops off my coffee and slides into the booth next to me.

"Nothing." It pains me to lie to her, even about this. She deserves the truth at all times, no matter what. It's a heavily contradictory way of thinking, given our situation.

"It's about the *other thing,* isn't it?"

Sometimes it weirds me out how in touch with my thoughts she is. All I was doing was staring blankly at the wall, how could she know what was on my mind?

"Yeah." I let out a breath.

"I'm off in"—she pivots to spot the clock near the cash register—"ten minutes."

Meaning, that's how long I have to figure out what the fuck I'm going to tell her.

Oh hey, Claire, girl that has literally been a fucking angel in this hell that I'm living. I'm sort of working for a notorious criminal, and I'm pretty sure I've been delivering drugs and weapons all over town because I was trying to help someone out who didn't deserve what was going on. I think the guy set me up and hired some brutes to beat my ass and steal a package, so he'd have a legitimate excuse to fire me, kill me, or go back on his end of the bargain. I have no idea what was in the package, and no clue how I'll locate it, but if I don't, by next Friday, you might never see me again. Basically, it was nice knowing you.

Something like that, right?

"Okay."

She goes back to work and leaves me with my destructive thoughts.

How do I tell her the truth without losing her in the process?

Things have been good between us; I don't want to complicate it with this mess I'm in.

But continuing to keep my secret will only deepen the divide between us, and as much as I hate to admit it, I don't think I can do this on my own.

I've gotten used to doing everything myself. That's how life has always been. This time, though, I might be in over my head.

"Hey." She appears at my side. "Bram said I could go since we're slow."

I shove everything into my bag and take a final swig of my coffee. "Let's get out of here." I lead her out of the diner and head toward our complex in silence.

She side-eyes me a few times but doesn't ask any questions. At one point, she checks her phone, types something, and puts it away.

I can't help wondering whether or not it was her ex, but I don't dare ask. If she wanted me to know, she'd tell me.

"Cora invited us to go out with her and her friends tonight."

"Oh?" I punch in the code to the gate.

"Yeah. I told her we were studying."

I continue across the courtyard and up the stairs, arriving at my place.

Claire follows along, her brown hair swishing behind her with each step.

I unlock my door but only open it enough to toss my backpack inside before shutting it again. Once I'm baggage free, I grab her hand and take her down the hall.

She lets me guide her but says, "Is this where you lead me to my untimely death?"

"You know me too well." I wink at her and keep going past all of the units on this side of the building until we reach a door she's probably never noticed.

We go through it and climb the dimly lit stairs to reach another entryway.

I push it and fresh air comes whooshing in.

She grips my hand tighter. "Is this the rooftop access?"

I reassuringly squeeze her back. "You'll see."

The moon casts a golden glow against the night sky, and from up here, the stars are decently visible.

I turn to her. "Do you trust me?"

Without hesitating, she nods, a mixture of fear and excitement dancing across her delicate features.

I walk her to the edge of the building, where another roof is just a few feet away. I leave her there for a second and rush over to grab what we need. I come back with a thick plank of wood, long enough to lay across the two buildings.

"You're not serious?" Her eyes go wide.

I grin. "Deadly." I place it in the same spot I've done numerous times in the past. "It'll be worth it, I promise."

And for whatever reason, she decides to believe me.

"I'll go first." I make quick work of crossing over, wanting to show her how simple it is despite seeming super dangerous. I hold out my hand and wait for her to follow.

She adjusts the hem of her jean shorts while peering over the edge. "You've done this before?"

"Yep. You got this." For a second, I doubt whether or not she's going to take the leap of faith, but my suspicions are quickly erased when the fierce version of Claire shines through.

She steps onto the board and wastes no time meeting me on the other side.

I grab onto her waist to steady her when she jumps off. "That wasn't so bad, was it?" I stare into her eyes, and although it's dark out, the intense blue melts right through me.

She swallows. "Nope."

A car alarm goes off in the distance, and we let go of each other.

"Anyway, um—" I point ahead, toward the section of this other building that is taller than ours. "This way."

We climb up a ladder that's fixed to the side of the structure and end up on a rooftop that provides a much better vantage point of the night sky; it also has plenty of privacy from the prying outside world.

"Wow." Claire slowly spins in a circle to take in the landscape, tilting her head upward. "It's…beautiful."

"Yeah." Except my eyes are trained on her, not the sky above. I lean against the stairwell access and allow her to bask in this hidden-in-plain-sight paradise.

"How did you find this place?" She finally turns toward me.

I think back to that night when I felt I couldn't breathe, like I needed to escape, to truly be alone. Not in my house, but where no one else would think to find me. "I kind of got lucky, really. I had to get away, you know? From everything. But in a town like this, that's not the easiest thing to do. I found the rooftop door and wandered over here. I was about to try a running jump when this big gust of wind had blown in, and I heard that plank rattle against the building.

"It was like a gift from the universe. A totally stupid one, because I didn't know if it would hold my weight or not, but I said screw it and tried. Had to be safer than jumping."

Claire waits for me to finish. "That's incredible."

I wiggle the toe of my shoe into the ground. "I've never shown this to anyone else." There was some part of me that needed her to know this. That this thing I hold near to my heart hadn't been shared with another person, other than her.

It might not be a big deal to her, but it is to me.

She comes closer and takes my hand. "Thank you."

In another world, this would be the perfect time to tug her to me, run my fingers through her hair, gripping the base of her head to tilt it upward, while my other hand rests on the small of her waist. I'd lean in, taking my time while my nose grazed hers. My lips would gently find their home—where they belong. I'd kiss her like it was the only thing keeping me alive. The earth would stop rotating and it would only be me and her, and nothing would ever be more seamless than that moment together.

But that would be unfair to her, given all the things I've yet to tell her. Without all the information, it wouldn't be right to push that boundary and not first allow her the choice to walk away. I've clung to this hope that maybe she won't react negatively to the mess I'm in, but that's a desperately bleak likelihood. Any person in their right mind would run the other way if they knew the truth.

"I can see it on your face." She breaks through my negative thoughts. "Spit it out."

I take a deep breath, doing my best to prepare myself for the fact that *everything* is about to be different. The way she looks at me, the way she treats me. What if she becomes afraid of me? What if she runs and hides and avoids me for the rest of her life? What if I somehow actually convince her that I'm the bad guy?

All of a sudden, the fear of how she'll react consumes me.

"I don't want this to change." I run my thumb along the top of her hand and savor the way it feels.

"It won't."

I meet her gaze. "You don't know that."

"Do you trust me?" She repeats my same question from a few moments ago.

And like a key, she unlocks part of me that I've never given anyone access to.

"I work for..." I struggle to finish my sentence.

She continues where I stop. "Something illegal."

I nod.

"You're a runner."

I narrow my brows. "How did you know?"

She smiles. "I'm not a complete idiot. You get called out at random times from unknown numbers. You're gone for hours at a time. You got mugged and had something taken from you. Which, by the way, makes no sense, because when I found you, your phone and wallet full of cash were with you. You had jewelry on."

I kick off from the building. "Wait, so, this whole time, you've known, and you..."

"Didn't care?" She shakes her head. "No. I mean, I *care,* but only because you clearly underestimate your occupational hazard and it's incredibly stressful. Every single time you leave I'm sick to my stomach that you might not actually come back. Do you know how many times I've genuinely thought you might be dead?"

My heart pounds, and I do the only thing that makes sense.

With both of my hands, I grab Claire by the face and press my lips against hers. It's not exactly how I planned it in my head earlier, but holy fuck if it isn't the best decision I've made in my entire life.

She steps closer and grabs my shirt collar with one hand, dragging me to her and weaving her other through my hair.

I walk our bodies toward the building and press against her small frame, backing her into the wall. I keep a firm grasp on her cheek and grip her around the waist.

She wraps her arms around my neck and pushes into me further, kissing me deeper with each passing second.

It's sweet and soft and hot and intense, all in one, and I cannot get enough.

I firmly take hold of her and lift her from the ground, wrapping her legs around my torso and pinning her in place.

She goes along with every bit of it, not seeming to want to stop in the slightest.

A vibration buzzes and tries to steal my attention. From this angle, it must be her phone, not mine.

I take a breath, resting my forehead against hers. "Do you need to get that?"

She answers me by digging her fingers in and pulling me back down, our mouths crashing together in the best way. Her kiss is decadent—her lips are soft and addictive, better than I ever could have imagined, no matter how many times I've caught myself staring at them.

Another vibration, now from my jean pocket.

This time, it's Claire that pauses. "You should check that."

I groan but do what she tells me. At this point, it's safe to say I'd do anything she asked of me. I keep her pinned against the building and slide my phone out. "Fuck."

She kisses the corner of my mouth. "You have to go?"

"Yeah. But I really, really, don't want to." And if there wasn't so much on the line, I would stay right here, melting our bodies together in a way I had convinced myself would never happen.

Claire releases her legs from around me, and I gently lower her to the ground. She takes out her phone and her eyes go wide.

"What's wrong?" I tuck her hair behind her ear.

"It's my…mom. She, uh, she has a layover, and she'll be here in a few hours."

"Holy shit."

"Yeah, you're telling me." She shoves the device into her pocket. "Talk about a buzzkill."

I rub my thumbs along her cheeks, gripping her face in my hands, and kiss her forehead, her nose, and then her lips. "You can stay at my place if you want to. You can have the bed, I'll take the couch."

She smiles and stands on her tiptoes to press her mouth against mine. "Such a gentleman."

"You'd be surprised. But really, the option is there if you want it. No pressure." I take a step back, and it's like I'm being separated from an extension of my being. I thought there was an invisible pull to Claire before, but now, it's out of this fucking world.

I weave my fingers through hers, and this time, it's different. I was right, things have changed, but in a way I could have never expected.

I may have only confessed the smallest part, but it somehow made us closer than ever. It's like I really have died and gone to heaven. Only, if that were the case, I wouldn't stop making out with the hottest girl on the planet to run some illegal contraband across the city.

We make our way down the ladder, across the platform, and through the roof access area to enter the confines of our complex.

I bring her hand to my mouth and gently press my lips against it. "I'll see you in a little bit, okay?"

"Deal."

I rush along the hallway and take the stairs quickly. The sooner I get this errand over, the sooner I can see her again. I jog through the courtyard with a little extra pep in my step.

I have to knock the grin off my face or Franklin is going to be able to tell something is up. I'd rather keep my personal life as far away from him as possible. Getting involved with Claire was already dangerous enough—I have to protect her at all costs.

I open the gate to the complex and nearly bump into someone as they walk in. Déjà vu hits me from my first interaction with Claire. I don't knock this person down, but I manage to spit out a "Sorry."

My phone goes off again.

Unknown: *???*

Me: *Be right there.*

I continue my pace but manage to reduce the level of happiness that seeps from my pores. What Claire and I have is special, and I won't dare risk that.

I'm a few blocks away from the complex when a weird sensation settles over me. My heart pounds as my mind races to catch up with itself.

That face, the guy I ran into...it was so familiar.

But where do I remember it from?

I try to match it with any of the current tenants but keep coming up short. I don't think we have had anyone move in recently, other than Claire.

Was it someone visiting? That would explain where I'd seen them before. It's Friday night, which might make sense. Could it have been someone from school?

Each wrong turn in my mind sends another spike of anxiety coursing through me.

Suddenly, it clicks into place.

I glance at the intersection, realizing just how far away I am. Panic consumes me, and I do the only thing I can, I turn around and I run.

I run as fast as I can, completely disregarding Franklin and any demand he might have of me. Nothing in the world could be more important than getting to her right now.

I sprint wildly, quicker than I ever have in my life. I rush past people on the street and don't give a shit that I must look like a total fucking idiot. I bolt across traffic, horns blaring and brakes locking up to avoid crashing into me.

I narrow my gaze on the building ahead; I'm almost there. Maybe I'm losing it, maybe I'm overreacting. Maybe it was a figment of my imagination, and it wasn't who I thought it was after all.

But if that's the case, why do I have this pit in my gut screaming at me to go, go, go?

I hear her voice first, confirming my fear. "Stop it, let go of me." She's pleading with him.

And it rips my heart in two.

I fumble with the code and frantically try to look through the gate separating us. The buzzer lets out a failure signal and flashes red.

"Claire!" I call out. "I'm coming."

"Who the fuck was that?" His voice is like thick poison.

"Please, Griffin, you're hurting me." She sniffles and chokes on her words.

I punch the numbers in and thank God it beeps and goes green. I throw the gate open, and it clangs loudly. I clear the courtyard in a flash and take the stairs three by three.

He has her at the top, gripping her forearms and shoving her closer and closer to the first step.

Tears are streaming down her cheeks.

"This is why you broke up with me?" He nods his stupid ugly head in my direction. "This fucking guy?"

I hold up my hands. "Just let her go, dude." I slowly position my body toward him and try to get him to shift his path in a different direction.

He's holding on way too tightly, and if I make the wrong move, he could easily send her tumbling down the stairs. Not a risk I'm willing to take.

I take a step and he counters, falling right into the trap I'm setting for him.

"She was mine first." He slurs his words, clearly indicating that he's been drinking.

"Griffin," Claire begs. "You're—" She winces.

"Wah, wah, wah. You're so dramatic." He digs his fingers into her forearms tighter and tighter.

"Stop, please," she says through a sob.

She takes the last and final step I need to make my advancement.

I jump forward, shoving my fist into this asshole's throat and causing him to release her from his death grip. I grab the collar of his preppy boy shirt and pull him closer to my face. "What the fuck is wrong with you? Who gave you the right to lay a hand on her?"

Memories from the first few days she was here trickle in; visions of her wearing long sleeves and hiding her skin, until one day, she wasn't, and she wore makeup on her arm to cover up bruises. Ones that this prick must have left on her skin before she escaped him.

She even had a nightmare when she passed out at my house where she was begging him to let her go.

Rage boils up inside of me. This isn't an isolated incident. Between what I *do* know, and the harassment and nonstop texting and calling, enough is enough.

I grip him firmly, not daring to let go, and shift my attention to her. "Are you okay?"

She's huddled on the ground, a few feet away, holding her arms close to her chest, shivering from the shock and stress he just put her through. Her eyes are red and puffy, and black streaks trail down her cheeks. Her lips tremble, the same lips that I kissed only minutes ago.

Griffin manages to do the unspeakable. He spits, directly in my face. "If I can't have her, no one can."

And between the anger and fury and sheer protectiveness I have over her, I yank him toward me and shove him forward, throwing him down the same steps he had just taunted Claire with.

I stand still and stare while his arms go out wide, matching the depth of his eyes, and his body thuds and rolls and slams into each stair, and lands with a final thump.

He lay there, motionless, in a contorted heap on the ground.

It starts to sink in exactly what I just did.

I may have saved her, but everything else I've sacrificed will all be for nothing when the cops come and I get arrested. If my plan was ever going to work, I couldn't get involved with the authorities. I managed to save one life, but I ruined another.

But the only thing that really matters is she's okay.

Doing what I did may have sealed Griffin's fate and mine along with it. Neither one of us will get to be with Claire. The difference is, my sacrifice was to protect her, and his actions were purely selfish and egotistical.

My only regret was not telling her how I felt before it was too late.

Claire looks at me with wild eyes. A new sense of vigor about her. She grips my shoulders and shakes me. "Go, Johnny! Fucking go! Get out of here!"

25
CLAIRE

Okay, Claire, pull it together.

You can do this.

I rush down the stairs and do the thing I always see people do in movies—I check for a pulse. I place my fingers under his neck and feel the slow but steady thumping of blood rushing through his veins.

I let out a breath. He's still alive.

But for the life of me, I don't know whether that's a good or bad thing. And that thought alone sends a shiver down my spine.

I drag my phone out of my pocket and dial those three numbers that I learned before I knew my own phone number. *Emergencies only,* we were told.

Right now, the situation seems pretty fitting.

A calm female voice answers. "Nine-one-one, what's your emergency?"

"I, um, I need an ambulance. My, my boyfriend, *ex*-boyfriend, he's fallen down the stairs. He's in bad shape."

"Okay, what's your name?"

"Claire."

"Claire, is he conscious?" The clicking of a keyboard sounds in the background.

"No."

"Is he breathing?"

I stare at his chest to find the rise and fall of life. "Yes."

"Claire, you're listed at eighty-eight Germain Street. Is that correct?"

"I—I think so. Yeah."

"There's a unit in your area, they're already on the way. I'm going to ask you a few more questions."

"Okay." I'm a terrible liar, what if I say the wrong thing?

"How old is he?"

"Um, twenty-one."

"And his name?"

"Griffin Thomas."

Sirens go off in the distance and get louder and louder by the second.

"Claire, are you injured?"

I glance down at my forearms. They're red and bruised already, and on one spot, there's dried blood from his fingernails cutting into my skin. "Not really."

"Is there anyone else there with you?"

"No." I guess when it comes to Johnny, protecting him comes naturally. He has enough going on, and the look on his face after he shoved Griffin down the stairs told me that he couldn't afford the risk of getting caught.

He gave me the greatest gift of all, he saved me, but this was my battle now.

I glance at the flashing lights illuminating the building across the street. "I have to open the gate; I have to let them in."

"Okay, Claire, help is there now. Do you see them?"

"Yes."

"I'm going to disconnect the call now, Claire. Do you understand?"

"Yes." I hang up and fumble with the latch, opening the gate and waving toward the approaching ambulance. "Over here."

A man jumps out of the passenger seat, and a woman opens up the back hatch and climbs down. Together, they rush over.

"What happened?" The guy asks me.

"He fell, down the stairs."

He spots Griffin from across the way and turns to the woman. "Grab a c-collar and backboard. I'll get on his vitals."

I glance at his badge: *Phillips K.*

"What's your name?"

"Claire," I spit out. How many more times am I going to be asked this tonight?

"Claire, is this your friend?"

"Um, he's my ex."

He nods. "Okay. I'm going to take over now." Phillips pokes around and verifies that Griffin is still alive. He opens this little toolbox thing of his and puts a device on Griffin's finger.

The woman approaches with the stuff Phillips requested.

"We've got to get him on a backboard," he tells her.

I stand there, in a complete daze while they do their job. The moments fade into each other, and I start to think I might be dreaming.

"Did you see her arms?" the guy whispers to the woman. "We're going to have to call this in. We can't leave her here."

It's not until the lady stands in front of me and waves her hand that I realize Phillips and another guy are carting Griffin away on the stiff board.

"Miss. Come with us. We can transport you to the hospital."

I go with her but take a final glance upstairs on our way out, noticing the few neighbors that decided to crack their doors and see what was happening. I've only been here for a few weeks and I've already caused a dramatic scene.

My gaze falls on my arms, and my hands do their best to cover up the marks. The automatic door opening and shutting with each frantic person entering the emergency room keeps me on edge. With every new body, the impending doom of when I will have to talk to someone rapidly approaches. I have no clue what I will say, and given the very fresh imprints on my skin, I can't exactly pretend I wasn't involved at all.

The one thing I'm certain of is I need to keep Johnny's name out of it.

I owe him that much, especially now.

A woman in scrubs comes into the sitting area. "Claire Cooper." Her tired eyes scan the room.

I stand from the stiff chair and walk over. "That's me."

"Right this way." She leads me to a room just feet from the receptionist desk. She motions for me to enter. "My name is Georgia. You can have a seat." She closes the door and shuts us in.

A strange sort of fight or flight response kicks in as I watch the outside disappear. I glance around at the standard-issue doctor room stuff. The paper-covered seat thing, the sink area with a jar full of tongue suppressors, and boxes of latex gloves. A trash can for hazardous products.

She sits, too, and lays a clipboard on her lap. "Claire, I'm here to help you, okay?" Her voice is calm and kind, despite her ragged features. "Can you tell me anything about why you're here this evening?"

"Um, my ex, Griffin, he fell." I shift toward the door and then back. "He's here somewhere."

She nods and makes a note on the paper. "I see. And what can you tell me about that?"

"About what? I don't know how he's doing; they won't tell me anything because I'm not family."

Georgia shakes her head. "No, not his condition, but the events that led up to it."

"He fell."

"I see." She stares at me. "Is there any particular reason why that happened?"

"I…" I have to come up with something. "I think he was drinking."

Georgia writes again. "Uh-huh." She leans forward and lowers her voice. "Claire, this is a safe space, okay? Everything you say in here is confidential, between you and me and the laws that protect people like you."

"What do you mean?" People like me?

"Honey." Her brown eyes fall to the arms I suck at covering. "How did that happen?"

I bite at my lip to try to stop the tears from starting again.

She raises her hands. "I don't want to make assumptions, but correct me if I'm wrong. That is not self-inflicted, is it?"

"No." Even if I did harm myself, the angle and fingerprints are no match to something I could have done.

"I didn't think so." She clicks her pen and jots another note. "Do you want to tell me how you got them?"

I remain silent. I don't know if this is a trick question or not, and I don't want to say the wrong thing. What if I confess something incriminating?

Georgia slides a pamphlet out from under her paper she's writing on. "Here." She hands it to me. "When you're ready, this is a great resource."

I glance down at the page and read the headline.

Dealing with Domestic Abuse.

A knock rumbles the door, and a second later, it opens. I expect it to be the cops, a person with a badge to come take me away.

Instead, it's a middle-aged woman who pokes her head in, her eyes going wide when she sees me. "Claire!"

Another lady appears from behind her. "Georgia, I'm so sorry, this lady wouldn't take no for an answer."

Georgia stands and tries to shove the intruder out.

"Claire, it's me." The random person narrows her familiar blue eyes at me.

"Mom?"

"Oh, sweetheart, you must be in shock." She shoves past the hospital workers and makes it to my side.

Georgia puts her arm out to block Beth from coming any closer. "Is this your mother?"

I study the arch of her nose, the curve of her jawline. I take in her stature and the scent of her over-the-top perfume. It's strange to only see someone in photos your whole life, and suddenly, they materialize in front of you.

"Yeah."

The next few minutes go by in a blur; a mother figure shushing and swatting everyone away, leading me out of the building and into a bright red BMW with dark tinted windows that's parked right in the valet zone.

The short drive to the complex is awkward as hell. Beth speaks, but I don't respond. She goes on about how she had some guy from her past that got rough with her and how she could relate.

Relate? She knows nothing about me and my life. I wish she would shut up and stop pretending she cares.

My heart dances wildly in my chest with each passing second.

Beth pushes a button to shut the car off, and I waste no time opening the door and getting out.

"Claire, wait." She jumps out to follow, clicking the key fob to lock the vehicle.

I don't stop, I just keep going. The last thing I want is to be forced to talk with this random woman, regardless of her role in creating me. I push the code into the gate access box and grant myself entry. It then dawns on me that although I've spent the last couple of weeks alone, this lady is going to be following me right into the place I was going to try to escape her.

I move through the courtyard, doing my best not to acknowledge the drops of blood still staining the ground where Griffin's body landed. I tilt my head up at the stairs, and all of a sudden, they become fucking terrifying. I pause and take in the seemingly endless mission ahead of me.

"Are you coming?" Beth says when she reaches my side.

I snap out of my trance and nod. "Yeah." I take each one slowly, not wanting to lose my footing and fall. I'd rather not spend any more time on them than necessary, but I'd also rather not end up like Griffin, splattered at the base of them.

I imagine Johnny's hand, his fingers weaved through mine, anchoring me safely, protecting me from any harm that comes my way.

I had yelled at him to go, and now I can't help but worry about him.

Did he return to the job he had blown off to save me from Griffin? Did he get punished for being late? Is he okay?

We never exchanged phone numbers, so I can't exactly call or text him to check in. He's probably equally concerned about me, and what I told the responders when they showed up.

I picture his face, the panic that wrecked him when he realized what he had done. He had gone into shock, and the only thing I could think of was getting him out of there. I couldn't let him take the fall for what happened, even if he did do it on purpose.

"What do you need me to do?" Beth breaks through my train of thought.

"Nothing." I stand awkwardly in the small foyer of her condo. This place feels strange and foreign now that she's here. "I don't need anything from you."

Not now, not ever.

"I could make you a cup of tea."

If she knew me, she'd know I find my comfort in coffee. But that's the thing—she doesn't, because in all the years I've been alive, she's shown absolutely no effort in playing the role of my mother. Why should she start today?

"No, I really just want to be alone." I cover my hands over the marks on my arms.

"We could press charges, you know?"

I ignore her words and make my way out of the suffocating space. "I'm going to bed." I pick up the pace once I'm down the hall. I shut and lock the door behind me and rush to the bathroom, closing myself in there, too.

I slide down the wall and sit on the cold floor. I bring my knees to my chest and hold onto myself tightly to keep everything from falling apart. I sit like that for a while, until finally, I bring myself to my feet. I approach the vanity and take a long look in the mirror.

Black faded streaks run down my cheeks, and my hair is a mess. I splash water on my face in an attempt to wash away the remnants of tonight. I catch sight of my forearms and it stops me completely.

The memory of Griffin's alcohol breath, inches from me—his fingers digging into my skin, holding onto me more aggressively than he ever has. He kept leading me toward the top of the stairs, hissing vile words and accusations at me.

All I could think about was how the other shoe had finally dropped.

One minute, everything was perfect, the next, it was ruined.

26
JOHNNY

The second I complete my delivery, I shove the white envelope into my pocket and take off toward the complex. The air whooshes by my face, stinging the new wound Franklin had one of his goons give me.

I was late, and it wasn't like I could tell them why. That would only complicate things more. So, I kept my mouth shut and took the beating he was going to give me either way.

I don't know whether she's home or at the hospital or at the police station, but I'll check each one until I find her and verify that she's okay. I've been away from her for as long as I could, and now that I'm finished with Franklin's task, I refuse to keep my distance any longer.

She saved me from both myself and the terrible reality that almost played out.

If I had stayed, the cops would have arrested me. I'd go into the system and be charged with whatever the crime was for pushing someone down a flight of stairs. Murder? Did I kill him? His contorted body definitely looked dead from where I was standing.

I rush through the courtyard and around the remains of

what transpired earlier. I jog up the steps and knock on Claire's door, hoping like hell she's home. I have no idea what time it is, but there's no way I'm going to wait until morning to find her.

"Johnny?" Beth's voice oozes confusion. "What are you doing here?"

I don't expect to see her standing in her own house. I had forgotten that message Claire received before we went our separate ways. "Claire, is she, is she here?"

"Yeah." She angles her head. "You met Claire? Duh. You two go to the same school." She shifts her tone. "You look a little rough. Are you okay? Oh God, you didn't have anything to do with that boy and the stairs, did you?"

"I'm back here." I spot Claire poking her head around the corner of the hall.

Beth turns in Claire's direction, and I take the opportunity to shove past her.

I rush toward her and follow her into the bedroom.

She studies my face, probably taking in the fresh cut across my brow and swollen lip.

I freeze, glancing her over, too. Her hair is damp, and she's in a fresh set of clothes, long sleeves covering her arms.

She wraps herself around me and buries her face in my chest.

I pull her closer and hold on tight. "Are you okay?"

"Yeah," she mumbles into my shirt. "I am now."

"Is he...?"

Her body goes tense. "He's still alive."

"Claire," I breathe. "I'm so sorry." I kiss the top of her head.

She pulls away and looks up at me with glistening eyes. "What?"

"I wasn't here for you when you needed me." I shake my head. "I'll never forgive myself for that."

I had walked right by that asshole and didn't realize it was him until it was almost too late. I had seen his stupid face pop up on her phone numerous times; it should have clicked sooner that it was him, her psychotic ex who would stop at nothing to terrorize her.

"Johnny," she cups my face in her palm. "You literally saved me." She averts her gaze. "I don't know what would have happened if you didn't show up when you did. That could have been me at the bottom of those stairs, instead of him." A shiver rolls through her.

I shift my attention to her fabric-covered arms. I swallow and hold onto her hand, gently pulling the sleeve up. I clench my jaw when I see the swollen, red remains of what he did to her. Although, I'm sure the effect on her is more than just skin deep.

A flashback from my childhood threatens to break me. My mom often hid similar injuries under layers of clothing and makeup. She was terrible at picking men, each new one seemed worse than the last, until one day, things went too far.

I blink away the image of her, the last time I had seen her outside of a casket, a vision that haunts me to this day. If only I had done more, maybe she'd still be here. If I had learned to stand up for myself and others earlier, maybe things would have played out differently. But, if they did, maybe I wouldn't have been here tonight when history almost repeated itself.

Fate has a funny way about it.

Claire drags her shirt back over the marks. "It's okay, really."

I run my thumb along her cheek. "No. Nothing about this is okay. What he did to you? That's not okay. You didn't deserve this. No one does."

Beth knocks on the door. "Hey, you all right in there?"

"Yeah."

"I have an early morning; I'm going to get to bed." She pauses. "Unless you want me to try to get someone to cover my flight."

"No," Claire blurts out. "I'll be fine. I just need to get some sleep."

"Okay...let me know if you change your mind." Beth's footsteps disappear down the hall and into her bedroom.

Claire tilts her head up at me, her eyes red and puffy. "I'm so tired."

"Right, of course. I'll go..." I attempt to back away.

She doesn't release me. "Will you stay?"

"Of course." I pull her into me once more. "But I'm going to have to run home and take a quick shower. I smell bad."

"You could shower here."

"I need clothes."

"Can I go with you? We can stay there. I just really don't want to be alone right now."

I grip her face between my hands and press my lips to her forehead. "I'm here for as long as you want me."

She slides on a pair of slippers and gathers her phone and keys.

Our hands magnetically find each other, and we leave her room behind. We quietly make our way down the hall and out the front door without drawing attention from her mother. A few seconds later, we're in my place.

"Do you need anything? Water? Food?" I pause when we pass my kitchen.

"Nope."

Given the circumstances, she seems to be handling this all pretty well. Although it's clear Griffin's abuse is nothing new to her, so I guess it's not at all surprising she's not freaking out more. She's become numb to that kind of treatment.

I walk her into my room and pull back the comforter on my bed. "Here."

Claire climbs in, leaving her slippers on the floor.

I cover her up and sit along the edge, smoothing a strand of her hair out of her face. "I'll only be a minute, okay?"

She nods and pulls the blanket to her chest. Her eyes are already getting heavy. "K."

I watch as her lids close.

How is it possible this angel is here with me now? After everything that's happened, she still chose me.

I make quick work of grabbing a towel and taking a shower. I don't want to waste another second where we aren't breathing the same air. It's stupid, feeling the way I do about her, so fucking intensely, so fucking quickly, but I can't help how fucking right it is.

It was like I knew the moment I bumped into her that she would forever change my world. I guess it just didn't dawn on me until recently what exactly that meant.

I walk out of the bathroom with a towel wrapped around my waist and go to my closet to rummage through a hamper with clean clothes that never got put away. I locate a pair of boxers and slip into them, letting the towel fall to the floor.

I do my best to stay quiet while I make my way to the recliner in the corner of the room.

Claire extends her arm and mumbles something.

I kneel by her side. "What is it?"

She tugs at my hand, scooting back in the bed and dragging me in with her.

"Are you sure? I'm like, almost naked."

"Yep." A smile spreads across her face and she peers through her heavy lids at me.

I climb in next to her and let her settle into the crook of my shoulder.

She nuzzles in close and sighs.

I wrap both arms around her and hold on tight. The warmth of her body settles into mine, and if anyone would have told me earlier that this is how my day would end, I never would have believed them.

I breathe her in and cherish every single second of this until sleep finally pulls me under.

I wake to her still in my embrace. Only now, we're on our sides, and her perfect backside is pressed into me. Our legs are intertwined, and she hugs my hand to her chest like she's afraid I might disappear if she lets go.

I slowly pull it from her grasp and graze it along her waist while kissing her hair. "Morning."

"Mmm."

"Do you want me to make coffee or get it from Bram's?"

She turns to face me, and my heart nearly stutters at seeing her beautiful face. She places her hand on my cheek and her gaze trails up to my brow and then to my lip. "Does that hurt?"

"Nah. It's been worse."

She frowns but leans forward, pressing her mouth gently on mine before pulling away.

I prop myself up on my elbow. "How are you feeling?"

"Bram's sounds good." She quickly changes the topic of conversation. "It's early enough that the donuts are probably super fresh, too."

"You sure you don't want to talk about it?"

Claire shakes her head. "I kind of just want things to go back to normal, if that's okay?" She sits up and crosses her legs. "I, uh, I don't want you to treat me any differently like I'm this fragile thing. I'm okay. I know I was sort of in shock last night and being super needy, but I'll be fine, really. You can even go to Bram's without me, and I promise I won't implode while you're gone."

I place my hand on her thigh and gently squeeze. "I think you're much stronger than you let on, actually." I've always known that about her, even if she doubts it herself.

Claire might have run into trouble with Griffin and let him take advantage of her, but that never made me question the strength she carries within.

She's a force that cannot be contained or extinguished, especially not by some pathetic douche like Griffin.

She may not recognize her power, but I do, and I'll be damned if I ever diminish that. There's a fire that burns behind her eyes, waiting to come to life.

"Do you mind? If I stay here while you go?" She stares at me with those ocean eyes.

"Not at all. Do you need me to get anything from your place? Your school stuff?" I don't want her to have to lift a finger if she doesn't have to. It's not about being fragile; it's about taking care of someone who has never been taken care of in their life.

From this point forward, I'll do everything in my power to be everything Griffin never was. I won't be perfect, and I'm sure I'll mess up, but Claire deserves someone willing to put forth the effort. To put her first.

"I'll go, actually. Grab some stuff and meet you back here?"

"Yeah, that works." I reach over and snatch my keys off the nightstand. I pull the little silver circle and slide my house key off. "Here."

Claire hesitates. "Won't you need it?"

I shake my head. "You'll be back before me." I push it into her hand. "Plus, if you happen to need to get away, you're welcome here whenever. It's not much but it's private."

"Really?" She bites at her lip like she's hiding something she wants to say.

"Yeah, really. Why do you sound so surprised?"

She lifts her shoulders. "You're not…dating anyone?"

I break out into a smile. "No."

"Oh." Her cheeks blush. "Cool." She flips the key between her thumb and index finger. "But really, I don't want to intrude."

"I think we're past that by now." An idea suddenly dawns on

me. I unplug my phone from the charger and unlock the screen. "Although, I don't have your number." I hand the device to her.

She takes it and punches her contact info in; a second later, her phone buzzes. "I sent myself a text, so I'd have yours, too."

Now I just need to take her on a proper date, and we'll have a somewhat normal-ish, age-appropriate relationship.

27
CLAIRE

Johnny is fucking adorable.

I mean, he started off in my mind as a total asshole, and now, he's leaving sweet kisses all over my head and giving me a key to his place.

It's probably way too quick and totally irrational, but I guess when things are right, there's no need to deny it.

In the short time that we've known each other, there has been an undeniable pull between us, and given everything that's happened, the little and big things, we've bonded.

I'd be lying if I said I wasn't freaking out, but deep down, I don't think it has anything to do with him.

What happened last night with Griffin, it was intense.

And I'm a little scared of how I'm reacting.

There is this mix of emotions—fear and shame and guilt, but also anger and rage. This part of me that is so pissed off at Griffin that I don't have any sympathy in me for his current condition.

He's lying in a hospital bed and there is no compassion left in me to feel sorry for him.

Doesn't that make me some kind of monster?

Griffin is twisted in the head. But does he actually deserve what happened to him? Does anyone?

Johnny is right to worry about me, because I'm worried about myself.

And right now, I'm clinging to the calming comfort he provides when he's nearby. I'm afraid that if he disappears for too long, I'll lose it all. I just need a little time to regain my composure and then I'll be back to the old Claire.

"I come bearing gifts." Johnny enters his front door and comes over to the couch where I'm sitting. "Aw, you look cute as hell."

He's referring to the gray sweatpants I borrowed from him.

"I hope it's okay, I got cold." I take the cup of coffee he hands me and breathe in the heavenly scent.

Bram really does have the best brew around. It's strong, but not too bitter.

"Of course." Johnny kisses my cheek. "Whatever you need." He plops down next to me and opens up the bag. "A famous Bram's breakfast sammy. And donuts, obviously."

"Famous? According to who?" I laugh but take it anyway.

"Me, duh." He feigns offense. "And Bram."

"Bram doesn't count."

"But I do?" Johnny winks at me and bites off a chunk of his sandwich.

Something about it just melts my fucking heart and has me feeling like I'm floating.

"Hey, I was thinking..." I hand him a napkin and set one on my own lap.

"Uh-oh." He wipes his mouth. "Breaking up with me already? Damn, that was short-lived."

I roll my eyes at him. "Shut up." Plus, you can't break up with someone you aren't officially dating. Right?

"So, it's not bad news? Carry on."

I test my coffee to see if it's going to burn my mouth off or not. "No, neither good nor bad. But I thought maybe we could focus on this *situation* of yours. The one you've been stressing out about. We're nearly caught up with our assignments, and it sure would be a great distraction from...well...you know."

"Is it that obvious?"

"Yeah. I get the feeling that you're not telling me something, that maybe it's time-sensitive?"

"You really should be a detective, Claire. What's your major?"

I laugh. "English. You?"

He avoids my eyes and grabs his cup. "Um."

I turn toward him. "I'm not familiar with that one."

"I'm still undecided." He seems embarrassed by this. "I've been a little preoccupied, and I pretty much failed my first year anyway. My second isn't looking that great either."

"What do you want to do?" I stare at him and try to predict what his interests might be. Is bad boy a major? Because he seems to have everyone there.

Except me.

"It's not really important."

"It is to me." This conversation is totally going off the rails here, but I'm dying to know more about him and the person he is outside of the nightmare world he created for himself.

"Photography." He side-eyes me and then focuses ahead.

"I can totally picture that."

He laughs. "A pun? Seriously?"

I giggle too but grab his arm. "I'm sorry, it sort of slipped out. I think it's perfect."

"Sure." He exaggerates the word.

"Let's put a pin in that one and get back on track. You said I was on to something, right?"

"Yeah." Johnny chews and swallows the last of his breakfast. "I have less than a week to find the package."

"Shit." Do I even want to ask what the consequences would be if he doesn't locate it?

"And I've pretty much come up with no solid leads."

"What *do* you know?" Or more like, what is he willing to tell me? I bite into my sandwich while he gathers his bearings.

He sighs. "Not much. A reliable source, that guy you saw me meet at the bar that night, he told me it's probably an inside job. I'm not exactly on good terms with the guy running this operation, and he's been trying to get me out since I started."

"And to confirm, that would be a bad thing?"

"Everything I've done would have been for nothing, so yeah, not a good alternative." He runs his hand through his thick brown hair. "There's this kid...Billy—you've met him."

My stomach clenches, the pieces of the puzzle all falling into place.

"His uncle, the guy he lives with, he's mixed up with some shady people. Children are so easy to manipulate and use, because I mean, who's going to suspect some ten-year-old to be doing this kind of shit? He was abusing him, using violence to force him to start making deliveries. I followed him one day to this slimy part of town, and it all sort of happened so fast, I didn't stop to think it through, I just knew that I had to do anything I could to get him out of that situation. I, uh, I pictured it was me, you know? This innocent kid who needed help. I couldn't just sit back and do nothing.

"Anyway, I made this big scene, and the guy in charge, his wife was there, so he agreed to let me take Billy's place, but I knew he didn't want to; he only did it because she wanted him to. Now he has it out for me. He can't get rid of me easily, cause then she'd be upset with him, so he's trying to find some loophole where I fuck up and it makes sense to cut me loose. Then he gets what he wanted all along." He pauses and turns toward me. "Billy."

I let the shock of his confession settle through me. I had

imagined that Johnny was doing this for some altruistic reason, but I never thought it would be *this*. His actions are noble and entirely self-sacrificing, and I refuse to let him do this on his own.

My mind wanders to Billy, the sweet boy I've had the privilege of talking to on a few occasions. The sun-kissed kid with bright eyes and a love for books. I recall the times I've seen Johnny sitting with him, the instance when Billy thanked Johnny and told him he was the best. I had overlooked it then, at how Johnny might be impacting this kid, but now, everything comes into focus. The grumpy man I assumed was Billy's dad is actually an abusive and manipulative uncle.

"Say something." Johnny meets my gaze.

"I'm processing."

"I've never told anyone any of this."

"Not even Bram?"

He shakes his head. "No."

I reach forward and take his hand in mine. What a terrible thing to have to go through by yourself. "We're going to figure this out...together."

Something in his features shift, a sadness replaced with something resembling hope. Like maybe he's finally realizing he doesn't have to handle everything on his own.

He lets out a breath. "Yeah?"

"You're stuck with me, remember?"

Johnny pulls me over and hugs me super tight, kissing all over my face. "I don't know what I did to get so lucky."

I can't help but wonder the same damn thing.

Sure, he's got some baggage, but don't we all? He might seem like a bad guy who doesn't care about anything on the surface, but he's actually got the biggest heart of anyone I've ever met.

Bram really was right after all.

"Okay, where's that list?" If we're going to figure this out, we need to get to work. As much as I'd love to be loved on, we have to prioritize to pull this off.

Johnny shoves his hand into the pocket of his jeans and pulls out the crumpled-up paper. He unfolds it and offers it to me.

I take it and skim it over. First names only, and some weird descriptors.

I point to the last one. "This foot guy, his name doesn't happen to be Jared, does it?"

Johnny nods his head. "Yeah, I think that's it. Do you know him?"

"If it's the same dude, he's in my math class. I made the mistake of sitting near him on the first day and now I'm sort of stuck in his stinky corner of the room." I scan the list again. "And this guy, Steve, sits near him."

"See, detective. You've already made more progress than me."

"What do you remember about that night?" *Other than almost dying in an alley and passing out in your bathtub.*

"Um..." He seems to get lost in his memory. "Besides you saving my ass?"

"Try to recall anything. No detail too small. Go back to the beginning if you have to, before it happened."

"Franklin was pissed, because I had been like thirty seconds late making a delivery. He had me go out on another run, but basically demanded I get it done immediately. Gave me almost an impossible time limit." He leans forward and rests his elbows on his knees while he goes through the chain of events. "Usually, I go home, change clothes and make a game plan, then head out. It's how I've managed to make it this far, but that night, Franklin left me no time for that. It was like he knew the quickest path and was certain I'd go that way. I walked into that alley and they came out of nowhere. They were expecting me."

I don't mean to, but I cut him off. "They? There was more than one of them?"

"Two guys. Bigger than me." He strains to consider something. "They had on ski masks. I couldn't see either of their faces."

"Did they say anything? Would you be able to recognize their voices?"

Johnny bobs his head back and forth. "No, not a word."

"Okay, anything else?"

"They knocked me to the ground pretty quick. And they kept hitting me. I could barely keep my eyes open, they swelled up almost immediately." Johnny's gaze steadies. "But there was this flash of white." He holds his palm to his rib. "His shoe." He turns to me with wild eyes. "What's that brand with the black stripes?"

"Adidas?"

"Yes! He was wearing those."

"This is good, this is really good." It's not much but in a matter of minutes, we've gotten closer to solving this mystery than Johnny has in the last week by himself. "And you're sure it's someone from this list?"

"No. It could be anyone, really. Franklin has hired hands all over. But Josey mentioned it was a new recruit, a younger guy. Cocky. I guess he was bragging about what happened."

I fight to keep my composure. There's something about someone being arrogant about hurting Johnny that sends sparks of fire shooting through me. I've never felt so...protective of a person before. Now that I know the truth about Johnny's situation and his motives, it only makes me want to crush anyone who mistreats him.

Kind of humorous considering what happened last night. The old Claire died on those steps; she was reborn the moment Johnny ripped Griffin away from me and shoved him down the stairs.

What Johnny said earlier about how he imagined himself in Billy's situation, and how he would have hoped someone stepped in for him? Well, he did exactly that for me, and I won't waste this gift of a fresh beginning.

From now on, I will not cower. I will fight.

"I have an idea." I grab my phone and swipe over to the text screen.

Cora: *Let me know about tonight.*

I haven't told her about what happened yesterday, and I plan on keeping it that way. I don't need her to pity me any more than she already does.

Me: *What are the details?*

Johnny turns his attention to me. "What is it?"

Cora: *House party, I'll send you the address when I get done at the gym. You coming?!*

Me: *Maybe!*

Cora: *Good! Bring that sexy man of yours.*

Johnny clears his throat. "Uh."

"She's referring to you, don't worry." I shove him teasingly.

"Hey now, guys can be insecure, too. But wait, your brilliant idea is a party?"

"Not just any. I overheard Stinky Feet talking to Steve about some big get-together they're having. And I'm pretty sure this guy Cora was talking to is friends with them, meaning... chances are, it's the same one. AKA, it's where they live."

Johnny sort of blankly stares at me like it hasn't fully clicked into place.

"The shoe, J. We can check their rooms to see if it's there. If it is, bingo, we've located the suspect."

"You...are fucking brilliant." He grabs me by the face and presses his lips firmly to mine.

A million butterflies float all around me, and I become completely immersed in his touch.

28
JOHNNY

I could watch Claire get ready for days, even if she's irritated. It only makes her that much cuter in my eyes.

"I have no clue what I'm going to wear." She snatches another thing from her closet and tosses it onto the floor behind her where a pile of stuff already sits.

I try to hide my smile with my hand from my spot in the corner.

She goes over to her bed and dramatically falls onto her back, spreading her arms out beside her. "It's not fair." She props herself up and glares at me. "You spent a total of five minutes getting dressed and you look like *that*."

I laugh and adjust the collar of my dark button-up, fixing my chain in the process. "Okay, first of all, you're out of your mind. Secondly…" I let out a breath and get up to walk over to her closet. "What about this?" I pull out a black, long-sleeved polyester crop-top that she's overlooked like twelve times. "And that high-waisted skirt you had on earlier?"

Claire stares from the shirt to me, then back to the shirt. "I totally forgot I had that." She hops up from the bed and rushes over to snatch it out of my hand. "You're the best." She kisses my cheek and goes to the bathroom to try it on.

I'd like to think she's being modest, but I have a feeling the real reason she's changing in the other room is so I can't see her arms.

"Claire," I say to her as she's shutting the door.

"Yeah?"

When I don't respond, she pokes her head out. "What's up?"

I glance down pointedly at the oversized sweatshirt she's been wearing all day.

She lowers her voice. "I don't want you to see it."

I step forward, closing the gap between us, the bathroom door the only thing in the way. "Please."

She sighs and steps back, allowing me entry. She sits down on the edge of the tub, and grabs the cuff of her hoodie, pulling the sleeves up on both sides.

I force myself not to react externally, not wanting to affirm whatever worries she has about showing me. It's a difficult thing to do, though, when my eyes settle on the red and purple skin covering both of her arms—something that I could have prevented if I would have been a little bit quicker, a little more perceptive to what was going on.

"Does it hurt?"

She bites at her lip. "Not really."

There's no way she's telling the truth. I've been covered in stuff like this pretty consistently since I got involved with Franklin, and I'm well aware of how shitty it feels.

I drop to my knees between her legs and gently take her hand into mine. I reach forward and kiss both arms. "Never again, okay?" I look up at her and will her to understand. "This will never happen again as long as I have anything to do with it."

"Don't make promises you can't keep." Tears well in her eyes, and one rolls down her cheek.

I wipe it away. "I'm stuck with you, remember?"

I don't really know when it happened, the shift in dynamic—maybe it was always there. This finality to us. This unspoken bond that forged us together. I tried like hell to shove it aside, to avoid it and be without her. But it was like I never had any control over the outcome at all. We were going to find our way to each other regardless.

Surrendering to her was the best thing I've ever done.

"So, what's the plan, since you're clearly the one in charge here?" I offer her my arm and she slides hers in. I'm extra careful to not apply too much pressure.

When I suggested the outfit to her earlier, I never imagined she'd look *this* fucking good. I'm suddenly regretting going out in public at all. I'd rather keep her tucked away safely for as long as possible.

But Claire's beauty is not something that can be contained, and walking out into the world with her by my side, I couldn't possibly feel any luckier. Some guys want to control their women, disallow them from dressing up and going out.

Me? I'm proud as fuck to say that she's with me.

The second someone disrespects or treats her poorly though, that's another story entirely.

Claire rubs my hand. "We're going to go to this party, and we're going to mingle. I'm going to sneak around and try to locate Jared's room, and you're going to work the floor and see if any of the guys from your list are there. Obviously, we're trying to spot these shoes."

"Wait, you're going to search his room?" I'm not thrilled about the sound of that.

"Yes, because I can innocently pretend like I'm looking for the bathroom, but if he finds you in there, and it was him that did it, shit will hit the fan."

"What does this package even look like? What's in it? If I'm going to be looking for the shoes, I might as well keep an eye out for it, too."

Oh man, where do I start? "He was always secretive about what was in them. I asked a few times in the beginning but learned it's best not to question him. Um." I hold out both index fingers. "It was about this big, this thick. One of those yellow envelopes, you know? I have no idea what was in it. Could have been anything."

"And if he set you up on purpose, it could absolutely be gone."

"Yes and no." I nod politely at a passerby on the street. "He plays a twisted game, but he's weirdly fair at times. If he's giving me two weeks to find it, I think it's still in circulation. That way his hands are totally clean—he gives me a chance, despite it being nearly impossible. If I don't find it, it's my fault, not his."

"Well then, let's hold on to that hope." Claire looks up at me and forces a smile.

"Oh, my God," a familiar voice calls out. "I knew it!"

Cora rushes over and nearly rips Claire from my arms.

Claire clenches her jaw to suppress the cringe of pain brought on by Cora's enthusiastic embrace.

Only Cora has no idea what happened last night, and Claire has asked me to keep things between us until she's ready to tell her friend.

Cora slaps my shoulder. "About damn time you make your move."

"Cora..." Claire deadpans.

"Sorry! You two are just freaking adorable together. From the moment he caught you falling off that pool table, and then paid off our entire tab... What a gentleman."

Claire turns to face me. "You did what?"

I attempt a distraction by pointing toward the green pedestrian light. "Our time to cross."

"Anyway, I'm Team Johnny." Cora sidesteps an old lady and continues on her path. "June's meeting us here. She's my plus one tonight."

"Where's Steff?" I ask her.

"She has a date. But I've been instructed to stay near my phone in case I have to call in a fake emergency."

"That's a real thing?" I glance over at Cora.

"Um, yep. Especially with the weirdos Steff finds on Tinder."

I grip Claire's hand, thankful that I don't have to deal with that. I haven't dated anyone since my senior year of high school, and granted we had both gone our separate ways because of college, I never really wanted to put myself back out there. Plenty of girls have shown interest since then, I just never felt connected to any of them until Claire stepped into my life.

Now the wait seems to make perfect sense.

We approach a row of houses that are college rentals, an area that I've gone past a few times while making deliveries. Weekends are usually full of loud and drunken debauchery, which is not my scene. Even before I took a position with Franklin, I was more of a low-key, small gathering kind of guy.

The puking in front of strangers and intoxicated bro-bonding was never my thing.

"It's the second one up ahead." Cora signals to the one with the biggest crowd gathered around it.

The two on each side seem to be for overflow traffic.

"Who lives here?" Claire asks her.

"Um…a handful of guys, I think. James, Randy, Doug, Jared… I can't remember the rest. Oh, wait, Steve, too."

Claire glances up at me, a silent confirmation of our plan.

We walk up the steps and join the crowd, funneling around people and making our way further into the packed structure.

"Do you want a drink?" Cora yells as she separates from us and heads toward what I assume is the kitchen.

"I'm good," Claire calls out to her.

I pull a flask out of my jacket pocket and spin off the top. I hold it out to Claire first.

She takes it gratefully and swallows a big swig.

"Easy, killer," I tease her. I drink some and tuck the thing back in its spot.

A girl with jet black hair approaches and waves at Claire. She either has a serious case of resting bitch face or she's pissed off about something.

"Hey." Claire motions to me. "June, Johnny—Johnny, June."

June lifts her chin to acknowledge me.

I lean in close to Claire and whisper into her ear. "I'm going to do a quick sweep. You good?"

"Yep. I'll keep an eye out, too. We're going to go find Cora."

I kiss her gently on the lips and watch as she tows June in the direction Cora disappeared. A tether to my soul tugs with each step she takes.

I rake my hand through my hair and focus on the reason why we came here—to gain information on who took the package. I weave my way through a group of girls gathered by the entrance to the living room area.

There's a DJ in the far corner. Or rather, a guy set up at a table with his laptop open and big chunky headphones on. Music blares and he dances along while pushing buttons on the computer.

I scan the crowd, looking for any familiar faces, or sneakers.

My heart nearly skips when I spot the black stripes, only to find them attached to some barely five-foot girl. I should have expected more than one person at the university to wear such a popular style. I accidentally make eye contact with her and she blushes, tucking her hair behind her ear.

Shit. I didn't mean to make it seem like I was checking her out. Although, the whole scanning of her body with my stare probably gave her the completely wrong idea.

I pivot and make my way further through the house, going

into a dining area where people are crowded around an intense game of beer pong. Both sides only have one cup left. The group around the table cheers loudly when the final ball lands and the winners throw their fists in the air and jump on each other.

That's when I notice him, Jared.

Unfortunately, he spots me at the same time.

"Dude, did you *see* that?" Jared rushes over and clamps onto my shoulders. "Johnny, you've got to play with me. My partner is bowing out and I need a new one."

"I, uh…" have no fucking idea what to say. *Hey, I was looking for you but didn't expect you to invite me to a game of pong?*

"Come on, man." Jared drags me over to the table with his arm thrown around my shoulder. "Us bros have got to stick together." He yanks me in closer. "If you know what I mean."

I take a breath. His words could be interpreted a few different ways, but the only thing I can think of is that another round would mean that he's preoccupied, giving Claire enough time to scope out his room.

"Yeah, why not."

"Ayyyy!" Jared cheers. He turns to the crowd and asks for a challenger.

I slide my phone out of my pocket and send her a quick text.

Me: *Beer pong table. You have fifteen. Go.*

I glance in the direction of the kitchen and see her beautiful face come around the corner.

She raises her hands and mouths, "What the fuck."

I nudge my head toward the stairs to signal for her to get moving.

Luckily, Jared is oblivious while he sets up for another game with the two newcomers, one of which happens to be Steve. This couldn't have worked out any better.

"You ready to lose?" Jared taunts our opponents.

"Shut up and throw the ball." Steve finishes securing the last cup.

Jared tosses and sinks his first shot. "Drink up, bitch." He nudges me. "Your turn."

I follow suit and land mine in the one next to his.

He laughs out loud. "Atta boy! Balls back."

Steve and his teammate bounce them across the table toward us.

Apparently, we get to go again, since we landed both shots. I'm a little rusty on my pong rules.

Jared throws but misses, cursing like a sailor, and I end up scoring another.

"Austin, you can go," Steve tells his partner.

The nervous red-headed kid takes his time lining up the shot. It swooshes into the beer and Jared grabs it up immediately.

"Can't have a death cup." Jared passes it to me. "You'll have Austin's, I'll take Steve's."

I down the contents. "What's a death cup?"

Jared swats away the ball that Steve bounces on the table. "Automatic win if you get two balls in the same cup. Or if you get one in a limbo cup, where someone hasn't drunk it yet, it counts, too. If you land on a bounce, two cups are removed." He dunks the ball into the cup of water and hands it to me. "Haven't you played before?"

I shrug. "It's been a while."

Jared takes out one of theirs in the back row.

If I'm going to keep this match going, I have to start missing mine. I aim it near the front, just a little off to the side, and end up hitting the exact spot I'm trying for.

"Ah, fuck man." He grabs my shoulder. "It's all right. Beginner's luck."

"Yeah, must have been."

Austin lands another and I make quick work of downing the booze and stacking the cup with the others.

Steve sinks his and Jared groans. We send the balls back to

the other team.

A skinny kid approaches the table. "Ay." He leans in close and whispers something into Jared's ear.

Jared's eyes go wide. "Oh yeah?" He turns toward us. "I'm going to have to ask for a brief intermission."

"Ah, what the fuck, Jare. That's not allowed." Steve throws one of the balls at Jared's head.

"Shut up, it's my fucking party, I'll do what I want." Jared grips my shoulder. "I'll be right back, partner."

I'm about to panic but he ends up taking off toward the kitchen instead of the stairs.

I go to reach into my pocket, but Cora grabs my arm.

"Have you seen Claire?" she asks me. "I thought she'd be with you."

"She probably went to the bathroom; I'll go find her." I turn toward the last place I saw her and spot Jared jumping up the steps, taking them two at a time.

A fire explodes inside of me as I shove through the crowd, with only one thing on my mind—what if I don't get there fast enough?

29
CLAIRE

I'm just finishing up in Jared's closest when the door to the dim bedroom creaks open. For a second, I assume it's Johnny, coming to help me do our detective work, but instead, my gaze settles on the six-foot-something, stinky-foot-smelling guy who this room belongs to.

I freeze, unable to speak or do a thing.

Come on, Claire, remember the plan.

"I… uh."

Jared places his fingertips on the door and clicks it shut. He turns his attention to me, a devious grin on his face. "Well, well, well, what do we have here?"

With each step he takes toward me, I slink the opposite direction, until I back myself up against the wall and can go no further.

"I heard you were asking around for me." He creeps closer.

"I was looking for…" But I don't get the chance to finish.

Jared advances and throws one hand up on the wall beside me, his foul breath assaulting me with the proximity. He inches his body up to where it's nearly touching mine. "I'm right here, baby."

I cringe at the mental image he's forcing into my head with his implications.

"I'm not interested," I manage to say.

"And I don't care."

I weigh my options. Clearly, I can't escape to my left, because his arm is in the way. If I bolt right, I have to side-step his desk and somehow make it to the door without him catching me.

"Thinking about going somewhere? So soon? You just got here." He slams his other arm up to block all of my paths.

His arousal grows against my leg, and I realize I only have one route out of here. If I'm going to make this work, I have to play the part.

I relax my body, giving myself a better vantage point. I place my hands on his shoulders to brace myself for what I'm about to do next. I draw my leg back, ready to blast it forward and into his man parts.

His eyebrows raise, telling me that he's buying right into it, thinking I'm going to go along with what he's suggesting.

The doorknob rattles, implying Jared had locked it when he came in.

There's a loud crash, and the door nearly flies off the hinges, but I'm already in full motion, blasting my knee straight into Jared's crotch.

"Fucking bitch," Jared yells, more distracted by my assault than everything else.

Johnny rushes in, his body a blur as he makes his way across the room, snatching Jared from his cowered position and pinning him against the wall with his hand around his throat.

Johnny tilts his head toward me. "You okay?"

I nod, holding my arms to my chest and backing away from that side of the room where I was trapped. "Yeah."

"What the fuck, man?" Jared chokes. "We were just having some fun."

Johnny slams Jared into the wall, squeezing his fingers tighter around his neck. "Didn't really look like it."

Jared grasps at Johnny's arms, trying to pry him off, but Johnny has a death grip on him. It's like there's an unbreakable surge of anger coursing through Johnny.

Jared easily towers over him but he's no match to Johnny's adrenaline-induced strength.

I inch forward, placing my palm on Johnny's shoulder. "Hey..."

"See, she's fine. Let me go." Jared attempts to rationalize with him. His words are choppy under the pressure around his vocal cords.

Johnny shakes his head. "No. Not fucking cool."

"Dude, she was in *my* room, what do you expect?" Jared should really keep his mouth shut if he knows what's best for him.

Johnny's other hand clenches, and I realize shit is about to get way worse between them. As much as I'd love for Jared to get what's coming to him, there are too many witnesses here to cover up for Johnny again.

Neither one of us can afford a repeat of the Griffin situation.

"J..." I come around and into Johnny's peripheral. I place both of my hands around his eager fist. "Come on. We need to go." Once I get his attention, I remind him, "It's not worth it."

Johnny seems to snap out of it, releasing Jared with one final shove. "If you ever so much as look at her, I will end you."

Jared gasps for breath and rubs at his neck.

I maintain eye contact with Johnny and drag him toward the exit. The second we're almost clear of the room, the idiot opens his mouth again.

"You're a dead man, Jones," Jared calls out.

But Johnny doesn't bother stopping. "Fucking try me."

We push through the crowd that had gathered in the hallway, a collective murmur in our wake. If we were trying to fly under the radar, we epically failed.

The worst part of it all, we didn't find what we came here looking for.

Johnny grips my hand firmly and guides us around the drunk people scattered about.

I glance behind us, scanning to make sure Jared isn't coming after us. My sights settle on another room, the door ajar enough for a person to barely squeeze through.

My breath catches and Johnny senses it immediately.

He snaps out of his stupor and focuses on me. "What is it?"

"Over there."

He follows my direction, spotting the white sneakers with black stripes sitting right next to the nightstand in the foreign room.

We might not know who they belong to, but we can officially rule one person out. And if anything, I call that a huge win.

"Hey." Cora grabs my arm to stop us at the bottom of the stairs. "Everything okay?"

I fight to hide my reaction to the impact of her fingers on my bruised skin. I may have fooled her, but Johnny notices the way my body tenses.

"Yeah," I yell over the loud music. "I'm not feeling so great. We're going to get going."

Cora narrows her gaze and throws her hand on her hip. "If you two wanna be alone to bone, just admit it. We're all adults here."

Johnny places his hand on my lower back to guide me away from the people behind us trying to make their way through. He scans the faces like he's waiting for a possible threat.

"Yeah," I laugh. "You caught us." I'd say anything to get her off our trail at this point. I need to get Johnny out of here before he explodes in a fit of rage.

She giggles and shoves me lightly. "Fine. Get out of here, then, lovebirds."

I waste no more time, weaving my fingers through his, and waving a final goodbye to Cora on our way out the wide front door. I have to nearly drag him to get him to follow.

His mind is obviously distracted by thoughts of going back in there and ripping Jared's head off.

I exhale once we're about a block away and the chaos of that frenzied street dies down behind us. "Are you okay?" I glance over at Johnny.

He shakes his head, his dark brown hair swaying with the movement. "Claire, I'm...so sorry. I shouldn't have put you in that position."

I cut him off. "You didn't. I did, remember? It was my plan, not yours."

Johnny stops completely, turning to face me. "Did he hurt you?" He places both hands gently on my cheeks and studies me over intently.

"No." He scared the shit out of me though, but I won't dare admit that. "I had the situation under control. If you recall, I kneed him in the nuts."

Johnny sighs. "Yeah, you did." He still doesn't seem convinced, which I don't blame him.

"You promised you wouldn't treat me differently," I remind him.

"Claire...no man in their right mind wouldn't be freaking out in this same scenario. That guy was triple your size. He could have..."

"But he didn't. I stopped him. *You* stopped him." I have to start taking care of myself. I can't rely on the Johnny's of the world to always come to my rescue. I will learn to stand up and stop people from pushing me around and trying to take advantage of me.

The days of the weak Claire are a thing of the past.

Johnny runs his thumb along my cheek, something he does often. It sends a chill down my spine every time, but in the best of ways.

It's strange to think that we only met a few weeks ago, and now we stare into each other's eyes like we've known each other our whole lives.

There's this sense of familiarity, of home.

I feel something with Johnny I've never felt before…safety.

With him, there's security—a safe haven I didn't realize I was longing for until he gave it to me. And with that, it gives me strength. Courage to be a stronger and more capable version of myself. I've always been weighed down by others, but with Johnny, it's a completely different story. He feels like the strong foundation I've always needed to stand on my own.

"I don't know what I would do if something happened to you." His emerald gaze melts into mine. "That's what I've been trying to avoid all along."

"What do you mean?" Although, I think I have an inkling to what he's going to say next.

"Since I met you, I've been…"

"Pushing me away," I answer for him.

"Yeah…I couldn't put you in any danger." He tucks my hair behind my ear. "But it's sort of impossible to stay away from you."

"The feeling is mutual." I recall how difficult it was to avoid him—how no matter what I did, I couldn't get him off my mind.

"I wanted you to hate me so it would be easier for you to stay away."

A loud group of boys cross the street and pass behind us.

Johnny continues once they've gone. "I just didn't realize how badly that would suck. And no matter what I did, whether I thought it was for the good or bad, I still kept hurting you. I thought I was protecting you from me, from trouble, but it seems like you're a magnet for it anyway."

"What about what I want?"

He lowers his voice. "You shouldn't want me, Claire. I'm no good for you."

And yet, if anyone asked me what the best part of my life was right now, I'd say him.

"You're wrong."

Johnny gently grazes his fingers along my covered forearm. "This, this is my fault."

I pull my hand from his grasp. "No. Not in a million years. That was going to happen with or without you, and honestly…" I stumble on the thought of my next words. "I'm not sure I'd be alive if you hadn't stepped in."

The depth of which Griffin was willing to take things had crossed my mind a few times, but I had always shoved it aside, given him the benefit of the doubt. Someone who was once kind and thoughtful could never be capable of such destruction, right? But I was wrong.

Griffin is a monster. A cold-blooded sociopath. And not like the romanticized villains in the movies where the heroine ultimately realizes he's the one for her. He's the gross, ugly one that everyone wishes would meet their timely demise and get the hell off the show. Griffin has gone through life doing everything selfishly—only for himself. He's sick and twisted and there is no way he could ever earn his redemption.

Johnny, on the other hand, has done pretty much everything he has for the greater good, or what he assumed was the best choice. He's perceived as the bad guy when in reality, he is the most self-sacrificing person I've ever met.

Griffin is just a wolf in sheep's clothing, his layers being peeled back to reveal a disgusting excuse for a man.

"But you are alive, you're here, and I was an idiot for leaving you alone tonight like that." Johnny can't seem to stop beating himself up for my decision.

"Hey." I place my hand along his jawbone, my fingers grazing under his ear. "We're in this together, okay? And that means we share the burden from now on. What happened tonight, it was a minor hiccup. No one's fault. We knew going into it that there might be risks. We're both fine, and things might have got a little rocky, but we managed to score a huge win with those sneakers. Let's focus on maintaining that momentum."

"We were quite the team, weren't we?" Finally, he shows a bit of optimism.

"Hell yeah, we were." I ignore the next set of rowdy college kids passing us and lean in, brushing my lips onto Johnny's.

His kiss is slow at first, gentle and sweet.

I pick up the pace and deepen the intensity, not giving a shit who might be walking by at this very moment. The only thing on my mind is the taste of Johnny.

He matches my tone and weaves his hands through my hair, pulling me closer to him. He trails his fingers down my neck and along my back, landing on my exposed waist to drag me in. His touch is like fire, igniting my soul.

Johnny relaxes, breaking away and resting his forehead along mine to catch his breath. "You're...incredible."

Suddenly, I'm realizing Cora might have been right after all. And when I glance around at our whereabouts, I'm desperately wishing we were capable of teleporting. We're at least a five-minute walk away from getting any kind of privacy to continue what we're doing.

"Your place or mine?" I say, weaving my fingers through his and dragging him in the direction of our complex.

30
JOHNNY

It's not that I don't want to have sex with Claire, because holy fuck I do—I just can't.

At least, not yet.

And maybe it's because I'm doing the very thing she asked me not to, treating her like she's this fragile person. It's not that I don't see Claire as a strong woman, it's that so many terrible things keep happening in her life, and I don't want to add to that. She deserves kindness and gentleness. To be treated like the goddess I see her as.

Everything bad is too fresh. The accident with Griffin, even what went down tonight. I haven't made a dent in redeeming myself for the way I've treated her the first couple weeks we knew each other. I can't bring myself to taint such an intimate experience because I can't keep it in my pants. I've been with other girls, but in hindsight, every time was totally meaningless compared to Claire.

And honestly, just processing all of this is a huge fucking surprise to my own system. She's absolutely stunning. Her body is a complete knockout, and I'd be lying if I said I hadn't imagined what it would be like to be inside her. What guy in his right mind would turn Claire down? But that's the whole point. I don't want to be like every other dude that crosses her path. Maybe I'm being a fool, constantly overthinking and trying to protect everyone else. I've already risked so much by being with her, and I have to be careful with how many more lines I cross.

I glance up ahead to see Bram standing on a short ladder out front of his shop. He fidgets with the lightbulb in his sign, and it flickers in response.

"You need a hand?" I say when we get close enough.

He turns it one last time and the light becomes steady. "Nope. I think I've got it. Thanks, though." Bram carefully climbs down. "What are you two up to?" He tries to hide his grin, but he fails epically.

"Just heading home," Claire replies.

"Actually." I point into the diner. "You hungry?" Without letting her respond, I add, "I'm starving." It's not totally a lie, but it's a surefire way to deter her from her previous train of thought.

Teenage me would kick me in the ass for not taking Claire home immediately.

"Great idea," Bram says while opening the door for us.

Claire sort of side-eyes me but goes along with my change of plans.

I grab the ladder. "This go in the storage room?"

"Yep, thanks, Johnny." Bram turns to Claire and smiles. "Sit wherever you want." He follows me into the back. "Right over there is fine."

I place the step stool on the hook and make sure it's securely in place.

"I'm glad you're taking my advice." Bram is terrible at being subtle.

"Yeah?"

"I'm telling you"—his gaze trails off like he's recalling a distant memory—"the moment I saw her, I knew you two would hit it off."

I laugh and lean against the wall. "Think so?"

Bram nods aggressively. "Absolutely. And I'm not often wrong about such things. I know you've been messed up with some stuff lately, and I get that you don't want to talk to me the way you used to, but you and Claire are good for each other... she's your light at the end of the tunnel."

Somehow, I understand completely what he's talking about.

"It's going to be hard, but try not to push her away like you have with everyone else." Bram unties, readjusts, and reties his apron. "It'll be worth it in the long run."

I let his words settle over me. It's nothing that I hadn't already thought of myself, but to hear him say it—to see it—it's refreshing to know I'm not just imagining it all.

Bram grips my shoulder and gives it a firm shake. "I love love, don't you?"

He leaves me behind with that single term.

Love.

Such a foreign thing in my life. Something I haven't known since I was young, and even then, I don't really feel certain that's what it was. A parent's love is strange, almost forced. There's no real choice in the matter. They either love you or they don't. Not that falling in love with someone is ever really in your control either, but it takes a conscious effort to maintain.

Love is deliberate; it's raw, it's powerful.

And I am fully consumed in it.

I wake to the sound of knocking. My eyes blink open and I take in the sight of the beautiful creature in my arms. Somehow last night I managed to distract her from having sex by putting her in a food coma. It was highly effective, considering she passed out shortly after we got to her place and she stripped out of her tight black crop-top and sexy skirt.

Trust me, denying the temptation brought on from her undressing in front of me was almost too much to handle, but I persevered.

Managing to control the nonstop boner she kept giving me was an added challenge, too.

"Claire." I gently nudge her.

She mumbles and grabs my arm, pulling it between her breasts to cuddle.

My skin grazes hers and I fight the desire that builds up inside of me to flip her over and do what I've wanted to do all night.

Instead, I regain my composure. "Were you expecting company?"

"What?" She lets go of me and sits up, rubbing her eyes in the process.

I bite the inside of my cheek to distract myself from her soft curves.

Baseball. Old men. Dirty socks.

Only, all of my thoughts come to a halt when I notice the discoloration of Claire's arms. Any thought of sex is quickly erased by murderous thoughts about Griffin. How could he ever think what he did was acceptable? Who in their right mind would do that to someone? Someone they supposedly care about. How can hurting a person make you feel better about them breaking up with you?

"If I can't have her, no one can." His words cut through me.

I'd rather die than hurt a hair on Claire's head. Even if she didn't want to be with me. That's a reality I'd rather face than doing what Griffin did. Losing her would kill me, but I'd do it ten times over if it meant her happiness.

The knock rattles again, this time a little louder.

She hops off the bed and reaches for the closest piece of clothing, which happens to be one of my fitted T-shirts. It's dark and hangs loosely on her body. She slides into a pair of cotton shorts and throws a knitted cardigan over her arms. "I'll be right back."

I raise on my elbows. "I'll—"

"No, stay here." She rushes out of the room and down the hall.

The front door creaks open and I wait impatiently for any sign of who it might be. There's a peephole, so I'm sure Claire was mindful in her decision to greet the random person showing up at her doorstep bright and early on a Sunday.

"Morning," a man says. "Miss Cooper?"

"Yeah." Claire clears her throat. "Yes."

"Officer Donovan. Do you mind if I come in to ask you a few questions?"

As in *police* officer? Fuck.

"Um, sure."

"It'll only take a few moments." He steps inside.

I stay quiet in her bed, not wanting to draw any attention to myself. It drives me fucking crazy not to be out there with her, but she's already done so much to protect me; I'd be stupid to ruin it now.

I listen intently to every single move they make.

Their bodies shuffle toward the living room, giving me a little better vantage point to hear what's going on.

"Do you, uh, want some water or something?" she asks him.

"No. Thank you, though."

She settles onto one of the seats in the awkwardly laid out space. Her breath catches, and even this far away, I can tell she's trying to steady herself.

She's nervous, for obvious reasons.

"I'd like to talk about what happened the other night, if that's okay?" The officer has a friendly, casual tone, despite the gravity of the situation.

"Sure."

I concentrate hard on sending Claire all of my strength to get her through this conversation. I'm sure it's meaningless, but it's the best I can do given the circumstances.

"Can you walk me through the events?" He clicks a pen and waits for her response.

"I was heading to my place when Griffin showed up out of nowhere."

"And this Griffin, how do you two know each other?"

"We dated, for a while, back home. But we recently broke up."

"I see...so you weren't aware of his visit?"

"No, not at all. It was a shock, really."

"What happened next?"

"Um, he..." Claire's voice trails off as she recalls the traumatic experience.

"Miss Cooper, I understand these types of things can be difficult to discuss." His words are followed by the sound of a shuffling of paper. "I'd like to show you something."

She must be looking the document over because there's nothing but silence.

Finally, she says, "I had no idea."

"But tell me, does this surprise you?"

She sighs. "No."

"This man has a history of violence littering his past. You weren't his first victim, but my hope is that you're his last. And with your help, I might be able to make that happen."

Rage builds inside of me at the idea of how much time Claire had spent under Griffin's thumb. It's a miracle he hadn't done something much worse.

"What do you mean, my help?" Claire seems confused.

"Your statement of what transpired. The state would like to

build a case to prosecute Mr. Thomas." The officer adds, "You're not in trouble for defending yourself, Miss Cooper."

Only, it wasn't Claire that shoved Griffin down the stairs, it was me. I'm the one who should be being questioned right now, not her. Claire's hands are clean, and I'm sitting in here letting her take the heat for something she didn't do.

Her voice cracks. "He, um...he grabbed me. He was really mad. Madder than I've ever seen him. He just kept...shaking me." She lets out a breath. "He had been drinking, I could smell it on him."

The officer mumbles something of an acknowledgment for her to continue.

"He kept guiding me toward the steps, just out there."

I imagine her pointing toward the spot outside her door.

"His fingers—he gripped my arms tighter and tighter until we were right on the edge. I begged him to let me go, I really did." She remains calm, despite the storm I know is raging inside of her. "It all happened so fast...one second he was screaming at me, the next he was tumbling down the stairs. I think he slipped or something. He must have misjudged his footing. I ran down after him and called for help immediately."

Clearly, she omitted the part where I showed up, guided him to move to get Claire safely away from the top, and then grabbed him by the collar. Plus, the whole shoving him with force when he threatened the implication of ending Claire's life.

"And to confirm, you were alone? No one else was with you?"

I cringe at the question, knowing damn well what her answer will be.

"No, I had just gotten done studying and was going inside."

I never meant to put Claire in the position where she would have to lie, especially to authorities. She could get caught, she could be charged with making a false statement, and that would probably ruin the State's chance of prosecuting Griffin, not to mention make Claire out to be a liar.

He doesn't press the topic of her company anymore. "You're correct about the alcohol consumption. The hospital did a blood test and it determined he was under the influence."

Claire doesn't respond.

"One more thing, before I leave you be."

"Yes?" There's a hint of anxiousness in her tone.

"You mentioned Mr. Thomas grabbing your arms, can I take a look?"

I can only imagine the dread consuming Claire. She does her best to conceal the bruises and not allow anyone to see them. Even me. It's clear she carries shame and who knows what else with the visual reminder of the assault.

She must pull up her sleeves, because the officer quietly clucks and sighs.

"I'm so sorry this happened to you," he tells her, compassion and sympathy lining his voice. "If I could just snap a few photos for the record."

Which must be another punch to Claire's gut.

It doesn't take him long, but I'm sure every second is antagonizing for her.

"I'll be in touch," he tells her. "I'm hoping to get a statement from Mr. Thomas, but I'm not sure if that will be possible."

"Oh?"

I strain to hear the rest of their conversation from their spot near the door.

Officer Donovan pauses before leaving. "You're unaware of his condition?"

Claire must shake her head because he continues.

"At this point, he's in a medically induced coma to try to give the swelling on his brain time to reduce. Doctors seem unsure of his prognosis."

The door opens, and I can't hear the rest of what's said.

I quietly hop up from the bed and impatiently wait for Claire to return.

She comes down the hall a minute later. "That was humiliating." Claire holds her arms close to her chest like she's shielding herself from the world.

From everything, including me.

31
CLAIRE

There are a million things on my mind right now, but the only one I can focus on is revenge.

For Johnny, for Billy, for all of the girls Griffin ever laid a hand on. For me. For anyone and everyone who has ever been mistreated in this cruel, cruel world.

How can people be so brutal and heartless? The Griffins and Jareds and Franklins…hell, even the Beths that plague this planet. What gives someone the right to abuse and neglect others the way they do?

"There's nothing to be embarrassed about." Johnny stands there, a hesitant look in his eyes.

"I just can't believe I let this happen, you know?" I've been a fool for how I've let people walk all over me my entire life. I thought I was doing the right thing, being passive and not causing any issues when someone wronged me. But what I've really been doing is silencing my voice and giving them approval to continue their sick and twisted games.

The more I allow shit to happen, the more they believe they can get away with it. The cycle will never stop unless someone puts their foot down and calls them out for what they've done or are doing. And maybe those types of people will never change, but the one thing I do have control over is disallowing them from doing it to me again. I will no longer be the victim, and I'll be damned if I let it happen to anyone else.

"Claire, you know it wasn't your fault, right?" Johnny takes a cautious step forward, like he's afraid I might explode if he makes any sudden moves.

"What time is it?"

Johnny pulls his phone out of his pocket. "Almost ten." He slides it back in place. "But listen, you can't answer a question with a question. Not with this. I need you to understand." He finally closes the gap between us. "You've done nothing to warrant the things that have happened to you."

I study his serious expression—the hard lines and his stern jaw.

His injuries are healing, but they will leave a lasting mark of what he went through. Scars from his journey to save an innocent. It's interesting to think about the external marks that show our trauma, when in reality, the damage done inside is much deeper than a faded line on someone's brow.

He's stronger than I ever could be, and I admire his ability to selflessly protect and fight for those unable. He's a noble man, one of the many reasons I...

My heart skips a beat, and my cheeks turn up into a faint smile.

There is a vast darkness consuming my soul, but Johnny is my compass, always guiding me home.

"What is it?" he asks with equal parts confusion and curiosity.

"Nothing." No way I'm going to be the one to spit it out first, especially this soon. We aren't even an official couple yet. And after he totally avoided having sex with me, I'm not certain he feels the same.

He runs his hand along my cheek and meets my gaze.

"Claire, I know this is the last thing you want to hear, but I'm worried about you."

I weave my arms under his and tightly squeeze his bare torso. I breathe in his scent and bask in the comfort he easily brings me. "You're right," I say into his chest. "I don't want to hear it." I pause and add, "I'm fine. Just processing."

"You know I'm here though, that you can talk to me?" His eyes bore into me with the lingering statement that is more like a question.

And despite us only being in each other's lives for a little over a month, I've grown more connected to him than I have any other human. It's terrifying and somehow incredibly exhilarating.

I rise onto my tiptoes and kiss the side of his face. "I'm going to be late for work."

Johnny sighs and his energy completely shifts. He wraps himself around me and picks me off the floor, dragging us both back to the bed.

I giggle and squirm and end up landing on top of him when he plops us onto the mattress.

He quickly grabs the comforter and throws it over us, cocooning us in. "Let's just stay here all day."

Moments like this, all of my doubts disappear about the way Johnny feels about me. It's as though his emotions pour out of him and into me, a direct lifeline of adoration. It's in the glimmer of his eyes when they look at me. The gentleness of his fingers upon grazing my skin. The care he puts into each kiss he plants on my lips. The change in dynamic when we're together. He goes from hardened bad boy to such a gentle sweetheart. He'd go to any length to protect me but would never hurt a hair on my head.

And for him, I'd do the same.

I run my finger along his forehead and swoop the unruly strand of dark hair out of his face. I trace the curve of his brow and the shape of his jaw. I study him so intently, desperate to memorize every single detail. I smile at the freckle I had tried to wipe away that night I had found him in that alley, beaten and left behind.

His beauty stirs something inside of me I've never felt before. A rampant lust and longing I haven't experienced with anyone else. I attribute the intensity to the powerful connection we have. The safety I feel with him allows me to let down walls I didn't realize I had, deepening that bond.

"Claire," his voice is barely a whisper. He reaches up and grazes my cheek, settling his fingers along the side of my face, cupping it gently.

Butterflies swarm my stomach at the way my name slides off his tongue.

"I..." His serious gaze consumes me.

His phone buzzes on my nightstand and he rolls his eyes at the intrusion, dropping his hand at the same time. It goes off once more, solidifying the ruined moment between us.

Johnny walks me to my shift at the diner, making sure I'm safe inside before he goes on his way.

I hate that he has to go, but I understand why he's doing it. He's too far in to back out now. I just hope whatever his plan is, that it works, because I can't stomach the idea of something terrible happening to him—or worse, losing him. Finding him in that alley was heartbreaking, and that was prior to our relationship developing the way it has now. I can only imagine how painful it would be for something like that to happen again.

Every single time he's called out, I'm a nervous wreck. Even when we were in that back and forth of not talking to each other, and he would disappear for hours on end, I'd be a ball of anxiety waiting for him to return safely.

Right now is no exception either.

Bram notices it, too. "You okay, kid?"

I approach the counter after delivering a stack of pancakes to the lone patron in the corner booth. "Yeah." I glance at the clock.

Johnny has been gone for four hours, and my shift ends in about forty-five minutes.

I grab a rag and walk to a newly emptied table to clean it off. My thoughts are interrupted when I overhear someone's name.

"Yeah, Jared and his buddy do it every Sunday."

I covertly follow the sound to spot a guy about my age talking on his cell phone. He brings his cup of coffee to his lips and takes a drink.

I drop my gaze and go back to wiping the table, listening attentively.

"Over on Sullivan. They pretty much got everyone from the building to go. Claim it's their hangover cure. Whatever. Steve was salty when I told him I wasn't coming." He pauses while the other person talks. "Probably another hour, but I'm not going." He slides a French fry off his plate and tosses it into his mouth. "Lifting weights is what they do, I'm more of a drown myself in greasy food type of guy."

And from the look of him, that statement rings true.

I check the time once more and glance at the door. Still no sign of Johnny. I could text him, but I don't want to distract him if he's in the middle of his delivery. I'd rather not add any more risk to his already dangerous situation.

I replay the one side of the conversation I just heard.

Sullivan. It's probably the gym in the community center that students at our school get free access to. Which is a hefty walk from their house. And if they're going to be there for another sixty minutes, I could easily pop over and rummage through that room Johnny and I had seen those sneakers in.

I'd be in and out in a flash, and if anyone catches me, I could easily say I left my purse behind at the party. Totally believable story.

I'd love to have the luxury of waiting, talking this over with Johnny, and coming up with a plan together, but considering the next time this guy mentioned they would be gone for sure is *next* Sunday, I can't exactly afford to waste this perfect opportunity.

Johnny isn't here, and I have no idea when he'll be back. He'll be pissed, but this is my chance to show him I'm not the weak girl he thinks I am. I can see it in the way he looks at me, like I'm going to break.

And maybe I am. But this is my time to prove those doubts wrong to both of us.

I convince Bram to let me go early, which is most likely going to be the easiest part of this plan. Bram can totally run the diner alone, with his eyes closed. Having me there is probably more for me than it is for him. I'm grateful for the job, and the opportunity to learn humility from such a good man.

I check my phone one last time and shove it into my back pocket. I still haven't heard from Johnny, but I have to hope that everything is okay. He's warned me numerous times about how long some of his errands can take, and yet it still doesn't make the wait any less unbearable.

Tugging the sleeves of my thin sweatshirt down around my wrists, I head out the front door of the diner and make my way toward my destination. I breathe in the warm fall air and squint at the brightness of the sun. I need to invest in a decent pair of shades and actually keep them on me if I'm going to continue living in a place that's always beaming.

I keep my arms tight around my chest and avoid eye contact with people on the walk to the building. Not that it's a difficult task, considering most of the pedestrians are so consumed by the device in their hands that they don't even notice me.

As I approach the house, I slow my pace to scope it out. Red solo cups litter the front lawn, but other than that, it's quiet. Honestly, it looks much different in the daylight. More... normal. If I hadn't already been here before, it would probably just blend in with all the other homes on the street.

I decide to waste no more time, considering the clock is ticking on when the hangover gym session will be finished. Considering my interaction with Jared last night, I'd rather avoid coming face-to-face with him again.

I bolt up the steps, careful to glance over my shoulder and confirm I'm alone. I walk in like I own the place, considering it's much easier to blend in when you act confident. My heart pounds wildly in my chest with each foot I put in front of the other.

The house is dead ass quiet. It's also a mess, although I'm not at all surprised. It's the home of a bunch of careless college party boys. The empty bottles of booze and discarded pizza boxes are clearly a staple of their décor.

I go down the hallway where June had greeted me and Johnny and turn to head up the stairs. Not a single person appears and stops me, leading me to think I might actually pull this off.

Quietly, I stroll along the row of bedrooms and go toward the one I came here for. I pause before it, listening carefully for any sign of life. The door is cracked open, those shoes still in the same spot they were. I place my fingers gently on the white wood and push it further.

The comforter hangs off the side of the unkempt bed and

clothes are strewn haphazardly around the room. I take the space in for just a moment, confirming no one is occupying it. I cautiously step in, letting the heaviness of the room settle over me. My gut tells me I'm in the right place; I only hope I find what I'm looking for in time.

I try to calm myself down and come up with where I would hide something if I was stupid enough to do what this guy did. Johnny might be in the same business, but he's never admitted to brutally beating someone up and stealing from them. And given Johnny's backstory, he at least has a reasonable explanation for why he's even involved with this kind of work. Anyone who signs up for this shit for the money is out of their mind.

I rush to the bed, dropping to my knees and shoving my arm between the mattress and the bed frame. I slide it around, coming up empty-handed. Letting out a sigh, I catch sight of the tall dresser. Immediately, I pull the top drawer back, cringing when I find this guy's underwear. I hold my breath and dig my fingers through the assortment. Something cold and hard startles me.

Without laying my eyes on it, I know exactly what I've stumbled upon.

I grip the deadly thing and pull it out anyway.

A gun. A small one. Compact.

I let the weight of it settle in my hand and do something completely insane—I tuck it into the back of my waistband. I'm not really sure what I'm going to do with it, but I can't stand the idea of leaving it behind in this room. If this person was willing to beat Johnny up, what else would they do? I won't allow the possibility of something worse to float around in the universe.

I shut the drawer and continue my search, the gun pressed against my skin, a reminder of the vicious and dark world I keep dipping my toes into.

Johnny warned me. He tried to keep his distance to protect me, but who's going to be the one to save him? Why should he have to go through all this on his own? Maybe we're more alike than we think—willing to dive headfirst into the fire to save someone we care about.

I rummage through the rest of the clothes, shutting the bottom drawer and sighing at my lack of finding anything else.

A person clears their throat behind me, and I freeze, praying like hell that I could make myself invisible. I guess I'm going to finally meet the person this room belongs to.

Only, when I slowly turn to see their face, it's Jared leaning in the doorway.

That same evil grin from last night.

"And what do we have here?" His large body easily blocks the entire exit.

There was one person I needed to avoid when I came here. If I would have run into anyone else I could have easily said I left something behind; but that story won't work on him. Jared knows too much, and if he's part of Franklin's organization, he's probably aware Johnny is not around to defend me.

Jared steps forward, his hand casually closing the door as he enters the room. "A little privacy, if you know what I mean."

I had hoped that last night Jared had too much to drink, and that's why he came at me the way he did. Aggressively, possessively, and in such a disgusting manner. But now, he's stone-cold sober and still approaching me with his greedy eyes, like I am his for the taking.

With the shutting of the door, the space of the room seems to shrink, confining me in and sealing my fate along with it.

"Aw, don't act so scared." Jared comes toward me, and my mind flashes back to the events that transpired during our first meeting. "I promise, you might even like it. I mean, you kind of owe me after what you did."

Kicking him in the balls for forcing himself on me? How does that even make sense?

But, despite every fiber in my being screaming at me to run,

I allow him to advance, because that's the only thing I *can* do. He's shut off the only viable exit, considering the owner of the room put their dresser in front of the window, blocking it from being accessible.

What a fire hazard.

Jared glides over and trails his finger along my covered arm. "You should really take that off." He pinches my sweatshirt and licks at his bottom lip.

My stomach flips from his words and the implications behind them.

His hot breath settles on my face, drawing away the attention from that familiar foot smell. Jared grabs my shoulders firmly. "What do you think?" His question is clearly rhetorical, since he's already made his decision of what's going to go down in this room.

Little does he know, so have I.

I slide my right hand back, gripping that cold, hard thing tucked into my waistband and without another thought, I yank it out. I grasp it with both hands and shove it against his belly. "Actually, I had something else in mind."

Jared's eyes go wide and immediately he removes himself from me.

This time, it's me that advances on him, pushing him further away, until he can't go anywhere else.

"Get your fucking hands off of me," I demand.

"Watch it with that thing," Jared spits out.

"Where's the package?" I ask him.

Jared narrows his gaze. "What are you talking about?" He keeps his arms outstretched and to the side, facing me.

"Don't act like you don't know. Where is it?"

He glances down and then back up at me, his resolve fading. "Do you even know how to use that thing?" Jared smirks like he's somehow got the upper hand despite the gun I'm aiming at him.

Without taking my eyes off of him, I slide my thumb down to switch the safety off. "You tell me." I shove the thing further into him, only this time, I aim for his groin. "Now, do I need to ask again, or should I shoot your fucking dick off?"

One of the perks of being raised by a gun-toting dad is learning how to use one at an early age. It wasn't something we did often, but enough for me to learn the basics and get comfortable with handling one. I've never been more thankful for those awkward daddy-daughter days at the gun range.

Sheer panic replaces the snide expression on his face. "Okay, okay, yeah. It's over there." He points behind me.

I don't dare break my concentration and give him an opportunity to disarm me. "You think you're clever? Tell me exactly where it is."

"The, uh, the closet. Behind his jackets." He practically spits out the words.

"You fucking move and I shoot you, do you hear me?" I keep the gun pointed at him but take a step back. I use my peripheral to glance out the location and slowly make my way in that direction.

He raggedly nods like he's afraid I might actually do it. There's something about the way he fears me for a change that is so incredibly empowering.

I take my left hand off the grip and feel around inside the space. I fumble through the T-shirts until I find the thicker, heavier stuff I'm searching for. I reach farther and graze my hand along the wall. I start to doubt whether Jared was telling the truth or not.

My heart seems to jump out of my chest when my fingers skim a section of tape. I trace the outline and rip the thing off the wall. With the weapon still pointed at Jared, I bring the package out into the open.

Yellow, just like Johnny had told me, the same exact size his hands had motioned toward. Except there's one thing he didn't mention. The dark splotches of his dried blood that were left behind.

I glance down at the gun in my hand, and then at Jared with an anger coursing through me that is all-consuming.

"Was it you?" I ask him through my clenched teeth.

"What?" He feigns confusion.

"Were you involved with the attack?" I extend the package. "To steal this?"

Jared places both hands up in the air and shakes his head. "No, I swear. I had nothing to do with it."

But why should I believe him? After what he might have done to me, who's to say what he's capable of. He could very well be lying right now to save his ass.

He seems to sense that I don't trust what he's telling me. "I didn't. It was Steve and Boston. They got the order; I only knew about it."

The memory of Johnny, lying there helpless on the ground, bleeding out and practically unconscious, assaults me heavily. I barely knew him but even then, the idea of someone hurting him like that was an impossible pill to swallow. He could have died. All because of some fucking *order*.

Why should I allow a person like Jared to continue to exist in this world? Even if he's telling the truth, he's still guilty by association. And Johnny aside, he's a threat to any woman he sets his sights on. He doesn't deserve to exist.

A chill creeps up my spine, reminding me that Griffin is still out there. Another menace to this world. I knew he was a monster, but when that officer showed me the numerous reports filed against Griffin, it solidified how terrible of a person he is. And the thing that concerns me the most is he's still capable of ruining more lives.

If Griffin wakes up and tells the authorities his story of what happened that night, Johnny could be in trouble. Sure, Griffin has a checkered past, but he'd be telling the truth, and if he's able to prove it, Johnny and I would be screwed.

But for now, I need to focus on the more time-sensitive problem in front of me. The two-hundred-plus-pound man nearly shitting his pants at the sight of a five-foot-something girl pointing a loaded gun at him.

The biggest mystery of all: Do I pull the trigger?

32
JOHNNY

I stop by the diner to pick up Claire a few minutes before her shift is over, and Bram informs me she's already gone. I try not to freak out as I send her a text to let her know I'm done.

Considering how nervous she always is when I leave, I assume she'll read it and respond immediately.

But she doesn't.

"Do you know where she went?" I ask Bram while attempting to hide my emotions.

He shakes his head while clearing off a table. "Nope. We weren't busy, so I let her go." He stops and faces me, seeming to pick up on my distress anyway. "Is something wrong?"

"No." I lie. "I'm sure everything is fine."

"Johnny…"

"I'm on edge. It's probably nothing." I make my way to the door. "Call me if you hear from her."

I bolt back to the complex. It's possible she went home to shower and change out of her diner clothes. Or maybe she's studying. There are plenty of reasonable explanations as to why she hasn't replied yet.

She could be in trouble, my brain reminds me.

I shake the thought away, not wanting to hyper-focus on that theory.

She has to be okay; I won't accept any other reality.

I key in my code, granting me access, and rush through the empty courtyard, hoping with all my might that she's upstairs, completely unharmed.

Griffin might be lying in a hospital bed, inches away from death, but countless other things could threaten Claire, especially in this world I allowed her to step into.

I pound on her door and peer through the window for any sign of her. "Claire, you in there?" A minute goes by and when she doesn't answer, I bolt down the hallway to my own place. I had given her a key to use, so maybe she decided to come over instead of going home. We've been spending so much time together that it seems like a possibility. At least, that's what I keep telling myself.

I enter my foyer and I'm greeted by the sound of my heartbeat thudding through the heavy silence. I pause and listen—nothing else. That could mean a number of things, like maybe she's taking a nap. Shit has been overwhelming lately, she could have needed some rest. But with each step closer to my bedroom, I remember her confession last night about not being able to fall asleep without me.

Who's to say she isn't trying, though?

I hold my breath and step into the room. A second later, I'm back out, rushing toward the front door. She's not here. She's not answering. She must be in trouble.

An invisible clock starts flashing in my mind, blinking a warning that time is running out. What if I'm too late? Like I almost was when Griffin came. Or last night when Jared was going to...

I can't even let my mind continue the vile thought. I've never killed someone before, but last night, the idea of ending Jared's life for what he could have done to Claire was insanely strong. If it wouldn't have only further put her in danger, I may have gone through with it.

I reach for the handle but startle when it turns, the door opening, and a beautiful angel standing on the other side.

"Claire." It's like I can finally breathe. I drag her in and wrap my arms around her. "Fuck, are you okay? I've never been more worried in my life." Each time Claire's life is threatened is a new and intense knife to the gut. Getting used to caring about someone so intensely is a shock to my system.

Claire hugs me tight, not saying a word. Her body relaxes into mine like she feels the same way I do.

It's then that I notice the protruding thing between us.

I break away, but only slightly, to look into her eyes.

She stares back and swallows thickly. She brings her hands to her stomach and fumbles under the thin sweatshirt she's only wearing to cover her bruised arms. Claire drags out a blood-stained package, and if I thought my heart was going to explode earlier, I was wrong.

I gasp, totally incapable of hiding my shock. A million things cross my mind in a matter of seconds, but each one of them ends with having no fucking clue how she pulled this off.

"What did you do?" I ask her in utter disbelief.

"I…I got this…for you." She shoves it toward me.

"How?" I take the package from her. And although I'm fucking thrilled it's here, I can't begin to imagine the lengths she had to go through to retrieve it.

She blinks and seems to snap out of her daze. "You promise you won't freak out?"

I breathe in deeply in a desperate attempt to calm myself from doing the very thing she thinks I'm going to do. We've only been in each other's lives a short time, but she already knows me well.

"Okay," I finally say quietly, not sure whether or not I'll be able to pull it off, but for her, I'll try.

Claire averts her gaze and reaches behind her, pulling out another surprise to completely throw me off balance.

I want to grab the gun from her—throw it into the ocean and get it as far away from her as possible. But the way she holds it, rigid yet loosely, with her finger running straight, showing perfect trigger control, tells me that she's either a natural or potentially experienced in this department.

Still, the urge to get any possible threat away from her is strong.

And so, her mouth opens once more, and she explains how she came into possession of both items. The conversation she overheard, the internal battle she faced on whether or not she should go, the gun, and Jared showing up when he did and how she forced him to tell her where the package was located. Part of me thinks she's leaving fragments out, not wanting to tell me the whole story. The other part of me is in awe of how she handled the situation.

Yeah, of course, I'm pissed that she was incredibly reckless, but damn am I proud of her, too.

"He said it was Steve and some guy named Boston?" She's sitting on the couch now, her elbow propped up on the back of it while she's facing me.

The stolen package sitting on the coffee table, the gun resting beside it.

I scan my memory for anyone by that name, only settling on a smaller built dude who's new to Franklin's organization. Clearly, there's no way he matches the description of one of the assholes who beat me up.

Meaning only one thing—Jared lied.

And if that's the case, he more than likely was involved in what happened, he was just too fucking afraid of Claire to admit it. He must have been genuinely concerned that she was going to shoot him if he wouldn't admit to his role in what went down.

That alone brings me a sense of comfort, knowing Claire put that much fear in him.

I've sensed it from the beginning—this hidden strength under the surface, something that no one has ever supported or allowed her to embrace.

Claire has been plagued by shitty people controlling her, bringing her down, and the time for that to stop has finally come. And I think she's realizing it, too.

"J…do you know a Boston?" She stares at me, waiting for a response.

I shrug. "I'm not sure. Maybe. I'm bad with names." If my gut is right, and Claire is willing to shoot someone because of what happened, I don't exactly want to admit the whole truth just yet. I need her emotions to settle down before she grabs the gun and finishes them off.

It's strange though, to have a person who cares this much in your life. I sort of got used to doing everything on my own. I fight my battles alone because that's what I grew up doing. I never knew my dad, and I lost my mom when I was young. My aunt got custody of me, but it was my cousin who sort of took me under his wing. Eventually, they both left, too. Her to an overdose and him to the army. I've known Bram most of my life, but I'd never expect anything from him. Hell, I even feel guilty when he won't let me pay for my food.

"Are you mad at me?" Claire's question snaps me back to reality.

I place my hand on her knee. "No, of course not." I rub my thumb along her silky skin. "Just promise me you won't do anything that dangerous without telling me first?" It's not that I want to control her, but more so that I can be there if something goes wrong. We're a team now, and I don't want her to think she has to do stuff alone, either.

"I wanted to; I really did. I just didn't want to distract you while you were working." Claire shifts closer to me. "Your job is already consuming enough."

Tucking her hair behind her ear, I tell her, "But you're more important, okay?"

She leans into my touch and her eyes close.

"I'm serious." I silently plead with her to understand the lengths I would go to protect her. It makes no sense how she could mean this much to me so soon, but she does, and I can't allow anything to get in the way of that.

Her lids open and that gorgeous blue stare pierces me. "What are you going to do?"

"Good question." I flit my attention to the contraband sitting on the table waiting for me to make a decision.

"You're sure?" Claire asks me, a hint of fear lingering in her tone.

I nod. "Yes." Although, I hate the uncertainty that threatens to wreck me.

Claire grips my face in her hands. "You'll let me know the second you're done?"

"Yes, not a moment later." That is, if I'm not dead.

"I could come with you."

"No, not this time. I have to do this alone." It's not my persistent fear of letting someone in that enforces this, it's the fact that this is entirely too dangerous to involve anyone who isn't already tangled up with Franklin. Claire has already put herself in harm's way by exposing herself to Jared, but I have to bank on the fact that he hasn't come clean with Franklin about what happened just yet. If what Claire tells me is true about how badly she scared him, Jared might not tell him at all. Apparently, her performance was pretty convincing.

"Okay."

I place my hand on her waist and pull her closer despite the package tucked into my waistband preventing us from touching our bodies completely together. I breathe her in and bask in this moment because it will be gone before I know it. I stare into her eyes and memorize every swirl of blue and fleck of gold.

"Don't you dare say goodbye," she tells me.

I press my lips to her forehead. "Nope, just a see ya later."

Claire stands taller, bringing her mouth to mine. Her kiss is soft and desperate and makes me wish I could stay here with her forever.

But I can't. Not with the way things are.

I walk out my front door, leaving a piece of me behind. I want to glance over my shoulder, to look at her beautiful face one last time, but *that* would only make me feel like it really was goodbye. And I refuse to believe this is the end of our story. There has to be more.

Her gaze burns a hole through me as I make my way down the stairs and across the courtyard. It lingers even when I exit the complex and disappear out of her line of sight.

I continue on my journey, crossing the street and taking my normal path to where Franklin is most Sundays. I haven't fully decided what I'm going to say, but one thing is certain: I have to get him the package.

Each step closer to him is one further away from Claire. I fight the desire to turn around, to run back to her and pack what we need and run far, far away from here. To use what money I have saved and seek refuge in another place. That's not an option, though. Not when so much is still on the line. If I quit now, all the progress I made with Billy will have been for nothing. I can't stop until everything falls into place. I just hope we can make it that long.

I round the corner to the dim and damp alley. Despite the sun still being out, the buildings cast a dark shadow, creating an ominous atmosphere that could be straight out of a mob movie. It's fitting, considering the circumstances.

"What's up, J?" Josey greets me from his usual spot near the back entrance.

I haven't seen much of him since our meeting in the bar. He's managed to keep his distance from me, and I don't blame him. If Franklin found out he gave me insider info on how to locate the package, I can only imagine what he would do to both of us.

"Boss in?" I ask him.

He stares at me like he's trying to read my mind and then finally says, "Yeah, give me a second." Josey opens the door, disappears inside, and then comes back out. "Go ahead, he's waiting for you."

I grip the handle of the metal door and pause to take a steadying breath.

Josey pats me on the shoulder. "Good luck, kid."

I step into the smoky area, making my way further until I'm standing in the same room I've been in countless times before. Each meeting was stressful, but nothing like what I'm feeling right now. The outcome of this visit could go any number of ways, and the majority end up with Franklin having someone put a bullet between my eyes. The rumors of Franklin's wrath are enough to worry anyone doing business with him.

Today though, I hope to take back a little of that power.

"This better be good." Franklin sets his crystal glass of brown liquid onto the table. He folds his arms across his wide chest and leans back in his chair.

I move my hands to reach into my waistband.

All four of the men posted up in each corner draw their weapons and aim them at me.

I stop completely, not wanting to die just yet. I'd at least like to see the reaction on Franklin's face when I show him that I was capable of pulling off the impossible. Well, Claire was, but I'll leave that part out of it.

Franklin nods at the goon to his left, somehow communicating with him to step forward and finish the task that I started out to do.

The large, broad-shouldered man approaches, lifts up my shirt, and retrieves the bloodied package and hands it to Franklin.

"Hmph." Franklin tilts his head to the side, a faint bit of disbelief showing through. "How'd you pull it off?"

"It's better not to ask questions." I boldly tell him the same thing he's told me when I got curious about stuff in the past. I shouldn't speak to him like this, but I'd rather avoid divulging any details if I can. It keeps everyone else involved safer. There's absolutely no way I'm going to admit Josey or Claire played a huge role in helping me.

Franklin laughs, which surprises me even more. "Fair enough." He examines the package for a brief moment and tosses it across the table toward me. "Keep it."

Not exactly the reaction I was expecting. Why was he so hell-bent on having me find it if he was willing to just let it go?

"What?" I say in disbelief.

"For your trouble." Franklin takes a long drag from his cigar and sets it onto the ashtray. Smoke billows from his mouth and he continues, "You've proven yourself quite resourceful, Johnny."

Am I supposed to thank him? He and I both know that this was a setup, but neither one of us seem to want to admit it.

Franklin cranes his finger toward the man behind me, motioning for him to come over. Franklin whispers something into his ear.

"Yes, sir. Consider it taken care of," the man responds, and then disappears out the door I entered from.

Panic rises within me at the idea of him going after Josey, but on the slight chance that he isn't, I can't react, because then

Franklin would absolutely know he was in on it. Instead, I remain as unaffected as possible.

Still, there's the lingering uncertainty of what happens next. "Are we, uh, good?" Meaning, is he going to go back on our prior arrangement and rope Billy back into this line of work? Or is something worse going to happen that I haven't already considered? With Franklin, it's like a game of Russian-fucking-roulette.

Franklin's dark eyes glare at me. "For now, yeah. Take the package and get out."

I do as he demands, swiping the stupid thing off the table and leaving without another word. I shove it into its home in my waistband for hopefully the last time. I pick up my pace without seeming too eager to leave.

I bust through the door and it takes my eyes a second to adjust.

"You good?" Josey's voice appears as my sights settle onto his big figure.

Relief settles over me along with the urge to freaking hug and thank him for all he's done, but I can't.

Instead, I grip his shoulder firmly. "Yeah." I try to telepathically say all the things I want to, and in a way, it's like he does the same. "I'll catch you later."

I leave him behind and drag my phone out of my pocket, following through with what I had promised Claire. I swipe over to the text screen and thumb a quick message.

Me: *I'll be home soon.*

And for the first time since all of this started, I feel like I might actually be able to pull this all off.

33
CLAIRE

I pace Johnny's foyer while I wait for him to arrive. Each minute is longer than the last, but the second the doorknob turns, and his gorgeous face appears, it's like the world slows and time halts and all is right in the universe.

I'd be lying if I said I wasn't worried I'd never see him again. His job is dangerous enough when his boss isn't plotting against him to fail. It's been incredibly nerve-wracking not knowing how he would react to actually seeing that package in Johnny's possession.

"You're okay." I rush to wrap my arms around him, nearly knocking him down in the process.

He embraces me and kisses the top of my head. "I am."

And like he had done to me earlier, I break away from him and motion to his stomach. "Um?"

Johnny fumbles to pull the same daunting package out and tosses it onto the counter. "He told me to keep it."

"What? Why?"

"I don't know. And I don't really care. Not right now." Johnny pulls me to him, his body finally able to get closer to mine without the package being there to interfere. He runs his hand up along my neck until he's cupping my cheek. "All I could think about was getting back to you."

"Yeah?" My voice is barely a whisper.

Johnny leans forward and gently grazes our noses together, his mouth skimming mine. "Yeah."

I push forward, not wanting to waste any more time without being as close to him as possible. I press my lips against his and drag my fingers up under his shirt.

The softness of the initial kiss fades into a frenzy of heated passion with our tongues desperately dancing together.

I didn't know it was possible to crave someone so intensely.

He runs his hand down my torso and grips my waist while keeping the other tangled in my hair.

I grasp the hem of his shirt and drag it over his head.

"Claire," he says breathily.

I continue kissing him, not wanting it to ever end. I reach for my own top and he stops me.

"Claire," he repeats, this time louder.

"Did I do something wrong?" I don't understand. I really thought we were on the same page here.

"No, never." He kisses the tip of my nose. "It's just..."

"Are you not attracted to me?"

Johnny chuckles. "That's definitely not it."

"Then why do you keep shutting me down?" I fight back tears I didn't realize were forming. His resistance seems like some sort of rejection. Maybe I've gotten all the signals crossed and he's not into me the way I think he is. Which makes no fucking sense at all considering everything we've been through.

His green gaze studies my face. "I don't want to shut you down, trust me, I don't...I just...I don't want to rush you." Johnny wipes a rogue tear off my face that escapes. "You've been through so much, Claire. I want you to be sure."

"But I am," I tell him.

"You're too important to me, and if we need to wait, we can."

I try my best to keep my emotions from boiling over. "You could have died today." I stare up at him. Something terrible could have happened to me earlier, too.

"I didn't, though. And I don't want that to be some default reason we do this."

I shake my head. "No. I choose you, a thousand times over. Life is too short, *especially* now. I'm done waiting for the perfect time to do what I want. I'm finally living for myself, and I know with complete certainty that this is what I want. *You* are what I want."

Johnny sighs, and it's like he's internally battling with himself on what to do with the information I just gave him.

I run my hand across his cheek. "Is that so hard to believe?"

"A little bit." He swallows and examines me once more. "You're sure?"

"Without a doubt."

He places his lips on mine, not wasting another second. Only this time, he kisses me in a manner he hasn't before. With longing and desire and a pure thirst that only I could satisfy. Johnny grabs me by the waist and lifts me from the floor.

I wrap my legs around him and let him carry me out of the room.

He continues caressing his tongue against mine each step of the way.

We stumble to his bedroom, the door swinging open and slamming into the wall. We giggle into each other and he drops me onto the foot of the bed.

I quickly remove my sweatshirt and toss it aside. I reach forward and unbutton his pants.

He glances at my bruised arms for a split-second before looking into my eyes. "You're still sure?"

"Yes." I tug his jeans down over his growing erection, which reassures me he wants this, too. "Are you?" I lick my lips in anticipation of his response.

He pulls at my hands to bring me to my feet. Johnny slides my black T-shirt over my head, revealing my bare chest. He trails his lips along mine and down my neck, nipping at my breasts on his way to my panty line. He kneels before me to unbutton my shorts and drag them over my ass with my underwear in one motion. He kisses my thigh, gradually inching further toward my center with hot breath along my skin.

I grip his head and drag him up to my face, no longer able to withstand his teasing. I pull his remaining clothes off and drag him onto the same bed we have spent the last few nights cuddling on. I spread my legs and tug him on top of me, our mouths never breaking apart.

He blindly reaches over and opens his nightstand drawer. A second later, the sound of a wrapper appears.

Johnny breaks our kiss one last time.

Anticipating his question, I tell him, "I'm sure, I promise."

You know those instances when you put such high expectations on something because you want it so bad, and when it finally happens, you're left wondering what the hype was all about?

Well, this is *nothing* like that.

No, being with Johnny is…everything.

Take all of the super cheesy clichés and toss them into a blender, and I doubt they would ever compare. I'm talking Earth slowing, mind-blowing, soul connecting, pure-fucking-bliss.

And that's only describing the first few seconds.

I arch my back, begging with my body for him to give me more.

Johnny stifles a moan against my lips, only driving my hunger for him that much more. He kisses me feverishly, and I match his intensity.

It doesn't take long until we find our groove, grinding into each other like we've been doing this all our lives. With our seemingly natural connection, I'm not at all surprised. What I didn't expect was for it to feel *this damn good.* Just when I think it can't possibly get any better, he switches things up.

He wraps his arm around my waist, lifting and angling me toward him.

I dig my nails into his back in response to this new wave of pleasure at the slightly different position. It's not much of an alteration but holy hell does it hit all the right spots.

His erection grinds against me, sending me higher and higher until I can barely hold on any longer.

He tugs at my lip with his teeth and pauses to whisper, "Let go."

And with that simple command, I spiral into the most intense orgasm I've ever had. The wave lasts longer than anything I could have imagined.

Johnny keeps thrusting all the way through, switching up his pace and guiding me exactly where he wants me to go. When my body finally stops shaking, he continues, somehow sending me right back to the starting line.

How can I be so eager for more when I've already been satisfied?

I force myself out of my head and right back here with him, noticing how his erection grows inside of me.

It's as though he purposely wasn't going to finish until I did, and now that I have, his desire builds that much more.

Which, if I'm being honest, fuels mine to heights that seem completely fictional.

I run one of my hands along his back and up his chest, finding its home on the side of his face, partially tangled in his hair. I grip it firmly and drag him closer. My breathing hitches, and I break away slightly. "Let go," I tell him just like he had told me.

And with that, he stares into my eyes before powerfully bringing his mouth back to mine, kissing me more intensely than ever, his release coming almost simultaneously with my second one.

I thought the first was intense—it's nothing compared to climaxing alongside him, his pulsing inside of me only heightening the sensation rippling through my body.

We slow our pace as each of us comes down from the insane high, our foreheads pressed against one another, our breaths ragged while we try to tame them.

Johnny carefully pulls himself out of me and collapses onto his back on the bed. He drapes his arm over his head. "That was..."

"Yeah," I respond. Because whatever he's about to say, I absolutely agree.

We lay there for a minute before he removes the condom and tosses it into the trash can by the nightstand.

He lowers himself back down and turns toward me. Carefully, he tucks a strand of hair behind my ear.

It's a simple gesture, and he's done it a million times in the past, but now, it's different, somehow more meaningful—like there's a hidden message behind the softness of his touch.

I become mesmerized by his beautiful green eyes and desperately wish I could stay in this moment forever. And maybe for a little while, we can.

"Come here." He holds his arm out for me and I inch closer.

Our still naked bodies intertwine, and I relax into the safety of his embrace.

When I wake, for a split-second I fear that this was all a dream. But feeling his skin against mine, I know my reality is better than anything my mind could conjure up.

He kisses the top of my head and nuzzles against me. "Hi."

"Hi." I breathe him in. "You hungry?" With everything that happened earlier, he hasn't had a solid meal in a while, and if we stand any chance of actually getting any sleep tonight, we should probably get up, at least for a little bit.

Life is crazy and all, but we still have classes to attend this week if he wants to bring his grades up and I want to get that scholarship.

My stomach sinks. I hadn't thought about the ramifications of my plan now that Johnny is part of it. I had come here with the notion that I would leave the moment the opportunity presented itself. There was nothing here for me other than an unfamiliar town and an estranged mother who doesn't care about anything other than herself. Now, though, how could I ever imagine a life without him?

Everything I've ever known is back home. But what if he's my home, too?

Johnny plants soft kisses on my face. "Starving."

Maybe I won't get the scholarship. Maybe I won't have to make that decision at all. There are still a few more weeks until the announcement is made—anything could happen between now and then. A couple months ago, if someone told me I'd be taking my second year of classes out here, I'd have dreaded it. But with him, it won't be so bad. I guess I'll cross that bridge when it happens.

"What are you thinking?" he asks me.

Instead of answering, I press my lips to his and savor the simple fact that he's here with me now. We played a game of cat and mouse for what felt like an eternity. It's heaven to finally bask in being whatever we are.

We stand in his kitchen, fully clothed and ready to head over to Bram's to catch a late-night dinner. The tainted package seems to glare at us with this big flashing neon sign.

"What's in it?" I glance over at him as the possibilities course through my head. Why would Franklin go to such lengths only to give it to him?

Johnny shrugs. "I'm not sure." He takes my hand and guides me over to it.

We sort of stare at it like it might explode or morph into something else.

"Are you going to open it?" I ask him.

He exhales and grabs a pair of kitchen scissors from a drawer. Johnny pauses, and for a second, I don't know if he'll follow through with it.

I pick up the package and hold it for him.

"Moment of truth." He slices through the top and takes it from me, dumping the contents out.

Stacks of hundred-dollar bills tumble on top of each other with bands marking a thousand-dollar denomination on them. There has to be at least a dozen of them. Outside of movies, I don't think I've ever seen anything quite like this.

I look to Johnny and wonder what he's thinking. I had some wild ideas of what might have been inside here, but this wasn't one of them. Maybe *some* money—not this much.

Johnny doesn't seem phased at all, but considering everything else he's been through, I shouldn't be surprised by his lack of reaction. Especially with the way he's constantly insisting on paying for everything.

He shoves the stacks back into the envelope. "I'm just glad it wasn't drugs. I don't know what the hell I would have done with a bunch of cocaine."

I side-eye him. "Was that a possibility?"

Johnny shrugs. "Honestly, I have no clue. With Franklin, I wouldn't put anything past him. He never tells me what's inside the packages."

I hate that for Johnny, how he has to blindly follow Franklin's orders and risk so fucking much to comply with his demands. Ignorance won't save him if he gets caught with something illegal. Hell, most of the time it's the runners that get punished, not the people actually in charge.

There's that age-old saying: good guys finish last.

I'll do anything in my power to make sure that doesn't happen to Johnny. I won't allow him to fall victim to Franklin's corrupt ways.

34
JOHNNY

I've never been much of a sports guy, but I imagine having sex with Claire is comparable to winning the Superbowl or something similar in nature. Or maybe it's more like traveling to the moon or winning the Nobel Peace Prize.

Visualize the best thing you could think of, and multiply it by ten billion. Yeah, that's probably closer to the experience we just shared.

Don't get me wrong, I've had sex. But not like *that.*

Passion. Intensity. Connection.

From the very moment I bumped into her that first day she arrived here, there's been an undeniable pull between us.

Call me crazy, but there's something about the way Claire looks at me. Like she knows me. Like she sees me. It's enough to set my soul on fire in the best way possible. I can be myself with her. Truly and utterly vulnerable. Nothing shakes her, and for once, I feel not so alone in the world.

"You okay?" Claire asks over the top of her cup of coffee. She's staring at me, which tells me I must have been zoning out.

I study her face—the soft edges and subtle glow about her.

Her lips, still a little puffy from our intimate time together. The freckle just a hair away from her brow.

"Yeah," I breathe.

I'll never have any clue what I did to be so fucking lucky. Not only is Claire pretty much drop-dead gorgeous, but she's incredibly smart, too. I wouldn't be surprised if she's carrying a perfect GPA. She's managed to maintain her grades and somehow help me raise all of mine. She's taken on a part-time job, and still somehow unraveled the great mystery of where the stolen package was located. All while making new friends and being braver than anyone I've ever met. She's kind and thoughtful and fiercely badass. Not to mention, all she's had to endure up until this point. She was forced to move across the country, live in an unfamiliar place with a mom she's never known, and deal with a psychotic stalker boyfriend. And that's just what I'm aware of.

Claire is a freaking angel.

"You ready to get out of here?" She reaches for the check, which completely snaps me out of my train of thought.

No way in hell I'm allowing her to pay for our food. I clearly have more money than I know what to do with, and she works hard for hers. It's the least I could do for everything she's done for me.

I manage to hop up and rush to the register to block Claire from intercepting the bill.

Bram smiles and cashes us out. "You kids seem happy."

Claire comes to my side, wrapping her arms around me.

I look down at her, her gaze meeting mine.

Something I haven't known, staring right back at me —happiness.

A loud pop sounds from outside—the kind that could be easily confused with fireworks.

I shift my attention toward the door and tighten my hold on Claire.

Another bang rattles through the diner.

I turn toward Claire and Bram. "Stay here."

Claire grabs at my hand. "What? No, you can't go out there!" Panic is written across her face.

"I'll be right back," I reassure her. I glance at Bram to help me out.

He seems just as startled as her.

I rush out the front of the diner, the doorbell dinging at my exit.

People are slowly rising from their cowered positions near cars and random stuff on the street. I make eye contact with an older woman and she points to my left. My stomach sinks when I notice the exact location.

I make my way over and poke my head into the dark alley with caution.

A large body lay on the ground, partially obscured by the lack of light.

I'm taken abruptly back to that night when I was beaten and left behind, only for Claire to come to my rescue.

This time, it's the person who beat me, lying bloodied on the ground.

The same guy who threatened Claire.

Jared coughs and blood flies out of his mouth. There's a gaping wound in his chest that he frantically tries to apply pressure to. His gaze flicks across the alley and when I follow it, I find another body.

This one completely lifeless. My beer-pong opponent. Steve.

Jared's partner in crime.

Footsteps rustle at the street entrance, drawing my attention.

"God damn it, Claire, get out of here." I plead with her to go.

She rushes to my side, her eyes wide with shock.

Bram appears next, along with random onlookers.

"Someone call 9-1-1!" I say into the mass of them.

Jared's red lips part, and he tries to say something.

"What?" I lean in closer.

He whispers his final words and takes his last, dying breath.

"Holy shit, is he…?" Claire latches onto my arm.

I let go of Jared's dead body and slowly stand. I look from Jared to Steve, noting the now incredibly visible guns at both of their sides.

This was meant to look like a setup. Like a double homicide. It's clean, tidy, and has absolutely no strings connecting what happened in this alley to anyone else. The police will come and think it was just an unfortunate altercation where both parties ended up dead. The only people who will have any idea of the truth are already too deep under Franklin's control to say a damn thing. It's fucking clever, really, but scary as fuck. If Franklin can orchestrate something so simple yet elaborate, what else is he capable of?

And the sheer fact that he staged it to happen in the very place where the two of these guys beat and stole that package from me… Well, it's twistedly poetic. Plus, a huge fucking warning of what would have happened to me had I not been the one to have gotten it back to him.

Franklin was out for blood, one way or another.

35
CLAIRE

It's been days since we found Jared and Steve shot in that alley, and Johnny is still acting strange. He's on edge. And I can't say I blame him. Two of his coworkers—do you call fellow criminal errand boys that?—were killed in a staged murder scene in very close proximity to where we live, where we hang out, and where Johnny was beaten only a couple weeks prior.

It's traumatic, to say the least. I wish I knew how to help him process what he's going through.

He's been attending his classes, but I have a hunch that's only so he can keep an eye on me and make sure I'm safe. He's barely left my side except for when it's absolutely necessary. He even stays at the diner during my shifts and studies in the corner booth.

Bram had tried to give me some time off, but I insisted I'd rather get back to some kind of normalcy.

If I'm being completely honest, I felt slightly relieved seeing the two people who did what they did to Johnny bleeding out in that nasty alley. I can't speak for Steve, but Jared was no gift to humanity. After the run-ins I had with him, watching him die didn't faze me the way everyone acts like it should. Maybe that makes me a bad person, but it's hard to feel sorry for someone who thought my body was for his personal enjoyment.

I round the corner to the hallway and pop my head into Johnny's bedroom. "You want some coffee?"

He quickly grabs the lid to the box he's looking through and shoves it on top. "I—uh...yeah. That sounds good."

I grip the doorframe and narrow my gaze. "J. What's up?"

"Nothing." He picks the plain cardboard container off his mattress and pushes it under the bed with his foot.

I want to press, to ask him what he was doing, but he's been in a funk lately, and I don't want to make it any worse by prying.

I can't help but notice the distance forming between us that I would do anything to get rid of.

Johnny walks over, kisses my cheek, and pulls me toward the kitchen.

My phone buzzes, and I pull it out of my pocket.

Rosie: *Hey! I'm back, bitch!*

My East Coast bestie had been on an impromptu writing retreat, and I only managed to find that out when I called her mom when I hadn't heard from her. I tried getting ahold of her after the whole Griffin debacle, but she had already left with her writing class. I'm glad she went, I really am. Had I still been back home, I would have been on the same trip with her, living a semi-normal-ish life.

"Call her," Johnny says. "I'll go grab us lunch."

"You sure?" I study his expression fanatically, looking for any sign of disapproval.

"Yeah. I could use the fresh air."

Does he mean from me?

I glance at the time on my phone and back up at him. "Please be careful."

Johnny strolls over, and it's like everything else fades away and it's just us. He glides his thumb along my cheek. "Always." He presses his soft lips against mine briefly and snatches his wallet and keys from the counter.

The door closes and I'm left alone in his place. I shift my attention toward his room, and the strong urge to look under his bed creeps over me. But if he wanted me to know what was in there, he would have told me, and I refuse to invade his privacy just because of sheer curiosity.

I shake away the thought and focus on what I had planned on doing.

I bring up the text screen.

Me: *About damn time! Call me!*

But instead of a regular call, she FaceTimes me.

I answer it anyway.

Her beaming and beautiful face greets me on the other side. Rosie's blonde hair bobs and her eyeliner is done in a perfect cat's eye. "I missed you," she feigns sadness.

"Oh whatever, you didn't even tell me you were going! I heard it from your freaking mom." I laugh and sit on the stool in Johnny's kitchen.

"Speaking of moms, did yours redecorate?" She brings her phone closer to her face to look into my background. "There's a total bachelor pad vibe going on."

I roll my eyes. "No. I'm—uh…do you remember that guy I was telling you about? From my complex?"

"Super dreamy yet illusive dude?" She narrows her gaze and then covers her mouth when it finally clicks. "You're sleeping with hottie McBadBoy?"

"You're the worst. You know that, right?" I sigh and bite at the inside of my lip. "A lot has changed since you've been gone."

"I'll say," she huffs. "Enough about boring writer camp, what the hell is going on with you?" She flops down onto her bed.

And so, I tell her everything. How we sort of avoided each other for a little while but ended up being stuck together by our teacher and her tutoring thing. About Griffin and how he potentially tried to kill me, and how Johnny saved me but the cops don't know the truth. How Johnny isn't really bad at all, just super misunderstood in his quest to save everyone except himself. I left out the details of the very obvious criminal underground but mentioned he had some issues with his boss, and how his job can be a little dangerous at times. I tried to make sense of how despite everything, there's this insane connection between us, but it's not exactly the easiest thing to explain to someone who hasn't experienced it themselves.

"Which leads us here, right now, to me waiting in his kitchen while he goes to grab us food." A strange weight seems to lift from my shoulders at being able to talk to her about almost all of this.

"You both drink the same weird-ass coffee? I mean, how adorable is that." She lets out a chuckle but then her tone changes into something darker. "I'm really sorry, Claire, about not being there when the Griffin thing happened. I can't imagine what that was like."

"It's okay; I'm fine."

She shakes her head. "No. You can pretend with everyone else, but you don't have to fake it with me. That dude terrorized you. He never deserved you. You know that, don't you?"

It's nothing that Johnny hasn't already told me.

"Yeah," I say, although it's not very convincing.

"I'm serious. Whatever happens to him, that's his fault. You hear me? The universe has its way of balancing good and evil. He can rot in that hospital bed for all I care. Actually, for what he did to you, I should fly over there and finish him off myself." She sighs. "What's your dad think about all of this?"

"I haven't really talked to him. The data on his phone is outrageous. We've exchanged a few texts but not much else. He told me he was getting settled in and adjusting to life there. Asked how I was. I don't exactly want to spring this on him, you know? I don't want him to feel like it's his fault. He deserves this opportunity, and I'm not going to make him second-guess it."

If I had told him, he'd probably have hopped on the first flight out of there to come be with me. Maybe if I had to go through this alone I would have reached out to him, but I didn't. I had Johnny, and he's been my constant throughout this whole strange experience.

"Yeah...I suppose." She turns over on her bed and props herself up on her elbows. "But I'm sure he'd want to know. You were his whole world, Claire."

"Beth was here, I forgot to mention that part."

Rosie's eyes go wide. "Holy shit, that's huge. How did that go?"

I stand from the stool and stretch. "Fucking weird. She showed up at the hospital and basically hijacked me from the nurse. Brought me back here, and I barely spoke to her. I hid out in my room until Johnny came by and then we snuck out after she'd gone to bed. She left for a flight early the next morning and I haven't heard from her since."

"You're kidding me. Wow. Freaking mother of the year."

I snort. "I'm not surprised. I mean, look at her track record. But, hey, no more about me. What's going on with you? How was the writing thing? Was it magical? Did you meet any cute boys?"

Rosie flips over onto her back and lets out a long dramatic breath. "Overall, sure, it was okay."

I stare into the camera. "But...?"

"It was like a couples thing, dude. Everyone branched off, and I was stuck with some random chick who barely spoke to me the entire time. I swear, it was like a fucking reality TV show where all these attractive single people got paired off and we were the losers no one wanted."

"Um, you're talking about my best friend."

"Whatever." She seems to perk up. "Does Johnny have any

hot friends? Come on, it's pretty much in the water over there, right?"

She's not wrong, there are a decent number of good-looking people out here, but none of them have caught my eye the way Johnny has. I've barely even noticed anyone else since he bumped into my life. "He doesn't really have any friends." Unless you count the dude from the bar. "Well...except for this one guy."

"I can work with that, what's he look like?" Her eyes are bright and cheery, totally ready for me to describe her dream man.

"He's kind of old, Rose." It kills me to burst her bubble.

"Like, dad old?" She tilts her head to the side.

"No, not quite." I haven't even told her anything else, but she already seems back on board.

I'd never consider getting her involved with someone in Johnny's line of work though. I trust Johnny, but I know nothing about this other guy. Johnny's motives for joining Franklin are entirely selfless—for all I know, his *friend* could be in it because he wants to be. What kind of friend would I be if I allowed Rosie to get tangled up with that?

"Go on..." she insists.

I walk over to the window and peer outside. I've been on the call with Rosie long enough that Johnny should probably be on his way back by now. Unless Bram was busy, and the food took longer than usual. Still, though, my anxiety sets in anyway.

That's when I see him approaching the complex from the street.

The tension in my shoulders releases. I glance back at my screen. "He's probably thirty, seriously."

Rosie cups her chin with her thumb and index finger in a total thinking pose. "I'm totally down for an older dude. Would be a nice change of pace, ya know? What's he look like?"

I deadpan. "Really?"

"Yes! Come on, Claire-bear. Humor me."

"He's not bad, at all, actually." It takes me a second to recall the details. "He's huge. Six-foot-something. Broad shoulders, but like built. Not a douchey gym-build though. Umm, what else…a beard…I think he had long dark hair. And visible tattoos."

I focus back on Rosie and laugh when I see her mouth hanging open.

"I'm in love already." She clutches at her chest. "The fate of my beautiful future babies rides on you putting in a good word."

"You're out of your mind! I don't even know him." I turn to see what's taking Johnny so long and spot him still outside of the gate.

Only now, he's not alone. There's a woman with him. From the looks of it, a pretty one. She's touching his arm and nodding her head, agreeing with whatever it is that he's telling her. She glances up toward the complex and shifts to where her back is facing me. She leans in, giving Johnny a way too friendly hug, and kisses his cheek.

I try like hell to calm the rage that builds within me. I've never been the type to get jealous, but considering the uncertainty of our relationship, I'm feeling hella insecure right about now. Didn't I ask him if he was seeing someone else? I could have sworn he had told me he wasn't.

"Earth to Claire," Rosie speaks up loud enough to break through my trance.

I shake my head. "Sorry."

"Did you see a ghost? What the hell happened there?"

"Nothing, hey, Johnny's back with food. Talk later?" I have to at least attempt to process my emotions before his arrival.

"Yeah, sure. But seriously, get the deets on that guy."

"Okay," I tell her, even though I have no intention of doing so. We're over two thousand miles apart, what good would that do her anyway? "Love you."

"Love you, bestie."

We hang up, and not a second later, the door swings open and Johnny appears.

So much for gaining some composure.

"You all right?" Johnny asks me, immediately sensing something being off.

I nod and unclench my jaw. "I was just worried."

He comes over and plants his lips on the side of my face. "You don't need to worry about me."

This would be a perfect chance for him to tell me why he was late. To explain who the random gorgeous lady was that greeted him outside our building. To help me make sense of the hug and lingering kiss she left on his cheek.

Instead, he goes over to the counter and unpacks the bag of takeout food, like nothing strange happened at all. "How was your chat with Rosie?"

"Fine."

Johnny side-eyes me while he puts a burger on each of our plates. He puts the container of fries between them. "I wasn't sure if you wanted onion rings or not, so I got them, too."

"Thanks." I walk over and hop onto the stool. I unwrap the napkin-covered utensils and set them both to the side.

"Do you want ketchup?" he asks me.

"Sure."

He dumps the rest of the bag out, and a dozen packets flop onto the counter.

I force myself not to look at him in an attempt to not make eye contact. It's obvious that things have been different since what happened to Jared and Steve, but he's been secretive lately. With the box in the bedroom, and now the girl in the street. If he wanted me to know, he would tell me, and he clearly doesn't. I thought we were past the whole keeping secrets thing. Haven't we already been through enough together? Why does he feel like he can't be honest with me about whatever is going on?

Does he not trust me?

I eat half of my burger in silence, shoving the occasional fry in my mouth here and there. If I wasn't hungry, I would have already left, but hey, a girl's got to eat. I poke the screen on my phone to light it up and see the time.

"I'm gonna head to class." I point to the rest of my food. "Do you want this?"

"Claire." Johnny grabs my arm gently and forces me to face him. "What's wrong?"

I avert my gaze. "Nothing."

He puts a finger under my chin and tilts it up toward him. "I know when you're lying."

The second I look into his eyes, I completely lose the ability to ignore him. That freaking connection we have just tugs at my heartstrings.

"You're being distant." It's not the complete truth as to why I'm acting strange all of a sudden, but it's a start.

He nods as if he understands. "I have a lot on my mind right now."

Still doesn't specifically explain any of the weird behavior.

"So do I," I say defensively.

Johnny frowns and the fading cut on his lip reminds me of all he's been through these last few months. Prior to that, he was doing this all alone.

I can't help but think he'd rather go back to that than have to include me in his life. Maybe the newness has worn off and he's not interested in our relationship anymore. He did warn me like five billion times that I shouldn't get involved with him. Is this when he pulls the plug on us?

Tears well in my eyes, and I hate myself for the overwhelming emotions that I can't control. I've been bottling everything up and now, with the idea of losing the one thing I thought was completely solid, I'm not sure how to hold it together. I take a deep breath to steady myself.

"Claire," Johnny's voice softens, and he pulls me into his arms.

It's unexpected, especially with where my mind was taking me. Perhaps a pity hug?

"Hey, shh, what's going on with you?" Johnny pats my back and kisses the top of my head. "Talk to me."

"Are you breaking up with me?" I mumble into his shirt. "I mean…it's not like we're a couple or anything, but you know."

Johnny quickly breaks apart from me, holding me at an arm's length. "What? No, of course not. Why? Who said we weren't a couple?"

I shrug and sniffle.

He continues to grip onto me and stares into my eyes. "Claire. I am telling you right now, we are more together than together can get, okay? Unless *you* end things, someone is going to have to pry my cold dead hands from you."

My heart flutters at his declaration. "Really?"

"I swear it." His serious gaze bores into me, like he's trying to telepathically get me to understand how sure he is.

But if what he's saying is true, who was that outside?

"You don't believe me?" Johnny studies my reaction.

"I want to…" And before the Jared thing, I probably would have without hesitation.

"Is this about earlier?"

Finally, he's starting to put it together.

"I, uh. I was counting my money."

"Wait, what?"

He nods toward the direction of his bedroom. "That box. It's the cash I've made from my *situation*. Well, some of it. It's sort of stashed all over the house."

"Oh." That actually makes decent sense. I'd probably be weird about my illegal income, too. Considering the size of the box to that of what was in that package we recovered from Jared, Johnny must be loaded.

"Yeah. I'm sorry, I didn't mean to make you think I was hiding anything from you. It was just a knee-jerk reaction. I'm not really used to having someone know about *that* stuff yet." Johnny runs his hand along my cheek, wiping the remnants of my tears away.

I bite my lip, unsure of whether or not I should spit out the question hanging on the tip of my tongue. "There's nothing else?" More like, *no one* else.

Johnny sighs and weaves his fingers through his hair, brushing it out of his face.

"Who is she?" I blurt without giving it any more thought.

He tilts his head and his brows furrow. "What?"

"The girl, from downstairs." I force myself to remain calm despite the bubbling nerves wanting to take hold.

"Oh, Claire," he sighs. "That's what has you worked up? Christ." He clutches his chest and lets out a breath. "You had me freaking out there for a second. Whatever you think that was, you're wrong. That's Isabella."

Still not totally sure why she was kissing his cheek.

"Billy's aunt."

As in kid Billy from across the way?

"I'm working with her, that's part of the plan. I just haven't told anyone because I don't want it to get out and something go wrong."

This time, it's me that cocks my head to the side. "What?"

"You didn't really think I was going to work for Franklin forever, did you?"

"I mean, I hoped not."

Johnny repositions in his seat to face me. "The system is flawed. When Billy's parents died, he was placed with his abusive prick uncle. His aunt, who lives out of town, has been trying to get custody of him but obviously, there are all these formalities in place. There's a court hearing coming up, and I'm set to be a character witness. If all goes well, Billy's guardianship will change, and he'll finally be free of that asshole. That's why I get stressed about my involvement with the cops; I don't want my reputation to be tainted. The judge could dismiss my testimony."

"But you literally work for a criminal."

Johnny shakes his head. "Franklin would never incriminate himself; he's an idiot, but he's not dumb."

All the pieces of the puzzle finally fit into place. Everything Johnny has been doing has been for this bigger picture.

"And Izzy? She's like forty-something and overly grateful for what I've done for Billy. Downstairs, what you saw was her updating me on the hearing and thanking me for helping her. The attorney she's using has high hopes of getting it moved up in the next few weeks."

"You're kidding me! That's great, right?"

Johnny exhales. "Yeah. It's been a long time coming."

And suddenly, all of my doubts are erased, and I find myself in disbelief that I had any to begin with. My insecurities were nothing that Johnny had done, but everything to do with myself and the things that haunt my past. For once, I have someone in my life who actually cares about me and the people around him.

"I'm sorry for making something out of nothing," I tell him.

"No, I should have told you." Johnny takes my hand in his. "It's hard for me to accept that you're here—that we're in this together now."

I think of the time Johnny and I have shared, the battles we have faced, the obstacles we have overcome. Somehow, if we can just make it through a few more, it will be smooth sailing. We'll finally get to be a normal-ish couple.

An image of Griffin pops into my head. Him having his breathing tubes taken out, regaining consciousness, telling the cops exactly what happened. Johnny being confronted by the police and questioned about that night. His credibility being lost and the entire plan falling apart, Franklin maintaining a grip on Johnny for the rest of his life.

Only, there's no way in hell I'd allow that to happen. I have to do something—*anything*— to make sure Griffin never speaks again.

36
JOHNNY

A week goes by in a blur of pretending things are fine. At least with Claire and me, they're absolutely golden. Our dirty laundry has been aired, and there are no more secrets between us, threatening to rip us apart.

To the outside world, we seem like an adorable couple, when in reality, we're constantly looking over our shoulders, wondering when the shit will hit the fan.

We're in it together, though, and that's all that matters.

Franklin has resumed his normal behavior toward me, demanding my services at whatever point he deems necessary. There haven't been any setups or beatings, just me delivering random packages across the city and bringing home more cash to add to the stockpile I'm hoarding—my contingency plan if anything goes wrong.

Only now that Claire is involved, I'm not so sure how that will play out.

She's managed to help me bring all of my grades up to solid Bs, all while maintaining her perfect straight-A record. She's freaking amazing, if you ask me. I'm not sure I could have ever asked for a better partner in this fucked-up life of mine. And that's why I have the cheesiest date planned for her birthday tomorrow.

Her birthday that she has no idea I know about.

Luckily for me, her wallet was sitting out on the counter a few days ago, and I did a double-take when I noticed the date being so damn close.

I'm not at all surprised she didn't tell me, since she goes out of her way to not draw attention to herself. She deserves that attention though, and I refuse to sit back and not give it to her.

Plus, I'm really banking on the possibility of tomorrow night doubling as a celebration, considering the court date for Billy's custody hearing was officially moved up.

Everything is finally starting to fall into place exactly how I planned. There's this beaming bright light at the end of the tunnel, and I cannot freaking wait to jump through it with Claire at my side and Billy safe with his aunt.

There's some preliminary stuff that Isabella asked me to show up early for, so I'll be there most of the day, which will only make my evening with Claire that much sweeter.

I grab Claire's notebook from the dining room table to go over some last-minute English homework while she's in the shower. A few papers slip out, and I kneel down to gather them up and stuff them back inside.

I don't mean to, but my eyes skim over the contents of one, stopping my heart completely.

It's a scholarship award letter. From a school nowhere fucking close to here. In her hometown, actually. I shift my attention to the top of the page and notice the date is marked from last week. She's had this that long and hasn't said a word to me about it?

I let out a breath and glance down the hallway and toward the bedroom we share. I thought all of our secrets were out in the open, why would Claire hide this from me?

The only thing that I can assume is that she's going to take it but she doesn't know how to tell me? Does that mean she's leaving? Was that *her* plan all along? Was our relationship some means to an end, something to occupy her time while she was stuck out on the West Coast?

Suddenly, my entire world comes caving in. I'm finally at the finish line with this Billy situation, except when I cross it, I'll be doing it alone? I guess that's how I imagined it from the start, but Claire was what gave me hope that I would actually make it through.

I hear the water valve shut off in the bathroom, so I quickly shove the paper into the notebook and set it back onto the table. I don't want to play pretend, not with her, but for now, until she decides to tell me, that's what I'll have to do. There must be some reasonable explanation for keeping this to herself. After everything we've been through, I have to at least give her the benefit of the doubt.

Even if it does kill me to think she might leave.

Claire's best interest has always been a priority to me, and if her returning to the East Coast to finish her college career is what she believes is best for her, I have to allow that to happen. I won't control her the same way Griffin did. Never in a million years will I do what he did.

I found Claire in the wild, and I will do everything I can to help her remain that way.

She pokes her head around the corner. "Hey." Her hair is dripping, and she's in nothing but a towel.

I swallow down the butterflies that appear with just one look. "Hey."

Claire raises an eyebrow, a devious grin on her beautiful face. "We have time."

I glance at the clock on the far wall and then back at her. "Yeah, we do."

Now, though, with that secret letter, I'm worried it's limited.

I jump up from the couch and rush over to her, pushing my negative thoughts away. I won't dare ruin whatever moments I have left with her, because even if this is it, these few months have been the best thing to ever happen to me.

The happiness Claire so willingly gave me is enough to last a lifetime.

I grip her around the waist and pick her up off the floor.

She giggles and holds on tight while I take her into our room.

I toss her onto the bed and her towel unwraps, exposing her flawless naked body. I rip my T-shirt over my head and toss it to the ground.

Claire snakes her fingers along my bare chest and unbuttons my jeans, wasting no time in tugging them down and letting them fall to my ankles. She grabs my cock firmly in her hand and teases the tip of it with her mouth. Within seconds of her guiding me in deeper, she already has me wanting to bust. Her moan reverberates against me, sending a spike of pleasure coursing through me.

I pull myself out and softly shove her back onto the bed. I push her legs apart and crawl my way between them, leaving a hot trail from her knee all the way up to her inner thigh.

Her body tenses in response but she pivots herself closer to me.

I breathe in her sweet and delectable scent before giving in to what we both want. I wrap one arm up under her leg and pull her into my face. My tongue dances in circles along the outside until she grabs my head and pushes me into place. I smile and comply, savoring the taste of her. I use the hand under her to reach up and find her perky breast. The second I make contact, her body arches and she lets out a moan.

I move the other hand up her leg and tease her entrance with my finger before gliding it easily in.

"Johnny," she breathes.

I glance up to find her eyes closed and her head tilted back, her hands gripping the sheets firmly.

My cock throbs, desperately wanting to be inside her. But not yet. Not until I make her cum once first.

I slip another digit into her, gently inching them in and out while I lick and suck on her clit. I pay attention to every breath, every subtle cue. She tenses around me, so I arch my fingers upward and rub the soft spot that drives her wild every time. I bury my face into her and slow my pace, creating the perfect mix of pressure that sends her right over the edge and pulsating against my fingers and lips. I keep my hand in place and rock it back and forth through the duration of her orgasm, while I climb up from between her legs.

Claire grips my hair and drags me to her, pressing her mouth against mine. Her tongue slides in, clearly tasting herself in the process.

I pull my wet fingers out of her and she brings them between our lips, dipping them into her mouth and sucking on them. My erection grows, urging me to hurry the hell up.

Claire's already two steps ahead, grabbing the condom she had sitting nearby and ripping the wrapper off and securing it on me. She positions her body to give me access.

I slowly enter her, savoring the sensation of her tightness around me. I let out a breath and bring my mouth to her neck, kissing all the way up to her lips. I thrust my hips back and forth while she digs her fingers across my back, pulling me further into her.

Her soft noises are enough to wreck me.

I wrap my arm around her waist and flip over onto my back, bringing her on top of me.

She grins against my mouth and grinds herself up and down along my shaft. Claire straightens herself, giving me the best fucking view I've ever seen of her tight body.

I run my hands along her torso and grab onto her tits,

thrusting myself into her and matching her pace. I weave my hands into her hair and drag her face down onto mine, kissing her deeply and feeling her tighten around me in anticipation of her second climax. I grip her ass, my fingers near her folds, and rock her toward me.

The buildup is intense, our bodies inching closer and closer at the same time. My pleasure is heightened by hers in this chaotic symphony of ecstasy. I've never had this kind of sexual chemistry with another person in my entire life.

Claire's pussy grips my cock and pulsates around it, sending me spiraling into my own climax in tandem with her.

I pump into her, slowing each thrust to prolong the sensation rippling through both of us.

We continue to kiss as if our mouths aren't quite done with the exchange.

She breaks away, resting her forehead against mine. "We're getting good at that."

I exhale and drop my arms to the side. "I'd say we're naturals."

Claire slides me out of her and plops down next to me, her elbow holding her up while she stares in my direction. "I haven't had sex like this before."

I turn my head to face her. "Me either." And it's the God's honest truth.

"Really?" She narrows her gaze. "Because you totally act like you know what you're doing."

I laugh. "So do you."

"True." She giggles too and leans over to kiss my cheek. "We're going to be late." Claire hops up from the bed and goes over to a pile of clean clothes near the closet.

I lay there, watching her get dressed, cherishing every single ounce of time I have left with her just in case it's my last.

"Take a picture, it'll last longer." She steps into her jean shorts and buttons them.

It's like she was reading my mind. I clench my jaw and think of what I really want to say to her but never will.

Please don't leave.

37
CLAIRE

Today is my birthday, and I refuse to tell anyone.

I've never been a huge fan of them. The whole not having a mom thing made it a little weird. Don't get me wrong, my dad did his best to throw me age-appropriate parties, but it got to the point where he was just overcompensating for her absence and it made things weird. After a while, I convinced him I was too old for the stuff he had planned, and that I would celebrate with my friends.

He seemed relieved, honestly. Like it was this burden he wasn't sure how to tackle, and me finally pulling the plug meant he was off the hook. I didn't resent him for it—truthfully, I was glad to have the attention shifted away from me.

Johnny wraps his arms around my waist. "You want to celebrate at Bram's tonight?"

It takes me a second to realize what the heck he's talking about. "Of course." I hold onto him even though I have to let him go soon if he stands any chance of getting to the courthouse on time.

A wave of pride courses over me at seeing him so damn close to the finish line he's sacrificed almost too much for. He put his entire life on the back burner to save an innocent kid and to protect his future. It's noble, honorable, and totally selfless. This cruel world doesn't deserve a man like Johnny.

Hell, I'm incredibly grateful he decided to pay me any notice.

"I'm gonna miss you." Johnny hugs me tighter and kisses my face. "You sure you're going to be okay?"

"I'll be fine." I pry him away from me. "Text me when you get there, all right?"

Johnny sighs and releases me, stepping back to smooth out his dark gray dress shirt.

I step forward and adjust his tie. "You look handsome."

He runs his hand through his hair, further proving my point. Johnny is hands-down one of the most gorgeous humans I've ever laid my eyes on. Something about that dark hair that makes his piercing green eyes really pop. Plus the simple fact that I'm absolutely enamored by him.

"You studying while I'm gone?" Johnny slides his wallet into his back pocket.

I nod. "Yep." It's not a complete lie, but it's not the whole truth.

There's something that's been nagging me for a while now, and with Johnny occupied with the custody hearing, I'm finally presented with the opportunity to follow through with my idea.

"Okay...call me if you need me?" Johnny hesitates by the front door.

"Of course." I open it for him. "Now get this over with so we can have celebratory pancakes for dinner later."

Johnny's lips part like he's going to say something, and for a slight second, I think it's going to be those three words I'm dying to hear. Instead, he replies, "Deal."

I lean against the door while he walks down the stairs and through the courtyard. As far as we know, Billy's uncle has no idea that Johnny is going to be a witness in their hearing today, and since it's not for another few hours, he shouldn't put it together, even if he does see Johnny leaving the building.

The plan has been perfectly executed, and now, all that's left is to win.

Although, I think it was such a pipedream that Johnny really hasn't mentioned what happens next. I'm not totally sure he knows.

Once Johnny is outside the complex, I make my way over to his couch. I fumble through the notebooks on the table and slide out the paper I've been keeping from him.

The acceptance letter for the scholarship I was desperate to get. The one that will allow me to return to the East Coast and finish college in my hometown, where I always planned to go.

Only now, everything has changed.

I've changed.

If I told him, he'd insist that I go. I'm not sure he'd take no for an answer. And the thought of leaving Johnny behind is almost too much to bear. I couldn't imagine asking him to uproot his life and come with me, which leaves only one viable option: I forfeit the prize and give it to the runner-up. Meaning I stay here, with him.

My education would be covered by my egg-donor mom's job, and if I remain living here, my expenses wouldn't be more than I could handle. I could keep my part-time gig at Bram's and potentially pursue intern options in the area to figure out which path to take for my career.

I could make sure Johnny finishes his degree and does something with his life other than what he's doing now. Rosie could visit, and I could save up and see her on breaks. She'd love it here, with the warm weather and much bigger pool of single guys.

It wasn't what I envisioned my life to be like, but sometimes, paths shift to make way for better options.

I push the paper back inside and toss the notebook onto the

table. My decision is made, and there's no reason to involve anyone other than me and the scholarship board. Monday morning, I'll inform them of my choice to decline the offer.

In the meantime, other pressing matters need my attention, something that I have firmly set my mind to and refuse to tell a soul about.

If I'm going to make it there and back on foot, I need to get a move on it.

The walk is refreshing, considering Johnny and I have spent a lot of our days outside of classes cooped up in the house either studying or having incredible sex. Don't get me wrong, I'm not complaining, but sometimes a little alone time with some fresh air does the body good.

Part of me thought that the fifteen-minute trek across town would clear my head, maybe knock some sense into me, but if anything, it solidified my rationale. I cannot continue to sit by and do nothing about what happened.

Today is my birthday, and there are only a few things I truly want, one of them being potentially in my control.

The automatic doors greet me, opening wide to grant me access. I go straight through the main entrance and turn to go down the long hall. The lights buzz and various machines beep in the background. I don't bother stopping to ask for approval or directions. There's something about faking confidence that really makes people not think twice about a random person being where they potentially shouldn't be.

I follow the signs posted and have no trouble locating the exact place I'm looking for. Ladies in various colored scrubs float by me and pay no mind to my being here.

I scan the last names written on dry erase boards outside the patient rooms until I find him.

Thomas, G.

Stepping into his sterile space, I'm welcomed by the computer screens beeping and recording Griffin's vitals. There are IVs hooked to him and cords running all over.

My chest tightens and the room seems to shrink in on me.

I walk closer, my shadow casting a darkness over him. It's strange for the roles to be reversed, him being the vulnerable one for a change. For so long, it's been him towering over me, controlling me, keeping his thumb pressed tightly against every single thing I did. It was subtle at first, and it came across like sweet thoughtful gestures that tricked me into thinking he cared. When in reality, it was all part of his sick game.

And I wasn't the first person he had done it to.

Griffin never mentioned the police reports and charges filed against him. Probably because he paid to have the victims drop them so he could pretend nothing ever happened and move on to his next target.

I take in the blond hair matted to his forehead. At one point, I was attracted to him, but now, all I can feel is disgust.

How is it possible he was able to convince so many people he was good? How did he become such a master manipulator?

"You stole a part of me I'll never get back," I whisper to his barely hanging on body. "My innocence. You duped me, Griff. You mentally beat me down until I had no choice but to cling to whatever you gave me. You tricked me into thinking I wasn't good enough. That what we had was normal, healthy." I shake my head. "You convinced me that love was this painful thing—that to get it, I had to sacrifice everything I was. You hurt me in ways I don't think I'll ever fully wrap my head around. You were this cruel and twisted part of my life, draining my soul with each second we were together."

He remains there, unmoving, unfazed by my truth.

"You tortured me, Griffin. And it's going to take me a long time to recover from everything you did. But I'll be damned if I ever allow you to control me ever again. Today is the day the dynamic shifts. It's my turn." I reach into my pocket, settling on the hard plastic. My way to guarantee he never lays a hand on me.

I glance over my shoulder at the closed door. There are no windows, no sign of outside life other than the faint noise of people passing by. Only me, Griffin, and the decision I've already made.

With Johnny at the court hearing, Griffin is no longer a threat to him. Don't get me wrong, I'd do absolutely anything for Johnny, but this? This is for me.

My heart picks up its pace, but I'm not sure if it's nerves or uncertainty or the power I finally have over this sick fuck boy.

I lean over, my silhouette consuming him. I steal a tissue from the holder next to the bed, and inch my hand forward. Using my knuckle, I prop his mouth open in the slightest. I spin the cap off the unassuming bottle and take one final breath.

I half-expect a wave of something to come over me. For my conscience to alert me that I'm making a terrible mistake. But that doesn't come. If anything, there's a surge of reassurance that I'm doing what needs to be done to confirm I'm the last person Griffin will ever hurt.

I tilt the bottle, allowing a few drops to fall onto Griffin's inner lip. I inch his head up and drain what's left of the container into his mouth, careful not to let any spill out. I keep hold of his chin while the liquid absorbs and use my free hand to secure the bottle safely into my pocket.

The Dateline episode I watched a year ago didn't really give specifics on a fatal dosage or how quickly it worked, probably for liability reasons. But I recall without a doubt how incredibly lethal this everyday item was, and when I saw it, sitting there plain as day in my mom's medicine cabinet, I knew what I had to do.

I relax my grip on his face and let him return to how I found him, only now, a deadly dose of tetrahydrozoline is seeping into his body. Completely undetectable on a normal toxicology report.

I crumble the tissue and shove it in alongside the bottle. "Goodbye, Griffin."

Without giving him another second, I turn my back on Griffin for what I hope will be the last time. A newfound power builds within me as I reassure myself that everything is going to be okay now.

38
JOHNNY

I practically skip home, the insane invigoration of winning coursing through me. I wasn't sure if it would happen, but it fucking did, and for once, I feel like everything I've done was finally worth something. The sleepless nights. The beatings. The risky illegal errands and the pushing everyone away.

Isabella was granted full custody of Billy, starting immediately. They didn't even bother going to his uncle's place to grab his few belongings. She wanted to get him as far away from that psycho as possible. And I don't blame her.

Billy had hugged me tight, tears streaming down his innocent face when the outcome was declared. "Thank you," he had said.

It was only two words, but it meant so much to know that I had helped him—I had saved him from a life he might never escape from if he got in too deep.

"Will you tell Claire bye for me?" Billy wiped his cheeks and sniffled. "I really like her."

I gripped his shoulders and smiled. "Me too, buddy, me too." I ruffled the hair on his head. "I'll let her know."

That memory will be engraved in my mind for all time.

Not much is better than putting your blood, sweat, and tears into something and it finally paying off. It just goes to show that hard work and determination can sometimes overcome insane obstacles.

I push away the recollection of Billy's uncle's hard stare as I walked out of that courtroom.

He was pissed, but at that point, there was not a damn thing he could do about it.

I'm working for Franklin, still being their bitch boy, so the fate of Billy's homelife shouldn't matter to them anymore. They got what they wanted—someone young and corruptible—me.

I punch my keycode into the gate and rush through the courtyard and up the steps. Excitement bubbles out of me and all I can think about is sharing it with the one person who means the most to me.

Claire jumps when I burst through the front door. She clutches her chest and laughs. "You scared the shit out of me."

"Sorry." I yank my tie down on my way over to her, a massive grin spread across my face. "We freaking did it."

Claire's mouth drops open and her eyes go wide. "Really?" She hops up and wraps her arms around me. "I'm so proud of you."

I spin her around in a circle and kiss all over her head. "Yes. It's done. He's already gone. Izzy took him straight from the courthouse." I carefully set her down and stare into her eyes. "He's safe."

She presses her lips to mine, and for once, everything feels right in the world.

Well, except I haven't fully come up with my exit plan.

Plus, there's a strong possibility that Claire has made the decision to leave me and return to her life back east.

But other than that, I'm fucking bubbling with happiness at

the way things are falling into place. And I refuse to allow anything to ruin this day.

"Let me get changed." I sweep her hair out of her face and tuck it behind her ear.

There's something different about her, a sort of glint in her eye I hadn't noticed until now. Maybe it's because she's feeling the same way I am about the overcoming of obstacles in our way.

"You hungry?" I glance at her on my way to the bedroom.

Claire smiles and nods. "I'll put this stuff away while you get ready." She shuffles through papers and stacks them onto the dining room table where she was sitting doing her schoolwork.

It doesn't take either of us long to get everything in order to leave.

I'm relieved when we step outside that the sun is already setting, paving the path for my cheesy evening.

She makes for the stairs, but I grip her hand firmly in mine and tug her down the hall.

"Pit-stop first," I tell her. I had wanted this to be the last thing we did tonight, but I can't wait any longer. The anticipation is killing me.

Claire narrows her gaze. "What are you up to?"

I bring her knuckles up to my lips and kiss them. "Do you trust me?"

"Of course." She follows along without asking any other questions.

I open up the door to the rooftop access and we climb the steps to the top.

Orange and pink light shines across Claire's flawless face, highlighting every impeccable feature. I fight the urge to stop and stare and lead her to the edge of the building.

Like the other time we were up here, I go over and grab the plank I had hidden against the building. One by one we cross over onto the other side and ascend the metal ladder to go even higher.

Once at the top, I tell her, "Close your eyes."

She rolls them first, but then complies. She bites at her lip while she waits for me to complete my surprise.

Not a minute later, I guide her over. "You can open."

Claire blinks, taking in the sight of a blanket laid out with rose petals flitting around the edges. It's not perfect, but the look on her face tells me that it is to her.

"Johnny," she breathes. "It's beautiful."

The sun dips under the horizon, and from here, we have the best view in the entire city. My original plan was to come up after dinner, when the sky was already asleep, but this worked out too well for me to not adjust my timeline.

Claire comes closer, her fingers trailing my cheek. "I love it."

I help her sit on the blanket and join her to bask in the beautiful masterpiece dancing across the sky.

A moment goes by and I break the silence. "There was something else."

She turns to face me, a hint of curiosity lining her features. "Yeah?"

"I, um..."

Come on, Johnny, get it together.

"The other day, you had mentioned being unsure of where we stood."

Claire opens her mouth to interject but I cut her off.

"I'm sorry I hadn't already made that clear." I place my hand on top of hers, allowing the warmth of her skin to calm me. "These last few months with you have been incredible, Claire. Truly. I really don't know if I would have gotten through all of this without you. Hell," I let out a breath. "I'm sure of it."

Her cheeks blush.

"So," I clear my throat. "I would like to take this moment to ask you, Claire Cooper, would you do me the great honor of officially allowing me to be your boyfriend?"

There are a few different directions this could go. She could say no. Confess to receiving that scholarship and break the news that she's going home. Or it could have nothing to do with that at all and she could just not be interested in a relationship with me.

Instead, my doubts are erased when a huge smile breaks across her face and she laughs.

I swear if there was some way to bottle that sound, it could cure cancer.

Claire leans over and kisses me through her giggles.

"Should I take that as a yes?"

"A million times over! Yes!" She climbs on my lap and continues running her hands through my hair and dragging her lips into mine.

Claire reaches down and pulls her shirt over her head, tossing it onto the blanket. She grins and does the same to mine.

This wasn't exactly the reaction I was expecting, but I won't deny that it's better for sure.

I slide my hands up her thighs and unbutton her shorts, dragging them over her ass.

She stands enough to slide completely out of them, and then straddles me. Claire licks and sucks on my neck while pulling my dick out of my pants.

I fumble to get a condom out of my wallet, something I've been sure to keep handy now that the sexual tension between us is at a staggering all-time high.

Claire doesn't waste another second. She slides herself down, inching me inside of her and immediately finding her groove.

I wrap my arms around her petite body, holding her tightly against my chest and rocking my hips up and down to match her rhythm.

We climb the mountain together, but I hold off, wanting to make sure she's pleased first.

"Don't," Claire breathes out against my lips. "Do it with me." She tightens around me.

I grip her waist and in one swift motion, flip her over onto her back and continue thrusting on top of her. I keep the movements slow and deep, driving her closer and closer to the edge.

Her nails dig into my skin, begging for me to give her more.

The night sky casts a stunning glow across her golden skin. For a second, I'm completely lost in her beauty.

Claire's body arches, angling up toward me.

My hands find hers, pinning them above her head while our explosive orgasms consume us both at the exact time.

She trembles as I decrease my speed and stretch her climax out.

I had planned on seducing her with my bad dance moves later, turning on some romantic music and slow dancing in the kitchen and then giving her a world-class birthday orgasm at home, but hell, the night is young, leaving room for plenty more celebratory sex tonight.

39
CLAIRE

This day couldn't be any more perfect.

Johnny's plan of saving Billy totally worked.

I may or may not have fatally poisoned my abusive ex.

My dream man asked me to be his girlfriend and followed it up with an earth-shattering orgasm on the rooftop overlooking the most magical sunset I've ever witnessed.

And now, we're at one of my favorite places, finishing off a massive stack of pancakes together.

"Hey." Johnny reaches across the table and looks into my eyes. "Promise me you won't be mad?"

"What?" His question throws me for a loop.

"Just promise."

"Fine, what did you do?"

It's then that I notice Bram approaching in my peripheral and everyone in the diner breaks into song.

"Happy birthday, to you..."

I turn back to Johnny, my eyes wide and my cheeks turning twelve shades redder.

"You promised," he whispers in between lyrics. "Happy

birthday, to *my girlfriend*," Johnny adds in place of my name. "Happy birthday, to you."

Bram beams and sets the plate with the blueberry old-fashioned down onto the table. "Happy birthday, Claire. Make a wish."

I glance at the lit candle, and then at Johnny. In this moment, what else could a girl want? I already have everything I could ever hope for.

Except, there is one thing.

I suck in a breath and blow out the flame, hoping like hell my wish comes true. There's only one more piece of the puzzle that needs to fall into place before Johnny and I can truly be free.

"Thank you," I tell Bram.

He grips my shoulder and smiles. "You have no idea how hard it was to ignore you this morning when you came in for coffee." Bram laughs. "I'm the worst with surprises."

"I thought you were acting weird." I poke my head around and wave at the cook, Carlos, before he makes his way back to the kitchen.

"And by the way, we've got your shift covered tomorrow, so no need to come in. Stay up all night doing whatever it is you kids do nowadays. Enjoy yourself." Bram grabs the empty plates from our table.

I glance at Johnny, a few ideas of how we could occupy our newfound time coming to mind.

He winks in response, and my heart nearly flutters out of my chest.

Yeah, tonight really is perfect.

I split my donut in half and give Johnny the other side. "How'd you know?"

"You leave your wallet on the counter." He breaks off a chunk of his and pops it into his mouth. "Good thing I pay attention to the details."

How can such a random thing turn me on?

I grin and shake my head. "I really thought I'd sneak it past you."

His expression shifts slightly. "Can't hide anything from me."

Suddenly, I don't think he's referring to my date of birth.

Johnny fidgets with his napkin. "When do you leave?"

"For where?" I nervously ask him.

He reaches back across the table to take my hand in his. "I get it." Johnny nods. "I really do."

"I'm not going anywhere, J," I tell him, straight-faced.

"Claire...come on, I saw the letter. I just wish you would have told me."

"Johnny, listen to me." I squeeze my fingers around his to help him understand how serious I am. "I didn't tell you because I knew you'd want me to go. I've already made my mind up. I'm staying here, with you."

He blinks at me like he's seen a ghost. "What?"

I stare into his radiant green eyes. "I'm going to tell the board on Monday to give the scholarship to someone else."

"But I don't understand. You worked so hard for this. I thought that's what you wanted."

"Home," I throw extra emphasis on the word. "That is what I've been after this whole time. Anywhere with you is exactly where I want to be."

Johnny sighs and runs his hand through his hair, leaning back into his side of the booth. "I've been holding my breath since I found that paper, scared to death you were going to leave."

"Nope. You're stuck with me, remember?" I cross my arms over my chest. "You second-guessing asking me to be your girlfriend now?"

He laughs. "Not in a million years." Johnny pulls out his wallet and lays a few bills on the table. "Let's get out of here."

I hop up and slide my arm around his as we make our way out of the diner.

A weight is lifted from my shoulders now that we have that out in the open.

Johnny kisses my temple and slides his hand down to grip mine.

Suddenly, there's nothing except me and him and this endless flow of happiness between us. Six months ago, I'd never have believed my life would end up like this.

We walk in tandem, smiling at each other like the love-drunk fools we are back to our complex.

A woman bumps into my shoulder, sending me stumbling into reality.

"Sorry," I tell her as she's offering me her own apology.

Apparently, we were both in our own little zone.

"I'm thinking popcorn and movie in bed," Johnny says while side-stepping another person on the sidewalk.

"That sounds great." I grip his arm and glance up at him.

A loud crack sounds, and Johnny's expression shifts to something of shock, fear, and confusion. Everything happens in a blur, our imperfectly-perfect world-shattering with the reverberation of a gunshot.

I lower my gaze to Johnny's torso, frantically hoping my imagination is playing tricks on me. That the figure who appeared from the dark alley didn't just do what I think he did.

Johnny drops to his knees and I fall to the ground with him.

"Oh God," I manage to spit out.

"Claire." Johnny holds his hands tightly to the seeping wound. His stare is weak but serious.

I apply what pressure I can. "No." I shake my head, tears falling down my cheeks.

"I..." He pants a little. "I need you to know..."

"No. Not like this. Don't you dare do it like this." I bring him closer to my chest to support his weight from settling onto the dirty ground.

"I love you, Claire." A bit of blood appears on his lips, and his body goes slack.

"No, no, no, Johnny!" I frantically plead with him. "Don't do this. No. Please, don't. Stay with me. You can't leave me."

But it's no use, he's already gone.

I turn toward the gathering crowd, desperate for someone to do something. "Help," I scream. "Someone help." My voice fades as my own will to live leaves me.

There's this old saying, about how when you die, your whole life flashes before you, but no one ever tells you what it's like to watch the light leave the eyes of the man you love. To see every ounce of strength wash away until you're left with nothing. I thought everything I had been through up to this point was a lot to handle, but not a damn thing could have ever prepared me for this.

For losing him.

It wasn't memories of the past that came—they were all of our potential future. Every single thing we never got to do. Stolen kisses in the rain. Shows we'd watch. The mornings I'd wake up next to him, or in his arms. We had so much left to do. All of it was gone.

I knew we had a long road ahead to figure out all the details, but I thought we had more time.

40
CLAIRE

Today is the first day since I've been here on the West Coast that it rained.

And it seems fitting, as I stand here wearing a solid black dress, next to Bram, watching Johnny's casket being lowered into the ground.

Nothing could have prepared me for this moment.

I wasn't sure if I'd cry or scream or be completely numb.

I guess I'm all of them. My soul is yelling at the top of its lungs to turn back the clock, to give me a second chance to change the events that played out. To try to reshape this reality that I'm currently living.

Silent tears cascade down my face, and my heart aches fiercely.

Bram wraps his arm around my shoulder and gives it a firm shake. "You're going to get through this. I promise."

But how can he be so sure?

The last few days have been utter chaos, making all of the arrangements.

I was supposed to be planning my future with Johnny, not organizing his funeral.

There weren't many calls to make, considering Johnny had no parents and his only close relative is currently stationed overseas.

A blacked-out SUV pulls along the lane and stops near us.

Josey appears from the driver's side and walks over to us.

Anger boils up inside of me.

"How dare you?" I yell and slap him across the face.

He takes the hit and wraps his arms around me while I pound my fists into his chest.

"How could you let this happen?" I blubber through my tears.

"I'm so sorry," he genuinely replies.

Bram tries to pry me away from Josey.

I keep hitting Josey, like my brain somehow thinks I can fix things this way.

"Come on, let me get you home." Bram finally breaks my hold and I stagger back.

I shake my head and sniffle. The rain picks up and my hair becomes matted to my cheeks. "I can't..." I drop to my knees beside the hole in the ground where Johnny's casket now lays.

The image of Johnny's lifeless body bleeding out in my arms is something that will haunt me for the rest of my life.

How can I ever move on from this?

My heart aches, being torn apart by everything that's happened.

"Let me help." Josey's large hands grip my shoulders in an attempt to raise me.

I flinch. "Don't you dare touch me. You've done enough."

"You heard her," Bram warns while coming between us.

"I'm sorry, I never meant for this to happen." Josey frantically tries to make me understand.

I shake my head, but before I can give him an earful, Bram interjects.

"What's done is done. I think it's best we go our separate ways now."

I numbly allow Bram to guide me to his old pickup truck and slide into the passenger seat. I wipe at my face and glance at myself in the side-view mirror. My mascara is streaked, and my hair is completely wild and unruly.

Bram climbs into the other side. "One day at a time, okay?"

I bite at my lip. "Yeah."

The drive into town is quiet, leaving me too much time alone with my thoughts. I replay the last few days over and over in my head, wondering if there was anything I could have done differently.

We pass Bram's diner, and I'm reminded of one of the many things I'll be giving up.

Bram cuts the engine in front of my complex. "Are you sure leaving is the best option?" he asks me once we're both out of his truck.

I nod. "I can't stay here, you know. It hurts too much."

"I understand." Bram sighs heavily. "It's not going to be the same around here, kid."

I wrap my arms around him and hug him tight. In such a short period, Bram has become this monumental person in my life. I don't want to walk away from him, but I have no other choice.

"Keep in touch?" Bram grips my shoulders firmly.

"Yeah." I walk away from him, punching my code into the keypad of my mom's building for what might be the last time. I stroll across the courtyard, remembering that moment from months ago that set off a chain of events I never could have imagined.

I climb the steps where Johnny had saved me from Griffin's grasp.

I pause, glancing toward Johnny's door one last time. So

many memories in such a short period. My heart aches, but I know I need to leave.

I unlock Beth's place and slide the key off my chain and lay it on the counter. Taking my final glance around, I grab onto the remaining piece of luggage I have yet to put in the car.

I pull the handle and say goodbye to my temporary home.

Without bothering to change my clothes or fix my makeup, I make my way down the hall and into the doorway that leads to the underground parking garage under my mom's complex.

I click the button on the bright red BMW and add my bag to the others in the trunk. I could have flown back to the East Coast, but I thought the drive would be good to clear my head and come up with a plan.

Luckily, my mom didn't seem bothered at all to offer her car up for me to take. I guess she's better at grand gestures than the little things. Regardless, I'm thankful for it.

I climb into the driver seat and push the button to start the engine. It roars to life, and I shift it into reverse to back out of the parking spot.

A few minutes later, I merge onto the interstate, glancing in the rearview mirror and watching the city that changed me become smaller and smaller the further I drive away.

"How was it?" His voice is soft but jagged.

I sigh, a mixture of relief and nerves coursing through me. "Terrible, you try going to my funeral and tell me how you like it. I slapped Josey."

He laughs, which only makes him cough. "Think they bought it?"

I shrug and look over my shoulder at the beautifully broken boy laying in the back seat. "I sure hope so."

Johnny holds the bandage wrapped around his torso and smiles. "Me too."

There are so many uncertainties left dangling that could threaten to break us. Franklin finding out Johnny faked his death being a huge one, and the whole me poisoning Griffin thing being another.

But even if the world comes crashing down tomorrow, at least we'll be together.

I don't believe in much, but I believe in us.

PART II

41
JOHNNY

I shouldn't be alive.

But by whatever fucking miracle, I am.

At one point, I truly believed I was dying. And that memory will forever be burned into my mind.

Claire held me in her arms, sobs rippling through her. I couldn't get the bleeding to stop, and despite the pain and numbness taking turns assaulting me, the only thing I could think about was leaving her behind.

That alone killed me in its own way.

In what I thought was my final moment, I uttered the words I needed her to hear.

That I loved her.

It wasn't really how I planned her birthday to go, but there was no way I was going to depart from this world without making sure she knew how I felt.

Luckily, our story didn't end there.

At least for us, it didn't. To almost everyone on the West Coast, I died in the street that brisk fall evening, in front of Bram's diner.

Tragically, poetically, and randomly.

I'd be lying if I said a part of that wasn't true. Because I did die that day. Claire and I both did. A traumatic situation will do that to a person. Break you down and mold you into another version of yourself. A darker one. One that you cannot come back from.

My shooter was never found.

The cops chalked it up to a robbery gone wrong, but there's no denying it was Franklin's doing.

From the moment I stepped foot into Franklin's world, he had been searching for a way to get rid of me. He knew I wasn't like the others. That I wasn't corruptible enough to turn into the minion he expected of me. I was obedient, but only to an extent. My goal was always to free Billy from his grasp and then make my own way out.

I was good, he was evil.

And he knew it.

The only way to ensure I would no longer do his business any damage was to take me out completely. He started with Steve and Jared—staging their double homicide—and followed it up with my incident. Franklin cleaned his slate of the mess I made and didn't think twice about the casualties that piled up in his wake.

Franklin is cruel and ruthless.

Getting away from him was my only chance of survival, especially now that Claire's involved. I couldn't risk putting her in any more danger than I already had. If anything, Franklin did me a huge fucking favor by setting the first piece in place.

I had been struggling to figure out how to make a proper exit from his clutches, and aside from it nearly killing me, it was the exact thing I needed to set everything in motion.

I put that life behind me the second the opportunity presented itself.

Josey crosses my mind from time to time. I wish I could have told him the truth. That I didn't actually meet my demise that day. But if I had, it could have ruined the whole plan. I needed him to believe I was dead if I wanted Franklin to buy the story, too. Josey had been such a brother to me, but I couldn't take that risk with the odds already stacked against me.

Claire played her part well, convincing everyone around her that she was grieving the loss of her boyfriend. I don't entirely buy that her performance was fabricated, given how emotional she was throughout the entire thing. I can only imagine how horrible it was to witness everything play out from her point of view. It was as though she bottled her anger and rage toward Franklin and channeled it into what everyone saw on the outside.

Hell, she even smacked Josey, which only made the entire thing that much more realistic.

"Hey," Claire calls out from the entrance of the bathroom.

My heart skips a beat, reminding me I am very much alive, and she is still an angel gracing me with her presence.

A towel clings to her wet body, and her dark hair cascades down both sides of her beautiful face.

"Hi." I sit on our new couch in complete and utter awe of her. It's like no matter how much time passes, I still can't believe she picked me. After everything we've been through, she's here.

It's been a rocky road, but we've traversed it together.

Claire's already flushed from the shower cheeks redden even more. She shakes her head. "We're already late, don't even think about it."

I grin and run my hand along my scalp, the hair prickling my fingertips. I haven't quite gotten used to the fact that my hair is short now. A potentially necessary change given the circumstances. "Come on, what's another fifteen minutes?"

She ruffles her head with a towel. "That's what you said earlier. I have to draw the line somewhere." Claire smiles and continues. "We won't be gone long. Just enough to watch the ball drop and do the *happy New Year* crap."

"You sure it's a good idea?"

"Rose said it's low-key. Her and a few friends. Remember Holland and Pax? They'll be there. We have to practice being *normal* if we're ever going to properly return to society."

She's not wrong. We've been here almost two months and we only leave the apartment when it's necessary. I keep waiting for something to go wrong. A sign that our plan failed, that Franklin found us and he's going to finish what he started. But weeks have gone by, and nothing has happened. Life really has been relatively mundane. So much so that Claire starts her second semester of college in a few days.

"No social media?" I ask her. It was something we agreed to when forming our escape plan. I can't risk my face accidentally being in a frame and Franklin finding out I'm still alive.

"Nope. There's a strict 'phone in bowl when you walk in the door' policy."

Claire's longtime best friend, Rosie, is mostly on a need-to-know basis for our unusual situation. She was the only person on the East Coast that knew of my existence, and considering her role in Claire's life, we had to come up with something. To her, I'm Johnny, but to everyone else here, I'm Theo.

Coined from my middle name, compliments of Claire.

It complicates things, but it's better than the alternative. I couldn't be Johnny anymore, at least not in the public eye. Not until I knew for sure that we were safe, and Franklin was a person from our past.

Although, I have no idea how or even if that will ever be possible.

He's a powerful man and will stop at nothing to fulfill his twisted desires.

"Did you get the mail earlier?" Claire snaps me out of my trance.

I plant my hands on my thighs and stand from the couch. "Nope. But I will now." I glance at my watch. "You better hurry."

"Thanks, babe." Claire goes back into the bathroom.

We've gotten into the habit of using cheesy pet names because it's much easier to remember than my own. There have been a few times she's slipped up and called me Johnny, but it's managed to go unnoticed by outsiders.

It's not ideal, to live this hidden life, but it's what makes sense for now until the dust has settled. I haven't even fully recovered from the gunshot wound and the surgery that followed; I certainly haven't had the time to mentally prepare for a war against Franklin if he manages to find out I duped him.

Claire has already sacrificed so much to be with me. I owe it to her to play along and attempt to bring some level of normalcy back to our lives.

I step into the crisp air and instantly regret not grabbing my jacket on the way out. The mailboxes aren't too far of a walk, but considering I was born and raised out west, I've never really known a true winter. I actually hadn't seen snow in person until a few weeks ago. It's sort of mesmerizing to witness, each little flake gently sprinkling down from the sky and slowly accumulating into a frigid, white wonderland.

My body shivers and each breath spouts out another small, misty cloud as my boots slosh through the mess of slush in front of the large community mailbox. Between the mail-forwarding service and the winter storm we had last Monday, mail has been running slower than usual. I slide our key into our lock and pull out the stacks of envelopes. I thumb through them, looking for the one Claire is anxious to receive.

Her scholarship information.

The financial aspect of our relocation has been difficult for her to process. Despite reassuring her that I can cover all of our expenses, she's still adamant about making sure the funds go through. Even after all of our moving costs, I could still pay her tuition ten times over if I needed to. Getting her to understand that, though, is a challenge in itself.

I assume part of it is because she's fiercely independent. She doesn't want to have to rely on someone else. Claire prefers to pull her own weight and handle things herself. And honestly, I admire that about her. That she's ambitious and self-sufficient—fully capable of handling pretty much whatever is thrown her way.

She's a badass, really.

But we're in this together, and I would have never made it this far without her. Pitching in and helping monetarily is the very least I could do. I owe her my life.

A slip of paper tucked between our water bill and a piece of spam mail catches my eye. There is no stamp, no return address, just a folded white sheet. I glance over my shoulder, the weight of eyes suddenly on me despite being completely alone.

I should crumple it up, toss it in the recycling, and not give it another thought.

Instead, I do the thing that I somehow know with certainty is going to change everything.

I open it up.

Red ink stares back at me, probably chosen for its dramatic effect.

Thought you could hide from me?

Suddenly, I'm not cold anymore.

My jaw tenses, and I clench the note in my fist. This is exactly what I had been worried about all these weeks, and part of me thought that maybe I had fooled him. That I had escaped his deadly grip.

Fear washes over me and my attention settles on our little apartment up ahead, with the one person who means the most to me tucked inside.

I slide my phone out of my pocket and scroll until I find the number I'm looking for. I scan the texts, noting the last few responses.

Since I've been on the East Coast, I've maintained one trusted contact back home. Someone to keep an eye on Franklin in case he leaves. He has many people working for him, but at this point, I think I've pissed him off enough that he would finish the job himself if given the chance. And that's why I keep tabs on his whereabouts, in case I need to make a move of my own.

His note could mean several things. It's possible that he only got wind of our relationship and has decided to provoke her. Maybe he wants to see if it can flush me out; his note could be a scare tactic to figure out whether or not I survived his attack. Or, he very well could know the truth of the situation and this could have been meant for me. He's such a sick fuck that there's a chance he could believe I'm dead but somehow *still* want to ruin me even after I'm gone.

Whatever his intentions, he's aware of Claire's whereabouts, and that alone is a big issue.

Tomorrow, I will start looking for another apartment, I'll switch our mail over to a post office box, and I'll do everything I can to ensure Claire's safety while allowing her to somewhat get back to her life. The cold air cools my raging nerves as I shove the message into my pocket and walk toward our apparently very temporary home.

"Anything important?" Claire asks me once I'm inside. She's changed into a dark green oversized sweater and black leggings. I swear that girl would look sexy wearing a paper bag.

I swallow down the truth and greet her with a lie. "Just some bills."

Her face drops and she nods. "Maybe this week."

I cross the space between us and tip her chin up to look at

me. “It’s going to come, okay? And even if it doesn’t, we’re going to be fine. No matter what happens.”

She bites at her lip. “Yeah.”

“We’re stuck with each other, remember?” Using the words she’s used on me many times, I wink at her. I still have no fucking clue how I got lucky enough to be with Claire, but I treat each day as a blessing—especially considering my close call with death, an experience I hope I don’t have to physically relive for a very long time.

Claire stands on her tiptoes and presses her lips gently to mine. “Good.”

Every kiss feels like the first with her, sending a swarm of butterflies through me. I keep wondering if that will ever go away, but with her, I wouldn’t be surprised if it lasts forever.

My only hope is that she experiences it, too.

The love and happiness she brings me is what keeps me going. What makes me believe that despite our fucked-up situation, as long as we’re together, we’ll be fine.

We will make it through.

Even with the looming note burning a hole in my pocket.

42
CLAIRE — ALMOST TWO MONTHS AGO

I've never been in more pain in my entire life.

My heart rips wide open watching the light leave Johnny's eyes and the blood pool around our bodies.

I scream for help, but I don't think anyone hears me.

I hold his body to my chest, begging him not to go. His last three words are a twisted lullaby I will never forget. If only there was a way to switch places with him. To sacrifice myself instead of him. I'd give anything, do anything, to give him a second chance at life.

Hands find my shoulders. Large ones. They threaten to tear me away from him, but I won't go. I can't. Not yet.

"Claire." Bram's voice finally comes through. He's frantic, for obvious reasons. He kneels next to us and applies pressure to Johnny's seeping wound. "Help is on the way."

I don't dare look up at Bram. If I take my eyes off Johnny, he might disappear forever.

Sirens appear in the distance and grow louder with their approach.

Tears roll down my cheek and onto the only man I've ever truly fallen in love with.

In a few months' time, Johnny had shown me more kindness and compassion than I thought possible. He respected me and taught me what love between two people was actually supposed to feel like. In a way, he repaired the damage done by my past with each gentle and thoughtful thing he had done. He gave me hope that the world wasn't really a terrible place like it seemed.

But watching such a terrible thing happen to such a great person, I'm not so sure anymore.

Johnny didn't deserve this.

After everything he's given up, his story should not have ended here.

How am I supposed to go on without him?

"Clear the way!" someone shouts.

A moment later, paramedics are in front of me. "What happened?"

Bram speaks up. "Gunshot wound to the abdomen."

"Ma'am, we're going to need you to let go."

I blink and Johnny is out of my grasp, lying on a stretcher, blood all over him. I reach out like I can somehow magnetically bring him back to me.

They do their work on the move, taking him further and further away from me.

I snap out of my shock and hop up from the dirty ground, rushing behind them.

An older man holds his arm out. "Family only."

Shock rattles my core. They didn't seem to care when it was Griffin; why do they all of a sudden have rules now?"

"I—I." My mouth seems to fail at forming a sentence.

"She is family," Bram says from beside me.

When did he get there?

"Are you his father?" asks the medic while climbing into the big flashing vehicle.

"No, but she—"

The guy cuts Bram off by slamming the door shut.

The air leaves my chest, and I find myself unable to breathe. "No," is all I manage to get out. This can't be it. He can't be gone.

I take off toward the medic, my arm extended to grab onto the door latch. I can't let them take him from me.

The brake lights illuminate, and it lurches away from me.

I call out, this time louder. "No, wait!"

Bram grabs me by the shoulders. "Come on, I'll drive." He turns me toward the entrance of the diner, where people are scattered about, staring at us.

I follow him over to the old truck and hop into the passenger seat without another thought. Once inside, I feel the invisible thread connecting me and Johnny being pulled apart.

I desperately bite at the inside of my cheek to stop the overwhelming wave of emotions threatening to completely ruin me.

Bram wastes no time turning over the engine and rushing out of the parking spot to catch up to the ambulance. The tires squeal, but he isn't bothered. He blows through a red light and cuts through traffic to place us right behind them.

A few agonizing minutes later, we pull up to the emergency room as Johnny is carted out of the back and brought into the hospital. I barely wait for Bram to stop his truck before I jump out and rush toward them.

Bram is at my side within seconds.

Machines beep. Automatic doors open. Other people in the medical field come rushing over to ask questions and start their assessment.

"Caucasian male, approximately twenty years old, gunshot wound. BP dropping."

I get stopped by two women in front of a set of doors. "You can't go back there."

I stand tall to glance through the small window and note the words *surgery* and *critical condition* that float back to me.

"Where are they taking him?" I blurt out.

The lady in the obnoxiously bright polka-dot-covered

scrubs says, "You can wait in the third-floor waiting room." She points across the way. "Elevator is to your left up ahead."

Bram places his hand on my back and leads me toward it without saying a word.

We rush over, despite knowing we have a long road ahead of us until we get any news on Johnny's condition.

I cling to the little bit of hope that he will make it through this. He has to.

We step into the elevator and an elderly woman holding herself up with a cane stares at us.

I go to the opposite side and glance down at my body. I'm covered in Johnny's blood and I can feel the hair that is matted to my cheeks from my tears. To her, I probably look like I just stepped out of a horror movie scene.

Bram and I get off at floor three and go into the empty waiting room.

"They're not going to tell us anything." I settle into a seat in the corner and pick at my thumb. I turn to him and finally meet his gaze. "Will you say you're his dad? Please?" I barely get the words out without choking on the sob that bubbles up.

Bram nods without hesitation. "Absolutely."

The tiniest bit of relief washes over me. It's not much, but at least now we won't completely be in the dark with what's going on with Johnny.

"Claire," Bram speaks quietly. "This wasn't an accident, was it?"

I clench my jaw. Johnny's done everything possible to make sure Bram was left out of this side of his world, but now, how can I lie to him given the circumstances? Doesn't Bram deserve to know a portion of the truth?

"No, it wasn't."

Bram runs his hand through his salt and pepper hair. "That's what I thought."

I expect him to ask more questions, but instead, he stays

quiet, like he's processing the little bit of information I just gave him.

Each passing minute is a vice being tightened around my heart. I flinch at every nurse or doctor that walks by, thinking it's going to be an update on Johnny.

A couple hours go by with no news. I hang tightly to the idea that he's still alive, because I cannot face a reality where he isn't.

"Do you want coffee?" Bram asks me. His features are riddled with nervous energy.

I nod, although there's nothing I truly want beyond Johnny.

In this same hospital is the man I visited earlier, the one that doesn't deserve the life left in him. Is this some kind of karmic balance for what I did to Griffin? Is what happened to Johnny somehow my fault because I was foolish enough to think I could poison Griffin and get away with it?

I'm not sure how long I'm lost in my own thoughts when Bram appears in front of me with a paper cup in his hand. "He's out of surgery."

I swear I feel my heart stutter in my chest. "What?"

"The doctor caught me on my way back. He's in recovery. The bullet missed all his major organs. Said Johnny must have had a guardian angel looking out for him. We can go back, but he's not awake yet. It could take a few hours before he's alert."

His words sink in one by one. The world seems to stop spinning. He's alive. Johnny is alive. By some fucking miracle, Franklin's plan failed.

Fresh tears roll down my cheeks. I rise to my feet; it's like a huge weight has been lifted off my shoulders. "Where is he?"

"This way." Bram leads me through a set of double doors and across a long hall. He pauses in front of a room and motions for me to enter.

I step inside, and all of my fears are quickly erased when my sights land on that beautiful, broken boy lying on the bed. The machines beep, telling me that he's very much still alive. That the world might not be as cruel as I had thought.

I silently thank the universe for sparing his life.

I'm at his side in an instant, gripping his hand in mine, but careful not to disturb him too much. A strong part of me wants to throw my arms around him and hold him tightly, kissing him all over and basking in the fact that he's here. I rein myself in, though, and settle for the comforting embrace of our fingers touching.

Bram pushes a chair forward for me. "Here."

I turn to him and swipe at the tears that won't seem to stop rolling down my cheeks. "He's alive."

Bram pulls me in for a hug.

I bury myself in his chest and put my arms around him.

"Everything is going to be okay," Bram reassures me.

And despite things being completely fucked up, knowing that Johnny made it through the impossible is enough to give me hope that Bram might be right.

"What do you need me to do? Can I get you guys a change of clothes?"

I wipe at my face and take a deep breath. I'm still covered in Johnny's blood and the debris from basically laying on the dirty street. I glance over to Johnny, sighing at just how young and vulnerable he appears. Rage tingles up my spine at the people responsible for putting him in this position. I shove it down—I can't focus on that right now. Not while things are in limbo.

Johnny may have escaped death tonight, but that doesn't mean he's in the clear just yet.

"Yeah, clothes would be good. I have an overnight bag already packed at Johnny's place. It's sitting on the couch in the living room. You'll have to grab his stuff, though. The gray sweatpants on the corner of his bed are his favorite. Maybe get his toothbrush, too. I'm sure he'll want to brush his teeth." I fumble in my pocket and pull out my keys. I slide the one

Johnny had given me off and hand it to Bram. "Oh, my access code, to the building—six two one three."

Bram nods his head with each one of my requests like he's taking an order at the diner. "Got it. Anything else?"

"No, that should be it." I glance over at Johnny and then back to Bram. "Thank you."

Bram leaves us behind, and I settle into the chair he had pulled up for me. I take Johnny's hand in mine and bring it to my lips. I press them gently along his skin and close my eyes, grateful for the warmth of life left in him.

I don't know what I would have done if I lost Johnny. A darkness creeps to the surface at the possibility. A version of me that would have stopped at nothing to make Franklin and his whole organization pay for what they had unfairly taken. It's still there, just simmering under the surface, partially at ease since Johnny really did make it through such a brutal attack.

I lay my head next to his thigh and hold his palm against my face, savoring the calmness his touch brings me. I imagine his fingers grazing my skin, his thumb doing that thing along my cheek that he always does.

Only, I'm not imagining it at all, it's real.

"Is that coffee I smell?" His voice is barely a whisper, cracking with each word spoken.

I can't help but break into a huge smile, tears streaming down despite having cried more than I thought humanly possible.

"Hey...it can't be that bad, right?" He grins and then winces, clutching his side in the process. "That feels terrible."

"Are you okay?"

Johnny reaches for me. "Come here."

I stand from the chair and approach him hesitantly. I don't want to cause him any more pain than he's already in.

He grabs my face with his hand, gripping it firmly while eyeing me over. "Are *you* okay?"

Leave it to Johnny to be concerned with someone else even though he's the one lying in the hospital bed, a true testament to how selfless he is.

"I am now." I smooth his hair off of his brow. "I thought I lost you."

He shakes his head. "Can't get rid of me that easily." Johnny pulls me toward him, gently kissing my lips.

I'll never quite get used to the feeling I get with him. It's a mixture of bliss and the best possible high. It's euphoric and unlike anything I've ever known.

"Is it any good?" He points to the paper cup I had forgotten all about.

I shrug. "Not sure." I grab onto it and take a sip. "It's pretty gross."

"Let me try." He takes it from me and brings it to his mouth. "Smells burnt."

The door to the room opens and a round-faced nurse holding a chart walks in. "You're awake, that's great." She looks at me. "Could we have a few moments alone?"

I don't mean to, but I squeeze Johnny's hand. The idea of not being with him is almost too much to handle. I just got him back, and now I have to leave again? What if something happens while I'm gone?

Johnny tightens his grip on me, too. "It'll be okay. I'm not going anywhere, unless it's to get a better cup of joe." He holds out the cup for me to take. "I promise."

Painfully, I walk away and out of the room, each step a twisted knife to my heart. I lean against the wall and lower myself to the ground, pulling my knees to my chest and holding them tightly. I refuse to cry anymore, even though the combination of everything going on is overwhelming. I have to be strong, if not for me, for Johnny.

There's the sound of footsteps, and when I glance up, Bram picks up his pace.

"Did something happen?" His eyes widen.

I rise to my feet. "No. Everything is okay. There's a nurse in there. She wanted privacy."

Relief washes over him. "Oh. Okay."

A second later, the same woman steps out. "You're good to go back in. I just gave him a dose of pain medicine, though, so he might not be awake too much longer." She points inside. "There are blankets in the cabinet, and you're more than welcome to use the facilities."

She must be referring to the fact that I'm covered in blood from head to toe.

"Thanks," I tell her.

Bram and I enter the room, each of us taking a side of the bed.

"You had us worried, kid," Bram tells Johnny.

"Sorry, old man." His voice is slurring.

"Everything go okay?" I nod toward the door where the nurse just exited.

Johnny nods. "Yeah, she wanted to make sure I was in a *safe environment,* since I got shot and all."

Bram sets a bag and a drink carrier on the table attached to Johnny's bed and hands me the overnight bag that I had asked for.

"Oh man, is that *real* coffee?" Johnny glances over at the paper cup on the other table. "That shit is gross."

I grin at him. "Told you."

"Yeah, it was pretty bad. Figured I wouldn't torture you any more than you already have been." Bram opens the bag. "Donuts, too. But I'm not sure if you're allowed to have either."

Johnny fumbles through his drugged-up state to snatch the sack and pull one out. "I almost died. I think they can make an exception." He pops the lid on one of the cups to let it cool.

With each thing he does, I feel the weight continue to be

lifted from my chest. The burden of thinking I had lost him nearly crushed me completely.

"Does anyone else know I made it?" Johnny asks us with a curious look on his face.

I tilt my head at him. "I've been here the whole time."

Bram adds, "I snuck in while everyone was busy. Didn't talk to anyone at the diner."

"What are the chances they actually think I'm dead?"

"Well, considering I was convinced until I heard the medic say your blood pressure was low, I'd assume they're pretty high." I hate recalling this entire nightmare.

"Why?" Bram meets Johnny's gaze.

With the most serious of expressions, Johnny blurts out, "We're going to fake my death."

"What can I do?" Bram stares at Johnny with the same intensity.

43
JOHNNY — NOW

It's difficult to pretend everything is fine when things could quite literally explode at any moment.

From the second this entire elaborate plan was put in motion, I've been looking over my shoulder nonstop.

I was a fool for thinking I could outrun him.

Franklin Sharp, the man with eyes everywhere.

How did I think a nobody like me could evade him?

"Here." Pax shoves a red cup toward me, and the golden liquid sloshes around.

I take it from him gratefully and down the contents in one motion. I wipe my lips and mutter, "Thanks."

Pax gawks at me with his beady eyes. He's been weird around me since the moment we met, but it's hard to blame him, considering he's known Claire for years and I'm a newcomer to the group.

She and I have been nothing but secrets and evasion, so it only makes sense to be skeptical of the random dude recovering from "appendicitis" surgery. I doubt the gunshot wound would have gone over very well, not to mention, it would have drawn too much unwanted attention to the truth of our double life.

were we supposed to know that Pax's brother had the surgery only a year ago? The recovery is fresh in his memory, alerting him to all the inconsistencies between the two.

Holland comes over and wraps her arm around Pax's shoulder. "How's my ginger friend doing?" Her words slur with the excess alcohol flooding through her. She blinks up at him and sways her body in a weak attempt to stand still.

He sighs and holds onto her in an attempt to keep her from falling down. "Hol. You're officially cut off." Pax carts her over to the couch and helps her sit. "You need water."

I turn my attention to the gorgeous girl across the room, the one with bright blue eyes and an ass to die for. I run my hand through my short hair, a habit I'm going to have to break. Another piece of the past I should put behind me.

I wink at Claire and she blushes in response, sending my heart galloping out of my chest.

Rosie rises from her seat and grabs the remote to the television, clicking the button to turn the volume up. "Thirty seconds!"

The small crowd gathers around. A few faces I'm familiar with, but the rest are friends of Claire's friends I've met but forgotten their names.

Slowly, like it's only me and Claire left in the universe, I make my way over to her, our gazes glued to each other the entire way.

"Ten…nine…" The old man on the screen counts down.

My hand finds her cheek, resting gently along her flawless face. I breathe her in and savor just how lucky I am to have her here with me now. "I love you, Claire Cooper."

"Two…one…"

Claire smiles and pulls me toward her, pressing her soft lips against mine as people in the room erupt into cheers for the New Year.

Our mouths dance together in a heated frenzy that has me wishing we really were the only ones around. Over the past few months, the chemistry between us has managed to keep growing despite being at an all-time high. I didn't realize it was possible to be *this* damn attracted to someone. But I guess when you completely fall for someone, the way Claire and I have, it makes sense.

You would think the shit that we've been through would have torn us apart by now, but it's somehow made us stronger. There isn't a person I trust more in the world than the girl standing in front of me. And if I had to wager, I'd say she feels the same about me. That's why we work so well—we can count on one another. That's something neither one of us has really known before. Safety, security, the predictability of having someone in your corner looking out for you and actually giving a fuck.

It's refreshing to finally have someone truly care.

Claire breaks away and leans her forehead against mine. She keeps her voice low. "I love you, Johnny Jones."

"Happy New Year!" Rosie calls out while gripping me and Claire both by the shoulder. She's had her fair share of booze tonight, but it's safe to say she can handle her liquor much better than Holland can.

"Happy New Year," I tell her.

Rosie was always the wildcard with our situation. The bond that she and Claire have runs deep, and there was no way she wouldn't be included in our future together. But managing what bits of information we gave her was like maneuvering through a minefield. Somehow, she did the impossible and surprised the hell out of me when she totally went along with the hidden identity thing. She didn't miss a beat in switching from calling me Johnny to Theo and, to this day, hasn't questioned us or slipped up on any of the details.

It's a lot to put on a person, especially without giving them the entire story.

But Claire and Rosie have something special. And because Rosie trusted Claire, and Claire trusted me, we built this circle of confidence in each other.

Plus, I really think having her friend somewhat know what's going on has helped Claire overcome the extremes of everything that has happened. I can't imagine how rattled Claire must have felt, given the insane things that have happened in the last six months of her life.

Not only did she have to move across the country to live with her estranged mother, in a completely foreign place, but she had to sever ties with an abusive ex, nearly get killed, get wrapped up in the mess of my life, only to move *again* while trying to protect my identity from a sick and twisted criminal mastermind. Plus, all the details in between, like the shit with Jared, thinking I died, and balancing her school life.

Claire is a freaking saint.

She slips her hand into mine and holds on tight.

"So, Theo," Pax says.

I accidentally hesitate but end up looking at him. "Yeah?" I watch his freckled face and wait for whatever is about to come out of his mouth.

He's easily a few inches taller than me, but I could probably take him if I had to.

I hate that things have resorted to me sizing other people up, *just in case.* This world has taught me that you can never be too sure about who will or won't turn on you.

"You're not starting classes this week with the rest of us?" Pax pushes up the sleeves to his navy shirt, revealing ink on both arms.

"Nope."

"Why not?"

What's with the twenty questions?

Claire speaks up. "He's taking some time off."

Pax takes a swig of his beer. "I think the man can speak for himself, right?" He tips the cup up, drinking the rest and then crushing it in his hand. He tosses it into the trash can a few feet to his left.

Is that supposed to somehow intimidate me?

"I'm taking some time off," I repeat Claire's words.

She tightens her grip on me.

Pax points to my stomach. "To recover."

"Sure." If that's what he wants to tell himself, then so be it.

This dude has some keen intuition alerting him that *something* isn't quite accurate in my story. It's hard to be mad at him, but it could very well ruin everything if he uncovers the truth.

I can't start school with Claire because I haven't gotten my fake I.D. yet. And without it, I can't exactly register for classes. Going about normal daily activities under an alias is difficult enough, but bypassing college registration is a whole other hurdle.

I'd give anything to be there, to continue my education, and most of all, keep an eye on Claire, especially with the new information that's presented itself tonight. But I can't. Not yet. Not until I have more pieces put in place.

And not while I'm trying to figure out how in the hell I'm going to end this thing with Franklin once and for all. I should have known that faking my death would be step one, not the final move. If I'm going to do this, I have to see everything through and find a way to sever ties completely.

Now that Claire's location has been compromised, the matter becomes that much more pressing. I cannot allow him to use her as a pawn in his twisted game.

"I think it's great," Rosie chimes in. "I'm considering taking a semester off, too."

Her lie is so good it even fools Claire.

"What?" Claire's eyes go wide. "Bitch, you better not."

Rosie winks at me and then shrugs nonchalantly. "People do

it all the time."

Pax keeps his sights trained on me for an extra few seconds before taking the bait and diverting his attention to Rosie.

I'm really going to owe that girl one when this is all said and done.

"Me too," Holland mumbles from the couch. She throws her arm into the air and rolls onto the floor with a thud. "Ow."

Pax sighs and picks her up, throwing her over his shoulder. "This one has had enough. I'm going to take her home."

The way he easily tosses her around makes me second-guess whether or not I actually stand a chance against him. Maybe it's best if I don't find out. I either need to avoid him or get him on my good side if I'm going to keep my secrets hidden.

He says his goodbyes and carries Holland through the front door, disappearing into the night.

"Are those two a couple?" I ask Claire when I realize I've never actually seen them hold hands or kiss, but they're always together.

Claire and Rosie laugh at the same time.

"They've been best friends since kindergarten," Claire tells me.

Rosie adds, "Meaning, they're in love, they just don't know it yet. We know it. Everyone knows it. But for some fucking reason, they're still absolutely unaware."

I raise my head slowly. "Ohh. That explains it." I shift the focus of the conversation. "Thanks for the save."

Claire darts her attention to me and then Rosie.

"Hey, what are friends for?" Rosie takes a sip from her cup.

"Wait, you're not actually contemplating taking time off?"

Rosie rolls her eyes and grabs Claire's wrist. "And miss a moment with you? Are you crazy?"

And it may only be a tiny fraction of relief, but at least I know that even if I'm not there, Claire will have Rosie there looking out for her.

44
CLAIRE

Johnny has been acting strange. But I'm not sure if it's a normal strange, or a new strange.

Clearly, life has been a bit weird since the whole *faking his death* thing.

If I had to guess, he's feeling a bit off since I'm starting classes today and he won't be there. I can only imagine how difficult it is for him to not be able to watch over me. But we have to move on from the darkness of our past if we stand any chance of making it through this.

We've been in my hometown for nearly two months, and nothing has happened. No sign of Franklin or his goonies. No indication that he's aware of what we did to escape him. No threats or dangers looming around us. Just normal, everyday life. Well, as normal as we allow.

And part of our plan was for me to go back to school. Because that's the "reason" why I'm here on the East Coast, to return to the college I wanted to go to, with the scholarship I worked my ass off for. Only, the paperwork still hasn't arrived, and Johnny is actually covering my tuition this semester. Something I very much did not want to happen.

He insisted, though, and continues to reassure me that it's not a big deal for him to cover it. Between all of the expenses we've incurred during our escape, he has to be running low on funds, right? How is it possible he managed to save that much money while working for Franklin?

We've moved into three different apartments, and he even bought a used car. He put it in my name, since he can't exactly use his. Johnny hasn't thought twice about the cash he's spending, and he doesn't seem to be stopping anytime soon. He isn't out buying pointless stuff, but even our necessities have to be adding up.

Johnny brings my hand to his lips and brushes my knuckles against them. "Let me know if you need me? I can be there in a second."

I can sense how nervous he is to let me go. At least one of the perks of our latest move is that it puts our new house within two blocks of the university. Johnny insists that I drive the little Volkswagen, but he'll be within walking distance if anything goes wrong. Another selling point of this unit is the gated entry and the fire escape access on the backside. It hasn't been easy to find what Johnny was looking for while making sure we could do month-to-month cash payments. Living under the radar poses its challenges, but he's done a damn good job making it all work.

"I will." I pull out my phone and show it to him. "Fully charged." I bring it toward me to let the facial recognition unlock the screen. I poke around until I find what I'm looking for. "And you have my location at all times." I zoom out and point to a few spots. "I'll be in this area the first few hours. Then this for the rest. I think the parking lot is here."

He sighs and bites at the inside of his lip.

I wish there was something more I could do to ease his nerves, like tucking him into my back pocket and letting him come with me for the day. I wouldn't mind it, really, having him around. But with things still so up in the air, we're trying to limit his public appearances. A little more time needs to pass and then *maybe* we'll feel safer.

For now, though, I need to keep up my own kind of appearances by being a normal person my age and following through with the plan of going to school.

I slide Johnny's fleece-lined denim jacket over my sweatshirt and toss my backpack over my shoulder. "You sure you're okay with me wearing this?"

His lip turns up in the corner. "Yeah. You look adorable." Johnny grabs my cheeks in his hands and kisses my mouth.

I'd be lying if I said I wasn't missing the heat of the sunny West Coast. I hadn't been there long, but damn if I didn't get used to that nonstop warmth, the ability to wear shorts and T-shirts, and the constantly beaming sun. In my time there, it had only rained once—the day of Johnny's fake funeral. It was fitting, really, totally setting the mood for our master plan. But other than that, it was bright and sunny and nothing like this winter doom and gloom it's been replaced by.

Don't get me wrong, the first day it snowed here, it was glorious. The look on Johnny's face was priceless. But once the newness wore off, and the messy slush replaced the bright white wonderland, I started crossing my fingers that the stupid groundhog won't see his shadow next month. A girl can still hope for an early spring.

I drive the short distance to school, making sure to avoid all of the new potholes created by the snowplows. I pull into my designated spot and put the car into park. Because I'm sure he's already stressed out, I send Johnny a quick text.

Me: *I made it. Miss you already xo*

Johnny: *Miss you more. Be safe walking to class.*

I swipe over to Rosie.

Me: *You here yet?*

Rosie: *I see you!!!*

I turn and look all around me until I spot her coming toward me. She's wearing a dark green sweatshirt and her golden blonde hair is in a neat ponytail, bobbing with each step she takes. There's a huge smile across her face, and it makes me feel a little less alone without having Johnny here with me.

"I'm so excited," she squeals when she opens my door.

I jump out and grab my bag, clicking the button on the key fob to lock the car. "Just like it was always supposed to be." I weave my arm through hers, and we take off toward the main building.

So much has changed since Rosie and I originally planned to go here. Six months ago, I was dating Griffin, held under his thumb and living a completely different version of my life, one that seems completely foreign when I reflect on it. Now, I'm stronger, broken down but somehow built up to a newer, better Claire. One that I don't think would have been possible without Johnny. He gave me the strength to find my inner power and overcome the shit life decided to throw my way. He helped shape me into the woman I am today.

Johnny gives me something I've never had before—a choice. A voice. The freedom to be me without judgment and concern that I won't be accepted.

All Griffin wanted to do was bring me down.

It's been weeks since I did what had to be done, and I'm still not sure what the outcome was. It's not exactly like I can call and ask if he's alive. I have to wait it out and see what happens. And then hope like hell I don't get caught.

There's a very real chance that poisoning Griffin did not work, but there's still a chance it did. Either way, I will keep that secret with me to the grave. Johnny has loved me through so much, but could he handle knowing I killed someone, and that I did it intentionally?

That might be too much for anyone to bear.

I wouldn't blame him for seeing me as a monster, but I'm not sure that's a reality I'm willing to face. What if I lose him? When I followed through with poisoning Griffin, I was trying to put him in the past. I wanted to sever ties with him and stop allowing him from controlling my life. But little did I know, there's no escaping someone who has their claws *that* deeply sunk into you.

"I've heard this creative writing class is the *bomb*." Rosie puts a little extra flair on that last word. "Hey." She glances over at me. "You okay?"

I nod and lie. "Yeah." I didn't realize being away from Johnny would be this…uncomfortable. We've been together nonstop for the past few months, aside from errands here and there, so spending *hours* away at school day after day will be the longest we've been apart. Maybe if we hadn't been through such traumatic shit, I wouldn't feel this way, but we have, and pretending to be a normal college kid is weirder than I thought it was going to be.

"Ah, you and JJ." She glances around. "Sorry, *Theo*." Rosie grips me tighter. "Makes sense. But listen, I'll be with you, so you aren't alone."

What if it's not me I'm worried about? What if it's Johnny? I have Rosie, and I get to at least play the part of a functioning person in society. Johnny is stuck all cooped up in our apartment worried sick that something will happen to me, or someone will come for him. There has to be *some* way to give him his life back so he's not constantly afraid of endless possibilities.

We walk into the classroom and go toward the back. I haven't been in such a crowded space since everything went down, so choosing a seat where I can keep my eyes on everyone puts me a little at ease. From here, I have a clear view of the door, too. Although, given there is only one exit, I'll have to get creative if something were to happen.

Is that what life is going to be like now? Constantly looking for a way out? Thinking everyone around me is a potential suspect? Until Franklin, I was naive to the world around me. I thought the shit that I witnessed first-hand was only stuff they made up in the movies. Witnessing Jared and Steve bleed out in that alley by Bram's, and Johnny getting shot not too long after, made me realize just how cruel people really can be.

Everything that Jared had done to me aside, did he and Steve really deserve to be shot and left for dead? They were someone's children, friends, maybe significant other. With all the time I've spent with Johnny, I know damn well that he never deserved the endless beatings and the near-death experience. Who gave Franklin the right to play God? To end someone's life because they inconvenienced him?

I guess at the end of the day, I'm not much better than him, considering what I did to Griffin.

But if anyone should be cowering in hiding, it should be me, not Johnny. He's given up so much and for what? To live in constant fear? How is that fair?

"You okay?" Rosie asks me.

I snap out of my trance and bob my head up and down. "Yeah, sorry, zoned out." I unzip my bag and pull a notebook out. If I'm going to be here, I might as well pay attention. I won't allow Johnny's hard-earned blood money to go to waste.

"Welcome," the curly-headed, middle-aged man at the front of the room says. "I'm Professor Adkins. If you're here with us now, please note that you are in Advanced Creative Writing. Course number 301.

A few students fumble with their bags and exit through that one door.

Our teacher lets out a chuckle. "Happens every time." He leans against his desk and scans the rest of us.

Rosie kicks my foot from under the table, drawing my attention. She raises her brows and cocks her head over at the professor.

"No," I mouth and shake my head.

She juts out her bottom lip. "Why not?"

"One," I whisper. "That's totally unprofessional, two, he's *old.*"

Rosie sighs. "Fine."

"You can grab your kits on the way out when class is dismissed." Professor Adkins crosses his arms. "Anyone have any questions about that?"

Shit. I have no idea what he said. Kits for what? This isn't exactly the best way to start my first class. Maybe taking some of my classes with Rosie was a bad idea after all. It's fun, that's for sure, but it's hella distracting, too.

"Great." He grabs a stack of papers from his desk and distributes them to the front of the class, mumbling something to the students and getting them to pass the pages back. "As you'll see, the ancestry results will be interpreted into your final paper, along with coinciding with most of your assignments throughout the course."

Ancestry? Is that what he meant when he was referring to the kits? That would make sense. What a strange thing to do in a creative writing class, though.

"I find that sometimes the best work comes from within, from our own experiences and those of our past. If we tap into that, and follow along with the prompts provided, I think there will be great results."

What, was he reading my mind or something?

"I'm sure you have your doubts, but trust me with this. Most people are completely unaware of their heritage." He goes back to leaning against his desk. "Now, on the other hand, if you already have an established knowledge, feel free to skip the test. You'll still be required to do the work, but if you're aware of yours, there's no need to do the analysis. We will be going back five generations, so if you have that covered, you're good to go."

What do I know about my lineage? Not much. Aside from my dad's mom, who died when I was little, it's always just been me and Dad. I never really asked about my own mother's family, since she was such an absent part of my life. I guess I assumed if there was anyone else, they would have cared enough to come forward.

My thoughts linger on Johnny and what little he's told me about his family. His mother died when he was young, and he never knew his dad. He has a cousin who's in the military, but I'm not sure if they were even blood-related.

There's Bram, but he was just a part of Johnny's found family, a father-figure role that Johnny never had. A piece of the past that I'm certain Johnny never wanted to give up.

I can't fix everything that's happening right now, especially in regard to Franklin, but what if there was a way I could bring Johnny some insight into who his family might actually be? Maybe that would bring him the littlest bit of peace in this chaotic time in his life. I owe him at least that.

45
JOHNNY — ALMOST TWO MONTHS AGO

I hate how fucking weak I am.

There's too much that needs to be done, and I'm in no shape to do it all myself.

The perfect opportunity has presented itself, and I have to take advantage of it.

Franklin may have thought he had the upper hand, but he underestimated my ability to adapt to whatever is thrown my way.

I never meant to involve anyone else in this twisted world of mine, but if I'm going to make it out of this, I'm going to have to get some outside help.

Starting with Claire and Bram.

The machines I'm attached to beep in the background. I keep my voice low but loud enough for them to hear. "I'll need a new burner phone and the contact to get in touch with someone at the coroner's office." I hold onto Claire's hand and brace myself for what I'm about to ask of her. "Claire, you're in charge of planning my funeral."

Her eyes go wide, but she doesn't say anything. I can sense

her unease but if this plan is going to work, we have to go through the motions as if it really happened.

"Do either of you trust any cops that are willing to take a bribe?"

Bram speaks up from his spot at the foot of my hospital bed. "I have a guy in mind."

"Good. But you need to be sure, okay? We can't make any mistakes with this."

"Got it." Bram stands from his chair. "I'm on it." He looks at Claire. "Call me if you need anything else in the meantime."

Bram goes, making sure to latch the door shut behind him.

"You okay?" I rub Claire's hand with my thumb.

"How are we going to pull this off?" Her blue eyes stare into me.

"Do you trust me?"

She blinks up at me. "Of course, I do."

"You're distraught, Claire. Your boyfriend just died. It makes total sense for you to leave this place behind and go home. You got a scholarship to pay for school, and have enough money saved to get your own apartment." I go over the story she's going to tell anyone from back home if it's brought up.

Rosie is the only one who knows about me, so she's the only one who needs to know anything. Everyone else? Claire followed through with her plan to win that scholarship and is returning home the way she always intended.

"But I don't have that kind of cash. And I have no clue when the award will be processed." Claire second-guesses my cover story.

"That part isn't important; I have it covered."

Claire narrows her eyes. "That's too much. And with everything else? There's no way."

"I'm telling you. The financial aspect of this entire thing is the last thing you should be concerned with." I don't know how else to make her realize her worries are misplaced without actually showing her how much money I have saved.

"What about that?" She points toward the bandage wrapped around my torso.

"I'll figure that out, too. We'll make stops along the way. Speaking of, I'll have to figure out a car, preferably with deeply tinted windows."

An idea seems to spark in Claire's mind. "Beth's BMW. It's the least she could do for being such a shit mom, and it totally fits in with the story we're telling." Claire's brief optimism is quickly erased. "Shit, what am I going to tell my dad?"

I soften my voice. "Have you talked to him?"

"No. But I'm going to have to. I can't just move back across the country and not let him know." Claire picks at her thumb. "What am I going to say to Rosie?"

I reach down and tilt her chin up. "We're going to figure this out, all of it." It suddenly dawns on me that I never gave Claire a choice in any of this. What if this isn't what she wants? To be with me? To risk everything and help me with this elaborate plan to evade a man that tried to kill me.

I'd do all of this again if it meant setting Billy free from Franklin's claws. But just because I'm willing to take insane chances doesn't mean Claire is, and I shouldn't assume this is what she wants.

"What's wrong?" Claire grips my hand tighter.

It's like she can see straight through me and into my soul.

One thing I always promised myself was that I would put Claire first, and the only way I can do that is by allowing her to make her own decision in this matter, even if it fucking kills me. "You're allowed to walk away."

She squints her brows. "What?"

"If this is too much. I'd understand if you didn't want to be a part of it anymore."

Claire pulls her hand away. "Are you trying to break up with me?"

"No." I reach for her but stop myself. "I'm just making sure you know you have a choice. That you're not forced to be here. And I wouldn't be mad at you if you've changed your mind. About any of this."

It rips my heart apart to open that theoretical door, but it would hurt me, even more, to not give her the option. I will never force myself—or this fucked-up situation—on her. After everything she's been through, she deserves much better, and I refuse to stand in her way. If Claire is going to stay, it's going to be *her* decision, not anyone else's.

"Do you want me here?" There's a slight hesitation behind her voice, like she might actually believe otherwise.

"You know I do, but I need *you* to be sure. This isn't up to me." Because at the end of the day, I care more about Claire than I do myself.

Claire weaves her fingers around mine and stares at me intensely. "I'm not going anywhere, not without you."

I should stop her. I should say no. I should tell her the risks over and over again until she realizes how insane all of this is. I should convince her that she isn't safe and that she should run far away from me. But I can't. I'm too weak to let her go. I've never needed anything like I need Claire.

I clear my throat. "Then it's settled, we do this. And we do it together."

There's so much left to plan. Like how to get out of the hospital without anyone noticing. Arranging medical care on our trip across the country. Getting everyone that will be involved on board with lying about my death and pulling off a believable funeral. I'll have to get my stuff from my place, plus all the cash stashed all over my house. I'll need a fake I.D. and a new alias to go by. Luckily, people are highly motivated by money, and with the excess I have, making this plan work might actually be possible.

I'll have to find us a place to live and secure us some kind of permanent transportation once we're done with Beth's car. Most of all, I have to do everything in my power to stay alive and keep Claire safe.

I've never traveled outside of my home state, but what better time to start than now? It's completely irrational, but it's the only thing I can think of to slip from Franklin's grasp. He's made it clear that he will stop at nothing to make sure I'm finished. Maybe if he truly believes I'm dead, he'll forget I ever existed and move on with his fucked-up life.

I will jump from this ledge, Claire's hand in mine, ready to dive headfirst into what I hope to be a fresh new beginning.

46
CLAIRE — NOW

How am I going to get Johnny's saliva on this test tube without telling him what it is?

It's not that I want any more secrets between us, but he's dealing with enough on his own, I'd rather present him with *good* news, not news that will make him nervous while we wait for the results.

What if his family is full of a bunch of serial killers? Or they're all dead? What if there is no one left and it really is just Johnny? I'd rather carry that burden for him until he's ready for it. But, what if he has living grandparents that own a bakery and go to bingo every Thursday and had no idea they had a grandson? There's a possibility that Johnny might have someone *other* than me and Bram, and I'd love to be able to give him that.

"You okay?" Johnny asks from his spot at our dining room table. He wipes his mouth on a napkin and takes a drink of his tea.

"Yeah." I change the subject. "How was your day?"

His jaw twitches, showing the slightest hint of tension, a cue that a random person would never notice. But I'm tuned-in enough to Johnny to recognize when something is bothering him. "It was all right."

I pop a French fry into my mouth. "Mmhm."

I guess we're both holding back from each other.

"I worried about you all day," he admits, although I'm not so sure that's the thing nagging at him.

I reach across the table and squeeze his hand. "But we did it. First day of school. No issues. Nothing major happened."

He glances over at me with the last part. "But something minor?"

I smile and shake my head. "No. It went smoothly, really."

"And the roads weren't bad?"

"Nope. Not with snow. There's a huge fucking pothole near the parking lot entrance, but other than that, it was fine." *Oh, and I want a sample of your DNA to see if you have any living relatives.* I keep that bit to myself though.

I could easily just ask him. Johnny would probably do anything for me. But there's the chance he says no. That he's fine not knowing about his family because he's okay with where he is—with me. That can't be it, though; if there are others out there, shouldn't he at least *know* about them? Then he can make the choice as to whether or not he wants anything to do with them. That's what I would want. But I shouldn't assume he has the same mindset. And that's why I'd rather figure it out first and *then* tell him if there's something that needs to be told. It would be unfair of me to unravel any unwanted emotions without having any details to follow them up with.

Johnny grazes my arm with his finger. "What's up with you?"

I glance over to meet his concerned look. This is where I open up my mouth and ask him the nagging question I can't get out of my head. When I learn the truth of how he really feels about the mystery behind his past.

Instead, I say, "Do you have any food allergies?"

His luscious brows bunch together. "What?"

I urge my raging heart to slow its pace. "Yeah, like dairy or gluten? Peanuts maybe?"

Johnny scratches his temple. "I'm not following."

I bite at the inside of my lip, forcing myself to come up with the rest of my lie. "In my nutrition class, we're doing this test to see if we have any. I was just wondering if you did."

It's not completely farfetched. I am taking a nutrition course. And we did discuss this very topic. But we're not actually checking for them, at least not that I'm aware of.

"Oh." Johnny blinks. "No. I don't think so." He pauses then adds, "Do you?"

I shake my head. "Me either. But I have an extra swab if you wanted to make sure." I let out a breath. "Hate to go through everything you have and then end up killing over from a random shellfish allergy."

Johnny hesitantly buys my story. "Yeah, sure. I'll take it with you. What do you need from me? Blood or something?"

I refrain from showing the emotion that's nearly seeping from my pores as I make my way over to my backpack and pull out the little vial. "Just a cheek swab." I hold it out and smile at him. I recall the details the professor had given us about making sure we hadn't eaten or drank anything within thirty minutes of taking the test. "But we'll have to wait."

Johnny holds out his arms to me, a seductive grin on his beautiful face. The faint outlines of scars linger on his skin. One near his brow, another on his cheek, the bottom of his lip. Memories from a time I hope he never has to visit again. "I can think of something we can do to pass the time."

I walk over to him, fitting myself between his legs while he sits on the barstool. "Yeah? What's that?"

"I was hoping you'd ask." His green eyes melt into me, trailing their way over my skin. He leans forward and brings his mouth to my ear, his breath warm on my neck. "Claire." His whisper sends a decadent chill along my eager body. Johnny runs his nose across my skin, leaving a wake of soft kisses on his journey to my mouth. He pauses, his lips lingering barely on mine.

My heart pounds heavily, but instead of it being because of my secret, it's for him, and him alone. The desire I have for him has never diminished in the slightest, and if anything, I want him more with each passing day. The more we explore each other, both sexually and emotionally, the stronger our bond becomes.

Some people go their whole lives not having the chance to experience what we share. It's solid and fierce and passionate. Raw and real, and unlike anything I ever could have imagined.

Every touch sends a beautiful fire rippling across my skin. Every look is enough to send a hidden message from one to the other. There's trust and devotion, loyalty, and selflessness. There's something magical that I would go to the ends of the earth to fight for, to hold onto as long as humanly possible.

The best part of all—it's mutual.

As absolutely crazy as I am for Johnny, I feel it reciprocated wholly. And maybe that's what stokes our flame higher, the constant flow of love we pour into our relationship. It's cliché as fuck to say, but we really are each other's ride or die.

I would do anything for Johnny. And I know he would do the same.

Johnny brings his lips to mine, caressing them softly. They're a perfect fit, like two puzzle pieces locking into place. Our mouths, our bodies, our hands, even our personalities, and the things we have in common…two beings that were made to complete the other. Where I end, he begins; we make each other whole.

He's in tune with my every breath and knows what I want before I do.

I bring my hands instinctually to his head, to tangle them in his hair. I smile into him when the short bristle of his new cut tickles my palms.

Johnny stands, causing me to take a step back. He grips my waist and guides me to the couch.

I clutch the hem of his T-shirt and drag it up and off of him. My fingers run down the front of his chest, pausing on his stomach. I sigh, taking my attention and shifting it toward his injury. "Are you in any pain?"

Johnny moves to unbutton my pants. "The only thing causing me discomfort right now is all this damn space between us." His intense stare bores into me.

We've been taking things slow since his accident, trying to be extra cautious considering we didn't want to have any unexpected complications with his recovery. It's one thing to find a shady doctor that won't ask too many questions to assess his healing, but it's another if he's rushed to the emergency room if something was to go wrong. He's pretty much made it out of the thick of it, but I still worry that our *extra-curriculars* could pose a risk, especially when he was obviously straining the first time we messed around after getting here.

"Claire, I promise. No pain. I'm good. More than good." He tips my chin up with his finger. "I want to feel you."

His words are my undoing.

I drop down onto the couch, grabbing his jeans and boxers in one motion, and yank them over his hips.

Johnny's hands tangle in my hair as I grip the base of him and swirl my tongue around his tip. A moan escapes his lips, and I continue to tease. I barely get a taste before he's pulling away.

"Turn over." He points to the couch.

Something about his demanding tone has me complying without another thought.

I climb up, my back to him as my knees rest on the cushion.

I glance over my shoulder at him, waiting for him to make his move.

Johnny weaves his fingers under the seam of my panties and slides them over my ass, exposing me to him. He lowers himself to the edge of the couch, bringing his face closer and closer until he's hovering his mouth along my slit.

I lean over the couch and arch my back, spreading my legs to give him better access.

He obliges by grabbing my hips and burying his face deeper, his tongue gliding up and down, his lips feverishly dancing all over me. If I was wet earlier, I'm soaked now—my desire to feel him inside me growing with each passing second of his playful exploration.

Johnny slides a digit into me, the thickness telling me it's his thumb. He rubs it in circles while he continues to lick in all the right places.

"Johnny," I breathe. I don't know how much of this I can handle. I need to feel *him*.

As if he reads my mind, he does one final pass with his tongue, nearly sending me over the edge. He leaves his thumb in place, gently rocking it back and forth while he fumbles to grab a condom.

I reach back, gripping and stroking him, trying to guide him closer to my entrance.

After what seems like forever, he bites off the corner of the condom wrapper and with one hand slides the sheath over his shaft.

I inch back, dropping my knees even further apart.

He glides his thumb out and up as he positions himself in place. His movements are slow and purposeful, where mine are rushed and greedy. This perfect dynamic of push and pull drives me completely fucking wild.

I rock back, allowing the length of him to enter me.

"Fuck," he moans.

I push against him, matching his rhythm and noting the steady build of his breaths.

His pleasure only continues to heighten mine.

For this temporary moment, there's nothing else in the world, it's only us, our bodies joined together in a beautiful chaos.

Johnny leans down while reaching for me, bringing his head closer to mine to tilt it to him and find my lips. He continues thrusting, a slow and steady, deep tempo.

The seconds our mouths collide, we hungrily kiss each other, rocking our bodies together more and more and more until our orgasms rattles through us at the exact same time, as though we're completely in sync with one another.

Johnny's breath fans over me as he rests his forehead against mine, his throbs inside of me send a vibration through my body that morphs into a shiver of pure pleasure. He kisses my shoulder softly, leaving a sweet trail on his way back up, then slides out of me carefully so we can both collapse on the couch.

I study the rise and fall of his chest, my eyes gazing down at the puckered wound from the gunshot that almost took him from me.

I'm forever thankful for whatever saving grace kept him in my life that day. But no matter how much I try to convince myself to leave the past in the past, I'm not sure I can. One way or another, I will find a way to make Franklin pay for what he's done. For torturing the man I love and putting him through things no one should have to go through. It might take me the rest of my life to figure it out, but Franklin will get what's coming to him if it's the last thing I do.

Johnny wipes at his forehead with his shoulder. He glances over at me. "Want to shower?"

47
JOHNNY

I keep waiting for something else to happen, but nothing does.

Part of Franklin's game is psychological warfare, and he does a damn good job at it. That one little sheet of paper slipped into our mail was enough to completely unhinge me. It was clever, if you think about it: a self-inflicted torture while he stays in the shadows, watching from the sidelines, waiting to attack.

If only I could find a way to end this once and for all; then I could go back to living my life, resume some kind of normalcy with the woman I love. Maybe we could go out on real dates and do things with her friends and not have to worry about someone posting us on social media. I could go back to school and focus on doing shit people my age do.

And maybe I could visit Bram without having to risk getting killed.

Leaving my old life behind wasn't too difficult, considering I had already given up so much in my attempt to save Billy from Franklin, but I hated having to say goodbye to the one person who stuck by me even when I went through some of my darkest days.

I wouldn't have made it this far without Bram. I'll never be able to repay him the kindness he showed me almost each and every day, and especially at the end, when he helped me and Claire orchestrate my escape. He did so without question, proving to me how much he really does care about me.

Claire's phone vibrates on the table, and after a quick glance at it, she pushes the button to silence it. She goes back to her studies without saying a word.

My old self would have ignored the weirdness of the situation and completely disregarded what just happened. But with things the way they are now, the unknown of who that could have been burns a hole straight through me. I open my mouth to speak, but I stop myself. If she wanted to tell me, she would. So why didn't she?

I'm not a jealous guy, but when Claire's life is in danger, I kind of need to know what the fuck is going on. It's a constant struggle to balance giving her the privacy she deserves while still keeping her safe.

I stare at the phone, wishing like hell I could set it on fire with my penetrating gaze so there was no way anyone could get in touch with her. At least, not until I figure out how to get Franklin out of our lives for good.

The thing buzzes again, alerting her to a voicemail.

I watch her intently and wait for some kind of reaction.

Finally, she sighs and swipes her screen to unlock it. Claire pokes at a few things until the crackle of the speaker comes to life.

Thank God, she put it on speakerphone. Now I won't have to be a completely overbearing boyfriend and ask her who it was.

A thick and familiar voice comes through. "Ms. Cooper, this is Officer Donovan."

Claire glances over at me and then back at her phone.

The officer continues, "If you could give me a call back at

your earliest convenience, it would be appreciated. You can reach me at my direct office line, or my cell. Thanks."

The line shuts off and a mixture of relief and confusion rolls through me.

It wasn't Franklin. It wasn't another weird message that could be interpreted as a threat. Since we relocated to this new, more private building, there hasn't been a single thing out of place to cause alarm. Although, it's only a matter of time until he finds us again. Hence why I'm jumpy at every damn thing.

But a call from Officer Donovan isn't great either, because that means it has something to do with Griffin, Claire's no-good, abusive, piece of shit ex who tried to ruin her life and even attempted to throw her down a flight of stairs. The one who I ended up sending down a flight of stairs instead and into a critical condition that might cost him his life.

If he's calling, does that mean Griffin woke up? Did he come to and tell the officer the truth about the situation? That I was the reason for his condition? That I assaulted him and that he's pressing charges? What if he has some kind of proof, or someone that's a witness to what went down that night?

Franklin isn't the only person who could potentially ruin my life. Griffin could, too.

And that sends another shockwave of fear rushing through me.

Who will protect Claire if I'm put behind bars? Franklin would sure enough finish me off if I got locked up. He has connections everywhere—a simple handshake full of cash would end my life quicker than a snap of the fingers.

Claire stares at her phone, not breaking her gaze until I walk over and sit across from her.

I place my hand on top of hers, reassuring her that I'm here, despite the unstable uncertainties rushing through me.

She flinches at my touch—a painful reminder of the fear Griffin must have put in her throughout their time together.

I never want her to be afraid of me. I'm the last person on the planet who would ever hurt a hair on her beautiful head.

"Hey," I say gently. "Everything's going to be okay." I'm not sure if I'm reassuring her or myself. Although, it's safe to say we both need it.

"What if it's not?" There's more than fear in her eyes, but I can't quite place it.

I tilt my head slightly and sigh. "Claire. We're in this together, okay? No matter what happens."

She must be just as afraid as I am that Griffin came to and told his side of the story. Claire thought she lost me once; what if she loses me again? I don't think either one of us could handle that reality.

Claire bites her lip. "Promise?"

I give her a gentle squeeze. "Always." There isn't a damn thing in the world I wouldn't do for her. We've made it through some insane shit, and there's no stopping me from fighting for us until my very last breath.

She exhales and forces a weak smile. "Okay." Claire pushes the contact for Officer Donovan and clicks on the call button.

A second later, it begins ringing through the speakerphone again.

"This is Officer Donovan."

Her voice cracks, "Hi, this is Claire...Claire Cooper."

"Miss Cooper, good afternoon."

I swallow down the fear that rises up my throat.

Claire stares at the screen. "What can I help you with?"

Donovan continues, "There's no great way to put this, but I wanted to call and inform you; Griffin Thomas is dead."

I do my best to hide my shock. *He's dead?*

"Oh wow, really? What happened?" Claire shifts slightly in her seat.

"There were some complications. It's not at all uncommon

in situations like this. There will be an autopsy performed, but the final report will take some time to come in."

I let out a breath. *Complications.*

Claire tenses beside me.

"This isn't exactly the outcome we had hoped for. I was really optimistic our case was solid enough to put Mr. Thomas behind bars." He sighs. "But you can rest assured that he'll never be able to hurt anyone else ever again."

"Yeah." Claire's voice is barely a whisper.

"Anyway, I thought you'd like to know. If anything, for a little bit of peace of mind."

"Thank you for calling me."

"Of course. I truly am sorry, for what happened to you and to his other victims."

Chatter comes through the background of his call.

Donovan covers the receiver and says, "Just a minute." He brings his attention back to the call. "If you need anything, don't hesitate to reach out."

"Will do," Claire tells him.

The line disconnects and we're left sitting there in the silence. A short moment passes, and I grip Claire's hand, staring intently at her profile.

She stays still while her eyes dart from left to right like she's lost in thought.

I swallow. "Are you okay?"

What a loaded question to ask someone in a situation like this. Of course she's not. Her ex-boyfriend is dead. And although he was a monster who treated her poorly, he was still a person. What's worse? He's no longer alive because of me.

I killed him.

What if the shock rattling her features is caused by the realization that the man she's with *now* is a monster, too? What if, in defending Claire, I turned into something she could never look past?

All I've wanted to do was protect her, not make her fear me.

Claire lets out a long breath. "Yeah. I'm fine." She forces a smile and finally meets my gaze. "You want some coffee?"

Is she really in that big of a rush to get away from me? How long until she's gone for good? What if she can't get over what I've done?

My heart constricts, like a giant hand is gripping it tightly, threatening to never let go.

"Claire." Her name is soft and delicate on my lips. A gentle pleading with her to understand I'd never hurt her. To know that she's the only thing that truly matters in this world.

"Yeah?" She bites at her lip, concealing whatever emotions that are bubbling to the surface.

"Can we talk about this?" I've always given Claire a choice, but damn if I don't want to drop down on my knees and beg her to forgive me, to stay with me.

"What is there to talk about? He's dead, that's all that matters." Claire's jaw tenses.

I'd give anything to read her mind, to truly hear what it is that she's thinking right now. I scan her face, desperately trying to uncover any hidden cue to help me figure her out. I always do my best to be in tune with Claire, her wants and needs, but at this very moment, it's as though she has a wall up against me, not allowing me in. She's blocking me out, and that only tightens the fist around my heart even more.

"I'm..." I start to apologize, but I don't want to lie to her—I can't. I'm not sorry for what I did. And if killing Griffin was the only way to save her, I'd do it over and over again. Deep down, I think Claire realizes this, too. There isn't anything I wouldn't do to keep her from harm's way. I'd go to the ends of the earth and stop at nothing to make sure she was safe.

I guess that's what happens when you fall for someone the way I have for Claire.

Deeply, powerfully, and without any fucking reservations.

I may have pushed her away, but I don't regret doing what I know with certainty was the right thing to do. Griffin would have killed her himself if I didn't step in and stop him. If I have to lose Claire, I'd rather it be like this than at the hands of Griffin or some other sick fuck.

"You're what?" Claire waits for me to continue.

I say the only thing I can. "I love you."

I don't miss the way her shoulders relax in the slightest, the release of tension that flutters out of her. She reaches out and runs her finger along my cheek. "I love you."

And maybe, just maybe, I haven't lost her after all.

48
CLAIRE — ALMOST TWO MONTHS AGO

In a dimly lit room a few blocks from our apartment, Johnny and Bram face each other for what will be the last time.

For now…maybe forever.

I try to give them distance to say their goodbye, but with the confined space and the pull on my heartstrings, it's difficult not to pay attention to such a beautifully tragic moment.

The two embrace but are careful not to be too rough with Johnny's injury.

Under his shirt is a bandage-wrapped torso that will have to be checked periodically to make sure it's healing and not getting infected—something that should be done in the hospital, or at the least in a proper doctor's office.

We don't have that luxury anymore, not if we want Johnny to live through this.

If Franklin catches wind that Johnny is still alive, he'll be furious, and there's no telling how many casualties will pile up on his way to end Johnny once and for all.

Pulling this off will be no easy feat, but there isn't anything I wouldn't do to keep this man alive.

Volunteering to drive us across the country to flee a psychopath is nothing compared to the idea of going through life without Johnny. I witnessed the light drain from his eyes, and I thought I had lost him. My heart shattered, and I begged the universe to bring him back to me. Maybe I used up my one allotted miracle, maybe it was some kind of divine intervention, but whatever it was—I refuse to lose him again.

"When will I be hearing from you?" Bram keeps his hands planted firmly on Johnny's shoulders, looking him in the eyes.

I can feel the sadness radiating off the two of them. Neither one of them are good at this kind of thing, but in reality, who would be?

"I don't know," Johnny says, his voice a bit tattered. He's hurting, probably in more pain than he lets on, both physically and emotionally, but he's well aware of what needs to be done.

Bram sighs, releasing Johnny. He shakes his head. "I can't believe this is it."

The scene resembles something of a teenager going off to college, only more heartbreaking and permanent.

Johnny clears his throat, wincing in the process and sitting down to catch his breath. "Thank you, for everything."

Bram stands there like there are a million things unsaid between them. Yet all he replies with is, "Of course."

Johnny may have his secrets from Bram, but he's still there for him no matter what. Bram knows with certainty that Johnny is a good person, and that whatever he was involved with was for good reason. He blindly trusts and supports him at the distance Johnny keeps. That's why the second Johnny asked for his help, he leapt at the opportunity without asking any questions.

I may have only been around a few months, but the relationship between Johnny and Bram runs deep, something that exceeds bloodlines and time. They are family despite the lack of DNA linking them together, something I'm not sure either one of them realized they had until now, when they had to walk away from it.

"Do you have everything you need?" Bram glances between us.

I approach him, reaching my arm around his torso. "Yeah. Thanks."

Bram pulls me in for a hug and grips me tightly. "You take care of each other, okay?"

I don't miss the way he fights through the words in his attempt not to cry. Johnny is like a son to him, and I can't imagine the way this must break his heart to let him go this way.

It would be one thing if there was a plan in place, a possibility of being in each other's lives again, but with the magnitude of the situation, this could be it. It would be unfair to give anyone unrealistic expectations of a future so unknown.

I'd like to think we'll slip completely from Franklin's grasp, but that's a reality that might not be possible.

As much as I harbor a boundless well of hatred for Franklin, actually getting the revenge I want will be an incredibly challenging task. Especially if I want to keep Johnny safe. And at the end of the day, keeping him far from death's door is my greatest priority.

Johnny brings himself to his feet once more, a massive task considering the freshness of his injury. It's a wonder at all that he's able to do what he has in such a short time, let alone while healing from his surgery after he was shot.

One thing is certain, Johnny is a fighter, and no matter how far he's backed against a wall, he will do everything in his power to overcome the situation. It's how he's managed to exist in Franklin's world this long.

I give Bram a final squeeze and let him go.

He turns to Johnny. "You'll call me if you need me?"

Johnny nods and steps toward Bram.

But Johnny is lying. He's already put Bram in too much danger involving him at all, and he won't continue to risk his safety any more.

Bram envelopes Johnny into his arms, his eyes glistening with all the things he wants to say. "I'll be seeing you."

Johnny palms Bram's back, struggling to maintain his own emotions. "Yeah."

Their moment is brief, but powerful.

My heart constricts at the enormous love these two have for each other.

All three of us walk to the door, Johnny leading up the rear at a little slower pace. How he's up walking around, I'll never know. It's probably all adrenaline and fear.

Bram plants his hand on Johnny's shoulder one last time. He looks to me, then to Johnny, and takes his leave.

We stand there in the doorway, Johnny hidden from sight behind me, watching Bram walk away. He never turns around; he doesn't glance over his shoulder one last time. He just keeps going, one step after another, until there's no more of him, until he's gone.

"I have to do this," Johnny says through gritted teeth.

"I don't doubt you."

"This is the only way."

I turn to him, wishing like hell I could take away every ounce of his suffering. "I know."

We're only on the road for a few hours when I glance in the rearview mirror and notice the sweat beading along Johnny's brow.

I look over my shoulder, confirming my suspicions. I try to reach back and feel for him myself, but I struggle to crane my arm all the way. I let out a breath, gripping the steering wheel and focusing ahead on the signs we pass.

There isn't another rest stop for almost fifty miles, and we're pretty much in the middle of fucking nowhere. A few cars litter the highway going in each direction, but otherwise, it's fairly empty. A whoosh of air hits the side of Beth's bright red BMW, throwing my attention to the semi that's passing us in the left lane.

Once it's just a blur in the distance, I check behind us again. Not a pair of headlights in sight, only a little bit of illumination from our own rear-end on the road.

We're eighty-three miles from our first stop, but with the uncertainty of Johnny's health, I find myself slowing down, signaling, and pulling off onto the shoulder. I make sure to get as far to the right as I can without going too much in the grass along the road. I push the button to put the sports car in park and reposition myself in the seat to take a better look.

Johnny stirs, but otherwise doesn't wake up. There's a pained expression on his face, one that I'd give anything to erase.

I carefully rest the back of my hand against his forehead, noting the damp warmth of his skin. I shift my body around to the front, poking a few things on the dash to get the air conditioning flowing toward him. I reach around, pointing the vents at him, and hope the cool air will ease his discomfort.

He mumbles something under his breath, and his eyes flutter open. His pupils take a second to adjust to the darkness and settle on me. "Claire, what's wrong?" His voice cracks, and he struggles to sit up.

"Shh, it's okay. Stay down." My intentions weren't to wake him, but to make sure he was okay. This entire thing is uncharted territory to me, and I'd be lying if I said I wasn't scared to make a mistake and put him in any more danger than he already is.

"Are we there?" He blinks through the dark.

"No." I shake my head. "You were…I thought you were running a fever."

Why am I so ashamed of being worried about him? Maybe it's because every single little thing out of place sets me on edge. It's difficult to determine which threats are worthy of our attention or not.

Johnny wipes at his brow, a bit of his own embarrassment settling in his features. "I'm fine."

We're on opposite ends of the spectrum—me overly concerned and him blowing things off completely. There needs to be some kind of balance between us, so we don't overlook something that is an actual concern.

"Really." He throws the cover off of him and sits up in the small back seat. Johnny holds his stomach, desperately hiding the twisting of his face.

I grab the bottle of water from the front cup holder and hand it to him. "Will you at least hydrate and take some meds?"

"If that'll get us back on the road."

Although I can pretty much tell that he knows he needs some reprieve from the damage to his body, he's been adamant about consuming the least amount of painkillers as possible, and if I didn't push him, he probably wouldn't take any at all. Must be some kind of pride thing. Which makes no sense—he was shot, almost died, and instead of receiving normal medical care, he's being bumped and tossed around in the back seat of a tiny car while he flees across the country to escape the man who wants him dead. It's safe to say he's more than deserving of a couple pills to ease the pain.

But I'll let him pretend it's all me if that's what I have to do to get them down his throat.

"Yes." I hand him two small, round tablets. "Thank you."

He swallows them down with a gulp of water and chugs down a bit more.

I hide the smile from forming on my face at correctly guessing he was thirsty.

This man can be completely selfless and do everything for anyone else, but when it comes to tending to himself, he's a lost cause. That's where I come into play. I will pick up the slack and look out for him the same he does for others. Because someone so noble deserves care and consideration, too.

The drugs might be a temporary fix, but it'll buy us a little time until we can get further down the road and to our first stop, where Johnny will get checked over by one of the few physicians we're scheduled to see along the way. It's not an ideal situation, but we're doing the best we can under our fairly shitty circumstances.

Regardless, I'm grateful for the opportunity, considering Johnny could very well have died the way Franklin intended.

49
JOHNNY — ALMOST TWO MONTHS AGO

"Are you sure you'll still love me?" I ask Claire, the device held tightly in my grasp.

When did I become so fucking insecure all of a sudden?

It's just hair.

Maybe I'm more attached to it than she is.

Claire deadpans. "Seriously?"

I shrug and stare into the mirror of our new apartment. It's not as nice as I'd hoped—the apartment, not the mirror—but it's the best I could do given our pressing situation. Now that we're here, on the East Coast, I can dig around to see if I can find us something better. Something safer, and a bit more comfortable than the cramped studio space.

I haven't left in the week that we've been here, but with the rest that Claire has sort of forced on me, I've garnered enough strength to finally do the thing I need to do before I can go out in public, even if it is only for very brief blips of time—like running necessary errands or going to get medical attention.

Faking my death means a new identity, and a different appearance. There's only so much I can change, but my signature long locks are a definite sacrifice I have to make. A piece of me that I weirdly hate giving up.

"What if you're not attracted to me anymore?" I meet her gaze in the reflection, her blue eyes staring seriously at me.

"I could shave mine, too, if you're worried." She holds her hair down and tilts her head around to get a better look. "Not sure I could pull it off though."

I turn around to face her. "You wouldn't."

She reaches for the clippers, a devious grin settling into her features. "Dare me?" Claire grabs hold of them and points them toward me. "You want me to do it?"

My eyes widen. "No."

Claire smiles. "I mean yours, not mine."

"Oh." My accelerated pulse starts to slow. It's not that Claire wouldn't still be smoking hot, it's that I'd hate for her to have to give up anything else for me. To be in my life. She's already surrendered more than her fair share at the cost of being with me.

"Let me prove you wrong," she tells me, a softness floating about her voice.

I swallow and nod. "Okay."

Claire flips the switch to the on position, and with a steady humming buzz, she swipes the first section of my hair off.

It lands in a heap on the counter, and she goes in for another. She carefully eyes each one, removing the thick mop on my head.

"Turn around," she tells me.

I face the mirror again, my gaze trailing slowly up to take myself in for the first time with this new look. It's still me, just different. But isn't that the point? It's not like I haven't already changed with everything that's already happened.

Claire stands taller to reach the back of my head. A few buzzes later and she stops, flicking the switch at the same time.

The quiet bathroom dances with my anxious energy.

I remove the white towel around my shoulders and toss it onto the counter. I run my hand through my short spiky hair, noticing a few uneven patches that I'll have to touch up. I fucking hate the way it feels, not because of the job Claire did, but because it's foreign. I'd gotten used to having long hair, running my fingers through like a nervous tick. Now it's bristly and unfamiliar, and I hate how exposed it makes me feel.

Claire presses her body against my back and rests her head along my side. "I'd still do ya."

Despite every terrible thing that's happened, that girl never fails to make me smile.

"Yeah?" I raise an eyebrow at her in the reflection and turn to face her.

She looks up at me, her eyes twinkling. "Mmhm." Claire reaches up and runs her hand across my cheek, settling it against my neck.

I wrap my arm around her waist and pull her up toward me. I'm not supposed to be lifting anything in my condition but screw the doctor's orders—I need to kiss my lady.

Claire kisses me back, tender and soft like she's afraid I might break. Her tongue darts into my mouth, her body reacting in succession to mine.

We haven't shared an intimate moment like this since we've been here, and it's showing through the heated passion that sparks at our touch.

"Johnny," she breathes into my mouth. "We can't."

But it doesn't matter; we can't stop what we already started. Not when it tastes this fucking sweet.

I run my hands down her frame, relishing every curve. I weave them under her shirt, allowing my skin to touch hers. It's smooth and everything I remember it to be.

It's not that we haven't been close since the attack on my life, but we've avoided anything that would exert too much of my energy and potentially hinder my healing. We sleep practically naked together every night, but this is the first time in a while we've let ourselves explore each other this way.

And damn if my entire being doesn't want more, more, more.

"Yes, we can," I tell her, grabbing her by the waist and leading her from our tiny bathroom into the open area that makes up our living space. "I hate how small this place is."

"What? Really? It's cozy."

I break away from her kiss and shove her onto the mattress, dropping to my knees in front of her and immediately finding the button of her pants. I drag them over her ass, wiggling them all of the way off her body and tossing them aside. I climb my way up, dragging my bottom lip along her thigh and tugging at her panties with my teeth.

I fight the breath that catches in my chest. We've barely gotten started, and somehow, I'm already winded. I refuse to allow my lack of endurance to stop us from crossing the finish line.

Claire senses my hesitation and props herself onto her elbows. "Johnny..."

I ignore her, wiggling my finger under the band of her undies and moving them to the side. Gliding my tongue over the remnants of a faded tan line, I make my way to her slit, where I allow myself a taste of her, my cock throbbing in response to her delectable sweetness. I trail down, savoring more of her.

She's wet, so fucking wet, like she's been ready for me this entire time.

I steady myself, trying to even out my ragged breathing in a desperate attempt to play it off like this is no big deal. But if I'm being honest, even if I wasn't recovering from a gunshot wound to the abdomen, I'd still be worked up from waiting this long to be close with the woman I love.

Claire sits up completely, severing the connection between me and her sugary bits.

I sigh. "I'm fine."

"You don't sound fine." She wipes at my lip with her thumb. "I don't want to hurt you."

Is this how she feels when I treat her exactly the same? How do I prove to her that I want this despite the danger it potentially poses?

"You're not hurting me." *Unless you count my pounding boner.* "I want this."

Claire's blue gaze scans my face.

I know she's struggling between being safe and frantically wanting this, too.

"Lay down," she demands. "I'm doing the work." Claire places her hands on my shoulders and guides me onto my back.

My heart picks up its pace, and I do my best to hide my triumphant grin.

Claire glides her hands to my waist, tugging my boxers and gray sweats over my hips in one solid motion, freeing my erection in the process. She brings her face to my dick, blowing a bit of cool air along the shaft before running her tongue teasingly over the base and up to swirl around the top.

I flop my head against the bed, my eyes practically rolling back as she licks the precum and spreads her lips around my cock. She takes me into her mouth, sliding it deep into the back of her throat. I throb against her teeth and revel in the pleasure it brings me.

Knowing how much I'm fucking loving this, she giggles and pulls away. She straddles my waist, teasing us both as she glides herself over me and reaches for a condom from the nightstand next to the bed. Claire finds one in my wallet, pulling it out and tossing the rest aside. She brings the package to her mouth and bites the corner off.

Who would have known using protection could be so fucking hot?

Claire pulls the rubber out, immediately moving to secure it around my ready member. Within seconds, she's positioned herself in place, sliding herself over me to continue this whirlwind of pleasure.

My wound tugs, a dull pain, reminding me that this is far from what we should be doing, but I ignore it and focus on the beautiful woman riding my cock.

Claire swivels up and down, her pussy tightening and telling me just where she is on her ascent to climax. One thing is for sure, in all the time Claire and I spent together prior to taking a break from sexual activities, I got very acquainted with her body and the way it ebbs and flows.

She brings her face to mine, kissing me with a feverish intensity.

I fight to pace myself, to revel in experiencing this fleeting moment with her.

Claire rocks herself steadily into me, shortening the strides but thrusting them deeper.

I run my tongue along her bottom lip and drag it into my mouth with my teeth, nibbling and sucking at it gently.

She reacts by digging her hands into the sheets near my head, getting a better grip to push herself into me. She lets out a soft moan, the sound fluttering straight to my cock.

"Together?" Claire breathes into me.

"Together," I mutter in response, grabbing her ass and taking over our rhythm, sending her spiraling around me the second I take control.

I explode inside of her, a wave of both pleasure and pain rippling through my body. Somehow the mixture of the two intensifies the sensation, and I welcome it all.

A perfect depiction of our lives together: so much darkness, yet so much fucking light.

50
CLAIRE — NOW

This past week has been strange.

Griffin is dead. And while that may be great news, considering what I did to ensure that happened, there's still the possibility that the poison I put into Griffin's mouth will show up during his autopsy, giving away the fact that he didn't actually die of complications from his accident.

That it was me that killed him.

I killed someone. On purpose.

Without so much as a second thought.

And not for one moment have I ever regretted it. The only thing that concerns me is getting caught—and what Johnny would think of me if he knew the truth.

He looks at me like I'm this sweet and innocent person, a fragile, delicate being. Would he run the other way if he found out what I did to rid Griffin from my life?

Even in death, he's still a lingering presence, threatening to ruin everything Johnny and I have worked so hard for.

I thought I was doing the right thing, to eliminate Griffin completely, but what if I made things worse by taking matters into my own hands? What if my actions are unforgivable in Johnny's eyes?

All I wanted was to take back the control Griffin had stolen from me so long ago.

Despite all of my worries, Johnny has somehow been sweeter than usual. If that's even possible. With me, he's this gentle, kind man, but with everyone else, he's cold and shut off, sometimes harsh. I'm the only one who gets to see his soft side, and I'm not mad about that one bit. I love that Johnny is comfortable enough with me to open up, to give me his heart and soul. But what if I don't deserve that?

Especially with the enormous secret I'm keeping from him. Along with the fact that I may have fibbed about needing a cheek swab for food allergies, when in reality it was for an ancestry test to see if he has any living family members.

The results of which happen to be coming in today.

Johnny wraps his arms around my waist and hugs me from behind. He buries his face in my hair and kisses my neck. "I'm going to miss you."

I hold him tightly and cherish the warmth that settles throughout my soul with his touch. I lean into him and sigh. "I wish you could come with me." I turn so I'm facing him, his hands still gripping my middle. "Maybe soon? Now that your I.D. came in?" I run my thumb along his bushy eyebrow and along his cheek. I'll never quite get used to how good-looking he is. Those emerald eyes shining against his long, dark lashes that any girl would pay a lot of money to have.

Johnny leans forward, running his nose along mine. Gently, he presses his mouth against my bottom lip. "Maybe."

I kiss him and cherish the sweet and savory taste of him. My tongue darts out, dancing elegantly with his. No matter how much time passes, I can never quite get used to the fluttering that appears with his touch. There's so much of us that fits perfectly together. Both physically and spiritually—as if we were once one soul, split in two, only to find each other again.

It's crazy to think that we've known each other less than a year, when it feels like we've been together since the beginning of time. Life before Johnny is a blur, and life without him, well, that seems completely unfathomable.

"As much as I want you to stay..." Johnny breathes into me, his fingers gripping me tighter. "You're going to be late."

I glance across at the clock on the microwave. "Shit."

He breaks away, a beautiful grin on his face. Johnny snatches my backpack from the dining room chair and hands it to me. "Here." He plants one final kiss on my cheek.

In a perfect world, Johnny would be coming with me. He'd be attending classes and taking the steps he needed to pursue whatever path he wanted. He'd hold my hand and walk me to our car, open my door and drive the couple blocks to our school. We'd meet each other outside of our classes when they let out and be a normal college couple.

But instead, I drive the short distance to campus alone, my only company the endless thoughts that float in and out of my head. Luckily, Rosie is there to greet me when I park, helping to distract me a little from my chaotic mind.

It's been wonderful to have her around, although she's only been informed of bits and pieces of the situation. Johnny and I already feel guilty about getting her involved, but considering she's my very best friend, there was no way I could go on without her in some capacity.

Rosie has actually been incredibly accommodating, given our super-secretive nature. Don't get me wrong, she's definitely tried to ask questions and get more details, but she's never once faltered or judged us for the weirdness of everything.

I guess when you've been friends with someone for so long, you roll with the punches when shit hits the fan.

"How was your date?" I ask her, happy to take my thoughts

away from my own drama. It's only a matter of minutes until I find out the results of Johnny's ancestry test, and if I don't focus on something else, I may lose my mind.

Rosie rolls her eyes and shakes her head. "Terrible. I'm telling you, the dating pool is absolute garbage. Not only was the guy twenty minutes late, but he also showed up piss drunk."

"You're joking!" I sidestep a pile of slushy snow and continue on our path to the main building.

"I wish I was." Rosie tugs her burgundy scarf closer to her. "I gave him the benefit of the doubt, you know, because I was already there. But then, he proceeded to order himself two shots of tequila, and then had the audacity to say he forgot his wallet."

I gasp and shoot her a look. "You have the worst luck with guys."

"You're telling me."

"I'm sorry, Rose." And I really mean it. Rosie is a catch. She's intelligent, has a great sense of humor, she's driven, and need I mention, gorgeous. She may be my longtime friend, but anyone would be a fool not to recognize how much she has to offer.

"Not your fault." She opens the door to our classroom and holds it for me to enter. "I'm meeting another guy tonight; fingers crossed it goes better. From his profile, he seems decent, but I've been fooled before."

"I'm rooting for you." I give her a smile and walk over to the table we've claimed as our own since school has started.

"Specifically doing a coffee date. Not giving him an opportunity to get drunk. I swear, this shit is like trial and error." She settles into her seat. "You're lucky you found what you did with JJ."

I sigh, my heart fluttering at the thought of Johnny. I am fortunate to have him in my life. But our journey has been nothing easy. We've had to fight tooth and nail, risking it all on numerous occasions to keep ourselves and our love alive. Our bond is strong and unbreakable, but the things we've had to overcome, I wouldn't wish that on anyone else.

"Class, the results are in." Professor Adkins strolls into the room, holding a stack of envelopes in his hand. "To get yours, you must turn in your assignment that was due today."

A few students in the corner groan, clearly letting the rest of us know that they haven't finished their paper yet.

"Those of you who are actually doing the work I assign, you can grab yours and head to the computer lab down the hall to access the records." The professor looks right at me. "Those of you who submitted more than one, make sure you pay the extra fee prior to pick up."

A fifty-dollar charge that I used out of my own funds. Johnny wouldn't have batted an eye about the amount, but I didn't want to involve him anymore in this lie than I already had.

Rosie and I make our way to the front of the room, our papers in hand, ready to exchange for the packages containing details about us that we're unaware of. Even Rosie doesn't know much about her ancestry outside of her grandparents on her mom's side.

"Ms. Cooper." Adkins nods and gives me two envelopes.

I swallow down the uncertainty that rises from the forbidden weight resting in my grasp. In a matter of moments, I'll know more about Johnny's past than he does, and I'm not sure if that will be a good or a bad thing. I hope like hell there's some kind of silver lining that will come from me going behind his back. He has me, but I don't want him to be alone in this world. No one deserves that. Well, Griffin or Franklin do—they both deserve to spend an eternity alone.

"You okay?" Rosie asks me.

I walk toward the door. "Yeah." I nod to her own envelope. "You're not worried?"

She shrugs and briefly glances at it. "Not really. Be cool to be related to someone famous though. Maybe royalty or something. I'm pretty sure I'm a mutt. I doubt there will be any big surprises."

I probably am, too, but it's not my results that have me flustered. It's Johnny's.

Now, with the way things are, there are so many possibilities. But this information will solidify if Johnny has anyone else in his family tree still alive. And I'm not sure if I can handle knowing the truth if it's bad news. I'm already keeping too much from him, how can I withhold that, too? I'll have to come clean, about this, and about everything, if we stand any chance of making it through these dark days.

We've already overcome so much, we can get through this, too, right?

I follow Rosie into the room and claim the computer next to her. The screen glares back at me, that cursor button blinking and waiting for me to make my move.

"Here, let me." Rosie reaches over me and types in the domain and hits enter. Her blonde hair wafts strawberries as it passes my face. She pokes at the page she pulled out of her envelope. "Looks like you just enter your code into there." Rosie points at the screen. "Whose are you going to do first?"

I avert my gaze, glaring at the two packages in front of me. "Um."

Rosie punches in her details and waits for her results to load. They're there within seconds. Her past and present right there for her to consume.

I slide my finger under the paper to break the seal, revealing a set of log-in instructions. Without allowing myself the chance to back out, I key the information into the browser quickly. I hover over the submit button as the severity of the situation comes around full force. Holding my breath, I push it anyway.

All too fast and too slow, the page loads, showing me more than I could have bargained for.

My heart pounds wildly as my eyes scan everything in front of me.

Genetic Ancestry.

DNA Matches.

DNA Circles.

I immediately click on the matches, frantic to finally satiate the burning desire to know the truth.

Only, the moment my gaze settles, my stomach clenches, my mouth dropping open.

"What's wrong?" Rosie asks me.

I blink twice, thinking I'm not possibly seeing clearly. I look again, sure that I'm reading this all wrong.

Lynne Jones, mother, deceased.

A piece of information I already knew. Johnny's late mother, who died when he was young. He barely speaks of her, but when he does, I can tell it pains him to relive the memory of her.

It's not his mom that unsettles me, though. It's the next line down.

"It's..." but I can't finish my sentence. It would make it all too real.

Luciano Bane, father.

But that's it. No deceased. No nothing. Just his name.

Meaning, his father is very much alive.

A father he has no idea even exists, let alone is still out there.

Here I was thinking I was going to find some long-lost grandparent or uncle, but I ended up with the name of his biological father. And I'm not entirely sure if that's good or bad. Clearly, this guy played no active role in Johnny's life, so maybe telling Johnny he's still out there would hurt him more, knowing he's alive and could have reached out, but never did.

I pull up a second browser, desperate to find out more information about this mystery man whose sole part in the creation of Johnny was as a sperm donor. Almost like what my mother had been for me, a vessel to bring me into this world, only to leave me once I was born.

I type in the name, noticing the Google search bar trying to complete my request.

Luciano Bane net worth.

Luciano Bane possible murder.

Luciano Bane owner of Bane Café.

Luciano Bane crimes.

Is it possible there's another person out there with the same name drawing this attention?

But, when I click enter and the first photo pops up, it's like I'm staring at Johnny, only he's aged, with a full, clean-cut beard, and there's a sort of darkness to him that my Johnny doesn't have. The resemblance is uncanny, almost like you put Johnny in one of those age simulators to show how he would look at the age of forty-something.

There's no denying that this man, this potential criminal, is Johnny's father.

Here I thought I was doing the right thing, but I may have just opened up a can of worms that can't be closed. I wanted to find a sweet old grandparent who could share their recipes and family photos, not add another layer of negativity to Johnny's life.

Rosie cranes her neck to check out my screen. She lowers her voice. "Is that who I think it is?"

I bite my lip and barely bob my head up and down, letting my eyes scan the news articles. My sights land on one from a local gossip paper. Dated only a few months back.

Possible Crime Syndicate Permanently Relocates.

I skim the details, my breath catching when I realize what exactly this means.

Not only is Johnny's dad alive, and into some bad stuff, but he likely lives within a few miles of us.

I sink back into my seat and let the weight of it all crash over me.

Rosie tightens her high ponytail. "What are you going to do?"

"What *should* I do?"

Tell him, my mind urges me.

But what if that's the wrong choice? Johnny already has enough on his plate, what if this sets him over the edge? Not only will he be upset that I went behind his back, but then knowing his dad is out there, and that he's a criminal on top of it? And there's still the truth of the Griffin situation. All of these secrets are piling up and building a wedge between us. I can't allow this to be what breaks us, though. We've been through more than our fair share, but what if this is too much? There has to be some kind of breaking point—something that we can't come back from.

Why did I ever think this would be a good idea? The way everything else has gone for us, I should have known this would result in nothing but disappointment.

"That's up to you," Rosie tells me. "How do you think he'll handle it?"

I scan the screen once more, sighing at the mess this man has gotten himself into. If these reports are correct, Luciano is basically the Franklin of the east coast. And knowing what Franklin has done to us, and countless others, there's no telling how Johnny will react.

"I don't know," I say honestly.

Johnny may have gotten wrapped up in some bad shit, but not for a second did he do so selfishly. Every single thing he's done has been for the sake of saving someone else. He's sacrificed himself time and time again to do the right thing, the noble thing. Johnny is a good man, one this world doesn't deserve. And here he is, bred from a criminal and a woman who ultimately went down bad path after bad path until she met her untimely demise. It would crush him to know what a bad man his father is. What if he loses himself thinking that he's going down that same road?

I can see Johnny's true self. The good one. But all he notices when he looks in the mirror is a bad guy. The one who's done terrible things. He doesn't believe he's worthy of anything good, or to be loved, when in reality, he's the best person I've ever known. Anyone who ever took a second to truly get to know him would say the same damn thing.

Even in the beginning, when Johnny partially had me fooled, Bram tried to convince me otherwise. Because Bram knew the truth. Johnny is a sheep in wolf's clothing. Don't get me wrong —he's fierce and intimidating, but it's only when those he cares about are in danger. He would risk anything to save someone who needed rescuing. And that's the difference between Johnny and everyone he's interacted with during his journey to the underworld.

"I'm going to find him." The words that leave my mouth surprise even me.

Rosie's eyes go wide. "What?"

"I have to. I have to see it for myself. I can't get Johnny involved until I know." Just as Johnny would do for me, I will do what I can to protect him. It's my fault I dug too deep, and now I will be the one to handle what comes from it.

51
JOHNNY

I hate it when Claire is gone.

This world is too dangerous to not worry my ass off every second she's away. I try to distract myself, following up on leads of where Franklin might be, keeping tabs on his whereabouts and his moves to note anything suspicious. But no matter what, my mind always floats back to her dark, honey-colored hair and bright blue eyes.

It's been a week since we heard the news of Griffin's death, and somehow, Claire has stayed with me. I keep waiting for her to realize that I'm a monster—a killer—but she doesn't. She hasn't even brought it up, which is equal parts relief and a concern.

I don't want her to suppress her feelings because she's afraid of being honest with me. I want her to be able to talk to me, even when it's uncomfortable. We're a team, and there isn't anything we can't handle together. Never do I want her to feel like she can't tell me something. I'd never judge her or try to gaslight her out of feeling a certain way. She matters to me, more than I'll ever fully comprehend, and I hope that she knows I'm here for her through it all—whatever life throws our way.

And if not being with me is what she truly wants, I will respect that, despite it being the most painful thing I can imagine.

Even worse than death itself.

And trust me, I've been pretty fucking close to knowing what that's like.

I wouldn't blame her for walking away. How could I expect her to understand that I did what I did to protect her? That everything I've ever done was because I thought it was the right thing to do. But why do I get to choose what's right or wrong? How do my bad actions get somehow justified based on my personal rationale?

I shake the thought and walk down the steps and into the front lobby of our building. I nod a hello to the kind-looking older woman picking up her tiny dog to carry it up the stairs. Walking out the main doors, the crisp cold air rushes to greet me, reminding me there are still a few more months until spring arrives, another season I'm curious to experience from the East Coast's perspective.

I glance left, then right, and cross the not very busy street, making my way to the post office to check our mailbox. Claire is still anxious about her scholarship details coming in, so I'm making sure to check daily in hopes that the letter will arrive and ease her nerves. No matter how many times I've told her that money is no issue, she hasn't let up with wanting to cover her tuition herself.

Just the thought of her brings a smile to my face. I can't exactly blame her for her rationale, I would probably be the same exact way if the situation were reversed. She's honestly handling it all better than I thought she would. Claire has been nothing but a wonderful surprise from day one, and I can only imagine that will continue with each moment spent together.

"Johnny?" A thick, familiar voice stops me dead in my tracks.

My heart clenches. I will myself to become invisible but it's no use.

Other than Claire and Rosie, no one, and I mean no one, should know my name out here.

I swallow. I could easily ignore the person, keep moving and pretend I didn't hear them. I could act like I'm tying my shoe, which would explain why I suddenly stopped. Or I could turn and face the person that voice came from.

"Johnny?" The person calls out again, this time a little closer.

My window of escape is closing. I've tried like hell to prepare myself for something like this, but I guess I always expected Franklin to be the one to come for me, not the man stepping around me to stand in front of me.

The guy I trusted, probably more than I should.

I raise my gaze from the ground ahead and up to meet his wild stare. "Josey."

He clutches his chest. "Holy shit." Josey steps forward, but I take one back. "Dude, seriously?" He closes the gap anyway, wrapping his wide arms around me, surprising me when he hugs me tight. "I thought you were fucking dead."

With my arms pinned to my side in a Josey hug, I mutter back, "Yeah, that was the whole point."

Josey lets go and clamps my shoulders. He grips me firmly and takes a solid look at me. "I can't believe it." He punches my arm. "Here you are, in the fucking flesh."

My attention darts all around, looking for some kind of exit. It's Josey, and although he's someone I once believed in, he could be here on behalf of Franklin to finish the job he had started back on the west coast.

"I heard rumors, man, I had to come see it for myself." Josey shakes his head. "You couldn't have picked some place a little warmer?" He rubs his arms. "It's frigid as fuck here." Josey kicks at a little pile of snow on the ground. "Even this shit is ugly."

Despite the raging panic coursing through me, it's strangely liberating to see him. We grew close in our time together, and I hated not being able to tell him the truth. But I couldn't risk

Franklin finding out, not just for my sake, but for Claire's, too. Honestly, I'm not sure I would have made it this far without Josey and the tip he gave me about that package being stolen from me being an inside job. Without that information, I might not have ever tracked it down and bought myself more time with Franklin. Josey risked his ass to help me out, which should show me where his loyalties lie. But one can never be too sure, especially in our line of business.

"Does anyone know you're here?" I ask the question that's nagging me.

Josey straightens up, easily towering over me with his height and build. Josey is a large dude. Someone I definitely wouldn't want to get into a fistfight with. "Told them I had some family business to attend to." He clears his throat. "I really do, my gran is sick."

"Ah, shit, Jose, I'm sorry, man." This time, it's me that slaps his shoulder.

It's like we're brought back to those nights behind Franklin's place. A difficult, but much simpler time. One when I wasn't running for my life, just running illegal packages all over the city.

"She's lived a long life." Josey sniffles and rubs his nose. "Anyway, no, boss didn't send me, if that's what you're wondering. But I wouldn't be surprised if he does come after you soon. Word on the streets is he might be putting a bounty on you. You really got under his skin, JJ."

I let out a nervous laugh. "What's stopping him then?"

Josey scratches his temple. "If I had to guess, I'd say it's because he wants to do it himself."

At least I was right about one thing—Franklin wants to be the one to finish me off.

It's probably a good thing I've gotten under his skin like I have, otherwise he would have just paid someone to end this weeks ago.

"Well, thanks for the warning?" I glance around at the oncoming passersby, scanning them for any kind of immediate threat.

They might not be there to kill me, but he could easily have someone capture and hold me captive until he got here to follow through with killing me.

"Had to see you for myself." Josey stares at me with such intensity. "I've got to say, man, you did a damn good job. You had everyone fooled." He chuckles. "Claire slapped the shit out of me at your funeral. She was pissed. Not that I blame her. I would have decked myself, too."

"What gave it away?" I've done everything I can to cover my tracks.

"Facial recognition shit. Some college kid posted you in the back of his Instagram story." He glances around, too. "Umm, Pax? Does that ring a bell?"

I knew I hated that guy for a reason. Had to have been the first time we hung out with Claire's friends, before we thoroughly enforced the no social media rule. He was live streaming and panned all around him, managing to clip part of my face before I realized what was happening. I turned as quickly as I could, but it must have been *just* enough to set Franklin off.

A chill creeps up my spine. He must have eyes reaching further than I thought he did.

Or, he's monitoring anyone Claire has ever been associated with, in case we slip up.

It was one time, and only for the briefest moment, but it was enough to cause Franklin to be suspicious of my death.

"How much time do you think I have?"

Josey shrugs. "Not sure, kid. He has some more pressing business he's taking care of, but probably another few weeks at max."

"Damn, okay." I take his words in, letting them be fully absorbed.

How in the hell am I going to weasel my way out of this mess? I thought I had escaped Franklin's wrath, but I only bought myself time. Time I haven't fully utilized, considering he could be coming after me at any moment. How does someone even go about getting out of something like this?

The only possible solution I can come up with is ending Franklin's life.

There's no other option. He's a man that can't be reasoned with. And at this point, killing me will be more satisfying than anything I could ever offer him. There's no chance I'd ever go back to working for him, because he'd only continue to put my life in danger until there was another *accident.* Not to mention, I'd never put Claire in that kind of danger.

But if I take Franklin out of the equation, what will happen next? Would someone replace him and want revenge? I may have worked for him, but I don't know enough about his organization to have the ins and outs of that type of system. The main reason I got to live as long as I did was because of his wife —does that mean she would be the one to take over once he's gone?

And how could I even begin to put myself in the position to kill him? He'd never be stupid enough to come at me unarmed or without guards.

I pull the buzzing phone out of my pocket.

Claire: *Me & Rose are going to grab coffee. I'll be a little late, love you.*

Me: *Be safe, please. Love you more.*

Usually, this is where I would ask Claire where she's going and have her keep me posted when she gets there, but Josey is standing in front of me, telling me I only have a few weeks to live. Claire only just got her life back; I don't want to ruin it already. I'll try to preserve what little bit of normalcy she has left for as long as I can.

"What can I do to help?" Josey surprises me with his question.

His expression is stern, showing nothing but candor.

"What?" I can't hide the surprise in my tone.

"Dude, I thought you were dead once, I think I'll pass on the real thing." Josey crosses his arms over his broad chest. "Listen, man, I didn't get the chance to warn you last time, and that shit ate me alive."

Ah, so Josey is here because he feels guilty. He's trying to clear his conscience.

"You're not a bad guy, JJ. And maybe not everyone sees that, but I do. I'm not trying to get all sentimental...but you're like the kid brother I never had."

Or maybe he's here because he actually cares.

I narrow my eyes at him. "Are you fucking with me?"

Josey grins and shakes his head. "I'm serious, you fucking idiot." He punches my shoulder. "I'm only in town for another week, but if you need me, I'm here."

I sigh and glance around, my breath a misty haze in front of me. Having someone other than Claire on my team would be huge, especially since I don't want to involve her just yet. But what if this is a trick? What if Josey really is a mole for Franklin, and he's using what connection we did have as a way to trap me? If it were only me, I would take Josey up on his offer of assistance without hesitation, but I have to give more caution to things involving Claire.

I would never forgive myself if something happened to her and I could have prevented it.

"Thanks, man," I finally say. I reach out my hand, letting it hang in the balance between us. "I'll let you know."

Josey rolls his eyes, which is hilarious coming from such a large and intimidating man. He grabs my outreached arm and pulls me to him, slapping my back in a manly kind of hug. "I'm glad you're not dead, kid."

I smile and smack him with the same intensity. "Me too, me too."

"If you need me, I'll be at a place called Bane's Café at noon every day."

And maybe it's foolish of me, but I make a mental note of the location. I have no idea what I'm going to do to make it out of this, and if it's a trap, I'll be walking right into it. Josey has already proven himself on more than one occasion, what's the harm in putting a little faith in him once again?

52
CLAIRE

I drive the three blocks from campus and park across the street from my destination.

It's eerily similar to Bram's, with the glowing signage out front and the large windowpane that shows the contents of the diner. Immediately, I'm taken back to the aroma of freshly brewed coffee and blueberry muffins. That home away from home feeling that cascaded over me the second I stepped foot into Bram's diner.

I hadn't been out west long, but I grew attached to that place and the man with salt and pepper hair and advice that was almost always on point. He was like a fairy-godfather, one that I would love to consult with on what the heck to do with this new information I've learned about Johnny's past.

I smile, thinking of Bram playing matchmaker with me and Johnny when we were in the *avoiding each other like the plague* stage of our relationship. The look on Bram's face when we finally started getting along was priceless, like he had hit the lottery. He looked out for Johnny as if he was his own flesh and blood, and I admired how much the two of them cared for one another.

Just goes to show you that sometimes the best family is found.

Which brings me to sitting in front of this knock-off Bram's, squinting my eyes to get a better look from my spot tucked carefully in my car.

I really could use a cup of coffee, so what's the harm in wandering inside for one?

I swallow down the nerves building up and do exactly that, hitting the lock button on my key fob and crossing the relatively empty street.

How have I lived here my entire life but never visited this specific coffee shop? Maybe because it's not within a walking distance of the house I grew up, and until recently, I've done the majority of my traversing on foot.

"Welcome to Bane's," a friendly teenage girl with rosy cheeks greets me.

A barista pulls a shot of espresso, and a middle-aged woman sits in the corner, tapping away on the keys of her laptop.

Taking everything in, I stroll toward the ordering area, where a large chalkboard has the menu listed. I study it over, out of curiosity more than anything.

"What can I get for you?" It's another teenager, this one with a beanie on his head and a sad attempt at a mustache hovering above his lip.

"Coffee, black. Please."

The guy blinks at me, like he's waiting for me to rattle the variations of milk and syrups I'd like to include with my order.

"With a dash of cinnamon."

"That's it?" He seems stunned by my sort of simple order.

"Yep."

He pushes a few buttons on his screen. "For here or to go?"

I bite at my lip, knowing damn well I should leave, but the nosiness in me not letting me go that easily. "For here, please."

"Miller," a deep voice calls out from the back.

The cashier turns his head to glance behind him. "Sir?"

My heart nearly drops when the man comes out. Dark, bushy hair with a hint of silver poking through. Bright emerald eyes and long, long lashes. He's easily six foot something, with a wide but not too wide build. Intimidating to say the very least.

The man catches me staring at him and he pauses. "Sorry, I didn't realize you were with a customer, carry on."

Manners? From a potential mob boss? At this point, I wouldn't be surprised if he sprouted a tail or set of wings and flew away.

Miller gives me his attention once again. "That'll be three dollars."

I slide him a five, take my change from him, and end up handing him a single back.

The kid offers me a smile. "Thanks." He turns around, grabbing a cup and a saucer from the stack by the kitchen window and setting it in front of me.

The man waits patiently for Miller to finish, and I do my best to avoid making eye contact with him. I thought maybe I would catch a glimpse of him, not be gawked at for minutes on end.

"Here you go." Miller sets the cinnamon shaker next to my steaming cup.

"That's how I take mine," the man says with a grin, stepping forward.

My pulse thuds loudly in my ears, and I do everything I can to stay firmly in place and not turn and run out of here. I never meant to garner *this much* attention from the guy I came here in search of.

I note the way his lips turn up: the same exact way Johnny's do when he's trying to hide his smile. The similarities between the two of them are eerie, confirming my suspicions of whether or not the results of the ancestry kit were accurate.

"Yeah?" I finally say.

"Mmhm. Adds just the right amount of flare without being too much." He points to the glass case of sweets. "Could I offer you something to go with your coffee? A muffin, maybe?"

I eye the case but shake my head. "No, thank you though, I appreciate it."

"I insist." He turns to Miller. "Bag up a blueberry old-fashioned for the lady." He winks at me. "I saw the way you hesitated." He takes the thing from Miller and sets it on the counter by my cup. "It's my favorite, too."

I dig my teeth into the inside of my lip to ground myself from losing control. Never could I have ever imagined *this* is how this entire interaction would go.

The man who looks just like an older version of the love of my life extends his hand. "Luciano."

I wipe my clammy palm on my pants and take his in mine. "Claire." It's not until the word slips from my lips that I realize I probably should have used a fake one. Now I've given him a piece of me that I can never take back.

Johnny is going to be so fucking mad when he finds out. And I don't blame him one bit.

This is stupid, completely foolish and irresponsible.

"Claire," Luciano repeats. "What a lovely name."

But there's something laced in his tone, something dangerous that sends a chill dancing up my spine.

His grip is firm but gentle, his hand consuming mine almost completely. "I'll leave you to it." Luciano nods toward my steaming cup and turns toward Miller. "There's a shipment in the back I could use your assistance with."

Miller makes eye contact with me and points across the room. "Sorcha can help with anything else."

"Thanks."

The two of them disappear, the door swishing in their wake.

And I'm left here, processing what the fuck just happened.

I came here to see for myself. To see if that man who showed up on Johnny's results was actually his father. To see if he was in fact, the crime boss that the internet claims he is.

I'm not sure what I expected, really. But for him to be so… charismatic…that was a surprise. There were layers of Johnny woven throughout him—in his mannerisms and even the sly twinkle in his eye. There is no denying that this man is his father.

But now, what do I do with that information?

He seems like a decent guy. Someone Johnny might not hate. He's the owner of a quaint corner coffee shop. Similar to his found father figure back home. Although, there's still the very real possibility that he's involved in illegal activities. And I guess that's what I have to figure out. Johnny is finally getting clear of that type of stuff; I won't be the reason he can't escape that lifestyle. He deserves to be free of the shit that wrecked the past year of his life and nearly killed him.

Plus, if he really is Johnny's biological father, he has some explaining to do on where he's been the past twenty years.

I take a sip of my coffee, savoring the bitter taste. If anything, the guy serves a decent cup of joe, giving him at least one brownie point.

I pull my phone out of my pocket, surprised when I don't have any notifications. Usually, Johnny would have followed up by now, but maybe he's busy with something else. I send him a text anyway in an attempt to calm his nerves in case he's trying to give me space.

He's done such a great job at balancing the strangeness of our situation. It's been hard on him, trying to play pretend that everything is fine, but he's gone out of his way to make things as normal as possible despite the raging nerves he deals with daily. He's still worried Franklin will come after him even though it's been months and nothing has happened.

At this point, the biggest concern should be whether or not the poison will show up on Griffin's autopsy.

Me: *Coffee is decent, I'll see you soon.*

Johnny: *I'm glad. You having a good time?*

I shouldn't have lied about being with Rosie. I should have told him a partial truth, that I was trying a new café. Or actually brought Rosie with me. The dishonesties add to the weight already pushing down on us.

Me: *Yes, just missing you.*

Johnny: *Me too, always.*

There's a sort of comfort to having Johnny around. A safety. A sense of home no matter where I am. Without him, there's this strange absence. Like part of me is missing. It's not that I'm dependent on Johnny, but instead, we somehow make each other stronger. It's difficult to wrap my head around and explain, but it's the only thing I've ever been absolutely certain about.

Johnny is my person. And I am his.

I take a few more swallows of my drink and push the cup forward, dropping my napkin on top. Hopping off the stool, I grab the paper bag with the donut inside and make my way toward the door. Once I'm outside, I exhale, allowing the slightest release of tension from my body.

"Over here," a person calls out from somewhere in the distance.

I turn toward the sound and take a few steps in that direction. A dark alley right behind Bane's Café. Almost immediately, my thoughts are transported to my birthday. That dreadful night where everything was perfect, until it wasn't. When Johnny's life almost slipped completely away from me. When I had been convinced I lost him forever. When a large piece of me was tainted with the thirst for revenge and the need to protect Johnny at all costs.

Watching something terrible happen to someone you love will change you.

With a mind of their own, my feet inch closer to the darkness beyond. It consumes me completely and a strange sort of calm comes over me. The shade a welcomed friend, saying hello to that part of me I try like hell to keep hidden from the world.

I tiptoe further, my back against the brick wall, slithering quietly toward the entrance of the back of the café.

A box van starts its engine, seconds later pulling away, leaving two people behind.

I stay in the shadows, lurking for any sign or clue of what's going on. Is this just an innocent delivery? Or something much more sinister?

"Net twenty thousand," the smaller of the two says.

It's Miller.

My eyes adjust, finally noticing the beanie resting on his head, and the silhouette of Luciano standing in front of him.

"Down ten percent." Luciano seems disappointed. "We'll have to put pressure on the north end if we're going to recoup costs."

"Who do you want to use?" Miller asks him.

"Viktor."

Miller looks up from the clipboard in his hands and stares at Luciano. "Are you sure?"

Luciano nods stiffly. "Yes."

"Okay, sir." Miller's voice cracks.

"Any word yet on what's going on out west?"

"No, sir. Only that it's a personal vendetta."

"Leave it to Franklin to get distracted by such things." Luciano lets out a breath.

And without meaning to, I suck one in. Did he just say what I think he did?

Out west? Franklin? As in the same Franklin we ran away from?

Personal vendetta.

Could he be referring to Johnny? Does that mean Franklin is aware Johnny faked his own death? Or is this all just some weird coincidence that Luciano knows someone by the same name and location?

Luciano shifts his sights from Miller and looks directly at me, squinting to see more clearly.

My eyes go wide and I freeze in place, hoping with all my might that he doesn't see me creeping from the dimness of the alley. I take a cautious step back, the ground betraying me by crackling under my shoe.

Luciano shoves Miller aside, his hand reaching back and resting on his hip as he makes his way toward me. Probably on a gun.

I could run, dart away quickly, but what if he decides to put a bullet in me before I can evade him? I have no option other than to stay put and hope he doesn't shoot me.

What a fucking fool I was—for coming here at all, and especially for thinking I could eavesdrop in a shady alley and not get caught.

I'm smarter than this, so why am I making stupid mistakes?

"Claire?" Luciano narrows his gaze and slowly takes his grip from his side.

"Hey, um, sorry. I thought this connected to Bradley Street." I tilt my head and put on my absolute best lost-ditzy-girl act.

Luciano continues to stare at me, as if determining whether or not he buys my story. "You shouldn't be on this side of town at night. It's dangerous." His voice is gravelly yet calm.

"Right, yeah. I'll just..." I turn toward the light of where I came from, but he reaches out and grabs my arm, stopping me completely.

"Claire." Luciano doesn't break his firm but soft hold.

I yank free of him, just to make sure I can.

He holds both of his palms in the air. "I was going to offer you a ride." Luciano points toward Miller, who stands waiting for Luciano to return. "These streets really aren't the safest."

I rub the spot where his hand once was. "No, I'm fine."

Luciano tilts his head. "Very well. Have a good evening."

"You, too." I waste no more time, making my way from him as quick as I can without raising too much concern at my speed. I feel his eyes on me the entire trek to my car.

I should have continued on foot, long enough to break his attention, but with the uncertainty of the Franklin situation still lingering, it wouldn't be safe to roam around in an area I'm unfamiliar with. I already risked too much by coming here alone, I shouldn't risk anymore.

The comfort of being inside of my car calms me only a little bit. I won't truly feel safe until Johnny is right next to me.

53
JOHNNY

I can no longer tell the difference between my own paranoia and real life.

Every single thing causes my mind to race.

I fucking hate hiding things from Claire, but I don't want to tell her about the note from Franklin, and Josey showing up, until I actually have some kind of plan put in place to get us out of this mess I've created. I was selfish for allowing Claire to waltz right into this chaos, and I refuse to let her fall victim to something that was my fault.

"What's on your mind?" Claire glances at me in the mirror as she braids her long brown hair.

I let out a breath and take in her beauty. "You're really pretty."

She rolls her eyes and blushes. "That was *not* what was on your mind."

I shrug and lay back on the bed, one arm behind my head, the other resting on my stomach. "Coulda been."

Claire plops down beside me and props herself up on her elbows. "Tell me."

I reach forward to run my fingers down her cheek. "You're beautiful."

"Fine then." She pokes me in the side and laughs. "Secrets don't make friends."

Oh, what I would give to just confess it all. To not harbor a single piece of information that she wasn't aware of. But if I'm going to keep her safe, I have to hold off a little longer. I don't want to ruin her mundane college experience any sooner than I have to. She deserves that, at least.

Her phone buzzes, and when she glances down at it, her eyes go wide. Claire answers it immediately. "Dad?" She presses her index finger to her lips to signal me to be quiet and then clicks the speakerphone button.

"Claire-bear!" The genuine happiness in his tone is heart-warming.

"Hey, Pops." Her eyes glisten with the tears she's holding back. "How's Africa?"

The line cracks slightly. "It's good, but hey, I don't have long, just a few minutes. The international rates are insane, I had to prepay just to make the call. Anyway, what's this about you being back home?"

"Yeah." Claire glances up at me. "I—uh—I got that scholarship I was trying for, remember? They went ahead and awarded it to me effective immediately, so I borrowed Beth's car and drove home."

"Wait, what? You drove two thousand miles, *by yourself*?"

"Um, about that, I wasn't exactly alone..."

Her dad sighs loudly. "Did Griffin have something to do with this?"

"Dad, actually..."

"I'm telling you, Claire, that boy, he rubs me the wrong way. You're an adult and you're going to do what you want, but so help me God, if he derails your college plans..."

I like this guy.

"Dad—" she interrupts. "It's not that. Griffin is..." Claire drags her bottom lip into her mouth and tugs on it before saying, "He's dead."

"What?" is all he manages.

Claire nods although he can't see that. "A lot has happened since you left."

Shuffling sounds in the background. "Griffin is *dead?* Dead? That's it. I'm done. I'm calling it quits. I'm coming back there. I should have never left."

She interrupts him again. "Dad, I'm fine. I promise you, I am. I have an apartment. It's really nice, safe."

"An apartment? How are you affording that? And hold on, you said you didn't come alone?"

Her eyes dart to me again. "Yes, I met someone, Dad. I brought him with me. He's nothing like Griffin, I swear it. Even Rosie approves."

"Rose met him?" Somehow, this seems to settle his nerves.

"Numerous times."

He lets out a breath. "I don't like this, Claire. I feel like I've abandoned you, that I'm failing you as a father by not being there. I mean Christ, your boyfriend, sorry, *ex*-boyfriend, he's dead? Did I hear that right?"

"He was drunk and fell down the stairs. He was in ICU for a while and ended up having *complications.*" She puts an extra emphasis on that last word.

"Jesus, Claire. I'm sorry I wasn't there for you. Are you...are you okay? I mean, as okay as you could be?"

I wish there was some way to reassure this man I've never met that I would do anything for his daughter. That the safest place she could possibly be is by my side, because I would quite literally stop at nothing to protect her.

"I am. Really."

And somehow, despite it being a terrible thing to admit, I

think Griffin dying was actually a good thing. He was a menace to everyone he came in contact with. He didn't deserve the air he was breathing. This world will be a better place without him.

"I can come back, Claire."

"No, Dad. I don't want you to. I mean, I do miss you, that's a given. But you're more useful there. Finish out your assignment and write the best damn piece you can. I want this for you, more than I want you here. Do it for me, okay?"

"If you change your mind, I swear it, I'll be on the next flight home." He pauses and adds. "This doesn't feel right. I should be there with you."

"Dad, there isn't anything for you to do. I'm in school full time. I'm working on getting a job. Between that, getting my assignments done, and my social life, there isn't space for much else. I'm telling you, stay there. If I need you, I pinky promise I'll reach out."

"And this guy, you're sure about him?"

She sighs and stares straight at me. "Absolutely."

And with that, the phone disconnects, his prepaid minutes ending abruptly.

"Well, that went well." Claire drops her butt onto the bed and covers her face.

"Could have probably gone worse, considering." I throw my arm around her shoulder. "He cares, though. You have that. Complete polar opposite of your mom. One great parent is better than two shitty ones."

She sighs and leans into me. "Yeah." Claire angles her head to look up at me. "Did you ever meet your dad?"

I avert my gaze, shifting it to the floor. "No." Childhood memories trickle in, none of them very pleasant. My mom, always with some douche who treated her like shit. "I don't think so."

"What if you could, would you?" She stares at me with such curiosity.

I've pondered this same question many times before. The answer always the same. Whoever that man was, he left us. He left her. And maybe her death was her own fault, for going down the wrong path time and time again, but it's hard not to hold someone at least a little accountable for something like that. She never told me anything about him, and at a certain point, I stopped asking. If he could leave her the way he did, he was never someone I wanted to get to know.

"No."

My response seems to surprise her. "Oh."

"Would you?" I ask her.

She shrugs and straightens up. "Maybe. I mean, I'm not you, and you have your own experience. But for me, I'm sort of glad I went out west to be with my mom. It sucked, don't get me wrong, it was a terrible time." She sort of humorlessly laughs. "I wouldn't have met you if I didn't, though. And I wouldn't have known for sure what kind of person she was. I didn't like the not knowing, the wondering if I had it all wrong, and she was actually a decent human. Now, well, now I can make my own judgments without guessing. That woman sucks. Maybe she's a good friend, or a loyal worker, but as a mother, she's the worst."

She has a point. The uncertainty that lingers is a fickle bitch. But there are endless possibilities and I'm not sure if I could handle the truth. And even then, I would have no fucking clue how to go about locating him, if he's even alive. I legit have not a single identifying detail about him. I don't know his name, where he's from, what he looks like—nothing. Only that he knocked my mom up and didn't stick around.

He could be dead. Or he could be a deadbeat. But what if he's actually decent? What if he's an investment banker or a freaking doctor? What if he has other children…a family? I could potentially have brothers or sisters.

I'll never know, though, because not only would it be like

finding a needle in a haystack, but I may also not live long enough to start the search. At this rate, Franklin will be coming for me any time now, and I need to focus on preparing for his arrival.

I kiss Claire's cheek. "You have the morning off from class, right?"

Her lips turn up into a smile, a devious grin forming. "Yeah, you thinking what I'm thinking?"

For once, sex is not on my brain. I grab her hand and pull her up from the bed.

Claire's smile immediately turns into a frown. "Ah, come on!"

"Let's get breakfast. We'll have time for that later." I wink at her and weave my fingers around hers.

I would absolutely love to do nothing more than lay in bed with her, rolling around the sheets until it's time for her to go to class, but if I'm going to get on top of the developing deadly situation, I need to do some reconnaissance.

"Are we driving or walking?" Claire slips from my grasp and walks over to her backpack that's resting on the couch in our living room.

"In this weather?" I snort. "Driving."

"I keep forgetting how much you hate the cold." She smiles at me and pulls a book from her bag. "I have to finish a chapter before class."

"It's not the temperature, it's all that wet nasty stuff on the ground out there."

Claire strolls over with a sultry gaze. She leans in close, whispering into my ear. "I could show you something wet and nasty."

Heat flushes over me. How is it possible she takes my dislike for the snow and turns it into something so fucking sexy? If I didn't want to extend the length of my life to give myself more time with her, I'd jump her bones right this instant. The throbbing in my pants is going to have to cool down until we get back.

I might not have long right now, but I steal a kiss from her anyway. I melt my lips onto hers and bring my hand up to grip the side of her face. I dance my tongue into her mouth, delicately caressing it against hers.

Her body reacts immediately, pushing into mine and silently begging me for more.

Instead, I break away, smiling and telling her, "You're out of control."

She grins back. "You made me this way."

The drive across town is quick, and I savor every second of Claire being beside me, my palm stretched out on her thigh as she reads from her book.

I pull into an open parking spot and put the car in park. I patiently wait for her to finish up the last page, watching her ocean blue eyes skim the words in such a captivating manner.

Every single thing she does drives me wild with love and lust and admiration.

I hop out, rushing around to open her door before she gets the chance to. I extend my hand for her to take and guide her onto the sidewalk.

She stops dead in her tracks and stares up at the building we're in front of.

I slide my fingers around hers and pull her toward the door. It clangs shut behind us, just like the one at Bram's had done.

A place I miss dearly. A place I hope to return to someday.

Bram was the father I never had, and I hate how I took for granted our time together. I had pushed him away when shit got rough, but somehow, he came through for me in ways I never could have expected. I owe him my life for helping me try to escape Franklin, even when he had no idea what was going on.

Claire clings to my arm, and I welcome her closeness.

I point to a booth in the corner. "How about there?"

She nods slightly, a sense of nervousness about her bubbling to the surface. Is it because she can feel my unease, too?

I slide into the seat opposite of Claire, giving myself a solid vantage point with the most optimal viewing of the diner.

A freckle-faced boy with a beanie approaches. He lays two napkins on the table and pulls out a notepad. "What can I get you to drink?"

I glance at Claire but she's fumbling with her thumb.

"Two black coffees. No cream or sugar, just a shaker of cinnamon, please."

The kid eyes me curiously, glances at Claire, and then walks away without another word.

I reach across, grabbing Claire's hand in mine, hoping it will calm whatever nerves she's experiencing. I scan the place, searching for any sign of something out of the ordinary.

The building has a strange resemblance to Bram's. A very old-fashioned diner kind of vibe. Same glass case with various sweets—some muffins, a few pies.

"Is this where you brought that donut home from?" I ask Claire.

She looks up at me, a wildness in her eyes. "Mmhm."

I narrow my gaze. "What's up with you?"

But before she can answer, the kid is back with two mugs and a pot of coffee. He sets down the cinnamon and slides it toward me. "What else can I get you?"

I shift my eyes to the menus near the packets of sugar, but decide to order our usual, in hopes that it's edible. "Two stacks of blueberry pancakes and two orders of bacon. That'll be it for now."

The kid makes a note on his paper. "Shouldn't take long."

He leaves me and Claire behind, our hands still gripping each other.

I sprinkle some cinnamon into her cup and nudge it toward her, doing the same with mine, and then scan the crowd again.

Old couple in the opposite corner booth. A middle-aged woman on her laptop at a table. A twenty-something guy standing near the register, waiting to pay his bill. Another guy kneeling by the donuts trying to figure out which one he wants.

There's the kid serving us, and another young lady wiping down a newly empty table. At least one person is working in the kitchen, but from here, I can't pinpoint how many for sure.

I release Claire and drag my cup to my lips, blowing gently on the steam rising to assault me. I take a sip, noting the decent flavor. Not too bitter but packs a solid bold punch. I will definitely be adding it to my list of coffee shops. Is that why Josey chooses to come here daily? I didn't peg him as a java snob, but maybe he enjoys the laid-back atmosphere and the fact that it's so fucking similar to Bram's. A reminder of back home.

A man appears from the kitchen area, his back pushing through the swinging door, a case of something in his arms. He turns, setting it on the counter and skimming the patrons. His harsh gaze settles over us briefly, but he does a double-take, staying on us longer than the rest of the diner. He glances over to the kid then points and mumbles something about the contents of the box, grabs a pot of coffee off the nearest burner, and walks over.

Claire's body goes rigid…as if she saw a ghost.

"Top you off?" He meets my gaze and doesn't look away.

I scan the shape of his face, the dark green shade of his eyes. The way his jaw is pressed in a tense manner. There's something so familiar about him that it's unnerving.

"Sure," I finally respond, pushing my cup toward him and dragging Claire's along, too.

"You take yours with cinnamon, too?" He fills us up and stands there, waiting for my response.

"Mmhm." I glance over to Claire in my peripheral, ready to throw myself across the table if this guy ends up somehow being a threat to her.

"Thought I was the only one." His lips turn up slowly, a strange kindness about the expression on his face. He glances at Claire. "Glad to see you back, Claire."

I fully focus on her again. Have these two already met?

"You and Rosie make friends everywhere, don't you?" I ask Claire a bit rhetorically.

The man raises a bushy eyebrow at her.

Claire forces a smile.

"They sure do. Rosie was a chatty one." He extends his free hand to me. "Luciano Bane."

My attention shifts to the branding on the menu, plastered on the front window...the name of the place. *Bane's Café.* It's no wonder he met Claire and Rosie last night, he's the freaking Bram of this establishment.

I grab hold and give him a firm shake. I catch the wrong word just as it's about to escape my lips and switch it with my hidden identity. "Theo."

"My pleasure." Luciano looks to Claire then to me. "If you need anything, let me know." He strolls away, going back behind the bar and setting the pot of joe on its warmer.

Our young waiter passes him on the way over, hands full of plates of pancakes and bacon.

I scan the room again, not really noticing anything out of place. Maybe I can meet Josey and see if he can help me figure out how to get out of this mess I'm in.

Claire takes a bite of her pancakes, mumbling about how good they are.

I focus on her, smiling at how happy she is with her breakfast. Good food and coffee are the way to my girl's heart, and it's one of the things I absolutely adore about her.

I notice the way her gaze darts across the room toward the kitchen, like she's watching out for something suspicious, too. Is it because of our already sketchy situation, or is there something else causing her to be extra concerned with keeping an eye out?

54
CLAIRE

Johnny shook his biological father's hand.

And neither one of them had a fucking clue who the other was.

Johnny probably assumes Luciano is just a random café owner, and Luciano thinks we're only another set of patrons who enjoy his place's food.

I should have paid more attention to where Johnny was taking us, but I really needed to get that chapter read before class, and I had no idea he would bring us to the one place on the entire Eastern Seaboard that we should avoid.

Last night, when I saw Luciano for the first time, I thought there was a strong resemblance, but seeing them together, practically side by side, it was startling how much they resemble each other. Their eyes especially—they're almost the exact same shade of emerald, which in itself is incredibly rare.

I wonder if they noticed it, the similarities between them? Or if they thought it was a weird coincidence that they happened to share a few physical qualities.

One thing that definitely drew my attention was Luciano's quick cover up when Johnny called me out on having Rosie with me. Luciano easily could have thrown me under the bus, but instead, he went right along with it, even layering a strangely believable detail about Rosie being chatty.

Luckily for me, that's how Rosie really is, which made Johnny buy into it even more.

Another lie added onto the stacks of deceit between us. If I don't come clean soon, it's going to raise too much suspicion and create issues with me and Johnny. We've been through too much; I can't afford for us to fight over shit that we can easily handle.

How do I tell him that I fibbed and got his DNA, not to test his allergies, but to see if he had any living relatives, and on top of that, that the man he met earlier for breakfast was his bio dad who I semi-stalked?

Oh, and that I'm pretty sure *I'm* the reason Griffin is dead.

You know, no big deal.

And on top of all of that, it feels like Johnny is hiding something from me, too.

He's been paranoid since the moment we initiated our plan in the hospital, but lately, he's taken it to a whole new level. Constantly looking over his shoulder, quite literally, scanning every single body that passes us, like he's waiting for a threat to form out of thin air.

I don't want to pry too much, because I don't want to draw attention to his paranoia if that's all it really is, but what if there's something he hasn't told me? A danger I'm unaware of. If there is, I should probably stop wandering off on my own, but if there isn't, I don't see any issue with doing a little more investigation into this Luciano Bane and seeing whether or not he's worthy of being in Johnny's life.

"J…" I place my hand on Johnny's shoulder, pulling his attention from the notepad he's jotting down stuff on.

"What's up?" He immediately pushes it aside and gives me

his full focus. He raises his arm to run his fingers through his hair but stops himself, realizing that his long locks are no more.

"Is everything okay?" I hate the idea that he might be holding back from me, but aren't I doing the same exact thing?

Johnny's brows scrunch together. "Yeah." His expression darkens. "Did something happen?"

I can sense the immediate shift in his heart rate. "No." I take his hands in mine. "I'm just checking on you. Making sure nothing had changed that I should know about."

Johnny sighs, and for a second, I think he's about to confess something to me.

Instead, he shakes his head. "No, nothing you should know about." Johnny brings my knuckles to his mouth and presses soft kisses along them.

Despite it feeling like that's not the whole truth, I don't push anymore. If it were a real concern, he would tell me. It would be foolish of him not to.

"Okay." I tilt his head up to stare into his beautiful eyes. "Good."

I guess that means I'm in the clear to do a bit of digging on Luciano before I decide when or if I'm going to tell Johnny the truth about his father.

I finish class and send Johnny a quick text.

Me: *Going to grab coffee again and study a little, want me to bring home dinner?*

Johnny: *Sure, surprise me. Be safe, okay?*

Me: *Always. Love you.*

Johnny: *Love you, more.*

"Hey." I pause before Rosie goes her separate way to her car. "You want to go over that Lit material?"

She shrugs and yawns. "If there's some caffeine involved, I'm game."

I smile. "Hop in." I open the door for her to climb aboard.

I grip the steering wheel firmly on our quick drive to the place I've been twice in the last twenty-four hours. Now about to be a third time. It's strange how I'd never been there in the entire time I lived here, and now I'm frequenting it multiple times in one day. I pull up and put the car into park, hesitating before cutting the engine.

"Wait, is this…" Rosie does a double-take on me and the building we're stopped in front of.

"Yep."

"Holy shit." She relaxes into her seat, allowing me to make the final decision on when we're going to get out. "I still can't believe they shook hands."

"Right? It was unnerving. Like watching someone meet themselves from the future."

Rosie squints to peer inside. "You think he's in there?"

I sigh. "It's possible."

"Good, I want to see him."

I reach into the backseat and pull my bag out. If I'm going to be here, I'd prefer to look like I really am studying and not as a total creep. At least this time I'm not alone.

I draw in a breath and grab the door handle, steadying myself for whatever is about to come next. Maybe what I heard last night was a total fluke, and Luciano is simply a café owner and nothing more.

Or there is the very real possibility that he's the equivalent of Franklin—a no-good criminal piece of shit that deserves to rot in hell.

Here's to hoping it's the former. For Johnny's sake.

Rosie and I walk side by side until we reach the entrance. I hold the door open for her and let her go ahead of me.

She goes straight in, claiming the same empty booth Johnny

and I occupied earlier today.

A deep voice sounds from behind me. "We really have to stop meeting like this."

I turn to see Luciano standing right there, a white towel draped over his shoulder, the same way Bram had done many times before.

I swallow down the immediate nerves that rise and force myself to act somewhat fucking normal. "I blame the coffee. It's really good."

Really, Claire? That's what you decide to say?

Luciano stifles a grin, the same way Johnny does. "What can I say, I've spent a lot of time researching and refining which beans we source. I'm glad you appreciate the effort."

Rosie clears her throat.

Luciano extends his hand. "You must be Rosie."

To my surprise, she blushes, but takes his outreaching palm into hers. "I am."

Leave it to Rosie to have the hots for my man's father. I'd kick her in the shin if it wouldn't bring unwanted attention my way.

"Well, ladies, what can I get for you? Coffee?" Luciano raises an eyebrow at me.

"And a lot of cream and sugar." Rosie plops herself into her seat.

"Two cups? Or is your man joining you?"

"Just us," I tell him.

He nods and disappears behind the counter to fetch our drinks.

Rosie's eyes go wide, and she lowers herself toward me. "Oh, my, God," she whisper-shouts. "He's *gorgeous.*"

I tilt my head at her. "Seriously?" I flit my gaze in Luciano's direction then back at her. "Cut it out. You're like half his age, and it's J's freaking *dad.*" I make sure to be extra quiet on that last part.

"Oh hush, I'm not going to do anything about it." Rosie folds her arms. "You were right though. It's a bit eerie."

I lean against my seat. "Right?"

A waitress brings our cups over and fills them, leaving and returning a moment later with Rosie's cream. "Are you ready to order?"

I shake my head. "I'm good with coffee." I promised Johnny I'd bring home dinner.

"Me too," Rosie adds.

I run my hands through my hair, scratching my scalp and tossing the long brown locks aside. "This is insane."

"Yeah, it really is."

I bring the cup to my lips, savoring the full, untainted flavor of the roast. Bold, a bit smoky, with a hint of something rich, maybe chocolate. It's damn good, to say the very least.

Rosie pours entirely too much cream into her mug and showers it with an ungodly amount of sugar. "What are you going to do?"

I only now remember that I forgot to ask for cinnamon. I take another drink anyway. "I'll be right back." Before I can overthink it, I slither out of the booth and through the front door without drawing the attention of anyone other than Rosie.

Once outside, I cautiously glance around and then sneak into that same alley as last night. I tiptoe quietly along the side of the building, careful not to make a sound. A bright light shines from the back, a few muted voices floating around. I strain to make them out to no success. I get a little closer, and then a little more.

I inch further and further until there's barely any shadow left to hide in. My heart races but more with exhilaration than fear. I shouldn't be here; I shouldn't be so foolish, but I have to find out more about this mystery man. I don't want to keep this secret from Johnny any longer than I have to, and I refuse to come forward without more information.

I press my side into the brick and brace myself with my hand to lean a bit more.

"Twelve shipments, East End," one of the people says.

"Should have been fifteen," the other corrects.

A long sigh. Some shuffling. The sound of a door closing, then silence.

I hold my breath, waiting for the voices to return. For something other than the very generic bits and pieces I've already heard. It's not enough to go on. Those deliveries could have easily been related to the café, not an illicit activity.

I blink and in a flash, my body is flipped against the wall, a hand wrapped around my throat, pressing tightly and pinning me in place.

Attached to it is the man in question, towering over me with a fierce glare. "Who are you working for?"

My mouth drops open, but words don't come out. I'm too stunned by the intensity of the situation. Still, this doesn't confirm whether or not he's involved with something illegal. Maybe he's just an incredibly protective coffee shop owner.

He tightens his grip. "Don't make me ask again, who are you and Theo working for?"

I narrow my gaze at him and attempt to shake my head. "No one." I clench my own hands around his forearm to try to pry him away.

"I don't believe you." Luciano clenches his jaw. "Out of nowhere, you two show up at my place four times, poking your noses around where you shouldn't be."

Four? I've only been here three, unless...unless Johnny came here without me?

But why would he have done that? He was acting rather curious when we were here this morning. Did it have something to do with that? Does Johnny somehow already know the truth about the owner of the café? How would that even be possible? I have only looked at the results once, and that was on campus, when Johnny wasn't around. If it's not that, maybe Johnny knows something I don't, that Luciano really is involved with a part of Johnny's past that he's trying to put behind him.

"I..." What am I supposed to tell him? The truth? That I'm lurking in the shadows because he's my boyfriend's father, and I'm trying to determine his worth prior to telling Johnny? But if I do, that opens up a whole new can of worms. And I'd rather Johnny know the truth before this random dude with his hand gripping my throat.

But if I don't tell him, he's going to suspect I'm working against him, and maybe he'll use the same professional courtesy Franklin has done to people who messed with him and end my life for the sheer fact that he can.

Luciano's nostrils flare as he lets out a breath. "Tell me who."

I frantically stare back and forth between his green eyes. They're so fucking similar to Johnny's.

"I am not a man you want to cross, Claire...if that's even your name." Luciano looks toward the street when a few people walk by, but we're tucked into the shadows no one would be able to see us without venturing down this dark path. "Are you here on behalf of Franklin?"

With that name, I practically see red. The person who nearly took Johnny from me. The man that I desperately hope gets what's coming to him.

Luciano cocks his head slightly. "You're not, are you?"

I slowly rock my head from side to side. "No."

Something seems to click within him, and his resolve softens. He doesn't let me go, but his grip loosens barely. "Why are you here?"

"The coffee," I spit out.

Luciano narrows his gaze once more. "I'm losing my patience with you." His fingers twitch around my neck, like he's about to squeeze it again and force the answer out of me.

I let my mind wander, to the very real possibility that Johnny finds out what happens tonight, and the reaction he'll have once he finds out what his father did. I cannot allow Luciano to leave a mark of what he did, because Johnny may never forgive him. Luciano isn't exactly winning any father of the year awards, but I'd be setting him up for immediate failure if he hurt a hair on my head.

The only thing I can do is tell him the truth, even if he doesn't believe me.

"Theo is your son."

Luciano stares at me, not saying a thing.

Is he in shock?

His lips part and his eyes wander then meet mine again. "That's not...possible."

"Lynne," I say.

"No." Luciano's hand falls from me, dropping to his side.

I bring my own up to my neck in an automatic response to being held so aggressively. I study him while an unrecognizable flurry of emotions rushes over him.

He rakes his fingers through his hair, another thing Johnny has a habit of doing. A second passes in uncomfortable silence before he looks at me again, a pang of sadness in his eyes. "I'm so sorry."

And somehow, I truly believe it. If he really is in the dark world I think he is, it's no shock that he reacted the way he did. I probably would have done the same if I were in his shoes. It's difficult to know who to trust when everyone is against you.

"You can't tell him," I blurt out.

"He doesn't know?" Luciano's brows bunch together in disbelief.

I rub my neck. "No, not yet...I..."

He tugs at his bunched-up sleeve, pulling it down. "How? How did you find out?"

I bite at my lip, hating to recall another one of my deceitful moments. "An ancestry thing."

"Why?" Luciano's stare is serious and intense.

"Joh—" I stop myself too late and hope he didn't catch that slip. "Theo doesn't have anyone else. It's just me. I don't want that for him. Heaven forbid, if something happened to me—he'd be alone. He doesn't deserve that."

Luciano stands there, shock rattling his features. He lets out a breath. "I'm…speechless."

I want to ask him questions, figure out why he left Lynne and Johnny, but this isn't exactly the time or place. Rosie will start to wonder where I've been, and I can't keep Johnny waiting much longer. He already worries enough; I don't want to make that worse.

"I have to go." I point my thumb toward the street.

That seems to snap Luciano out of his trance. "Sure, yeah." He holds his hand out between us, signaling me to wait. "Listen, I really am sorry." He motions to his neck. "I…" Luciano shakes his head. "I shouldn't have done that."

"Water under the bridge." Because if I don't put it in the past, and Johnny finds out, there will be hell to pay. And I don't blame him; I would do the same. I turn to walk away but stop myself, something he had said earlier nagging at my thoughts. "You mentioned four times that we had been in. I've only been in three."

Luciano averts his gaze slightly before returning to me. "My mistake. I'm probably just paranoid."

But I'm not stupid, and Luciano is in the type of business where you can't make those types of errors. He had covered up for me with Johnny about the Rosie thing, and now he's doing the same for Johnny.

Why would Johnny come to the diner without telling me? What is he hiding?

I know damn well it's not another woman, so it has to be something that involves the past we're trying to escape. That would be the only reason Johnny would keep a secret from me.

55
JOHNNY

One of my favorite parts of living with Claire is watching her get ready in the morning.

From that first moment of opening her sleepy eyes, it's like I fall in love again every single day. Each time deeper than the last. My heart never really sure how it's possible to feel the way I do about another person but allowing it to happen without reservation.

Sure, the possibility of her leaving me fucking wrecks me to consider, but I cherish the moments I have with her, just in case it's my last. One day, Claire might realize she's too good for me, and decide she's had enough of hiding in the shadows and living a half-life. She deserves more than this constantly looking over your shoulder existence that I've drug her into.

Claire pauses, her hand on her jutted-out hip. Her black lace panties hug her in such a way it makes the blood rush straight to my dick.

"This is where I tell you to take a picture, so it'll last longer." Claire grins at me and steps closer to the edge of the bed.

"And I'd respond with something stupid, I'm sure, like...can

I?" I reach up, grabbing her by the hands and tugging her on top of me.

Claire giggles but doesn't protest, climbing up and straddling my waist. "We don't have time." But instead of hopping off of me, she leans down and presses her lips to mine, our bodies coming alive in a flash.

"Then we'll be quick," I breathe into her between kisses. I wrap my arm around her and flip her onto her back. I break away from her mouth and make a trail straight down her neck, her stomach, and hover around her panty line. I tug them to the side, swirling my tongue confidently in all the places I know drive her wild.

She arches her body toward me, telling me that I'm doing exactly what she needs.

I slide a finger in place, rocking it gently while my mouth does most of the work. Sucking and licking and appreciating her like the goddess she is. I feel her tension build, my own pleasure rising with hers. I reach up with my free hand, twisting and teasing her nipple gently.

Claire's attention shifts as she fumbles with the stack of condoms sitting on our bedside table. She rips one open and drags me up, her lips cascading onto mine while she tugs down my boxers and secures the thing over my ready cock.

I'm careful sliding into her, partially because entering her might just be my favorite thing ever.

She lets out a moan in response and pivots herself toward me. Her hands grip my back, inching me into her even more.

I lift her with one arm, the other propping me up. I thrust gently in and out, deeper and deeper, and when I sense her climax, I let mine ride along with hers in tandem.

"Johnny," she whispers. Claire's mouth meets mine in a chaos of lust and passion and desire that could never be satiated. An intense love that is impossible to replicate.

With one final plunge, we come crashing down together, maintaining a slow and steady pace to lengthen the pleasure.

It's everything all at once, the most extreme high I could ever imagine.

Every single time, I think it can't possibly get any better, yet somehow it does. The more we're with each other, the stronger our connection becomes, the more powerful the experience.

Claire grins and brings her plush lips to mine once again. "I really have to go."

And although I'd love nothing more than to keep her here with me, tucked safely away from any kind of harm that could come her way, I sigh and hop off the bed, letting her escape me.

I have work that needs to be done anyway—strategizing with Josey in an attempt to figure out how to evade Franklin for good. I had met with Josey yesterday, but it was cut short when his pressing family situation called him out. We only had a few minutes in that Bram's lookalike diner before he had to go. I'm hopeful that today will give us a bit more room to come up with something, considering I'm at pretty much ground zero on what I'm going to do.

Claire finishes getting ready and stands by the front door, waiting for our almost ritualistic goodbye: a hug that never seems to last long enough, and a kiss that puts those Hollywood romances to shame. We both hate being away from each other, that's for damn sure. But she needs to get her education, and I have to work on preserving our lives.

After killing a couple hours once she's gone, I slip out of the security of our apartment and onto the street. I could easily take an Uber across town, but I use the time to get a little more acquainted with my surroundings, just in case. Plus, I hear exercise helps in the recovery process, and I'd like to do what I can to get back to one hundred percent.

I definitely don't recommend getting shot, especially the way that I did. Most people would have spent a few extra days in the hospital, stayed on bed rest, and recovered normally. Me? I planned an elaborate fake death and spent close to three days in the backseat of a car, stopping occasionally for medical care and constantly worrying that my attacker would be hot on our tail. It wasn't ideal, but we did what we had to do, given the circumstances.

I'm pretty much fine now, just a bit achy here and there. Something that probably wouldn't be an issue if there wasn't a psychopath wanting to finish me off.

The air is crisp and cold. I hug my arms around me and continue along the main road, coming up on Claire's university. The invisible thread tethering us together tightens with her near proximity. There's a strong pull to wander toward it, just to see her, to confirm that she's safe and sound, but I ignore it and keep on my way. There's no real reason she should be in any immediate danger—not yet.

I glance at my watch, noting the time and how long it took me to get here. The walk wasn't as bad as I expected, not with the snow being mostly gone. I grip the metal handle of the door, the little bells jingling when I pull the door open. I stroll in like I own the place and go straight to the booth in the corner. The one with the best view.

Two older women sit at a small table, sipping their tea. A guy close to my age, with thick-rimmed glasses, is nose-deep in a book a few feet away from the ladies. The kid with the beanie is working again, wiping down a table.

He glances over at me and tips his head up to acknowledge me. "I'll be right there."

I repeat the gesture. "You're fine."

The door to the kitchen swings open and Luciano appears. His eyes widen when he sees me.

What the hell has gotten into him?

Luciano grabs a cup and a pot of coffee and comes over. He

pours it without saying anything, his hand almost shaking a little.

"Thanks." The word sort of comes out of my mouth like a question.

"Mmhm," he mumbles. "Can I get you anything else?"

The beanie kid comes over. "I can take over from here, boss."

Luciano shoos him away. "I've got it, Miller."

Miller side-eyes him but shrugs and walks away, probably grateful for the reprieve from working. For such a young fellow, he sure does seem worn out. The bags under his eyes are dark and heavy.

"No, I'm fine," I answer Luciano's question. "I'm just waiting for someone."

Luciano bobs his head up and down. "I see. Claire joining you?"

At just the sound of her name leaving his lips, a fire ignites within me, the possessiveness of keeping her safe overpowering the very normalness of the inquiry.

I relax my clenched jaw. "No. A friend."

Luciano's eyes dart to the seat across from me and then back to me, like he's nervous about something. This is not how he acted the night I met him with Claire. Then, he seemed confident and cocky, arrogant even. Now he's being...weird.

"Are you all right?" I'm not really sure why I ask this.

"Yes. I—um."

The bell dings, alerting us to another patron in the diner.

Josey strolls over, slapping Luciano on the back like they're longtime pals. "Lucy." He slides into the unoccupied seat and points to the pot still in Luciano's hand. "I'll have a cup."

Luciano blinks at him, then at me, then at him again. "You two know each other?"

"Ah, yeah, we go way back." Josey points his big-ass arm at me.

I watch as the wrong name forms on his lips, but he immediately catches it.

"Theo just moved to town. I was going to show him around."

Luciano meets my gaze again. "Is that right?"

I nod. "Yep."

Why does he act like he's doubting what we're saying? Who does this guy think he is? And why does it matter either way? Who is he to Josey?

Luciano lets it go, focusing on Josey. "I'll get you a mug." He turns toward Miller. "Another coffee over here."

"Yes, sir," Miller replies obediently, going straight over and fetching a cup.

I stare at Josey. "What was that all about?"

"What?" He stirs some sugar into his java, completely oblivious. Finally, he meets my gaze. "Lucy? That was nothing. He's just nosy. Don't worry about him."

I glance toward the kitchen, catching Luciano peeking out from behind the open window area. He moves quickly to avoid eye contact. That was definitely not nothing. The dude is creeping me out.

"I mean, don't cross him, that's for sure. But you're a new face. He's letting his need to know everything get the best of him." Josey tilts his cup to his lips, taking a hearty swig even though steam is pouring from the piping hot brew. "Honestly, this is the safest place for us to meet. You don't have to worry about anything shady here." He nonchalantly sets his drink down and throws his arm over the back of his seat. "So, you wanted to talk to me."

But with the sudden weight of Luciano's mysterious stare, I no longer think that involving Josey is the best idea. Maybe I should stick with my gut and handle all of this on my own. Without his help, though, I'm up shit creek without a paddle. I don't know which direction I'd row even if given the opportunity.

Ever since Claire walked into my life, I haven't had to do any of this alone. Even when I tried to keep her out of it, she managed to barge in and take control of each situation, navigating me through the thick of it. I wouldn't have made it this far without her, and I'm a fool for thinking I'll get through the rest of it. She helped me find that package, plan the entire faking my death scheme, and has managed to nurse me back to health. Shit, she brought up all of my grades, maintained hers, and scored a competitive scholarship, all while navigating a criminal underground.

We're a team, and we've made that known. That's not going to change. Why am I struggling so damn much to involve her?

Because I don't want her to get hurt. That's why.

There have been too many close calls. Too many moments when Claire could have been seriously injured. With Griffin. With Jared. With all of this. What if that shooter missed on her birthday and shot her instead of me? The idea of Claire being caught in the crossfire is enough to make me want to wrap her up in a bubble and never let her go.

"You've got this wild look on your face, JJ." Josey takes another drink.

"There's got to be something I can do to stop him, right?"

Josey rakes his hand across his jaw. "I mean, other than putting a bullet between his eyes?" He glances around the diner and then back to me. "You really pissed him off."

If only he'd tell me something I don't already know.

"Why does he care so much? Doesn't he have better shit to deal with than chasing me down?" It's petty, even for a mob boss.

"Principle. If word gets around that he knew what you did and he let it slide, people will think he went soft." Josey lets out a breath. "This *business* is ruthless, you've seen it."

One too many times. I shake the thoughts out of my head,

not wanting to relive the things I've witnessed Franklin have his men carry out.

That sick glint of power that Franklin always had. He enjoys his job more than he should.

"What about..." I lower my voice and lean forward. "The feds?"

Josey laughs. "You think people haven't tried? The dude's hands are clean. That's what he has cronies like us for."

He's right. Franklin was sure to be careful about that kind of thing. Making us do his bitch work. But he's only human. He could have slipped up at least once.

My phone buzzes in my pocket, and I drag it out to see Claire's face across the screen. I press my finger to my lips to signal Josey to not say a word. I hit the green button and accept the call.

"Babe, what's going on?"

Claire sniffles. "I didn't want to call you, I tried to fix it myself. I'm sorry."

My heart picks up its pace, a million different situations run through my head. "Claire, where are you? What happened? I'm coming right now." I hop up from the booth, digging my hand into my pocket. I throw a five-dollar bill onto the table and make my way to the door, completely ignoring everyone in the place.

"I'm in front of the parking garage." Claire exhales. "I got a flat tire."

And like I can finally fucking breathe again, I clutch my hand to my chest. "Oh, sweetheart. It's okay. Shit happens."

Of all the things I had thought of, this was definitely at the back of the list. This outcome being the best worst-case scenario.

"Hop in the car and wait for me. I'll be right there."

"Okay," she says with such defeat in her tone.

"Everything is fine. Don't worry. I'll be there soon. I love you."

"I love you."

We hang up and I turn around to see Josey coming after me.

"Car trouble, dude. I've got to go."

"You need a hand?" He points in the direction I was heading.

"Not a chance. She still doesn't know you're in town."

Josey widens his eyes and nods his head. "Ah. I got it. She's a feisty one, though, I'd be careful keeping secrets from her."

Ain't that the damn truth. I fucking hate that I haven't told her about what's going on. I just want to attempt to have some kind of solution to the problem before I spring it on her. The last thing I want her to be concerned about is how to help me. I should be the one taking care of her, not the other way around.

"I'll catch you later, man." My sights land on Luciano as he pretends to clean off a table; in reality he's eyeing us from his place inside the diner.

There's something seriously off about that guy, and once I figure out how to live a little longer, I'm going to find out what his deal is.

I jog the rest of the way to Claire's location, pleased with my ability to not completely get out of breath despite the lack of exercise since my near-death experience.

Claire jumps out when she sees me. "Why did you come from that direction?" She narrows her gaze at me immediately.

"What?" Fuck. "I was uh—out for a walk, when you called." I tap on the trunk. "Will you pop it so I can grab the spare?"

She reaches down and pulls the latch but doesn't take her eyes off of me. "Johnny."

I lift up the mat in the back and sigh in relief at the sight of the full-size spare. At least I won't have to track down a tire shop and get a replacement. One less problem despite the many others piling up.

Claire leans her hip on the side of the car and crosses her arms. "Where were you?"

This is my moment to come clean. To tell her about Josey. About Franklin. The note he left in the mailbox of our old apartment. To confess that I'm scared, that I'm completely in over my head and I'm not sure how I'm going to get us out of this mess. To apologize for ever getting her involved in the first place. To drop to my knees and beg her for forgiveness for everything I've put her through since she met me. To stomach the pain of watching her walk away when she realizes there's no coming back from the darkness Franklin has consumed us in.

My mouth opens, ready to say the words I've held in for far too long. Instead, I blurt out, "Can you grab that tool kit?"

"Seriously?" Claire snatches it out of the trunk and tosses it onto the ground next to me.

It clangs loud enough to gather the attention of the two college kids on the opposite side of the street.

"What happened to us being a team?"

Without looking, I can tell there are tears in her eyes—a sixth sense developed from loving someone so fucking intensely.

I focus on the task at hand, walking around her and getting the jack out of the trunk, bringing it around, and positioning it in place.

"You're not even going to say anything?" This time, there's anger in her voice.

It's not at all misplaced. I'd be pissed at me, too.

"Can we talk when we get home?" I don't dare tilt my head up at her because I know the second I see her face I'll lose every single bit of strength left in me. "Please."

"Whatever." She turns on her heel and takes off, kicking up a trail of wet debris in her wake.

"Claire." I sigh and stand. "Wait."

Somehow, this stops her. "I need a moment away from you."

There's so much hurt written across her delicate features. "I'll be home soon. Right now, I just need some space."

That familiar tether pulls taut, threatening to rip my heart in two. How did I let things get this out of control? To the point that she doesn't want to be around me. All because I wanted to keep her safe.

I run my hand through my stupid short hair, gawking as she disappears around the corner and out of sight.

I will let her go, for now. She's not in any immediate danger with Franklin still in place. She just needs to cool down. Then she'll come back to me, and I'll tell her anything she wants to know. I refuse to allow anything else to break us apart.

56
CLAIRE

When did Johnny and I decide to keep secrets from each other?

What happened to us?

We've been through some of the worst shit anyone could imagine, and here we are, being fools and hiding shit.

If I know Johnny, he's doing what he thinks is protecting me. The same exact thing I'm doing to him. But are we really saving each other from anything if we're putting a wedge between us? At the end of the day, aren't *we* the most important part?

It doesn't make his omissions any less painful to experience. And I imagine if he knew I was withholding something, he'd feel the same.

I round the corner, already my emotions settling with the distance from him. Now, all I can think about is running back to him, wrapping my arms around him, and hugging him tightly. Confessing everything I've been keeping from him and airing every single piece of dirty laundry.

Why did I think *space* is what we needed? It's to tell the damn truth. To be honest with each other and stop assuming that secrets are what's going to help our relationship.

I glance up, noticing I've mindlessly walked myself over to Bane's Café. Part of me wishes I could teleport to Bram's, sit down at the counter, and have him give me a slice of his world-class wisdom. That isn't possible, though, at least not with the newness of faking Johnny's death. Maybe in the future, I could play pretend as the grieving girlfriend, but I'm not sure I could stomach being in the same vicinity where Johnny was almost taken from me forever.

As much as I love Bram and his diner, it's been tainted red.

Instead, I go inside Bane's and walk to the register. I wipe at my face, hoping I don't appear like a total mess. "Two coffees, to go."

A peace offering of sorts. The ice that will break the tension, which will lead to us working through this weird rough patch.

I reach into my pocket to pull out my phone, where I have my cash and cards attached to the case. Except, I come up empty-handed. I feel around the front and back.

"Fuck," I spit out. I dig my fingers into my tiny front pockets, relief washing over me when I feel a bill tucked inside. I wiggle it out, even more relieved to see it'll at least cover our drinks.

Luciano comes out from the kitchen area. "It's on the house." He nudges Miller aside and pushes a few buttons on the screen.

Miller rolls his eyes but grabs our cups and pours them full.

Grabbing the cinnamon shaker on his way, Luciano strolls over. "Do you have a minute?"

After the biggest fight Johnny and I have ever had? "Not really."

"Those tables need cleaned," Luciano tells Miller.

Basically, in a *give us some privacy* kind of way.

I put a dash of cinnamon in each of the coffees and secure the lids.

Luciano tilts his body toward me, away from the rest of the diner. "I believe you."

I meet his gaze. "Why would I have lied about something like that?"

He lifts his shoulder. "People have done crazier things to weasel their way in and out of my presence."

Who does he think he is? "I didn't know who you were until a few days ago. Don't act all high and mighty."

I probably shouldn't take this tone with him, but my emotions are still running wild given the evening I'm having. All I really want is to go home and tell Johnny how sorry I am for storming away. For being childish and reacting the way I did. He's not the only one keeping secrets. We're both guilty, and if we had to weigh them all out, mine is probably worse. He must be worried sick about me, especially now that I know I left my phone in the car. In any other instance, he could track my location and make sure I'm safe and sound.

With Griffin, he demanded I keep that turned on for him, but in a way to control me, to keep his thumb on me and make sure I wasn't cheating on him. With Johnny, he really does put my wellbeing at the top of his priorities. He didn't even want to turn it on, because of my past with Griffin. I insisted, though, knowing it would ease his nerves about me going back to school full time. I wouldn't be going far, but he'd have the ability to check if something had happened and I was taken off course.

Franklin is such a wild card—we haven't been fully confident we escaped him just yet. Maybe with more time. It's still a little too fresh, though.

"You're right," Luciano admits. He runs his hand along his bearded face and into his hair. "This has been…a shock, to say the least. Something I didn't see coming."

I can tell he wants to talk, to vent about the situation. And if I had more time, I would sit down and hear him out, but I can't allow the gap between me and Johnny to grow any larger.

"It wasn't expected on our end either." I shift my tone to be softer. "But I can't get into it right now. I have to get home. We'll discuss this soon, okay?"

"Yeah?" This seems to calm him.

"Yeah."

He sighs, a twinkle appearing in his emerald eyes. "Okay."

I walk out into the cold, grateful for the warm cups in my hands. Was it this chilly when I came here? Or was I fueled by my emotions to the point I ignored the nip at my skin?

I glance both ways, suddenly realizing that I don't have my phone's GPS to guide me. I'll have to figure this out from memory. I'll follow the signs leading me to campus and make my way from there. It shouldn't be too difficult to manage, each step getting me closer to the man who is my home.

Commotion from behind me catches my attention, but when I look, the people scatter into an alley. My heart stutters, the very realness of being out here alone, in the dark of night, creeping into me. The measly streetlights only do so much to illuminate my path.

I turn back, stopping abruptly when a man wearing a ski mask is standing directly in front of me. Without thinking, I throw one of the still steaming coffees at him.

He flinches and I shift the other direction, only to find another man there, too.

Panicked, I toss the other one and try to evade him.

Anticipating my attack, he dodges out of the way, hissing insults. He grabs hold of my arms, holding me in place while the first guy puts something over my head, completely concealing my vision.

Fuck.

I kick and scream, but it all happens too fast. My body being picked up, the sound of a van door opening, the thud of them dropping me inside and closing me in, the squealing of the tires. I slam against the side of the cold interior as we whip around a corner.

I reach for the burlap sack on my head, ripping it off in one motion. I blink, blink again. But there's nothing but darkness. The back of this vehicle is pitch fucking black. I desperately try to get my eyes to adjust but I struggle to see even my hands in front of my face.

I grip the metal floor, bracing myself for the turns and accelerated motions.

I breathe deeply in an attempt to calm myself.

Okay, Claire, how are you going to get out of this?

My mind shifts to Johnny, and the continued distance between us.

He has to know something is wrong, right? For once, I pray he doesn't listen, that he doesn't actually give me the space I asked for. But even then, how will he find me? I left my phone in our car, and I didn't exactly tell him where I was going.

I shake my head in the dark. I'm on my own. And if I want to make it out of this, I'm going to have to fight.

I feel around the side until my hands locate the back door. I tug at the handle. Of course, it's locked, what kind of kidnappers would leave it in any other position?

The van slows so I do the only thing that comes to mind.

I play dead. Or well, in this case, passed out.

I lay there, my eyes shut enough that I can still see the darkness through them. My arms limp to my side.

We come to a complete stop, my body shifting forward at the abruptness. The engine cuts. Two doors open, then slam shut. Mumbling ensues.

"You do it," one of them says.

"Whatever, man, you're such a pussy."

"She doesn't even look eighteen, dude. You know how much trouble we can get into if we get caught?"

They approach the tail of the van.

I struggle to keep my breathing shallow and my body still.

"You're worried about *the cops*? Seriously?" The guy chuckles.

"You clearly haven't been in this business long."

The door cracks open, a bit of light peering in.

"See, she's fucking out. This is cake."

One of the guys climbs in after me, I'm not sure which, and I don't really care.

He does exactly what I want, moving right into the trap I've set for him.

The second he's in place, I bring my leg up as hard as I can and kick him straight in his man parts.

"Fucking bitch," he wails, falling against the interior with his hands gripping his privates.

I jump up in a flash, darting out and around the stunned guy still standing at the door.

"Get her, you fucking idiot."

For the smallest fleeting moment, I think I've duped them. But the man I assaulted gathers his bearings and takes off after me.

I break into a sprint, the sound of his footsteps fueling me to run even faster.

But it doesn't matter, I'm no match to the length of his strides or the adrenaline-induced dash from being temporarily taken down by a girl.

Frantically, I glance around, hoping like hell I can find some escape. Darkness all around me. A vast open area. Empty industrial buildings, all of them looking exactly the same. Deserted, empty, promising no way out.

The guy grunts loudly while extending his arm, grabbing the mass of brown hair flowing behind me.

I scream out in pain, but it's no use. No one can hear me. And that's exactly why they brought me here. They knew what they were doing. The one guy may be inexperienced at this kind of thing, but the one with his fist tangled in my hair is at least a bit seasoned enough to take me some place remote. Isolated from people hearing my cries for help.

"Come here, you bitch."

I grit my teeth through the throbbing ache on my skull. I swing my fist, landing the side of it on the guy's throat.

He coughs but doesn't let go. Instead, he grips me tighter, dropping me to my knees with the control he has over me.

"Are you going to help me or just stand there?" He calls out to his accomplice.

I struggle to get a look at him, the dark obstructing my view of his face.

The other guy approaches, binding my hands behind my back, but not as aggressively as I would have suspected the guy holding onto me would have done.

"There, try punching me again." The meaner of the two drags me to my feet, pulling me toward the van we arrived in.

"I can still kick you in the nuts," I say through gritted teeth.

He digs his hand in further, tilting my head toward him. "I'd like to see you fucking try."

It's then that he comes a little into focus. His face is riddled with scars, a large one on his brow and across his cheek. Dark, piercing eyes. A cold, unpalatable expression. Is this what Johnny would have eventually turned into if he never escaped Franklin's grasp?

No, that's impossible. Johnny is too good, too pure of a soul for that to have happened.

The man in front of me is nothing but a pathetic waste of oxygen.

His friend might not be as hostile, but he's just as guilty by aiding him.

I'm dragged into one of the vacant structures and tied to a putty-colored metal chair.

With the pull of a chain, a single bulb illuminates the space around us. I want to roll my eyes at how cliché all of it is.

I wiggle in my seat, my stomach sinking at the realization that it's secured to the concrete floor below my feet. The smell of bleach fills my nostrils and only furthers the panic that courses through me.

Someone was killed here. And the mess was cleaned up.

It's very possible that my life will end here, too.

The only thing on my mind is the regret of not making it back to Johnny in time, to tell him the truth, and to come clean about everything between us. Our last memory can't be of us fighting.

The brown-eyed guy hands the other a tablet. "Here, you figure it out."

My sights take in the other man, much younger than his partner, probably close to my age, maybe a little older. He casts a glance at me and focuses on his task. Regret hangs in his blue eyes. He's well aware that what he's doing is fucked up, but he goes along with it anyway, probably knowing he has no other choice.

With a final click of a button, ringing sounds, followed by the connection of a call.

He flips the thing around, and my suspicions are finally confirmed.

"Claire Cooper."

A chill creeps up my spine. I've never actually seen him before, but he's exactly how Johnny had described.

"Franklin," I greet him.

He brings a cigar to his lips, taking a drag and letting the smoke billow from his mouth. Slowly, he places it in a crystal dish and leans back into his chair. He's sitting at a table with white linen, hideous red and black paper lining the wall behind him.

Oh, what I wouldn't give to hop through and wring his neck for what he did to Johnny.

"So, you do know who I am." A wicked grin snakes its way up his face. "Quite the elaborate setup you and Mr. Jones pulled off."

I tighten my jaw but don't say anything.

"Listen, Claire, you and I...we have no qualms. Sure, you helped orchestrate Johnny's escape, but I'm willing to put that aside and spare your life." Franklin drums his fingers on the table. "The things you kids do for *puppy love*." He lets out a grave chuckle.

Is he really insinuating what Johnny and I share is comparable to a juvenile crush?

Brown-eyed guy repositions himself, shifting his weight from one foot to the other.

Franklin continues, "All I want is Johnny. It's that simple."

Finally, I ready myself to speak. "You killed him." It's not entirely a lie. Johnny and I both died a little that day.

"You actually expect me to believe that?" Franklin leans forward. "You think I didn't have my nephew followed?" His tone is condescending, as if I should know what he's talking about.

"Your nephew?"

Franklin laughs dryly. "Josey."

Josey? What does he have to do with anything? Is he here? Is that why Johnny has been so fucking weird lately? Because he's been meeting with Josey? Johnny isn't foolish enough to make such a stupid mistake, is he?

He trusts Josey, and Franklin played right into that. If anyone could squeeze him out, other than me, of course it would be Josey.

"I don't know what you're talking about." Which is the honest to God truth.

Franklin nods at the cruel man standing in front of me.

The guy steps forward, draws his arm back and slams it against my face.

Sharp pain spreads through me, and hot sticky liquid runs down my chin. I jut out my tongue to feel the split in my lip then clench my jaw through the pain. I refuse to show them any weakness.

"Is that all you got?" I shouldn't taunt such a twisted fuck, but I do it anyway. Chances of me living to tell the story are slim to none, might as well make it interesting while it lasts.

"Cocky little spitfire, aren't you?" Franklin points his finger through the screen. "You know, Johnny used to do the same. Take his beatings like a good little boy."

Franklin knew the exact thing to say to get me to react, and I do that very thing.

I yank forward, my arms being held back behind me by the ropes, pulling tighter as I fight to get away. As if somehow getting loose would help me get any closer to the man calling the shots. Only, he's probably thousands of miles away, technology the thing linking us together.

"You're a fucking coward." My insult is thrown at Franklin but applicable to everyone standing in this room.

All for what? Because Johnny refused to let Franklin abuse an innocent child. Because he saw someone in need of help and did everything he could to free said person. How does Franklin not see how fucking sadistic he's being?

Franklin clears his throat and taps at his nose, a signal of sorts.

The evil guy lets out an annoyed sigh and reaches into the waistband of his pants, pulling out a pistol. He slides the chamber, securing a bullet in place and pointing it directly at me.

My heart stutters. Is this really happening? I'm going to be killed because I didn't cooperate? Why am I surprised? This is the kind of bullshit Franklin does. He plays God, because he can.

"All you have to do is give me an address." Franklin's tone is softer but still harsh. "The rest will be taken care of, and I assure you, you'll never hear from me again."

"I'll pass."

The kid's eyes go wide. His mouth slightly parts like he's in disbelief of my words.

The side of the gun slams into my face, a newfound wave of pain following in its wake. Blood trickles down, and I have to squint to see straight.

"Are you sure, Claire? I'm a reasonable man. I'd understand if you reconsidered."

I stare straight at the screen. "I'd rather die."

"Very well." Franklin seems completely unbothered. "I'll find him with or without you."

I wouldn't put it past him to have wanted to do this for the fun of it. Just to watch someone suffer at his hand. And to twist the figurative knife into Johnny that much more. To show Johnny that he calls the shots, and that he won't be trifled with.

The guy brings the barrel of the gun only inches away from my forehead.

This is it. I'm going to be murdered, my blood cleaned up with a splash of bleach. What will happen to my body? What will my dad think? How will Rosie react? Will Johnny ever forgive me? I'd give anything to turn back time and change the outcome of this situation, at least the part where Johnny's under the impression that I'm mad at him.

Does he know how much I love him? From the moment I met him, our souls were intertwined in a way I'll never fully understand. I'll be forever grateful for our tiny infinity. The feelings I have for him will traverse whatever follows—in this life and the next.

I squeeze my eyes shut and whisper, "I love you, Johnny."

Franklin may control the outcome of what happens here, but he won't take my final words.

I'll be waiting for you, I urge the connection between us to give him this parting message.

The last thing I hear is the sound of a gunshot echoing through the building.

57
JOHNNY

Something doesn't feel right. Something deep within my gut.

Claire and I never fight. Even with everything we've been through, we've never taken time from each other. Maybe a walk to the other room, but not like this. In the beginning, before we were a couple, we avoided each other like the plague, but there was always the undeniable pull to be near each other. It's what eventually drew us together.

I could just be being paranoid, given everything else going on. But what if I'm not?

She asked me for space, I should give that to her.

I pull my phone from my pocket. If I can just see where she is, that little red dot, and know that she's safe, I'll continue to respect her wishes. I unlock the screen and click over to her contact, impatiently waiting for the circle to zoom in and show me her whereabouts.

It's nearly next to my own dot.

She's home?

I rush to the front door, peering outside for her. My heart pounds wildly, like I'll be seeing her for the first time ever.

Everything in me is aching to be beside her, to drag her into me and tell her how sorry I am. To confess everything.

But she doesn't appear. I glance down at the screen again, frantically hoping her dot gets closer to mine. It doesn't move.

I let the door shut behind me as I make my way toward her. I rush along the hallway, down the stairs and into the large foyer of our building. I take another look at my phone and continue my approach to the red circle. I pop outside, startled to find myself standing in front of the car I bought for Claire.

Was she so upset with me that she's hanging out in there instead of coming upstairs?

I peer through the windows, no Claire in sight. Opening the door, my stomach drops upon settling my sights on the corner of her phone case peeking out from under my jacket she had been wearing. I reach forward and grip it in my hand. Everything is in its place—her ID, debit card, cash. If it's here, where is Claire?

Panic completely consumes me. The only way I could keep tabs on her was her phone's location service. Now, she could be anywhere. And that thought alone spikes a fear in me I've never known.

"Claire," her name is a whisper on my lips.

I punch in her passcode and dial the one person I'm praying she's with.

"What's up, bitch?" Rosie answers.

"Rose, is Claire with you?" I can barely hide the alarm in my voice.

Her tone immediately changes. "JJ? No, she's not here. Is everything okay?"

"Call me if you hear from her." I hang up the phone, not wanting to waste another second.

Claire isn't with her best friend. She's not with me. Where could she be?

If she didn't go to Rosie, she sure as shit didn't go to Pax's or

Holland's. And without her phone or any money, she couldn't have gotten too far.

The café, something inside me shouts.

She loves their coffee; maybe that's where she went to clear her thoughts before coming home.

I slam the door to the car shut and take off on foot. With all of the one-way streets and potholes, it'll be quicker if I make a beeline there, plus I can get a better look without being distracted by driving. I sprint straight there, taking the shortest route and peering down every single alley on the way. Each step closer, my soul pleads with the universe that she's okay. That she's sitting in the corner booth sipping a cup of cinnamon java, thinking of how mad she is at me. Because I'd have Claire pissed at me any day over the alternatives threatening to ruin me.

I can beg for her forgiveness, but I'll never forgive myself if something happens to her.

I grip the café's door and swing it open, rushing inside, frantically looking around, my eyes scanning every single patron.

The tired kid with the beanie stares at me. "Can I help you?"

"Claire, the girl I was in here with earlier." I rush over to him. "Have you seen her?"

He scratches his head, not seeming to understand the urgency of the situation.

His nonchalance annoys me to the point I grab the collar of his shirt and shake him. "Has she been in here tonight?"

"What the fuck, man?"

The door to the kitchen flaps open, and Luciano comes through. He seems less upset than he should that I'm assaulting his worker.

"What's the problem?" Luciano puts his hand on my shoulder.

I shrug it off. "Don't fucking touch me."

He puts his palms in the air. "I can't help you if you don't tell me what's wrong."

"Claire. Have you seen Claire?" I don't mind the eyes of the customers staring in disbelief at the sight of a psychotic man in their presence.

Luciano nods. "Yeah, she was in here. Got two coffees to go. Forgot her wallet. Said she had to get home. Sounded urgent."

I drop the kid's collar and pat the fabric down. "How long ago?"

If she was on her way home, I would have passed her on the way, right?

Luciano glances at his watch. "Maybe half an hour ago."

My shoulders slump. She definitely should have made it back by now. Is it possible she took another route? She's clueless with direction without her GPS.

Come on, Claire, where are you?

I leave the two of them and the rest of the café behind, popping out the front door and flipping my attention from left to right. I spot the sign for the university ahead. Maybe she went that way because it was familiar.

"Theo, wait," Luciano calls out.

I ignore him and take off in the direction I think she went. Scattered trash up ahead draws my attention. I run up to it, dropping to my knees when I realize what it is.

Two coffees. Just like Luciano had said.

I clutch my hand to my chest, afraid the world is going to fall out from under me.

"Over here." Luciano points to the street. "Tire tracks."

I drag my hands through my short hair. "It was Franklin, it had to have been Franklin," I mutter out loud, not caring if anyone else hears.

If Franklin has Claire, it might already be too late.

The memory of Griffin gripping Claire at the top of those stairs runs through my mind, the frightened look on her face as he pushed her closer to the edge. If I was only a minute longer, I would have lost Claire.

What if I've already waited too long?

I should have never let her walk away. I should have chased after her. Told her the truth right there. Made things right between us and never allowed her to wander off in the dark. Why did I think I should give her space, knowing damn well that Franklin was back in our lives?

"You're working with Franklin?" Luciano steps in front of me, demanding that I give him my attention.

I shake my head. "No. Well, not anymore." I pause. "Wait, you know Franklin?"

Luciano's fist tightens. "If Franklin took her, I know where she is. Come on."

And for some crazy fucking reason, I go with him, because right now, it's the only lead I have. It's foolish to trust this stranger, but he might be the only shot I have at getting to Claire before it's too late.

I trail him as he sprints back to the café and down the alley. An unnerving feeling trickles over me at the idea of going blindly into such a hauntingly familiar setting. I push it away, Claire being my sole focus. I will risk anything to get to her, to save her from whatever hell she's going through.

I should have told her about the note in our mailbox, about Josey showing up out of nowhere. Then she would have been on higher alert. Maybe she wouldn't have stormed off. She could have stayed with me, been mad at me at home, where she was safe.

I climb into the passenger seat of Luciano's black sedan. I ignore how nice it is, the deeply tinted windows and immaculate condition it's in. Café ownership isn't the most lucrative of professions. Maybe he's good at investing or into cryptocurrency. Whatever the hell that is.

He pushes a button to start the car, the engine roaring to life.

I hope this thing is as fast as it sounds and not a phony like those frat boy cars around town.

"How do you know Franklin?" I ask, despite being hesitant to know the answer.

Luciano peeks at me out of the corner of his eye. "He's blood."

I let my head fall back against the seat. Great. I just got into the car with my adversary's family. I should have just mailed myself to Franklin's doorstep with a glittery bow and saved Claire the misery of getting wrapped up in this nightmare.

"It's bad blood, though." Luciano grips the steering wheel with one hand and shifts aggressively with the other.

At least there's that. Perhaps we share a common enemy. Maybe this isn't my funeral after all. But what about Claire? What does Franklin have in store for her?

"He's forbidden from this territory. If he was in town, I'd know it." Luciano blazes through a red light, completely ignoring traffic laws. "Doesn't mean he didn't have someone do it for him, though."

If Franklin wanted to expose me, this is the perfect plan. Of course, because I'd do anything for her. But if there were no hints on how to find her, Franklin was probably more clueless than I thought. Which means that he's trying to get information out of Claire. And if I know her the way I think I do, there's no way in hell she'll give him any details on my whereabouts. As much as I would sacrifice for her, she'd do the same for me. Meaning if she doesn't spill soon, he'll end her life just for fun.

"How do you know Franklin?" Luciano repeats the same question I asked him.

I sigh, running my hand over my face. Where would I even begin? With Billy? No, that would show weakness, and without knowing a damn thing about Luciano, I don't want him to have any insight into what kind of person I am.

He skids the car sideways and onto a nearly hidden path, leading down rows of abandoned industrial buildings.

"It's a long story," I finally say.

"Keep an eye right, I'll look left." Luciano points to the access passages between the structures. He slams on the brakes and points ahead, where a lone van is parked in the distance.

Immediately, I hop out of the car and take off on foot.

Luciano catches up to me within a second, reaching behind him and pulling out a gun.

If he was going to kill me, he would have had the chance numerous times again. I allow the uncertainty of this man to be pushed aside as I run with all my might toward where my soul is screaming at me to go.

I only hope I'm not too late.

I hear her voice first, a soothing melody to my aching existence. But it's her words that breathe a new wave of fear in me.

"I'd rather die," she tells someone.

Followed by the uncanny sound of Franklin. "Very well. I'll find him with or without you."

I step into the open space, only a dozen feet away from my beloved. My heart seems to leap out of my chest at the sight of the weapon pointed in Claire's face.

I reach over, grabbing the gun from Luciano's hand, not a care in the world about what consequences could come from my actions. I point it at the man in front of Claire and just as he realizes there's a weapon aimed at him, I pull the trigger. The reverberation crashes through my wrist and up my arm, settling in my chest. My ears ring, the casing of the bullet rattles against the concrete floor. I shift my mark, pointing the end of my barrel at the other guy. I don't allow myself to think, I just do what I have to do, Claire's safety my only concern at the moment. I fire another shot, the loud noise secondary to everything else.

I glance at the screen in his grasp as it falls to the ground with the man's now lifeless body. Franklin's face pressed up close to get a better look, in total disbelief of what he's witnessing. I rush over, take one look at the still connected call and aim the gun one more time.

"You'll pay for this." I don't give Franklin time to react before I shoot the tablet and end any chance he has of saying a damn thing to me.

I turn around, dropping to my knees and grabbing Claire's face in my hands. Her eyes are pressed shut, her hair caked to her face with a mixture of blood and snot.

"Claire, I'm here." I hold my breath and frantically wait for some kind of response.

Did the man get off a shot before I could finish him? Or maybe his finger pulled the trigger in his final moments?

Slowly, she peeks through her lids at me. Her cheeks are swollen on both sides, a massive cut on her lip. If I hadn't already killed the two men who did this to her, I'd torture them until they begged me to end their lives. Now, it's Franklin who has to pay for what he's done to Claire.

"Johnny." Claire lifts her gaze to meet mine. A tear rolls down her cheek. "Are you really here?"

I quickly get to work untying the binds that hold her in place. "I'm here. I'm here. You're safe now. I'm here." I help her from the chair and bring her to my chest.

"Johnny? I thought your name was Theo?" Luciano whips his head toward me.

"I…" I really don't care what he thinks. The only thing on my mind is that Claire is safe. That I found her. That she's in my arms.

I hold her tightly against my chest, not wanting to ever let her go.

Claire grips me with an equal intensity. Her bloodied face pressed into me. "I'm sorry," she mumbles.

"Shh." I kiss the top of her head. "It's my fault. I'm sorry. I'm so sorry, Claire."

Rage, unlike anything I've ever known threatens to

completely unhinge me. Franklin will pay, if it's the last thing I do. It's one thing to fuck with me, but to hurt Claire? He has no idea the beast he's unleashed.

My gaze flits to the bodies lying on the floor, dead at my hand. Not a bit of remorse or regret. Just cold fury.

"Get out of here." Luciano takes the gun near my feet. "Use my car. I'll handle all of this." He pulls his phone out of his pocket and pushes a button. He presses it to his ear, "Five-oh-four. Mmhm. IDB." Luciano disconnects the call and hands me his keys. "Seriously, go."

And for the second time tonight, I put my faith in this complete stranger and hope like hell he doesn't prove me wrong in trusting him.

58
CLAIRE

I thought I was going to die, and my last thoughts were of all that I would be leaving behind, most importantly, the man that holds my heart in the palm of his hand.

My face aches, and yet, all that's on my mind is the beautiful being in front of me.

Johnny dabs at my cheek with a towel, wincing like it hurts him more than it does me. I smile, knowing all too well exactly what he's going through. Every single time another mark was left on his body, a piece of me was lit on fire with a rage to inflict twice as much injury on the person who did it.

Sadness consumes Johnny's features as he delicately tries to clean me up.

I grip his hand, stopping his motion. "Johnny..." I force him to meet my gaze. I'm sure I look like shit, but I need him to understand. "None of this was your fault. I can *feel* it—you blaming yourself."

His jaw tightens, his demeanor still solid. "I shouldn't have let you go."

At this, my lips turn up. "You think you could have stopped me?"

Johnny tilts his head. "Claire, I'm serious. I…I should have told you."

Ah, the thing he's been hiding from me. His secret.

He runs his hand along his short hair—that old habit he still hasn't broken. If we ever make it out of this chaos, I hope for his sake that he can grow it out again.

"I need to tell you something, too." My voice cracks, but I can't keep this mountain of deceit between us any longer. "A few things, actually."

I've almost lost Johnny more times than I'd like to admit. If a war is on the horizon, I want to go into it on the same page, with everything out in the open. Even if he decides to hate me, I'll stand by him in this next chapter, fighting to free him from that sick monster once and for all.

But where do I start? With Luciano, or with Griffin? Both secrets are massive, and I'm not sure which one to lead with. The two of them could ruin us, but it could wreck us more if I continue to keep them from him.

"Whatever it is, Claire…" Johnny tucks my still gross hair behind my ear. "We'll get through it, okay? You can tell me anything."

My heart clenches.

He means well, but what if the truth is too tough to handle? What if it's more than he bargained for? What if he thinks *I'm* the villain in this story?

That's a reality I will have to face, because Johnny deserves better than this, better than the lying by omission. He's given me plenty of opportunities to choose my own destiny—to decide whether or not I wanted to stick around through all of the turmoil. I owe him that choice, too.

"The morning of my birthday…" Somehow, this moment is more terrifying than when I was staring down the barrel of that gun. Losing Johnny is a greater loss than dying. "I went to the hospital."

Johnny shows no reaction, just waits for me to continue.

"To see Griffin."

Finally, a bit of confusion as his brows bunch together.

"I…I couldn't go another day with him still out there. Alive." I let out a breath, the weight of what I'm about to say growing heavier and lighter all at once. "I poisoned him, Johnny. With a lethal dose of tetrahydrozoline. That's why Griffin is dead—because I killed him."

Tears well in my eyes, but not because of what I did, because I don't know how Johnny will react.

"Claire." My name is a whisper on his lips. "Why?"

"I had to break free of him." I sniffle. "I couldn't allow him to continue to control me. To potentially wake up and hurt anyone else. To come between us. I couldn't stomach the idea of him walking free."

Johnny's emerald eyes flit back and forth between mine. "Claire." He cups my face between his hands with such a gentleness like I may break at his touch.

This is the moment I lose him. The one where he tells me I'm just as bad as Griffin, as Franklin. That he can't be with someone who could do something so very cruel. The last time I'll get to be this close to him, to feel his warm skin on mine.

Instead, his words surprise me.

"You are so brave."

My lips part, total disbelief washing over me. Brave? What I did was out of cowardice. *Fear.*

"Today, every day since I've known you, you continually surprise me with how fearless you are." Johnny pauses. "You're stronger than you think. Stronger than I give you credit for. Which is why I should have told you…I should have told you that on New Year's Eve, when I went out to check the mail, there was a note inside. From Franklin. I thought I could handle it on my own." He lowers his gaze for a second. "But I was wrong to keep that from you. I know that now. And I'm so sorry."

After what I just told him, *he's* the one apologizing?

"You were only doing what you thought was right." Because that's the same rationale I've told myself to excuse the withholding of information from each other.

"That's not all." Johnny lowers his hands to rest them on top of mine.

"Josey," I say with a sigh.

He blinks up at me. "How did you know?"

I clench my jaw, my memory flitting to earlier when I was kidnapped and tortured for information that I would rather die than give up. "Franklin."

"I'm going to make him pay for what he did to you."

I bring my fingers to his face, running them along his brow and across his cheek, feeling the raised skin where scars remain. "We. *We* are going to make him pay."

"Together," he sighs.

And although I've told him one truth, I have to admit the other before we can continue with our quest for vengeance. It was difficult to spit the first out, but it's nothing compared to the bomb I'm about to drop.

"There's something else." I go to bite at my lip, realizing all too late that it's busted.

"Oh, baby." Johnny snatches the towel and rests it at the bottom of my mouth.

"I understand if you hate me for what I'm about to tell you. I should have never gone behind your back."

Johnny stares into my eyes. "You're telling me now, and that's all that matters. I'm just as guilty, so how could I hate you? No more secrets, okay?"

I nod and swallow, forcing the words to come to me. "Remember when I told you about the food allergy thing?"

"Yeah?"

"Well, I lied. It was actually an ancestry test."

"Okay…?"

A knock rattles our front door, causing us both to flinch.

My heart nearly jumps out of my chest from the intrusion and the confession I was about to make.

Johnny sucks in a breath and presses his finger to his lips. "Shh." He tiptoes to the door and peers through the peephole. His shoulders relax slightly, and he glances back at me before opening it up.

"How did you get in here?" Johnny keeps his foot firmly pressed against the bottom of the door so it can't be opened any further.

"I own the building." The sound of Luciano's voice flutters over to me.

Of course he does. What isn't this man involved with?

"Can I come in?"

What weirdly convenient timing.

"Now?" Johnny tries to hide the annoyance in his voice, but he doesn't do a very good job.

"No, tomorrow." I can almost hear Luciano rolling his eyes from here. "Yes, now. Why else would I have asked?"

Johnny lets out an exaggerated breath and slides his shoe away, shutting the door to unlatch the security chain and opening it wide.

Luciano strolls in, shifting his gaze all around while making his way toward me. "I know a guy." He points at my face. "I can have someone look at that."

"I'm fine." Although, it really does feel like I got hit by a fucking truck. Can't say I've ever been punched in the face by a man or pistol-whipped before. I guess there's a first time for everything. And hopefully a last.

"What are you doing here, Luciano?" Johnny comes over and

stands in front of me, like he's protecting me from any potential threat.

Luciano sits down on the chair opposite of me, making himself right at home. "I need to know what I'm dealing with here. Clearly, you and Franklin have some kind of feud. I'm just trying to put all the pieces together. What's a guy like him have against someone like you?"

"The details aren't important." Johnny remains firm in place.

I raise my hand to rest it on his back. "Hey," I say calmly. "Sit." I manage to tug him down next to me.

Still, he pivots himself like a shield across me.

Luciano adjusts the cuffs of his black dress shirt. "I just disposed of two bodies for you. The least you could do is not act like I'm the dangerous person here."

I wrap my fingers around Johnny's, hoping it anchors him in this unsteady time.

"I worked for him, and then I didn't. He didn't exactly take my parting very well, tried to kill me." Johnny raises his shirt to show Luciano the scar on his torso. "I took the opportunity to fake my death, and here we are."

Luciano leans forward. "He put a hit out on you?"

"Why is that surprising to you? I thought you knew Franklin."

"Oh, I know him all right." Luciano shifts his gaze to me and then back to Johnny. "You two haven't *talked* yet, have you?"

I speak up. "We haven't exactly had the moment." I circle my finger around my face. "With this going on and all."

Johnny tenses beside me. It's one thing for me to have a secret, but to share one with this stranger, it's probably enough to unhinge him.

"What is it?" Johnny turns toward me.

"Well, um..." I point to Luciano. "He's part of your family tree."

There, I said it.

Johnny looks at Luciano. "What, like an uncle or something?"

Luciano runs his hand through his hair, the dark locks billowing in response.

"Actually." I brace for the bomb that I'm about to detonate. "He's your father."

Johnny shakes his head side to side slowly. "No."

Luciano sits there, waiting for the shock to wear off. But something like this, on top of everything else that's happened, could take Johnny a while to process.

"Wait." Johnny scratches his temple. "If this is true." He stares at the man with a striking resemblance of him. "And you're my...dad." He emphasizes the last word like it might bite him. "What does that make me to Franklin?"

Now I'm the one thrown for a loop. What does Franklin have to do with any of this?

Luciano sighs. "His nephew."

I sit up straighter, trying to get around Johnny to get a better view of Luciano. "He's your brother?"

Luciano nods. "Unfortunately. Yes."

I am at a complete loss for words. Never in a million years did I imagine taking that small sample of Johnny's DNA would result in finding a birth father, let alone forever linking him to the man who tried to kill him. The sick fuck who almost ruined Johnny's life. Who was going to have a bullet blasted into my head a few hours ago because I wouldn't give him the information he wanted.

Nephew.

Wasn't that the same thing Franklin said about Josey? Which would either make Johnny and him brothers...or cousins. Either way, the plot thickens with them somehow being related, too.

59
JOHNNY

"Honestly, Claire. I'm not mad."

She reaches out to stop me from pacing back and forth. "J. You've barely said a word since last night. Sure, you're here, you haven't left or kicked me out. But we have to talk, please. This silence is driving me insane."

I face her, seeing the hurt that runs much deeper than the damage Franklin's men caused. I've stayed with her every second since I found her in that abandoned building, afraid if I don't keep her within arm's reach, something terrible will happen.

Everything keeps falling apart, and the one thing I refuse to let go of is her.

"I'm not going to *kick you out.* This is *our* home. You." I press my finger to her chest. "And me."

A quiet resolve settles over her. Did she really think I'd bail on her? Yeah, I'm freaking out. About Franklin. Luciano. Literally, all the shit that's happening. But choosing to walk away from her because she was looking out for me? That would be foolish.

I absolutely wish she would have told me the truth, but I understand why she didn't.

Our bond may be deep, but our relationship is still fresh. We're figuring each other out. This is just part of the process. Good things don't come easy, and what Claire and I have, it's better than great.

What happened was not betrayal, and for that, I refuse to allow it to get between us.

If only I could figure out how to articulate all of this to her while managing the shit storm that keeps coming our way.

After Luciano left last night, I took Claire into our bathroom and finished tending her injuries as best as I could. I drew a warm bath and helped her undress and slink down into it. She had asked me to join her, and with my heart still aching from nearly losing her, I removed my clothes and slid in behind her. Her head had rested against my chest, and I fought to balance feeling so incredibly lucky for this beautiful angel in my presence and so fucking infuriated that I allowed her to get hurt.

I held her until it was time to get out and dry off, and even then, I made sure she was moisturized and that her hair was combed. I carefully slipped one of my T-shirts over her head and let her borrow a pair of my boxers because I thought it would be the most comfortable option. I tucked her into our bed and climbed in with her, desperate to show her how sorry I am.

I didn't sleep a wink, my mind wandering between rage and regret, fluttering every now and then to utter confusion.

I have a dad. Well, I knew I did, I just had no clue who he was, or that he was alive.

I thought it was just me, my mom's death leaving me on my own. I have my cousin, but that was it. He was never around. And from what I knew, his family was long gone, too. It wasn't really something we talked about, since we were too busy trying to figure out how to fend for ourselves. I had a strange childhood, one I wouldn't wish on anyone else—another reason why I was so adamant about Billy staying as far away from Franklin as possible. At least I managed to succeed at something.

Questions rattle my brain. Like the major one—why did Luciano fail to ever be a part of my life?

Plus, who the hell is he?

The dude is clearly loaded. He owns a café, which is more than likely a front for whatever criminal enterprise he's running. Diner owners don't have guys on call for body disposal.

He's related to Franklin. They're brothers.

Does that mean Luciano is the other side of the same coin?

And how does Josey know him?

Luciano mentioned them having bad blood—what does that mean?

"Johnny." Claire snaps her fingers in front of my face. "You zoned out again." She frowns, which comes out even sadder with the condition she's in. Swollen, puffy, redness turning into various shades of bruising, butterfly bandages holding together the cuts. "Did you sleep at all?"

It's difficult to even look at her. Not because I can't stomach stuff like that; I've definitely had my own fair share of bloody noses and busted lips—but the fact that it's Claire, my sweet girl. It makes me want to rush out of this apartment and rip apart every single person standing between me and Franklin and then slowly torture him, ensuring he feels every ounce of pain I can possibly inflict on him.

I was never a violent person. Not until I had something worth fighting for.

Now? There's no stopping what I would do to get even with him and anyone who ever dared lay a finger on her.

"Yeah, a little bit." We both know that's a lie.

I glance at my watch, the secondhand ticking by slowly while we wait for Luciano to show back up.

He had said he had some calls to make, some things to arrange, and that he'd be here at nine in the morning to regroup and figure out a plan of action.

I hate staying cooped up, but it makes the most sense at the moment. It's safer here, since Franklin clearly doesn't know where we are.

We can't risk exposing ourselves—not yet.

The only upper hand we have is that Franklin hasn't figured out my location. He made that clear when he tried to torture it out of Claire last night.

"Are you hungry?" Claire walks over to the kitchen and opens up the fridge. "I can make you breakfast."

It's then that I see her, truly see her. The kindness of her pouring out. The concern she has for me when she's been through hell herself. Not for a second has she shown weakness, despite terrible things happening to her. She almost died, and she's trying to make sure I eat.

What did I ever do to score such a beautiful soul?

"Come here." I hold out my arms and go over to her, pulling her in and nudging the refrigerator door shut with my hip. "I should be taking care of you. Not the other way around." I plant my lips on the top of her head, savoring her sweet scent.

She opens her mouth to respond but a knock thuds against the door.

I lower my hands to her shoulders and hold her at an arm's length, peering into her eyes. "It should be Luciano, but if it's not, you remember the plan?"

Claire swallows and nods, grabbing a butcher knife from the block and backing herself toward the window with our fire escape access.

It's something we practiced a few times at each of our new homes, just in case someone came for us. And now that the threat seems very real, so does the need to use our exit strategy.

I glide across the room, making sure not to make a sound on

my way to the front door. I hold my breath and peer through the peephole, relief washing over me when I see Luciano nonchalantly picking at the cuticle on his middle finger. I scan the hallway, my heart picking up its pace when I see Josey is leaning against the wall.

Luciano didn't mention Josey coming with him. And from what Claire mentioned, Franklin had him followed. Surely Luciano wouldn't be dumb enough to expose me like this, would he?

He might be my biological father, but he owes me no loyalty. He could easily throw me under the bus and go on with his life like nothing happened at all.

But I know Josey. I trust him. And he wouldn't do me like that…I don't think.

I crack open the door without sliding off the chain and keep my foot firmly in place. It's not much, but it would be enough to give Claire the chance to escape if they forced entry.

"Were you tailed?" I say through the small opening.

Luciano rolls his eyes. "You think this is my first rodeo?"

How am I supposed to know? I just met this dude.

I narrow my gaze, not appreciative of his condescending tone.

He sighs, and Josey pops around to step in front of him.

"That's what took us so long. Lucy picked me up, and we had to drive around like idiots making sure we were good. Took the service entrance, no cameras, no eyes. I wouldn't do you dirty, kid." Josey grabs a large duffel bag from the floor and slings it over his shoulder, then picks up a drink carrier with what I assume is Claire's kryptonite.

I sigh and shove the door shut to unlock it then swing it wide.

Luciano barrels in, acting like he owns the place. I guess in his case, he does.

"These apartments could definitely use some remodeling." He glances around.

"Let's worry about that another day." Josey hands me the drinks and a paper bag I didn't realize he was holding, then walks over to the couch, dropping the massive duffel with a clunk.

Claire comes around to my side, still clutching the butcher knife in her hand. She puts her arm around me but stays firm in place, a reminder of how strong she is in the face of evil.

"Damn, girl, you've seen better days." Josey scrunches up his face at Claire. "You okay?"

She nods stiffly. "You should see the other guy."

A bit of dark humor, I like it.

"I did, actually." Josey reaches forward and slides a cup from the holder, popping the top and taking a sip. He winces. "Shit, I must have got one of yours." He pushes the thing toward me and takes another, making sure to check the lids this time. He settles into a free spot and throws his arm around the back.

Luciano clears his throat. "Coffee." He gives one to Claire and takes one for himself. He points to the paper bag. "Donuts."

Claire slides away from me and returns with a stack of napkins.

Josey is the first to grab one, clearly being the ice breaker of our awkward group.

It's been less than twenty-four hours and I have no idea how to act around this man who happens to be my father. Who is also some kind of criminal and happens to be related to the man who would stop at nothing to end my life.

Luciano starts. "I have eyes all over the city. Franklin won't get in without me knowing. For now, we're in the clear, but that doesn't mean his mercenaries aren't already in place. We have to be vigilant." He turns to Claire. "After what happened to you, it's best to stay put for now. This is war, and we can't afford to make any mistakes."

Josey wipes his face and leans forward. "Listen, this is great, and I'm totally on board with whatever is about to happen, but will someone clue me in on what the fuck this is?" He points between me and Luciano. "When did you two become best buds?"

I raise my hand to my hair, that stupid habit of mine. I catch Luciano doing the same damn thing out of the corner of my eye.

"Theo—excuse me—*Johnny*, is my son," Luciano says matter-of-factly.

Josey's brown eyes go wide, and he nearly spits out his coffee. "What?"

"It's true," Claire assures him.

"Wait?" Confusion settles over Josey. "Does that mean...?"

Luciano lets out an exasperated breath. "You're cousins, yes. Now, can we get back to business?"

"Holy shit, man." Josey hops up from his seat and grabs my arm, pulling me into a breath-squeezing hug. "I knew I liked you for a reason."

"The feeling is mutual." I slap his back, the same thought running through my head. I've always had this weird trust in Josey, despite not really knowing why. He's always been nice to me, and we've had this sort of unspoken comradery.

My phone buzzes in my pocket, which is cause for alarm considering the only person who talks to me on a daily basis is in this very room.

I pull it out, the text from my contact back home sending my heart rate a bit higher.

"He's on his way," I say to anyone who might be listening.

"How do you know?" Luciano stares up at me.

"I have a reliable source." I pause and add, "He left an hour ago."

Luciano's gaze seems to dart away, like he's lost in thought. "He's on a private jet. Estimated four hours travel time, giving us three until he arrives. If I'm right, he's flying into a small airport right outside my jurisdiction. I'll make a few calls to see if I can get exact details on tracking. If we're going to do this, we'll have to attack the second he lands."

"Isn't that against your agreement?" Josey breaks through Luciano's planning.

"He already broke it when he tried to kill my son."

A chill goes up my back. I don't know if it's the usage of the word, or the sheer determination on Luciano's face to end Franklin. He might be doing this for his own reasons, but the fact that he wants him dead almost as much as I do forms a strange bond between us.

It may be temporary, but it's there, nonetheless.

"What do we do?" Claire readies herself next to me. Her face is swollen and bruised, and I'm sure causing her a great deal of pain. Still, she puts that all aside to prepare herself for battle against the man who keeps trying to ruin us.

Luciano nods at Josey, signaling him to open up the bulky black bag.

With a hint of excitement about him, Josey complies, unzipping it and pulling out a shotgun onto our living room table and reaches in for another. A pistol this time, with a tactical-looking scope secured to the top. Then, two smaller revolvers. He places them all gently side by side and keeps going back for more.

"Dibs on this one," he says as he lugs out an AR-15.

Luciano rolls his eyes. "You're a child."

Josey continues to pull weapons out of the bag. Knives, more handguns, even a few smoke bombs.

"There's plenty more where that came from," Luciano tells us. "I'm assembling a team to back us, and I'm sure Franklin has already done the same. He's ruthless, but he's predictable. That will work to our advantage."

Claire reaches forward, hovering over the smaller guns and picking one up.

The rest of us stay quiet as she examines it.

She confidently thumbs a button near the trigger, dropping the magazine into her other palm. She grips the slide and pulls it back, eyeing the barrel and then releasing it. Claire shoves the magazine back into the gun and sizes up the weight of it in her hand. She narrows her gaze along the rear sight and then lowers it, finally looking at the rest of us. "I'll take this one…if that's okay?"

Luciano chuckles and splays out his hands. "By all means." He latches onto a smaller, more compact one and extends it to her. "This one will conceal nicely, too."

Claire takes it from him, repeating the same motions she had done on the other one. "Thanks."

"You didn't tell me you were dating a badass." Josey brings his coffee to his lips, reminding me that I have one of those, too. "Although, I should have known when she slapped the shit out of me."

I catch Luciano raising an eyebrow out of the corner of my eye.

"Is that so?" Luciano seems intrigued.

Claire shrugs, blowing it off like no big deal. She tucks the bigger of the guns into the back of her waistband. "Don't expect an apology out of me. You had it coming."

I can't help but be proud as hell. Claire is a remarkable individual, continually surprising me with her resiliency and loyalty.

A grin spreads across Josey's cheeks. "I did, didn't I?"

"If you need to make any further preparations, now is your time to do so. I'll be back for you at the top of the hour." Luciano checks his expensive-looking watch. "You have roughly twenty-two minutes." He stands and focuses on Josey. "Come on, you buffoon."

Josey slaps Luciano's shoulder. "Lucy, you know I'm your favorite nephew."

Luciano straightens out his shirt. "You're my *only* nephew, Joseph."

The banter between them is a welcomed distraction from the clock ticking down, a steady reminder that the end is coming. My only hope is that we're the ones who get to call the shots.

The two of them exit through the front door, leaving me and Claire alone.

"Are you ready for this?" I ask her.

A wildness flickers in her eyes, telling me all I need to know without saying a word.

60

CLAIRE

Is it bad that I'm not nervous?

I'm not scared. There is no fear coursing through me.

Only rage. Anger. The thirst for sweet revenge.

I used to be afraid of the world. I allowed people to walk all over me, control me, take me for granted. But now? Now I've shed that unwanted skin and transformed into a person who looks scary situations in the face without a bit of hesitation.

There's a sort of calmness about giving in and overcoming the things holding you back.

It's probably reckless, completely foolish of me. But I do so without reservations, because the only way we're going to take Franklin down is if we refuse to cower to his intimidation tactics.

I've had enough of him calling the shots.

Luciano, in the passenger seat of this blacked-out SUV, reaches behind him and pulls out a handgun. He turns and holds it out to Johnny. "Here."

Johnny wavers. "I already have one."

"I insist." Luciano nudges it forward.

The shots being fired last night replay in my memory. I had clenched my eyes shut, thinking I was going to die, only to open them to see my beautiful man kneeling before me, both men who kidnapped me lying on the floor of that building, dead. A gun next to Johnny's foot. The one he must have used to kill the two people who took me. The one Luciano must be trying to give him now.

"I'll take it if you don't want it," Josey chimes in.

Luciano fires him a death glare.

Josey raises his large arms. "Just saying."

Johnny decides to grab the gun, probably to settle the tension of the offering. "Thanks."

Luciano nods and turns back to the road.

Another SUV like ours is in front of us, and another follows behind. Both of them are full of armed men that Luciano was able to scrounge up on short notice, only confirming my suspicions that he's in the same line of business as Franklin. I just hope like hell he's a better man, at least for Johnny's sake.

I'm sure learning he had a father was difficult enough to handle, but if Luciano turns out to be the same as Franklin, I'm afraid of how Johnny will react. He's already been through so much. He deserves to have some kind of silver lining in his life. It can't all be one bad thing after another. Johnny has sacrificed everything to do the right thing; it's time for the right thing to finally happen to him.

We pull onto a gravel road, following the lead of the first vehicle in our entourage.

Johnny's hand grips mine tightly.

I take my free hand and double-check that my weapons are in place. It's not like they could get up and walk away, but in this kind of situation, it's better safe than sorry. I accidentally elbow Josey and mumble, "Sorry."

"You nervous?" Josey turns his attention from out the window to me.

"Not at all."

"Good." He winks at me. "You got any older, crazy friends like you running around out there?"

Johnny tilts his head toward Josey. "Seriously? Right now?"

Josey shrugs. "What better time?"

Our driver, a middle-aged guy who hasn't said a word this whole trip, presses on the brakes, slowing us down and pulling in next to the other SUV. A large building, I'm assuming a hanger for an airplane, blocks our view of the runway.

Luciano points ahead. "They'll taxi over there." He moves his hand. "We'll be waiting there." He glances into the back at us. "Any questions?"

I look to Johnny and then at Josey, neither one of them saying a word.

"Very well." Luciano hops out, which triggers everyone from the other two vehicles to disperse, too.

Johnny climbs out of his side, holding his hand to help me onto the ground. He'd rather me not be here, that much is clear, but he knows damn well I'm going to see this thing through with him. We may not have started this journey together, but we're sure as shit going to finish it side by side.

I catch sight of a familiar face—that kid from the diner, the one with the beanie, who seems entirely too young to be here. We make eye contact, but he carries on without any sign of wavering. He doesn't seem bothered by the condition of my face, unlike the others, who flinch a little when their gaze lands on me. It makes me wonder what kind of things this kid has seen to make him so blasé.

It's not that I want his pity—hell, I appreciate the fact that he carried on with no concern. It's just that I hope he doesn't lose himself to this kind of life. The darkness that will take over and consume him with no disregard for his humanity. I don't wish that kind of thing on anyone.

One by one, we make our way over to where Luciano had

told us to wait. He does some elaborate hand signals and directs a few of the armed men here and there.

It suddenly dawns on me that I'm the only female here. Not that it's a bad thing. It just goes to show what kind of world I've found myself in.

Luciano takes point at one corner of a building, and Josey makes his way to the other.

"Stay behind me," Luciano tells me and Johnny.

A silent fury bubbles up within me at the command.

Johnny tenses like he feels the same exact way.

After everything that Franklin has put Johnny through, it's no wonder we both want to shove everyone aside and handle this situation on our own.

The one thing stopping us is wanting to actually make it out alive.

We've had too many close calls, and ending Franklin will be for nothing if we don't make it through to the other side still breathing.

I hold a pistol firmly in my grasp, careful to maintain trigger control. I say a mental *thank you* to my father for those random shooting range sessions we had taken when I was a child. Who would have known that they would come in handy so much in my adult life?

Luciano glances at his watch. "Any minute now," he whispers back at us.

Like clockwork, we hear the sound of whirring somewhere above us in the sky.

My heart picks up its pace, ready for this to finally be over. In a perfect world, I'd tie Franklin to a chair and torture him until he begged for reprieve, but an ambush and a bullet to the head will do, too.

Just as long as he's the one who dies when this is all said and done.

A screech comes from the runway as the plane touches

down, the brakes locking up to slow its speed.

Luciano holds his hand up, all of us staying in place, waiting for his sign to move.

It's strange to think that a few days ago, we barely knew this man, and now he's leading the attack against Franklin, his own brother.

The plane continues to taxi, moving to the exact location Luciano said.

Finally, it stops completely.

I can barely make it out from my spot tucked behind him and Johnny. I strain to peer around them, but Johnny is like a shadow in front of me, moving when I do to block me from harm's way. I'm not even sure if he realizes he's doing it, or if it's just a reflex reaction.

After a minute, the door to the aircraft finally opens with a whooshing sound.

A single man steps outside of the plane, walking down the small set of stairs without a care in the world. Perhaps he's the pilot? It's difficult to tell from my vantage point.

Luciano drops his arm, a slew of men running around us with their guns drawn.

The guy immediately throws his hands up in the air and stops in his tracks. "Don't shoot."

Johnny and I take off behind the crowd, rushing to catch up with Luciano and Josey.

A few of our guys rush into the belly of the plane and come back out.

"Clear," one of them says.

Luciano curses under his breath. He points his gun at the man's head. "Where is he?"

The pilot shakes his head. "I don't know. It's just me."

"Why are you here?" Luciano stares at the man such intensity, proving just how very similar he is to Franklin.

"I—" the guy struggles to speak under the pressure of the

many weapons trained in his direction. "I got paid, twenty large. To fly here. I didn't ask questions. I need the money. My kid has this medical—"

Luciano cuts him off. "That's enough." He looks to one of his men, "Get his phone."

The pilot's eyes glisten, "Please, I have..."

Luciano interrupts him again, and just when I think he's about to shoot this guy because he can, he motions at him. "Get out of here."

Making damn clear that he may be in the same line of business as Franklin, and they may share blood, but they are not cut from the same cloth.

And that alone gives me hope that Johnny may be able to have a relationship with this man after all.

Luciano turns toward the gathering group of men. "Tear that plane apart. I need any clue you can find." He flits his attention toward me and Johnny. "He knew you had a spy on him. And he played it right into his hand. We've been busy orchestrating this, distracted." He hesitates before finishing, "I wouldn't be surprised if he's already here."

If he snuck in without Luciano finding out, that could mean that he's anywhere.

No place is safe. No one is safe. It's only a matter of time until he comes for us.

Until he comes for Johnny.

"Hey..." I sit on the edge of this unfamiliar bed, watching Johnny pace across the room Luciano gave us to hide out in. "Come here." I pat the lavish comforter next to me.

Johnny pauses, his gaze meeting mine. His eyes are full of

immense worry that will only be erased when this is all said and done.

I can't rid him of that apprehension, but maybe I can take his mind off of them for a little while.

Johnny lowers his butt onto the mattress, his shoulders slump despite the tension flowing through him. "I have a bad feeling."

I place my hand on his arm. "We're going to get through this."

I hate how difficult it is to hide my own uncertainty.

He turns toward me, doing his best not to flinch at the sight of my face. "I can't believe I let that happen to you."

"Johnny, stop. Stop beating yourself up about something you ultimately had no control over." I inch closer to him. "Let's focus on the here, the now."

Johnny tilts his head. "Claire..."

I press my finger to his lips to quiet him. "No. I don't want to hear anything else. All I want to do is get lost in the only thing that truly matters to me in this world. *You*. There's no point in focusing on anything else when there's nothing we can do right now."

He sighs, his gaze carefully fluttering over me.

"Give me that, at least for one last night."

Johnny rocks his head back and forth. "See, that's the thing, I can't stomach the thought of this being the end."

"Then don't." I graze my fingers along his cheek. "We're going to win this, no matter what it takes."

And maybe it's a stupid thing to say, but I refuse to give Franklin any more than he's already stolen from us.

"I love you." Johnny closes his eyes and leans into my touch. When he opens them, it's as though there's a fire behind them, sparking him to life.

I run my thumb across his bottom lip and bring my face

forward, pressing my mouth against his. If I'm careful, I can do so without bumping into my cut.

Johnny kisses me softly, paying special attention to my wound, but somehow intensifying the moment between us. He tilts his body, mine shifting back in response, giving him more space to climb on top of me. "Are you sure?" He breaks away and stares at me seriously.

I nod with absolute certainty. "Yes." I grip the hem of his shirt and pull it over his head, tossing it aside, running my fingers up his chest and then down to unbutton his jeans.

He hops off the bed and tugs them down, never once breaking eye contact with me as I slide out of my own bottoms, leaving me completely naked aside from my loose top.

Johnny grips my thighs and comes forward, his mouth hovering its way further and further up until he swirls his tongue over where my panty line would be. He inches closer, the build-up driving me wild.

I reach to grab onto his hair, annoyed with the shortness of it and the difficulty it poses on being able to navigate him where I want him more easily.

Anticipating my desire, he licks deeper, starting at my clit and gliding down, down, down. He brings his fingers closer, teasing my entry until I'm angling myself toward him greedily.

How is it possible that we've barely just started and I'm already dying for a release?

Johnny presses his index finger against my hole, and I rock my body onto it.

A moan escapes my lips, my head tilting back at the pleasure of the slightest penetration.

He obliges me by giving me another digit, curving them upward and putting gentle pressure on my G-spot.

I clench around him and he slows his movement, pulling them both out and dipping them into his mouth. I let out a frustrated sigh at having been so close, but I'm well aware Johnny knows exactly what he's doing.

This time, he fills me with three, a new wave of pleasure rippling through me at the resulting stretch and fullness. He continues to lick and suck my clit, dragging it carefully between his teeth and intensifying the feeling.

I grip the sheets and clench my jaw.

He slides his other hand up my thigh, positioning it right under my ass, his thumb caressing me in ways that only heighten my enjoyment.

When I initiated this sexcapade, my intention was to get his mind off things, but damn if he isn't completely consuming my every thought.

Johnny keeps this up for a few more minutes, bringing me closer to the edge and then pulling me back, with full and utter control over my climax. I no longer fight it; I embrace that I will come when he wants me to, despite the frustration it may cause.

Finally, he stops, breaking away completely and stroking himself with his soaked hand. He climbs his way up, shoving my shirt aside to take each of my nipples into his mouth and giving them some desired attention. I nearly come undone both times, and he's fully aware of it.

His mouth meets mine, and the taste of myself on his lips.

I kiss him deeply, reveling in the sting of my split lip. I spit onto my palm and reach down, gripping his hard cock, desperate to bring him pleasure, too.

I drag him to me, massaging and bringing him to my eager entrance.

"Claire, we don't have a..." He breathes against me.

And maybe because this might actually be the last time, or because I cannot possibly spend another second without feeling him inside me, I tell him, "I don't care."

I'm on birth control, and we don't have any other active partners. There's no reason we can't live life on the edge during this moment of intimacy—just like we are in every other aspect of our lives.

Johnny must be on the same page as me, given the fact that he doesn't question any further. Instead, he positions himself in place and as slowly as humanly possible, inches himself into me.

I dig my nails into his back and spread my legs wider to give him more access. I savor this new sensation, wishing there was some way to freeze this moment in time, the one with our bodies intertwined, his gaze focused on me, nothing in the world except me and him.

He picks up his pace, cruising from a slow thrust to a deeper, steadier rhythm. "Is that okay?"

I huff a snort of disbelief and his eyes flutter shut at the resulting squeeze on him. "Yeah."

He grows inside of me, throbbing and filling me full of him.

I tighten around him, but I don't dare come, not yet, not until he wants me to. I ride that edge and fight the desire to throw myself over without him.

Johnny weaves his fingers through mine, dragging them over my head and holding onto them with one of his hands. He holds himself up with the other, but drops his face to my neck, kissing and swirling his tongue along my collarbone and up to my ear. He tugs on the lobe, breathing against the sensitive skin. Johnny slows down, lengthening his stride and tilting himself just right to hit my clit in the process.

I moan again, nearly losing this battle with myself.

"Let go," he whispers, thrusting into me again, with just the right amount of pressure to send me spiraling.

Johnny exhales and continues to plunge in and out, fierce in a way I've never experienced before.

My body ripples with an intense gratification, consuming me from head to toe as our orgasms go off in tandem, one being propelled higher by the other, forming a peak of beautiful rapture.

It lasts longer than I could have imagined, and honestly, even when he stops moving, I convulse with the aftershock of the high.

Johnny stays inside me while bringing his face over to mine, resting his lips against my mouth. "I love you."

I smile and sigh, having never felt anything more powerful than what I do for him. "I love you."

I don't know what this war will bring, but one thing is for damn sure, I would do anything for my man and will stop at nothing to bring him the victory and subsequent peace he so deserves.

61
JOHNNY

I feel like everything is spiraling out of control. For the smallest moment, I thought I had a hold on the situation, but now it's like I'm walking through a constant minefield, wondering which step is going to cause a massive explosion.

Things were sketchy enough when Franklin was two thousand miles away, still unsure of whether or not I was alive. But with the momentary video chat where I killed two of his men, confirming his suspicions, he could be anywhere. Around any corner. Lurking in any shadow. Waiting, preparing, planning the perfect opportunity to strike.

I have no idea how to keep Claire safe when things are so fucking uncertain.

On the West Coast, I knew his hangouts, the places he frequented. I had a solid grasp of who was part of his organization. Out here? I'm totally blind to which moves he'll take, to the people he has on his payroll.

Luckily, my sperm donor is just as powerful as Franklin is, if not more.

For the last twenty-four hours, we've been tucked into one

of his safe houses. The only way in or out is with a retinal scan and a code that very few know. Luciano added us to the list and gave us access to our own side of the massive loft. He assured us that the windows are bulletproof, even if someone was able to get a shot off at this height, and that the place was pretty much impenetrable.

That's all fine for now, but eventually, we will have to leave.

Luciano scratches his beard and leans up against the doorframe. "I still haven't located Franklin." His green gaze meets mine and then shifts to the floor. "This is very unlike him. He is usually much more predictable."

I guess Luciano doesn't know Franklin the way that I do. Sure, most of his moves can be anticipated, but he's also completely irrational and impulsive. There is no rhyme or reason to some of the things he goes through with, other than to feed his twisted desires.

Claire's phone dings, and all three of us turn our attention toward the device.

She picks it up, her shoulders relaxing once her eyes settle on the screen. "It was just an email. From one of my professors."

I've forced Claire into a life where she has to lie to her teachers to excuse her absence. I hate myself for everything I've put her through, and if I don't figure out how to end this for good, all of this will have been for nothing. She deserves better than what I've given her, and I won't stop until I make sure that happens.

"I still don't understand why he's so hell-bent on killing you." Luciano crosses his arms. "I mean, to risk coming here, on my turf, to settle a petty dispute? We have people quit all the time. You don't see me chasing them down."

"It was never about Johnny quitting," Claire speaks up for me. "J was actually still technically working for him when he gunned him down."

"Then what was it?"

Claire meets my gaze and then looks to Luciano. "Johnny outsmarted him. He saw an opportunity to help someone, and he did. He basically sacrificed a year of his life to free this innocent person for no reason other than to do the right thing." Claire takes a breath, shaking her head. "J convinced everyone that he was this bad guy, and don't get me wrong, he did some bad shit, but it was the most selfless thing I've ever seen anyone do. And once Franklin realized Johnny had the upper hand, he did the only thing he could. He had him shot."

Luciano cuts in at this point. "Then you outsmarted him again when you faked your death. Making him look like a complete idiot."

I shrug. "In a nutshell."

Claire continues, "If we're being honest here, I think Franklin is weirdly intimidated by Johnny's altruism. Threatened, even. Like this one person could potentially ruin whatever he has going. I don't think anyone has ever done what Johnny did and got away with it. So he's making a point to follow through with his threats, to keep his reputation intact."

"I could see that," Luciano adds.

"But what about you?" I ask the man offering us a safe haven. "You said there was bad blood?"

Luciano twists his foot into the floor and glances over his shoulder briefly. "This line of business definitely isn't for the faint of heart. But, to go about it the way Frankie does…it's wrong. I'm not saying I'm a better man than him, we just don't see eye to eye on the way we handle things. We never have. He was always competitive and so damn spiteful. Honest mistakes would turn into these huge pissing matches. It was childish and absolutely reckless. Petty stuff, like I couldn't even show interest in a girl around him because he would stake this weird-ass claim.

"I tried and tried to keep the peace, but it got to the point where it was impossible. Nothing I could do was right. He got fucking mad over everything." He lets out a long breath. "I—uh, I had gained the East Coast sector, and after that, there was no coming back. It didn't matter that we were blood, that we were brothers. There was no reasoning with him. One day, things escalated too far. People got hurt. Good people. I couldn't allow him to stay here and continue to fuck everything up. He went west, somehow weaseled his way into the position he's in now, and we've basically been rivals ever since."

I've been in denial about Luciano's *professional* life since the moment I caught wind of it being similar to Franklin's. He's my father. And to think that he could be this cruel person like Franklin—it turned my stomach. I couldn't fathom that I had been brought into this world by that kind of person. Not when everything I've done has been for the good of others.

But hearing the way Luciano talks about Franklin, about how he disagreed with his ways to the point that he essentially disowned him, it gives me hope that perhaps I was wrong about the kind of man I worried Luciano was.

Sure, he's a criminal—but he is nothing like Franklin, and for that alone, I am grateful. Maybe there is a future for us after all.

Claire breaks the silence, keeping her sights trained on Luciano. "Sounds like Franklin saw a little bit of you in Johnny."

Is it possible we're more alike than I thought? There are definitely some striking physical similarities, but what if Franklin noticed it, too? I could have reminded him too much of his brother. The man he would never be. I threatened him because I showed him the error of his ways. That I was good, and he was evil.

And that in the end, I think deep down he knew I would win, just like Luciano had.

I'd like to think that I would have walked away from Franklin, gotten out from under his thumb, and gone my separate way. But in hindsight, I'm not sure if I could have allowed such a sick fuck to go free. It's possible that Franklin knew I'd come for him before I even did.

Claire's phone buzzes again, this time longer instead of the single vibration earlier.

She holds it out for me to see the screen. "It's Rosie. She's FaceTiming me."

"She's probably checking in to see how you are."

"Do I answer it?" Claire glances at me and then Luciano, then back to me.

"I don't see the harm in it," I tell her.

Claire slides her finger across to accept the call. She holds it out in front of her and allows it to connect. Within a split second, her expression shifts from a smile to something of utter terror.

"Claire," Rosie wails.

I rush over to Claire, taking her phone from her to get a better look at what could be causing her such alarm.

A spit-soaked rag dangles just below Rosie's mouth. Her blonde hair is matted to her mascara-stained cheeks. She's secured to a chair, her arms and legs in place the same way Claire's were last night.

Never in a million years did I think Franklin would go after Rosie, but I guess no one is safe when it comes to him. He went after who was important to me—Claire. And when I got Claire safely away from him, he did the same to her.

The screen pivots, a person coming into view.

The man behind this all.

Luciano rushes over but I hold out my hand to him.

He furrows his brows but complies with a subtle nod.

Franklin may hate us both, but I don't think he knows we're working together. And if we can maintain the slightest advantage against him, I'll graciously take it.

"Mr. Jones, what a pleasure." Franklin slides a butcher knife off a metal tray, twirling it gently in his hand. "So glad to see you alive and well." He exhales. "We haven't had a chance to catch up." Franklin stares into the camera. "How's the weather?"

I clench my jaw. "Let her go, Franklin." My gaze flicks to the doorway, where Josey has now taken up residency.

Franklin completely ignores my demand. "Yeah, it rained a bit back home on and off. Beats this cold, though."

"Tell me what you want." Although I know exactly what he's going to say.

Despite already having my attention, he lifts the blade toward Rosie, running the tip of it down the side of her temple. "Sure would be a shame to mark up another pretty lady's face."

My blood boils at the implication behind his words. He already did the unthinkable to the woman I love, there's no telling how far he'd take it with Rosie. She's just another disposable pawn in his gruesome game, and I'm not entirely positive she'll make it out of this alive.

I thought I had already put Claire through enough, but having her witness the brutal murder of her best friend? That would be a line crossed we could never come back from.

Franklin pulls the blade away and faces the camera again. "How about an even trade? You for her. Easy enough. Then we can chat in person."

"When and where?"

Claire tenses beside me, but I refuse to look her way. I can't allow my concentration to waver while the call is still connected.

"Good answer." Franklin grins a toothless grin. "You can bring Claire. I'd hate for Rosie here to have to walk home in the dark. I'll text you the details. And Johnny…" He waits until he has my full attention to continue. "You two come alone, or you don't come at all. If you bring anyone else, I'll carve this girl up like a pumpkin on Halloween."

And with that final threat, the call is disconnected.

"He's going to kill her." The words we are all thinking leave Claire's mouth first.

"I'm not going to let that happen." It's true, he really does want me, and I have a feeling this is one of those situations he's giving me that I can actually succeed at. Even if the prize at the end is my death.

Claire's best friend will not die because of me.

"You can't go." Claire tugs on my arm in an attempt to pull my attention to her.

Defeat crashes over me. I've always found a way to slip out of Franklin's grasp just in the nick of time. There has always been some kind of escape route in place. But now, I can think of none. I'll be walking right into his palm, with no means of a way out. For once, he finally outsmarted me and put me in a complete checkmate.

All that's left is finding the courage to say goodbye.

Slowly, I tilt my head toward her. My heart aching at the pain I've put her through since the moment I stepped into her life. I bumped into her that fateful night, knocking her down, and all I've done since is continue to ruin everything. I was a coward for not having the strength to stay away from her then. I was selfish and idiotic for thinking I could ever be the type of man that Claire deserves. We may have formed something beautiful and rare together, but at what cost?

I cannot allow my angel to fall.

"Don't look at me like that." Claire's bottom lip quivers.

"Like what?"

"Like you're about to say goodbye."

Luciano finally steps forward, metaphorically and literally putting his foot down. "No one, and I repeat *no one*, is saying goodbye."

"Yeah, what he said." Josey comes into the room, his muscles nearly bulging out of his T-shirt.

"There's no way around it," I tell them. "I've run countless scenarios through my head. The only way I can save Rosie is to give him what he wants. And once I'm there, there's no turning back. He won't let me escape for a second time."

"You stopped me from coming into view for a reason." Luciano stares at me intensely. "He doesn't know we're working together. He'd never see it coming."

"How does that help me, though? He said for us to come alone. I wouldn't put it past him to follow through with his threat if we do a damn thing to make him suspicious. I won't let Rosie get hurt."

"Wait, who's Rosie?" Josey rubs his chin.

Claire's phone goes off in my hand, the details Franklin promised beaming across the screen.

The wheels in Luciano's brain seem to start turning as a plan formulates in his head. "I have an idea."

62
CLAIRE

If Rosie dies, I'm going to lose my mind. If it's Johnny instead, I'll still lose my mind. I should have known that I'd be putting her in danger by running back to my old life. I was foolish to think we'd actually get away with it. I underestimated just how far Franklin would take things to get his way.

Now, it feels like all hope is lost, and that there's no chance at saving any of us.

If we can get Rosie to safety, I'll stay by Johnny's side and go headfirst into whatever fate has in store for us. I refuse to walk away from him, no matter how difficult things become.

He is my person, the only reason I'm still here today.

It was never about owing him anything; it was that we solidified ourselves as one. We share our challenges, our successes, any hurdle or obstacle, and we rise to the top together.

Keeping secrets was stupid. We thought we were doing the right thing for each other, when in reality, the best thing we could have done was to be honest. We're a team, and we've already overcome mountains. What's another impossible feat?

Johnny grips my hand firmly as we march down the dark street. He glances over at me, his eyes silently pleading with me to turn around, to go back. But he knows better. He wouldn't walk away, and neither will I.

The cold metal of the guns presses up against my bare skin under my shirt. Each step we take, we get closer to the possibility of death.

"This isn't right," Johnny says under his breath.

"I know."

He pauses under a dim section of the sidewalk. "What if it doesn't work?" His green gaze traces over me, sending those all too familiar butterflies dancing around my belly.

Even in the darkest of times, my love for him flourishes.

I graze his cheek with my hand and savor every detail of him that I can make out in the darkness of night. I run my thumb along his bottom lip, every single kiss replaying in my memory. "At least we'll have tried." And it might be an influx of desperation, but I tell him, "We're going to make it through this."

Because I can't accept the alternative. I refuse to think Johnny sacrificed everything for nothing. That we were placed in each other's lives only temporarily. There's more to our story than what we've already been through. There has to be a light at the end of this darkness.

If not for me, for him.

"I want to believe that." Johnny carefully raises his hand to my cheek, hesitating along the skin. "I'm sorry, Claire, for everything. For this..." He hovers over the wounds on my face, still aching from the beating from Franklin's goons. "For not being able to stay away from you when I knew I should have."

"Hey, you don't get to carry that burden. I regret nothing. Okay?" I stare into those beautiful emerald eyes. "I'd do it all over again if it meant being with you."

Maybe I'm foolish, but the time I've shared with Johnny has been the best moments of my life. And I truly think that in order to appreciate the good, you have to endure the bad. Our highs were higher because our lows were so damn low.

I stand on my tiptoes, sliding my arms around Johnny's neck and pulling him down into me. I don't care that he's afraid to kiss me with my injuries, I press my lips to his anyway.

I can be beaten, but I will not be broken. If I'm going to die tonight, I'm going to cherish these final moments with my man. Almost dying after fighting with him was awful. I'm going to make sure he knows how much I love him.

Johnny is gentle, extra careful not to apply too much pressure. His touch is soft and delicate, just like he has been our entire relationship. Never once did he show an ounce of aggression or control over me. It's not that he isn't capable of it; he just reserves it for anyone who threatens someone he cares about. He is fierce, and strong, but he is kind and thoughtful.

Johnny is a man that I am grateful for having known. To have shared my life with, even if for such a short period.

He gave me the strength to step into the woman I am today.

"I love you, Claire Cooper," he whispers against my mouth.

"I love you, Johnny Jones."

Johnny rests his forehead against mine. "Together?"

It's as though he finally realizes the magnitude of my love for him—the lengths I would go to have him with me.

I smile through the pain, both physical and internal. "You're stuck with me, remember?"

Johnny lets out a breath, breaking away and studying me intently. "Yeah." He rocks his head back and forth gently, a sort of disbelief in his expression.

I weave my hand around his, uniting us again. We are stronger together, and I want to make damn sure that Franklin sees that.

He fucked with the wrong power couple.

The rest of our walk is brief and quiet, aside from the occasional car that drives by. The location Franklin sent us wasn't too far from Luciano's hideout, but we couldn't use one of his vehicles without risking Franklin realizing our alliance. And going back to our car seemed foolish, so here we are, hand in hand, strolling to another abandoned building in the industrial district.

We approach the clearing leading toward where we need to go, loose gravel crunching under our shoes, a train passing in the distance. My heartbeat is steady, my grip firmly on Johnny.

It's clear that our chances of survival are narrow, but I appreciate the fact that we get to do this together. It's totally bat-shit crazy, to have such a mindset—I'm well aware of that. There's something to be said about fully giving yourself to someone, though. Mind, body, and soul. Often, people find this very thing, but it's one-sided. It's rare when that connection goes both ways, but with it comes the ability to do anything for the person you love without reservation. Because at the end of the day, what's more important than that?

I sacrifice myself because Johnny does, too.

A metal door creaks open up ahead, and a large man steps out into the night. His arms are crossed over his chest, and his face is solemn. He studies us each continued step of the way.

Johnny tenses slightly and glances down at me.

I can sense his hesitation. I'm sure he'd rather push me away, forbid me from going into that building, and handle this himself. I know the feeling all too well, given it's the exact thing running through my mind, too. There's no convincing either of us otherwise, and there's no point in trying.

For a split second, I replay a million possible scenarios through my head, but not of the outcome of tonight. Of Johnny's future.

I watch as he graduates from college, starts his photography business, decides to dabble in cinema and goes off to win some kind of award. He maintains a relationship with his father, and it builds over the years. Wrinkles appear on his face, the scars fading with time. He's smiling, he's free…and I'm there with him each step of the way. We bounce around the world, traveling and exploring, and he surprises me with a party when my first novel is published. His character never falters, and somehow, he grows kinder with age. At one point, I even catch a glimpse of us running our own coffee shop. A very Johnny and Claire thing to do.

The massive man at the door puts his hand up, signaling us to stop. "Arms out. Turn around." His voice is thick and coarse.

So much for the guns we had tucked away.

We comply, outstretching side by side.

He pats Johnny down first, pulling out the two pistols tucked into his waistband. He slides them across the ground where another nameless man picks them up. He flips Johnny around, checking his front, and once he's confident Johnny is clean, he moves his attention to me.

He starts at the top of my head, moving his way down, across my shoulders, along my arms, up under my armpits. He hesitates for a second too long, his grimy hands hovering over my tits. Before Johnny can react, because I know damn well he's about to, I thrust my elbow back and slam it into the guy's face. I probably shouldn't have, but I'd rather it be me than Johnny.

There's a crack, followed by a slur of curse words. I immediately go back into the arms-out position like nothing happened at all.

I flit my gaze over to Johnny, a look of shock and pride on his face. I stifle the grin on my own.

"You idiot," the other guy says. "You let a girl break your nose? Seriously?"

"Viktor, she fucking decked me."

Viktor? Why does that name sound so familiar?

With my back still turned, I have to guess what's happening. There's a mild sound of shuffling, and a grunt.

"Get in there, clean yourself up." The new guy tells the one I injured. His footsteps approach behind me. "Sorry about that. Gleb can get a little *handsy,* if you know what I mean." He sighs and goes to work patting me down, but not in the creepy way Gleb had done. "Can't have these." He pulls the pistols from around my waistband and tucks them into his own.

Well, we tried.

"Turn," the new guy says.

I glance at Johnny, his jaw tense for obvious reasons.

I take in the man's face. It's nothing special. Dark eyes. Dark hair. Cookie-cutter mob-looking guy. Forty-something, and probably wishing he'd gone to college instead of choosing this as a career path.

He taps around my ankles one last time and throws a thumb behind him toward the door Gleb disappeared into. "You're good to go."

Johnny and I meet each other's gaze, a silent exchange speaking volumes between us.

He winks at me, and with that subtle gesture, I prepare myself for any possible outcome.

Our hands find each other, almost like their magnets, locking us together.

We step through the threshold, a familiar stench tickling my nostrils—the same one from when I was taken. A chemical sort of smell—a mix of bleach and the remains of whatever was produced here years ago.

It takes my eyes a second to adjust, but when they do, I spot Rosie tied to a chair in the center of the room, Franklin standing at her side, that same knife from the video call pressed to her neck.

I want to break into a sprint, rush over and free Rosie, but I can't. Not yet. Any sudden move could cause Franklin to react more irrationally than he already is.

"Well, well, well, what do we have here?" Franklin calls out to us. With his free hand, he motions us over.

A fresh set of goons come up behind us and shove us forward.

Still hand in hand, gripping each other tightly, we make our way closer.

I try to scan the space, count the sets of eyes on us, but it's too much. There are too many of them, and every time I think I've finished tallying them up, someone else appears from the shadows.

Franklin was no fool; he came prepared.

Which if you think about it, is slightly hilarious. He's *that* damn afraid of Johnny that he brought an army to fight his war. Fucking coward.

Johnny attempts to position himself in front of me, but I make sure to stay by his side. He's already handled so much on his own, I refuse to let that happen anymore.

"Let her go," Johnny tells Franklin.

Franklin tilts his head to the side. "Now, what's the rush? We're only just getting started." He looks down at her and runs the flat of the blade across her cheek.

Rosie squirms under him but it's no use. She's tied in place with no chance of breaking free. Panic seeps out of her, which only fuels my rage.

The door we came through slams shut behind us, a row of men in black blocking the way. The room seems to shrink as a wall of men close in around us. Franklin in the center, two guys at his back, and Rosie at his mercy.

Johnny gravitates toward me, or maybe me toward him, and either way, we inch together, as if we can somehow combine our strengths to find a way out. Our plan suddenly falls flat with the sheer magnitude of the effort Franklin is putting in to keep us confined. We stop within six feet of my best friend and the man threatening her.

I stare at her, pleading with her to understand how sorry I am, and that we will do everything in our power to get her out of this alive, even if it means sacrificing ourselves for her.

A man approaches Franklin, whispering something into his ear before retiring to his spot in the line.

Franklin's eyebrows raise and he nods his head. "Interesting." He focuses on Johnny. "You actually listened. I have to say, I wasn't sure you'd actually come alone."

Johnny stiffens. "Who was I supposed to bring along? We did everything you asked. Let her go."

"You know…" Franklin circles Rosie slowly, the knife still in his grasp. "I'll never relate. This whole *good guy* act you put on." He stops, holding the tip toward us. "What's the point? It makes you weak. Vulnerable. Easily predictable. I mean, how simple was it for me to find you? All I had to do was locate her." He points at me. "And once I knew you had her, I just took this one." Franklin nudges Rosie. "It's like taking candy from a baby. What's the point? You're willing to *die* for these people? What's wrong with you?"

"You got what you wanted." Johnny grips my hand tightly. "Take me instead. Kill me instead of her."

Franklin strolls over to stand behind Rosie. "Oh Johnny, I don't want to kill you, not yet. I want to *torture* you. I want to make you pay for every little inconvenience you've caused me. I want you to beg me to stop. And when you do, I'm going to keep going." Franklin shakes his head. "You won't die tonight, boy. Not the way you think you will. This is only just the beginning of your end."

A different but similar man appears at Franklin's side, telling him something quietly.

Franklin sighs. "It appears our fun here will be cut short, as I have an urgent family matter to attend to." He nods to someone behind us. "Let's wrap this up and pick up where we left off later."

I watch in horror as he grabs Rosie by the hair, tilting her head back and pressing the blade of his knife to her throat. Everything speeds up and slows down all at once, the sudden realization that none of us are going to make it out of this alive.

And if that's the case, I am going to do everything in my power to make sure I take Franklin with us.

Franklin moves first, a twitch of his wrist.

I drop Johnny's hand, leaping away from him as my scream ripples through the air at the sight of blood on my best friend's neck.

Rosie's frantic gaze meets mine, and a loud bang echoes throughout the building. Chaos erupts, and with that, the execution has turned to a war.

63
JOHNNY

Gunfire, smoke, bodies flailing and voices crying out.

I duck and squint through the mayhem, desperately searching for the most important person in my world.

My breath catches in my chest. Where the fuck could she be?

My vision blurs, and a person stumbles into me, nearly knocking me down.

Their body hits the concrete with a thud.

I ignore them and continue my search, moving in the direction my soul urges me. "Claire!" I call out.

She was right here. Right at my side. Literally connected to me. And in one flash, she was gone.

In a matter of seconds, dozens of scenarios play through my mind, none of which diminish the panic coursing through me. The idea of something happening to Claire unleashes a tidal wave of fear unlike anything I've ever known.

I will rip apart every single person in here if a single hair on her head is harmed.

I shuffle toward the chair bolted to the ground. The one

with Rosie attached to it. The one Claire had rushed toward after Franklin drew his blade across her best friend's neck.

My heart aches. All I wanted was to keep Claire safe. To save Rosie. To get Claire far, far away from this madness and give her the life she deserved.

The shape of her comes into my line of sight, relief washing over me. I'm not sure if my feet have ever moved as quickly as they do, dodging every person and flying debris that comes my way.

I skid to a stop beside her. "Claire, are you..." But other than the damage already on her face, there is nothing physically wrong with Claire, just the terror raging through her as she keeps her hand placed firmly against Rosie's bleeding neck.

She turns to me, a helpless look I've never seen on her before. "Johnny, help me."

I immediately go into action, reaching across and into the waistband of Claire's pants, pulling out the small, concealed knife that the man who patted her down missed. I drag it along the zip ties holding Rosie in place, one by one freeing her from her restraints.

She collapses forward, Claire and I both catching her. Rosie drags her hands to her own neck in an attempt to stop the bleeding.

"Here." I tug the fabric out of her mouth and pull it down over her throat, then motion for them to put pressure on the wound again.

I barely get it in place before the entire building flashes with light and a loud explosion bows my eardrums.

"Fuck!" I throw my body over Claire and Rosie the best I can, shielding them from the debris.

Splintered wood and concrete chunks are raining down, and I look down to see a severed hand skidding to a stop a few feet from us.

A large figure barrels toward us, and I raise my arm to throw the knife in their direction.

Josey throws his arms up. "Whoa, it's me." He drops to his knees beside Claire, ducking when gunfire goes off near us.

We are surrounded by absolute chaos, corralling us in the center of this battleground.

Josey reaches behind him, drawing two guns and holding them out. "Here." He nods to Rosie. "I'll take her."

Claire meets my gaze, then Rosie's. She doesn't want to let her friend go, but she needs medical attention if she's going to live through this. And considering Claire and I are both unfamiliar with this kind of thing, it makes sense to let someone more experienced take control.

"I'll keep her safe," Josey tells Claire. He extends his arm and blocks a body from barreling into us. "But we need to go, *now*."

I can sense Claire wavering, resisting putting her faith in someone other than herself—other than me. It's her call, but I hope like hell she makes the right one.

Whatever that may be.

"Okay," Claire mouths the word, her fingers still pressed against the half-assed bandage around Rosie's neck. "Rose, this is Josey." Claire grabs one of the guns, hands it to me, and takes the other. She pushes Josey's hands around Rosie's throat. "Do *not* let her die."

An automatic gun goes off in the distance, and people scream and cuss and do their best to avoid the crossfire.

Cries of agony ring out, bullets finding their targets.

"I won't." He turns to Rosie, pressing his hand against hers. "Keep pressure on that, you hear me?" Josey scoops Rosie into his arms with ease. He gives us one final look. "Stay safe." And with that, he's off.

Josey only takes a few large leaps when a man appears from a cloud of smoke, a knife raised over his head. Josey pivots, missing the guy's first attack, but he's not so lucky on his second. The blade lands in Josey's upper thigh, nearly dropping him to his knees.

From my crouched position, I aim the gun in my hand, not wanting to waste another second. I pull the trigger, ending the life of the guy who attacked Josey in one fell swoop.

Josey lets out a muffled grunt and, holding Rosie in just one of his arms, pulls the knife out of his leg with the other. He tosses it to the side and takes off running toward the closest exit, disappearing.

Claire steadies herself, drops the magazine from the gun in her possession, examines it quickly and shoves it back in. She inhales, her gaze meeting mine. "Are you ready?"

There was a fierceness about her before, but it's been replaced with something deeper, something darker, something unstoppable.

There are infinite reasons why I love this girl in front of me, and each day I'm surprised to see more added to the list. The fact that she's prepared to go, guns blazing, by my side, is more than I deserve, but only continues to make my heart swell for her.

"Let's end this." I stand as she does and push my back to hers.

Together, we pivot and scan the room, looking for the one person whose death will end this nightmare.

The swarm has seemed to die down, quite literally. Countless bodies litter the floor, bloodied and tangled together in a sea of death and destruction.

Luckily, it seems Franklin has become too concerned with his potential sudden death to continue his pursuit of us. My only hope is that he wasn't able to escape when he had the chance.

A loud crack sounds in my ears and smoke flits from the barrel of Claire's gun.

Her target falls to his knees, then drops over. A straight, clean shot to the temple.

My heart picks up its pace. What have I done? What kind of world have I brought Claire into? Why did I ever think this would end in anything other than disaster?

"Over there." Claire catches my attention, whipping her pistol toward the largest section of people left standing.

I squint until I see a familiar shape. And then another. And surprisingly, another.

Franklin. Luciano. Miller. Plus, a bunch of people gathered around them, firing their weapons haphazardly.

Two large men rush toward me and Claire, malice on their faces. They bare their teeth and draw their guns.

"Claire," I spit out while raising my firearm, popping off shot after shot, securing our temporary safety.

The reverberation shakes my wrists, but I refuse to let it steal my attention. The smell of gunpowder and death fills the air.

I dash over and snatch their weapons, tucking one into my pants. "Here." I toss the other to Claire, which she takes without a second thought.

A commotion flows from the throng in the corner, and Franklin and his goonies bolt from behind their cover and across the room. Luciano steadies his aim, taking out one of Franklin's guys.

But Franklin's men manage to eliminate three of Luciano's.

Rage, unlike anything I've ever seen, illuminates Luciano's stone-cold features. He lets out a battle cry and takes off after his brother, Miller and a couple of others in tow.

Without backup, they're clearly outnumbered, meaning only one thing.

Franklin is going to win.

I rush toward the chaos, Claire like a shadow behind me.

Maybe Franklin was right, maybe it's stupid to care for people the way I do, but I refuse to think the life he chooses is the one more worth living. I will not allow anyone else to die at his hands, not if I can help it.

He has to be stopped.

Another violent explosion ripples through the building, dropping me to the floor. Bits of concrete rain down all around, and I do what I can to use my body as armor to protect Claire from the wreckage.

"Are you okay?" I scream at her over top of the ringing in my ears.

She nods, her eyes squinted to block out the dust floating through the hazy air.

I allow my gaze to float through the crowd, ignoring the blood all around. I grip my gun, firing a bullet and somehow landing it in the chest of one of Franklin's men. Another unfortunate sacrifice in the grand scheme of things. These types of guys will not be reasoned with, not with Franklin still alive. There's too much loyalty, too much hatred in their eyes. And for what? A pretty penny?

I was like them once, blindly following that same sick and twisted excuse of a human. But the difference between me and them is that I never would have gone along with this. Not the kidnapping and torture of innocent people. The slaughter of many with no disregard because of some personal vendetta. Because I *outsmarted* him. How do they not realize the error of their ways? Of his ways? How is any of this justified?

One by one, Claire and I bolt across the dimly lit battlefield of a building to catch up to Luciano and Miller and the only other guy left on their side. The five of us run to duck behind a shipping container and catch our breaths.

Panting, Luciano grabs my shoulder. "You're alive."

"No shit. So are you." I flip my head toward where we came from. "What the fuck are we going to do? We're outnumbered."

Luciano runs his hand through his hair, sweeping it out of his sweat-soaked face. He drops the empty magazine from his gun and pulls another from his pocket. "I'm out after this." He dips his head toward a few bodies nearby, to their weapons at their sides.

Claire stares eagerly ahead, waiting for us to come to some kind of decision. Whatever it is, she'll be on board. She wipes her head on her shoulder, and her tongue traces the cut on her bottom lip.

Luciano sighs, glancing at the few faces left. He lowers his voice. "We'll have to charge them. I don't think he'll expect it."

Franklin calls out. "Brother, are you hiding from me?" He laughs, a sick and twisted sort of cackle. "Just like when we were children. Strange company you keep, though."

Luciano and I exchange glances.

Franklin is still unaware of our connection, the reason for our alliance. He has no idea the line he's crossed numerous times in Luciano's eyes.

"Luce, let's call a truce." Franklin giggles to himself. "That rhymed."

"He's getting closer," Miller whispers to us.

"Brother, I have a bit of unfinished business with your friend there," Franklin continues. "I'm all for answering to breaking the treaty and coming onto your territory, but can we do it another time? This doesn't have to be answered in bloodshed, not between us."

"He's not my friend," Luciano grits through his teeth, standing up and stepping out into the open.

The three of us dart after him, our weapons drawn with our fingers resting against the triggers.

The smell of burning flesh and the taste of metal reminds me of what's on the line. My head throbs and a lingering odor stings my eyes.

Franklin raises his gun, pointing it at the man standing between me and him. "Then, you wouldn't mind me..."

"He's my..."

Franklin doesn't wait for Luciano's response; he simply shoots. He doesn't care about anything, or anyone, other than the stupid fucking vendetta he has against me.

"Son." Luciano's word hangs in the balance as the bullet pierces his chest.

My mouth drops open, my heart clenching. I extend my arms, catching my father before he tumbles onto the disgusting floor. We collapse together—red instantly seeping through his shirt.

Another shot rings out, then another.

I glance up, complete shock rattling Franklin's features, his men dropping like flies beside him. Claire and Miller take them out one by one with Franklin's momentary distraction.

Claire glides around like she's floating, maneuvering herself strategically as if she was an elegant ice skater, but instead she's a ruthless assassin. Really, she's just an angry soul, hell-bent on getting the revenge she's been hungry for.

For once, I'm not worried about her, because I know damn well she can take care of herself. Who I fear for is the man in my lap, bleeding out at a rapid rate.

"Johnny," he mumbles.

I focus my attention on him, pushing on the leaking wound. "Shh."

Luciano stares at me, and it's like I'm looking in the mirror. "I didn't know," he tells me.

"What?"

Luciano coughs and winces. "I didn't know. About you. I would have been there if I knew."

And somehow, despite all of my doubts up until this moment, I believe him, because in a matter of a few days, he's proven more to me than I could have imagined.

"You're going to be okay." It's like my reassurance is more for me than it is for him. I only just got him in my life. I won't accept that he's gone this soon. Bad things keep happening but this, no…I won't accept it.

Red trickles from the corner of Luciano's lips. He wheezes, blood splattering out. "It didn't matter that I wasn't there…"

I shush him again but it's no use, he's determined to say his piece.

"You turned out exactly…" His lids become heavier as he forces himself to meet my gaze. "Exactly the man I would have hoped for."

"Johnny!" Claire's voice pulls my attention.

She's standing there, the barrel of the gun aimed at the man on his knees in front of her. Miller is within arm's length of her, there in case she needs him, but not overstepping.

Franklin. The man I have been tormented by for way too long. The man who ruins lives. Who will stop at nothing to hurt every single person in his path for no good reason other than to fill his twisted desires. Who shot his own flesh and blood, his brother, because he stood in his way.

Who will now die at the hands of the most beautiful angel I've ever seen.

My fallen angel, sweet and fearless in all her glory.

"It's up to you now." Luciano's voice is a choked murmur.

"Do it," I say through gritted teeth.

Franklin's eyes go wide, his hands rise further in the air, he opens his mouth to speak, but it's no use—we're not here to negotiate, not with him.

And with that final command, Claire pulls the trigger, blasting a bullet into the side of his head.

The shot rings out, a loud and thunderous echo in the largeness of the open space.

Franklin collapses with a thud onto the floor, ruby-red pooling around him.

Claire towers over him, firing off shot after shot into his

chest, blood spattering all over her body and face, until the magazine in her gun runs empty.

I allow myself to see it through her eyes. To feel the liberation through her.

This would be the perfect moment to sigh in relief. To relish in this bittersweet triumphant victory. But when my gaze cascades from her to the man dying in my arms, I find it a bit too difficult to celebrate.

64
CLAIRE

Franklin is dead.

And I killed him.

I ended him, and honestly, the rush that consumes me is euphoric.

But it's also short-lived, considering the dozens of dead bodies surrounding us, and the dying man in Johnny's lap.

His father. Luciano Bane. Bleeding out and taking me uncomfortably back to the night of my birthday when Franklin ordered someone to shoot Johnny. I thought I had lost him then. The wound wouldn't stop oozing. The light in his eyes flickering until they closed for what I thought was the last time. If Johnny remotely feels anything like I did that night, I hate that for him.

I hate that he has to continue suffering at the hands of Franklin, even after I emptied countless rounds into his body.

It was probably excessive, but I had to be sure. Sure that Franklin had no chance of coming back from the dead and ruining Johnny's life any more than he already has.

I drop to my knees next to Johnny, helping him hold the weight of Luciano.

Miller drags his phone out of his pocket and pushes a few buttons, quickly putting it to his ear. "Immediate code eleven. I repeat, code eleven. Location incoming. We need all crews available." He scans the devastating contents of the building. "*All* available crews." Miller disconnects the call and clicks the screen again. He kneels beside us and takes Luciano's hand in his, flipping it over and pressing his fingers to Luciano's wrist.

Luciano can't be dead. I won't permit my mind to wander in that direction. He has to be okay. For Johnny's sake. If I force my thoughts on him making it out of this alive, it will come true, right? Isn't that how manifestation works?

When I pictured Johnny's future earlier, Luciano was a part of it. He played an active role. Fluttering in and out, sharing laughs and successes and making up for the lost time. A positive role model in this otherwise negative world. A sliver of good coming from this terrible situation.

But as the blood continues to flow out and onto the ground, I worry that my premonition was a false hope. A reality that may never come to fruition. Sealing Johnny's fate to be alone in this world, aside from me.

Except now he has Josey—a cousin he never knew existed. The two worked side by side in Franklin's organization and had no idea they were related.

And there's Bram—Johnny's found father. Now that Franklin is gone, we can return to see him once the dust settles.

Maybe Johnny can become Johnny again, just fade back into the person he really is, and put all the secrecy behind him. Behind us. We can go on and live our lives like the age-appropriate people we are.

Who am I kidding, though? This shit has changed us. And I'd be lying if I said we'd ever return to the people we were before this. I wouldn't want to, anyway. A darkness has taken hold and I embrace it for what it is.

Johnny's gaze trails over to mine, fear seeping out of him.

Our connection runs deep between us, giving us the ability to tune in directly to each other. It's one of the reasons we work so well—we can anticipate one another's needs.

This is something I'm not sure how to fix. I'm not a doctor. The only things I can handle are the occasional bumps and bruises Johnny stumbles home with, not a gunshot wound to the chest. I couldn't even help him when he was the one bleeding out in my arms.

Commotion draws my attention from the entryway. Countless people run inside the building, jogging in various directions. A trio approaches us and drags Luciano from Johnny. Two of them lift him onto a stretcher and the other cuts through Luciano's clothes.

I grab Johnny and turn him away from the sight of his father, near death.

The second Johnny's attention is away from him, he fully focuses on me. His gaze scans my frame, looking for any kind of injury.

I almost wish there was one so it would distract his mind from the more pressing situation—his dying father.

Kind of like how all of this has stolen my direct attention from freaking out about my best friend's slit throat.

I shove that thought away. I refuse to break down when Johnny needs me most.

Once Johnny realizes I'm completely free of any major damage, he reaches forward and pulls me to his chest. "Claire," he breathes. "Christ, you are brave." He says the words with equal parts admiration and annoyance. "Are you hurt?"

I shake my head against him and wrap my arms around his torso. "No."

Truthfully, I'm absolutely unscathed, aside from my prior wounds. The fact that Johnny and I are both alive, and Franklin is dead, feels like a miracle.

We did the fucking impossible.

We defeated Franklin.

Miller steps up to us. "They're taking him to Methodist Hospital. He has a room there, but it'll take a bit to get everything in order. I'll text you the details." He flits his finger at us. "I'd use the time to get cleaned up."

"What about...?" I wave my arm around us, halting my question when I notice the room is already tidier than it was.

Most of the bodies have been carried out. The weapons are piled into one general heap in the middle and cleaning supplies are stacked along the wall.

"Taken care of, ma'am."

Did Miller seriously just call me what I think he did?

Johnny goes stiff beside me.

I follow his gaze to the lifeless form that caused all of this destruction.

Franklin.

"You're sure he's..."

Miller and I both respond, "Yes."

Johnny seems to relax slightly, his body still rigid.

I take in a breath, steadying myself before I allow myself to speak. "Have you heard from Josey? Do you know if Rosie..."

Miller trains himself on me. "Josey would have taken her to the same hospital. Luciano has staff on call there. I haven't spoken directly to him, no. But if they're anywhere, it would be there."

Miller appears young, but he seems to have his shit together. He knows the ins and outs of Luciano's operation, and immediately stepped in when Luciano went down. If I didn't know any better, I'd say Miller was Luciano's right-hand man. But Miller is barely out of high school, that can't be true?

"Claire, Johnny." Miller looks to each of us, as if confirming that's our names. "You may have won your war, but this is only the beginning of what's to come. With Franklin gone, and Luciano hanging in the balance, it's only a matter of time until things erupt. The feud between these two has gone on for decades, a thick line drawn in the sand, with loyal men and women on both sides." Miller glances at the door where Luciano was carted out of. "If he makes it out of this, he's going to need your support."

A life I never wanted for Johnny: crime and danger. A world he has been desperately trying to escape since the moment he stepped foot into it. One that has nearly killed him on numerous occasions and put countless others in harm's way—including me.

We thought ending Franklin meant we could finally be free of this chaos.

In reality, it was the start of something much bigger.

Because who am I kidding? We can't walk away now. Not after everything we've been through. If there are more out there like Franklin, there's no way Johnny will sleep soundly at night knowing he could have done something to stop them.

And there's no chance in hell that I'd forsake the man who has done more for me than anyone else. Who has proven time and time again that doing the right thing is, in fact, the right thing.

He'll have his doubts, but not because he doesn't think he should offer his assistance, but because he won't want to involve me. His main reason for ever shutting me out in the first place was to shield me from any danger, to protect me. What good did that do, though? We were drawn to each other in an uncontrollable way, even when we both tried to keep our distance.

Where Johnny goes, I go.

I would follow Johnny to the ends of this earth, and I confirm that when I look over at him, his beautiful green eyes staring down at me, and say, "You're stuck with me, remember?"

He stares at me, a sudden seriousness about him, like he realizes for the first time that I really am here to stay. No matter what, I am with him.

"He's not answering," Johnny tells me from our closet. He throws a dark T-shirt over his head and pulls a top out for me.

I rush over, dragging it onto my clean body while letting out a muffled groan. Does this mean that Josey doesn't want to tell us the bad news over the phone? That Rosie didn't make it? Sure enough he'd find some way to let us know if she succumbed to her injuries.

Rosie was someone who never should have been involved. An innocent bystander that didn't deserve what came to her.

I sigh, realizing how Johnny must feel toward every single person who's been wrapped up in this nightmare.

I love Rosie like a sister, and that only compounds the rage inside of me. If there was some way to resurrect Franklin and end his life again, over and over, that still wouldn't be retribution for what he's done.

My only consolation is hoping whatever he faces in the afterlife is far more tortuous than what I'd prefer to do to him.

"Claire." Johnny plants his hands on my shoulders, steadying me and staring into my eyes.

Within a second, calm rushes over me. How does he have that kind of power over me?

"Josey probably doesn't have his phone. And I can't imagine he has my new number memorized. We're going, now. Okay?"

I study the way the green in his eyes swirls together with a golden amber. A dark fleck here and there. An even darker rim around the outside of them, nearly onyx, and contrasting beautifully against the emerald. His black lashes highlight them even more, giving a wonderful depth to his gaze.

My attention falls to that freckle I tried to scrub away many, many moons ago. The first night I saw just how vulnerable this man before me could be. I had no idea, but I was falling for him then. My heart had a mind of its own, tethering me to that beautiful soul of his. From the moment we quite literally bumped into each other, there was no escaping the magnetic pull that brought us together.

Life may have thrown us both some incredibly difficult curveballs, but it brought us to one another. We've fought like hell to be here, and we will continue fighting, because that's what you do when you find something this incredibly rare.

"Okay," I finally breathe.

We both have lives hanging in the balance, but at least we have each other to anchor us in place.

Johnny's phone buzzes, and he reaches for it without hesitation.

I look over his shoulder, the screen lighting up with details from Miller, the kid who isn't exactly a kid.

"You ready?" Johnny shoves the thing into his pocket and grabs the handle of the backpack containing a few essentials: phone chargers, clean clothes for Rosie, toothbrushes, change for the vending machine.

There's no telling how long we'll be there, and I'm sure Rosie will be anxious to get into something fresh that doesn't tie in the back. Although, if anyone can pull off a hospital gown, it's definitely her.

If she made it through Franklin's attack.

How will I even begin to explain to my best friend what happened to her? And how it was my fault? I've already been so fucking secretive about everything in an attempt to not get her involved, and here she is, near death because of it. Because of me.

It just goes to show that being open and honest with the people you care about is far better than keeping secrets. At least to those who could potentially be directly involved.

It'll be difficult, telling her the truth, but she deserves to know anything and everything she wants to help her make sense of the situation.

The drive to the hospital is short but somehow feels like an eternity.

Johnny grips my thigh in an attempt to settle my nerves and his own . He glances over at me every now and then, like he's checking to make sure I haven't evaporated into thin air.

My jaw stays clenched, my mind wild at the possible outcomes we may find.

We've already lost so much, and it's likely that the losses keep coming.

We pull up to the place where Miller told us to park, and a man dressed in black greets us. Johnny goes rigid, but recalls the text he received, telling him that a guy would be waiting to take our car.

The man holds out his hand, waiting for the keys.

Johnny plops them into his palm and rushes around to get my door, but I'm already halfway out before he gets there.

I cannot stand being this close and not knowing if Rosie is dead or alive.

We've been friends almost our entire lives. Surely I would *know* if she was gone. There is an empty pit in my chest, but maybe it's from the worry, not the result of this unfortunate winter night.

Johnny weaves his fingers through mine and guides me up the few concrete steps leading into the back of the hospital. It's private, secure, and totally what I imagined given our *criminal* circumstances.

The sterile air hits me the second we walk through the threshold. Bright, fluorescent light shines down on a single hallway. I grip Johnny tighter, the uncertainty of things becoming increasingly dire. Within a matter of moments, I will know if Rosie made it out of this alive. And in a few hours, the fate of Luciano will follow.

We walk the path, each step closer causing my heart to beat that much harder.

The entry swings open, my eyes taking a second to adjust to the empty waiting room area. My gaze settles on the man I slapped, the man who carried my dying best friend away from me only a little while ago.

He stands, meeting my gaze, a sad but hopeful smile written on his hardened face. Josey nods, telling me everything I need to know.

Rosie—she's alive.

65
JOHNNY

Waiting is the hardest part.

We've faced half the battle. Claire's best friend making it out of this with her life. But now, what will happen to Luciano? Will he survive, too? Is this what Claire felt like when she was stuck in a stupid hospital room, waiting for the outcome of my surgery?

Josey clasps my shoulder, forcing me to look at him. "He's a tough man, give him some credit."

"Yeah," I mumble.

It dawns on me that Josey knows this man who happens to be my father far better than I do. Luciano is practically a stranger to me—one that sacrificed himself by going into battle against Franklin to save my ass. He easily could have stayed out of it, not charged headfirst into that building, risking his life in the process. Sure, there was already a war between the two of them, but like Miller had said, it's been going on for decades; it could have easily waited for a few more.

His last words flutter through my mind—that he didn't know. That he wasn't aware I was ever created, let alone existed in the world. That he would have been there, had he known.

What would life have been like if I had an involved father? Would I have stayed out west? Gone east with him? Would I be like Josey or Miller? Would I be something similar to Luciano, or worse, like Franklin?

In a way, Luciano and I have things in common: our stubborn-headed need to do the right thing, and to help those that need help. The apple didn't fall too far from the tree on that one.

But why wasn't he aware? Why did my mom never tell him? She and I never spoke of the man who played a role in creating me, and honestly, I just assumed it was another one of the low-life idiots she hung around. I never asked questions, because I wasn't totally sure she knew herself who my father might be.

And maybe she didn't.

Things could have been so different if she did, though.

I'd like to think that Claire and I would have crossed paths at some point, regardless of what path we were on in life. I mean, hell, she lives in the same town as my father now. Perhaps we would have stumbled into each other on the street out in front of the café, and I would have offered to buy her a cup of coffee. Then we'd laugh over bumping hands while grabbing for the cinnamon shaker at the same time, and our love story would have begun there.

I would have found her, in any universe, in any lifetime.

And in each one, I'd know it was her with a simple look.

Even before we really knew each other, we were never strangers. There's always been this undeniable familiarity between us. Like our souls met long ago, and our bodies were only just catching up.

Claire is the part of me that I never knew was missing until she filled the void.

"Hey," she whispers softly. "Rosie is awake. Will you go back with me?"

There's this sadness about her that tells me she needs me; I can recognize it easily because it's the very thing I'm feeling, too. After everything we've been through, I don't want to be away from Claire either, not even for a second.

"Of course." I clasp her hand and follow behind the male nurse that came for us.

Rosie's room is right off the hallway of the waiting area, which is right next to the one Luciano will be in if he makes it through surgery. He's been in there for hours, and we still haven't heard one way or another if he will survive. I guess no news is better than bad news.

The twenty-something nurse holds open the door for us.

Claire tugs me along, rushing to Rosie's side. "Rose."

"Cla—" Rosie struggles to speak.

There's a bandage wrapped around her throat, and she looks like she could use a shower, but other than that, she's very much alive. And considering the alternatives, I'd say she's lucky. Franklin had no intentions of sparing her life, and had Luciano not stormed in when he did and started firing, she would have met the fate Franklin had decided for her.

"Shh, don't say anything." Claire drops my hand and smooths Rosie's blonde hair back from her forehead. "I'm so sorry."

The same words I've told Claire over and over for getting her involved in this twisted web of peril.

Rosie furrows her brows and tries to shake her head. She winces and pulls her hand to her neck. She sighs, clearly annoyed with not being capable of speaking freely.

"Truly, I never meant for you to get hurt." Claire lets out a breath of her own. "I'm so glad you're okay. That you're *going* to be okay."

Rosie's lips part, and despite her injury, she speaks anyway, "Are you?"

Claire glances over at me, and then at Rosie. "Yeah." She hesitates before continuing, "The man who did this to you…"

I place my palm on Claire's shoulder, a small gesture to let her know I'm here, that I'm always going to be here.

Claire straightens up, her jaw tensing slightly. "He's gone."

"Like, he escaped?" Rosie croaks.

"No, he's dead," I tell her before her panic sets in.

"I killed him," Claire confirms.

Rosie blinks a few times, soaking in what Claire just said.

Is she going to freak out? Is she going to be afraid of her best friend? Someone she's known her whole life is suddenly a killer standing before her. Will she be devastated by the news or will she understand, the same way I have for everything Claire has done? Every single brave and fearless choice she's made to take control of her life, to protect those that she loves.

In the time it takes Rosie to form a response, I can imagine the range of emotions Claire speeds through. It's the same I've experienced every time I've told her something that could threaten to break us apart. There's this terrifying uncertainty of how someone will react that makes time slow to a crawl.

"Good," Rosie finally sputters.

And just like that, the tension in Claire's shoulders relaxes, a feeling I know all too well.

Acceptance. Understanding. Insecurities being thrown to the side.

Claire grips Rosie's hand. "I have so much I need to tell you, but it's late." Claire glances at the clock above Rosie's bed. "Get some rest. We'll talk in a few hours, okay?"

Rosie nods, her lids already heavy from the pain medication they have her on. We knew she wouldn't be awake long, but it was enough for Claire to get her little bit of peace from seeing her best friend open her eyes.

Claire and I start to make our way out of the room when Rosie speaks up.

"JJ..." She stares right at me.

"Yeah?"

"Thanks," Rosie tells me, her expression and tone speaking a million words despite having just said the one.

She is a part of Claire, and for that, I will do whatever it takes to save her, too, even if it means risking my own life.

"I can't believe you did it." Josey shakes his head. "You two are fucking crazy."

Claire lays her legs across me in an oversized chair in the waiting room of this hospital. She keeps dozing in and out while we wait to hear something from one of Luciano's doctors.

It's like we're stuck in this weird limbo of not being able to be happy he made it or start the grieving process if he didn't. The uncertainty is fucking killing me.

Even Miller's nerves are beginning to show. The dude is sitting at the opposite end of the room, making phone call after phone call and glancing at the main door every few seconds.

"You're perfect for each other, that's for sure," Josey adds. He holds his leg and repositions himself, groaning a little in the process.

I tighten my hand around Claire's calf, pulling her closer to my chest. Claire's face is bruised and swollen, her bottom lip busted, but somehow, she's the most beautiful human I've ever laid my sights on. I still can't believe I get the honor of calling her mine.

"How you holding up?" I ask him, eyeing the bandage wrapped around his thigh.

He shrugs like it's no big deal. "Meh. I'll be fine."

"You took a flying knife to the leg, dude."

"I did, didn't I?" Josey chuckles. "Thanks, by the way, for saving my ass when it happened."

"Of course, man."

Josey sighs and leans back. "I never did care for him. Guy was always a dick."

"You're telling me," I laugh.

His tone shifts to serious again. "Franklin. Dead. Never thought I'd see the day. I'm relieved. Honestly." Josey lifts his shoulder. "A little terrified of what's to come, though."

I flit my gaze across the room at Miller, recalling what he had said about what would happen now that Franklin is gone, and Luciano is in limbo. Hearing it from Josey makes it that much more real.

Solving my one problem may have created a fuckload of others.

And that alone makes me feel guilty as hell.

What if Luciano doesn't make it out of this? What will that mean for his organization and for everyone that works for him? Will they be overthrown by Franklin's minions? Who will take over for either of them? Franklin had a wife; she was there when I petitioned to take Billy's place, and she was the only reason Franklin decided to take me on. Will she take on his responsibilities? And if she does, what will she think when she finds out I was the reason why her husband was killed? What will happen to Josey? Will he go home, or will he stay here? Why was he ever involved with Franklin to begin with?

"Josey," I say when the question strikes me. "The fuck were you doing working for Franklin anyway?"

Josey leans forward and exhales. "It's a long, very fucked-up story. Family obligations and shit. Ended up biting off more than I could chew, kind of got stuck there with him. But..." Josey rakes his hand across his beard. "Now that my Gram is on her deathbed, it kind of changes things."

Grandma? Oh right, he mentioned that's why he was out here. Does that mean...?

Josey shakes his head. "On my dad's side, not my mom's. By

the way, my mom was your aunt, if you're wondering how we're cousins. Franklin, Luciano, and Cecilia were siblings."

His use of the words *'was'* and *'were'* come through loud and clear. Past tense.

Josey must notice the way my expression changes because he continues. "Now it's just Luciano."

If he manages to live past the gunshot wound to his chest.

Miller stands from his spot and comes over. "Sorry to interrupt, but Josey, if you have a minute?"

Josey stays in place. "Yeah, sure, man, what's up?"

Miller glances over at me and Claire and then at Josey.

"They're family, anything you have to say to me, you can say it to them." Josey slaps me on the shoulder and winks.

"Very well." Miller clears his throat. "Who's left in charge on the West Coast?"

Josey scratches his temple. "Dominic, probably."

"Who's directly under Dominic?"

"Um...let me think. Cohen, Magnus, possibly Simon."

"Do you know if Franklin delayed any shipments while he was away, or if he carried on with business as usual?" Miller takes notes on his phone.

"He was dealing with some shit from up north. I overheard it before I left. Not sure if he squared it away or not. I can't imagine he would have slowed down for this. He probably thought he'd be in and out in a few days."

"Think you could give me a list of his known suppliers?" Miller stares at Josey.

It's such a strange sight. The two of them couldn't be any more different. Josey clearly has over ten years on him, plus at least eighty pounds. Josey is a large man, big-ass muscles, intimidating as hell. And there's Miller, this freckle-faced kid who doesn't look like he should be running numbers or making the arrangements for a café, let alone a criminal underground. Miller has basically taken over Luciano's operation since he's been incapacitated, and if Luciano makes it out of this alive, I'm going to suggest that he give Miller a raise. I don't know what this kid makes, but it's probably not enough for the work he's done. And if anything, I could stand to learn a thing or two from him, especially if I'm going to be living in this kind of world permanently.

"What can I do to help?" I ask him.

At this, he seems stunned. "You want to help?"

"Yeah." I point toward the motionless door. "This waiting game sucks. If there's something you need me to do, just tell me."

Miller juts up his lip, his brows raised with surprise. "Cool. Thanks." His expression has him looking totally his age.

"I do have to ask though, how old are you?"

Miller rolls his eyes. "I'm twenty-one."

Now it's my turn to be shocked. "Holy shit, no way."

He folds his arms across his chest. "Come on, get it out. I know. I know."

Here I thought the kid was maybe still in high school, and it turns out he's older than I am.

"You must have good genes," Claire chimes in.

The latest talk seemed to wake her up a bit from her dozing in and out.

My heart nearly lurches out of my chest when the door we've stared at for hours now opens. A stern-faced man with gray hair walks through, a clipboard clutched in his grasp.

I desperately try to read his face. To determine what he's going to say before he says it, in some pathetic attempt to brace myself for whatever the outcome is.

On one hand, I could be fatherless. The man I only just met could be dead as a result of a bullet from his own brother. I've gone my entire life thinking my dad wanted nothing to do with me or my mother, I guess having him in my life for a few days is better than nothing. He'll be dead but I'll know that I was wanted—that he didn't abandon me, and that he was a decent man.

On the other hand, he could very well be alive. My dad could be living, breathing, and still potentially capable of being in my life. There's so much left that we've yet to do. Endless firsts between a father and a son—things I never got to do with him because of our weird circumstances. There's still time to make up for all of the lost years between us. To take back what was robbed from us.

I hold my breath and wait for something, anything to rid me of this hell I've been locked in.

The doctor glances anxiously at each of us, like he's not sure which person to focus on for this news. "Mr. Bane did not make it through surgery."

He's *dead?* I must not have heard him correctly. Maybe the excessive gunfire and explosions fucked with my ability to hear, not to mention my pounding heartbeat thudding loudly in my ears.

I jump out of my seat, Claire joining me at my side. Josey and Miller stand huddled around this newcomer who wields more information than we do.

"He's dead?" Miller asks the question all of us have on our minds.

The doctor nods, a formal sadness on his face. "I'm sorry."

A collective silence fills the room.

"The bullet damaged his ribs and nicked his lung. We were able to remove it and repair what we could, but the damage was too extensive. We couldn't get the bleeding under control." He shifts his glance around again, still uncertain who he should be speaking directly to.

He continues to say words, but it all becomes a blur.

I reach to grab onto Claire's hand, allowing her touch to calm my aching heart. I didn't realize how incredibly scared I was to lose this man. I thought there was hope. I was sure that he would make it through this. That one day, this would fade into our past. But that's not how the world works. No, time and time again, it reassures me that bad things happen to good people.

My chest tightens, strings pulling and tearing at a loss so fresh. It was one thing when I thought he didn't want to be a part of my life, to think he didn't care. But to know he did, and to lose him, it hurts worse than I could have imagined. Tears well in my eyes but I force them away. I will not break. Not here. Not now. Not like this.

It can't be possible, but it is.

He's dead.

My dad is dead.

66
CLAIRE

Luciano is dead, and Rosie is alive.

I'd be lying if I said I didn't believe like hell that we'd all somehow make it through this unscathed. But the universe was not on our side, reminding me that only so many miracles are allowed to happen in such a short time.

Franklin is gone, no longer a threat to our safety. But our loss was massive. Not to mention, we unleashed a whole new world of danger into our lives. It might not be immediate, or lurking around every corner, but we are fully consumed in a world we thought we were going to escape from.

If it's the price I have to pay to be in Johnny's life, I will gladly go running into the fire to stay with him.

If someone would have pulled me aside a year ago and told me that this is how things would play out, I'd never have believed them. I knew things were going to change, that I was going to get away from Griffin, but I didn't think it would happen *this* way. I never would have guessed I'd become *this* version of me. The Claire that was always there, just under the surface, waiting for me to realize and unleash her.

This *"face whatever comes her way and fights for what's right"* kind of woman.

One that would manipulate and poison and shoot those in her path to save the ones she loves.

It's dark, darker than I imagined I could be, but it's me. And honestly, I don't regret any of it, because it got me to where I am today. If anything, I embrace it.

I glance across the room, my sights settling on Johnny, Josey and Miller at his sides. They're talking strategy on how to overcome the shit storm that is heading our way.

Within moments of finding out Luciano's fate, Miller went straight into executive mode, pushing aside his emotions and focusing on the task at hand. Johnny mirrored his hardened exterior and followed suit, and for the last few hours, they've been huddled in the corner of this dank hospital waiting area, discussing some kind of plan.

Worry courses through me at seeing Johnny put up such a cold front, but I don't take it personally. He's around other people, and I'm confident he doesn't want to appear vulnerable in front of them. The soft version of Johnny is reserved for me, and once we're outside of these walls, behind the privacy of our own, Johnny will feel safe enough with me to let his guard down.

People grieve in different ways, and I have to accept that for now, this is Johnny's.

My role is to harden myself into his rock, anchoring Johnny from spinning out of control.

Rosie sits in the chair across from me, the bandage still wrapped around her throat, but with the doctor's approval that she can get up and walk around a little. As soon as she got the go-ahead, she hopped into the shower in her attached bathroom and changed into the spare clothes I had brought her. They're not her style, but they're comfortable and clean. She was grateful to get out of that hospital gown, just like I imagined she would be.

"I can't believe you didn't bring me any makeup." Rosie cups her hand toward me and lowers her voice. "You didn't tell me how *cute* JJ's friend was."

"I told you on FaceTime, remember?" I glance over at Josey. "He's too old for you."

Plus, he is sort of a criminal. But aren't we all, if you really think about it? Mainly, it's the age difference. He's way more experienced, in every imaginable way, than Rosie. I don't want her to get hurt if she doesn't know what she's getting involved with. I've only been around Josey on a few occasions, I don't know him well enough to give my stamp of approval.

He did get her to safety and maybe saved her life. I guess he gets brownie points for that. And he gave Johnny insider information on that package situation. Okay, a few more points.

Rosie tilts her head to the side and deadpans. "Is not."

Somehow, no makeup, freshly tortured, she still looks like a supermodel.

Josey glances over his shoulder like he suspects he's being talked about. He winks at Rosie, turning around and focusing back on the boys.

Rosie blushes and starts to speak but ends up wincing, being completely taken out of the moment.

It feels wrong to even consider anything cheerful given the magnitude of the situation.

I shake my head back and forth. "Nope. Not happening. See, you're already getting hurt."

But if I know the power of love, if those two are meant to get together, there's nothing any of us could do to stop it from happening.

I settle my gaze on my own dark prince, the one I tried like hell to stay away from.

He runs his hand through his stubbly hair, growing irritated with himself at the lack of length.

"At least you can grow it out now," I whisper to him from across the room.

He probably can't hear me, but I tell him anyway.

Johnny pivots his head and looks right at me. He puckers his lips, blowing me a soft kiss and going back to the conversation.

Despite the heavy dark cloud over him at losing his father, there's a sort of lightness about him that hasn't been there before. A weight that was lifted from his shoulders. The burden of doing everything on his own is now replaced by the ability to count on others.

When I met him, he was alone. Relying on himself and no one else. He had Bram, but he kept him further than an arm's length. He didn't tell Bram the many struggles he faced, just handled them all on his own.

Since knowing Johnny, I've done my best to take some of that burden from him. To help him even when it's hard for him to let go. To show him that *sometimes* people can be trusted.

Johnny Jones is not a good man. He's a damn *great* one, and he deserves the same benevolence he puts out into the world. His soul is pure, and he is easily the most selfless person I've ever known. I am forever grateful that our paths crossed, and that I get to be his partner in this life.

He supports my hopes and dreams, empowers me to be a better woman. He is gentle and compassionate, intelligent and hilarious, not to mention, drop-dead fucking gorgeous. Most of all, he is the type of human I aspire to be. That everyone should want to be. He may be good at fooling people into thinking he's a bad guy, but his heart is big and when he loves someone, he gives it his all. And he will stop at nothing to make sure they're safe.

Even if he has to push them away. Even if he has to sacrifice himself for their wellbeing.

I let out a breath, allowing this new chapter to wash over me.

"So, what's next?" Rosie asks me, her expression solemn.

I take a look at the man who holds my heart, and the unlikely friends and family surrounding him.

Johnny holds out his hand, inviting me over to him.

It was only a matter of time before I was drawn back to him.

I grab Rosie's on the way, leading her out of her chair and over to sit with the guys.

Josey seems to gravitate toward her, cutting Miller off and sort of pushing him out of the way.

Miller rolls his eyes and moves to the other side.

Johnny meets my gaze. "We're coming up with a plan."

A memory of a scene incredibly similar flickers into my head: Johnny in the hospital, figuring out his move against Franklin. He may be dead, but his ghost still haunts us.

I repeat the words Bram had said that day, fully meaning them. "What can I do?"

Miller clears his throat. "Well, with the way things are, and everything kind of up in the air, I need to pull myself from the café full time. Which leaves it pretty much unattended." He gives Johnny a glance before settling on me. "I heard you had some experience in such."

"Waitressing maybe," I laugh unenthusiastically.

He isn't implying what I think he is, is he?

Johnny slides his hand over, resting it on top of mine. A silent but powerful gesture.

"It would be great if you could take over. You'll be trained on the operations, but you have some pretty solid references." Miller looks at me with a hopeful stare. "It's your choice, obviously, feel free to think it over."

I mill it around in my mind, coming to the same conclusion every single time.

"Okay, I'm in."

Miller's brows raise, a hint of surprise in his voice. "You are?"

I squeeze Johnny's hand. "Without a doubt."

"Great." Miller lets out a breath. "We can begin tomorrow, if that works for you."

I'll have to figure out how to factor in school, but now, without the pressing threat of hiding from Franklin, it should be simple finding a balance between everything. It's not like I haven't already done crazier things. The best part of all is that I get to do it with these people surrounding me.

"Yeah, tomorrow," I tell Miller.

Johnny nudges me to him, wrapping his arms around me from behind. He whispers into my ear, "I love you."

I weave my fingers around his, pulling him tighter. I tilt my head up to him.

He brings his lips down to gently rest on mine in a brief, but completely heart-melting moment of bliss.

"Get a rooooom!" Josey calls out.

Johnny shoots him a death glare. "You're just jealous you're alone."

Josey narrows his gaze. "Am not."

"You two sound like children," Miller adds.

Josey and Johnny both turn to Miller.

"*Sound*, maybe, but you look fourteen." Josey nudges Miller teasingly in the shoulder.

And so it begins, the comradery between these three. An improbable bond that will form because of circumstances I never saw coming.

Rosie remains quiet, as if watching our situation play out as an outsider.

"I'd like to ask something." I shift my gaze between them.

Miller perks up his brows, clearly the de facto one in charge here. "By all means."

"Given my new position, am I allowed to hire anyone?"

Miller blinks at me, allowing the question to soak in. "Well, they'll have to be vetted, considering our unique situation. I could imagine you would need the help. So, yes. Yes, you can."

"What about Rosie?" I point to her, totally putting her on the spot but not caring.

She's my best friend, the one person other than Johnny I trust completely. I don't see anyone more perfect for the position than her. I'm not sure if she's even willing, but she's mentioned to me before about finding a side-gig, making this an opportune prospect for both of us.

"She has my full support," Johnny confirms.

My heart swells with joy at having my two favorite people get along so well.

"And what are your thoughts about this?" Miller asks Rosie.

She glances at me briefly and focuses on him. "I—I'd love to help, whatever way I can."

"Okay," is all Miller says in response. A simple word, confirming so much.

I wasn't confident either of them would be on board, but I had to at least try. Rosie is my own right-hand woman, and to have her at my side during this huge transition, it would be monumental.

Josey grips Rosie's shoulder, "Welcome to the team."

She glances up at him, careful not to tilt her head too much, and smiles. "Thanks."

I think back to the three of us out west in that hospital room —me, Johnny, and Bram—and how none of us would have ever imagined *this* would have resulted from our half-assed plan to fake Johnny's death.

But the thing about fate is you never really know where it will take you until you're there.

Because never in my wildest dreams would I have imagined bumping into a boy on my first day in a new town would lead me here.

My phone buzzes from its spot on the armrest of the chair across the room.

Johnny steps back, giving me space to get up, a mixture of concern and confusion on his face. Things couldn't possibly get any worse, right?

Maybe it's a telemarketer, trying to sell me some extended car insurance.

The contact on the screen sets my heart racing.

I glance back at Johnny, hoping that looking at him will somehow erase the panic now racing through me.

There was only one other thing left in limbo, threatening to ruin us.

The lethal dose of poison I used on Griffin.

The whole room goes silent, as if sensing the new danger.

I swallow the lump in my throat, click the green button, and drag the receiver to my ear. "Hello."

"Miss Cooper. This is Officer Donovan. How are you?" His usual formalities.

I force myself not to stammer. "I'm fine. You?" I keep my eyes trained on Johnny's.

"I'm well." His tone immediately shifts. "Listen, I don't want to take up any more of your time than I already have, but I wanted to call and let you know."

Oh God, this is it. He's going to warn me that the authorities are on their way. Or that they're starting an investigation based on the chemical they found dancing around Griffin's bloodstream. That it wasn't *complications* and something much crazier that happened. That Griffin didn't die from an accident, that he was murdered.

I force the thought of being taken from this group of people before me away.

Even if the eye drops showed up, surely what's left of Luciano's organization is powerful enough to help me make this go away.

But that would be wrong. I killed Griffin. And I deserve to face the consequences that come from taking his life into my own hands. I've already shed enough blood.

"It appears I was correct in my preliminary assessment." A bit of static comes through Donovan's end. "Griffin Thomas died as a result of his injuries. His heart gave out."

His heart. The thing that the poison impacts. It causes a decreased heart rate and lowers the pressure, eventually killing a person if the dose is large enough and it goes untreated.

I did, in fact, kill Griffin. It just went completely undetected, like I had planned all along.

"Anyway, I know this experience has been traumatic, and I do regret that I was unable to get the justice that you and many others deserved."

Little does he know I got it for all of us.

"Miss Cooper, are you still there?"

I blink, throwing myself back into reality. "Yes, sorry."

"No worries. I understand this is a shock. If there's anything I can do, feel free to reach out."

"Of course. Thank you."

"Take care, Miss Cooper."

"You, too."

And with that, the line disconnects, severing the last major uncertainty in my life.

Johnny makes his way to me within a second, his hands gripping my face. "What did he say?"

I should have thought to put it on speakerphone, but then I'd have to explain the entire situation, and I think my best friend has had enough of me being a murderer for one day.

"It was complications. He died from complications."

A new wave of relief crashes over me.

Ever since Donovan told me there would be an autopsy, I feared that I would be found out. That the poison would be uncovered, and that eventually, they would trace it back to me.

It wasn't getting in trouble that scared me, it was the thought of losing Johnny. The idea that my actions would be unforgivable and that they would take me away from him permanently.

But now, with the confirmation that they went undetected, I realize nothing is standing between us. We defied the odds stacked against us, overcoming things that threatened to break us apart. Time after time, we have been thrown into impossible situations, and somehow, we fought through the darkness and found the light. We never gave up, even when our backs were against the wall.

Only proving that no matter what, we will make it through, and we will do so together.

We are stronger as a team, as one.

"You had me worried there for a second." Johnny runs his thumbs gently along my cheeks. "I thought I was going to lose you, too."

A smile breaks across my beaten face, and despite my heart breaking for this tortured man in front of me, I remind him that I'm here to stay. "You're stuck with me, remember?"

EPILOGUE – JOHNNY

I flinch when a knock rattles the front door to our apartment.

Claire stops writing in her notebook and glances toward it. She's in a mad dash to get caught up on her college assignments if she wants to pass this semester. It wouldn't be the first time she's pulled off that kind of miracle, leaving me with no doubts she'll do it this time, too.

It's only been a week since the war with Franklin, but we're both clearly still on edge. The intensity of the situation hasn't worn off, and despite the immediate threat being eliminated, there's that lingering worry that remains.

"I'll get it," I tell her as I stand and make my way over toward it.

Glancing through the peephole, I catch Miller flipping his head both ways, eyeing the hallway while he anxiously waits for me to answer. A short man in a business suit at his side, a binder in his hands, a pair of black-rimmed glasses on his face.

I open the door, shifting my focus between them. "What's this about?"

"Mr. Jones." The guy holds his hand out toward me. "Bruce Green."

I hesitate, not really sure what the hell is going on.

"I'm here on behalf of Mr. Bane's estate management team."

I finally take Bruce's palm into mine and give it a firm shake. "Oh, right. Come on in."

Claire jumps up from her spot on the couch and moves toward the kitchen. "Can I get you anything to drink?"

Bruce shakes his head. "No, I won't be long, thank you."

Claire continues on her task anyway, grabbing four glasses and filling them with water. She carries them over and sets them down in front of each of us at the table. "Just in case."

"Thanks," Bruce says politely.

"You hungry?" she asks Miller, who in the short amount of time we've known him has become like a sibling to us.

Another addition to our strange found family.

"Maybe in a little bit," he tells her.

Claire settles into the seat beside me, sliding her fingers around mine in a subtle but powerful gesture. She knows how much I hate uncertainty, and this situation is bursting with it.

Bruce carefully unclips the tie around his binder, flipping it open and skimming the edge until he settles on a blue tab. "Mr. Jones." His gaze skims the page. "As the beneficiary for one Luciano Bane, you are entitled to the majority of Mr. Bane's assets."

My heart skips a beat and then thuds loudly. Did I just hear him correctly?

Beneficiary? Assets?

I swallow the lump rising in my throat.

My mouth drops open, but I find myself unable to speak.

"I'll provide you with a list to encompass the entirety of your inheritance, including, but not limited to, Bane's Café, the penthouse on Water Street, Front Street, and Walnut Avenue, Loose Change Laundry, and numerous other enterprises. You will also be taking over his…" Bruce stops to turn his attention toward me, lowering his glasses to get a better look. "Less official ventures."

This can't be true. I must have died back in that warehouse and this is some weird afterlife.

"Mr. Bane gave specific instructions that one Samuel Miller would be staying on with a salaried position to be your…" He runs his finger down the page to find the exact wordage. "Advisor." Bruce pauses. "Miller was also given a piece of real estate, a vehicle from Mr. Bane's collection, and a sum of cash."

Miller and I lock eyes briefly.

"Josey got the same, too," Miller adds. "He's part of your advisory board." He glances toward the door. "He should be here soon, actually, he just had to pick Rosie up first."

"Miss Claire Cooper?" Bruce turns to Claire, snapping me out of my stupor at the mention of her name.

"Yes," she confirms with a bit of a question mark in her tone.

"Mr. Bane left you money, too, with the instruction to use it for your tuition, and then the rest at your own discretion." Bruce flits his gaze at me. "And gave you co-ownership of Bane's Café, with Mr. Jones."

Claire releases my hand and points to the page he's getting his information from. "That must be some mistake." She shakes her head. "I don't need anything. That's…"

Bruce puts his palm in the air to stop her. "I don't determine these affairs, and I'm unable to make changes to them. I'm just the guy who gets to divvy them out. What you choose to do with them is up to you, but I must respect Mr. Bane's wishes and follow through with his estate plan."

Claire and I share the same thought process.

I did nothing to deserve any of this. I only knew this man a week, and he left basically his entire fortune to me? There had to be someone else in his life that this could have gone to. Hell, he and Miller had a better relationship than we did, why didn't he get all of Luciano's stuff? I was practically a stranger that shared the same DNA.

Luciano's final words cross into my mind. There was such sadness in his eyes when he told me he didn't know. That he would have been there if he did. Maybe this was his way of making sure I knew that he meant those words. That regardless of when our paths intersected, he would always be looking out for me.

I tilt my head toward Claire, disbelief wrecking both of our features.

The bruising on her face has nearly faded into a pale green that is easily covered up by a little bit of makeup. The cut on her lip has scabbed over, and will more than likely leave a lasting scar, a forever reminder of the day she was almost taken from me. Her brow and cheek have healed nicely, and with some extra care, may continue until they're good as new. The only remnants of them being the brutal memory that will never leave me.

But with every mark on both of us, the realization that we made it through, that despite everything that's happened, we're still here today.

Together.

Six months have passed since Luciano left us, and finally, Claire and I get the chance to do something we've been dying to do the second we broke free from Franklin.

I pull our black Audi into a parking spot across the street from our destination and hop out to open Claire's door. I scan the vicinity, disallowing any negative feelings to come rushing in at being near a place that caused so much trauma.

"My lady," I tell her.

"Why, thank you," Claire beams back.

We hold each other's hands tightly, the sun cascading down on our skin.

It's much hotter than I remember, especially after spending the winter out east. Now, it's the dead of summer, and the sun is making damn sure we're aware of it.

I reach toward the handle, gripping it firmly and grinning at Claire.

The bell on the door does that familiar dinging I've heard a million times before.

I breathe in the scent of home—a mixture of coffee and freshly baked muffins. A smell that could never be replicated, that is reserved for one place and one place alone.

"Sit wherever you want," a waitress tells us from a few tables down. She goes to work dumping the remaining plates into her plastic dishpan.

Claire makes her way straight to the counter, disregarding the odd looks she gets from a couple in a booth, and flips up the partition to step behind it. She holds it for me and I slide in after her.

Just then, the door to the kitchen swings open, a tall, gray-haired man appearing in front of us.

A mixture of shock, surprise, and then complete joy washes over him and into me.

His mouth drops open, and he reaches his arms out to envelop us both.

"Bram," I sigh.

He sniffles and continues to hug us tightly, despite the scene we must be causing.

"Johnny, Claire." Bram finally lets go. A bit of concern flits across his face. "Is everything okay?"

"Yeah," I breathe.

I'd be lying if I said life was easy, because taking over numerous businesses, properties, employees, and essentially stepping into the expensive wingtips of the powerful Luciano

Bane has been a huge fucking challenge, but along with it, a sense of security to go with that risk.

And I mean literally, I have a security detail now that pretty much shadows my every move. Claire has one, too, as do Josey and Miller, and even Rosie. Basically, every vital member of Luciano's legacy. The wrath of Franklin didn't stop when he did, because his death caused a series of events to take place, throwing his entire organization into utter chaos and sending various threats our way. For the most part, it's been stabilized, at least enough that we could finally break away and visit someone who played such a huge role in shaping me into the man I am today.

"Here." Bram reaches for the nearby pot of coffee. He points toward the booth in the corner, the one me and Claire pretty much claimed as our own during our time here. "Go sit." He shoves us back through the way we came and motions for the waitress who greeted us. "Three cups, a shaker of cinnamon, and a half dozen blueberry old-fashioneds."

Claire and I slide in next to each other, our backs against the wall so we can scope out the diner, a habit that has only continued to intensify with each passing day.

Bram joins us a second later, the petite waitress on his heels.

He waits for her to finish setting the mugs on the table to speak. Bram sighs. "I can't believe it."

Claire puts a dash of cinnamon in both of our coffees before stirring them. She nudges the one toward me and looks at the bright-eyed man across from her. "We missed you, Bram."

"The feeling is mutual." He fidgets with his spoon. "I was so damn worried about you two." His serious gaze cuts right through me.

I fucking hated leaving him the way I did. He had done so much for me, and I thanked him by disappearing into thin air, barely holding onto my life. I can only imagine the endless possibilities that ran through his mind and the countless times he must have thought the worst had happened.

I became a ghost, one that was hiding from a man that tried to kill me. I had given Bram close to nothing to hang on to, other than the weak possibility that if I was ever able, I would reach out to let him know I was okay. I couldn't risk contacting him after I had left, because there was no telling the lengths Franklin had gone through to keep tabs on me. I needed Franklin to assume that all Bram was to me was the dude who owned the coffee shop I liked to frequent. If he knew anything else, he would use it against me, just like he did with Claire, and with Rosie.

I couldn't protect Bram from two thousand miles away, so I did what I had to do to keep him in the dark. The less he knew, the better.

I reach across the table, resting my hand on his and forcing his gaze. "I'm sorry."

Bram's eyes glisten and he lets out a breath of air. "You have nothing to apologize for. I understand."

A father's love is unconditional, and I may have lost the man who brought me into this world, but the man sitting in front of me is more of a dad than I ever deserved.

The waitress sets a plate full of donuts on the table, pulling us out of our bittersweet moment. "Can I get you anything else?" She seems to notice all too late that she interrupted something. "Or I can come back?"

Bram wipes at his eye and forces a smile. "What do you say? You two kids hungry?"

Claire sets down her cup. "I could go for a stack of blue and a side of B."

Bram points his finger at me. "How about you?"

"Sure," I grin. "For old times' sake."

"Three orders, please," Bram tells the girl.

I take a long sip of my coffee, savoring the perfect combo of bitter and bold with a hint of spice. "Still the best cup of joe around."

And it's the truth. Even being part-owner of a café, our roast will never compare. There's just something about being at home that makes things that much better.

"One more stop, then we can get going," I tell Claire.

Our time out west is drawing to a close. We only had a limited window, but we had to make the most of it. Visiting Bram was a given, something that was well overdue, but the last thing I have planned is a bit of a secret.

"We're going to miss our flight," Claire whines.

I tilt my head at her. "It's a private jet, it can wait."

Claire scratches at the blindfold around her eyes, and for a second, I think she's trying to look.

"No peeking," I remind her as I pull over and park our West Coast car.

I jump out and open her door, grabbing her hand and guiding her blindly out. I punch the code into the gate, watching the light illuminate green, granting us entry.

"Um, was that what I think it was?"

Can't get anything past Claire.

"Maybe, maybe not."

I take in a breath, glancing around to make sure everything is in place. String lights float like stars across the courtyard, dozens of candles illuminate the darkness, and flower petals gild the paved ground we stand on.

"Claire." I gently remove her blindfold and pat down her hair.

My heart thuds with anxious energy. The choice I'm about to give her—the one that could make or break everything.

Claire blinks to adjust her vision, taking in the spectacle I've made. She brings her hand to her chest. "Johnny."

"It was right here"—I point to the spot we're standing in—"when I saw you for the first time. One of the darkest periods of my life, and an angel literally dropped right in my path. My soul knew before my mind did that you would be the person to guide me through. I was stubborn, stupid, and I tried like hell to push you away. To protect you. But the universe had a different plan. It was over there"—I point to the picnic table at the far end—"that I got the privilege to spend time with you, to get to know you, to see what a brilliant and wonderful person you are."

"J..."

"It was there"—I point to the rooftop access that no one uses—"that I shared with you the pieces of me that I had never shared with another. I was so scared of losing you, but I knew I had to give you the option to walk away, that you deserved to decide for yourself." I let out a small chuckle. "You accepted me without question, which led to the most insane first kiss ever."

Claire blushes, and I run my hand through my hair, grateful at the length that's growing back.

"This building is home to some of our best and worst memories. But without them, Claire, it wouldn't have brought us here, to this one. And maybe that path was a little jagged, but I am eternally grateful for whatever force brought us together." I drop down onto one knee, the light from overhead twinkling in my face. "Claire, would you do me the great honor of allowing me to be your husband?" Opening up the small black case, I finish my speech.

"Will you marry me?"

I've given her a choice numerous times before, and each one, I thought the uncertainty of her response would drive me insane. But it's nothing compared to the fear I feel right now. I know with all of my heart that Claire loves me, but there's still the slightest chance that she might change her mind about being forever hooked to my wagon.

Claire cups her hands over her mouth, tears springing from her eyes. She bobs her head up and down, her brown waves dangling along her bare shoulders.

My heart nearly jumps out of my chest.

"Is that a yes?" I fight to hide my excitement.

She reaches down to grip onto my face, pulling me up to her. "Yes, a million times over, yes." Claire presses her lips to mine, smiling and laughing and kissing me all at once. "Of course, I'll marry you. Are you really second-guessing that?"

I wrap my arm around her waist, picking her up and spinning her in a circle. I gently lower her to the ground, the petals dancing near us. Sliding the ring out of the box and onto her finger, I didn't think it was possible to be any happier than I already was, but each day with Claire only continues to remind me that even in the darkest of times, if you look for it, there is light.

Claire, my sweet and destructive angel, you are mine.

Want to know what happens in the aftermath of Franklin's demise? Curious who could take control of the West Coast next? Join June, the seductive take-no-shit vixen, and her brutal mafia men in *Untamed Vixen,* a dark mafia reverse harem romance set following the events of *Broken Like You.*

ACKNOWLEDGMENTS

Every book I write, I seem to go on a journey with my characters. One of growth and change and evolution. I shed layers of myself and uncover parts of me I didn't know existed. This one was no different. It was an absolute honor to tell the beautiful and broken story of Johnny and Claire, and I am thrilled that you came along with us for the ride.

This book would not be possible without a handful of absolutely incredible women.

Sam and Michelle, what would I do without you? Thank you both for sharing my love of bad boys and being advocates for my books.

Tiffany, Tori, Cassie—this book wouldn't shine the way it does without you.

Victoria, you're my bestie, and I hope I get to keep you forever.

My tiny human—the reason I work my butt off, to show you that chasing your dreams really is possible in this soul-crushing world we live in.

My mom—I'm glad you finally found your prince charming.

My Patrons—for the constant support, thank you so very much for coming along on this epic journey. Clayton, James, Tyler, Michelle, Ashley, and Victoria.

To anyone who ever broke my heart—thanks for the raw material that makes my stories so damn real.

Finally, to my readers—those of you who have followed me

from my other pen names, and those of you who are new to me. Thank you for giving my books a chance, and falling for my characters the way that I have. This wouldn't be possible without you.

ALSO BY LUNA PIERCE

Sinners and Angels Universe

Broken Like You (Standalone)

Untamed Vixen (Part One)

Villain Era (Part Two)

Ruin My Life (Standalone)

The Harper Shadow Academy Series

(Paranormal academy reverse harem)

Hidden Magic

Cursed Magic

Wicked Magic

Ancient Magic

Sacred Magic

Harper Shadow Academy: Complete Box Set

Falling for the Enemy Series

(Paranormal reverse harem)

Stolen by Monsters

Fighting for Monsters

Fated to Monsters

ABOUT THE AUTHOR

Luna Pierce is the author of gritty romance, both dark contemporary and paranormal. She adores writing broken characters you won't help but fall for on their journey to find themselves and fight for what they love. Her stories are for the hopelessly romantic who enjoy grit, angst, and passion.

When she's not writing, you'll find her consuming way too much coffee, making endless to-do lists, and spending time with her daughter and cats in small-town Ohio.

Join the exclusive reader group: Luna Pierce's Gritty Romance Squad

Join Luna's newsletter to receive updates at: www.lunapierce.com/subscribe

If you enjoyed reading Johnny and Claire's epic story, please consider leaving an honest review on Amazon, Goodreads, and/or BookBub.

Printed in Great Britain
by Amazon

17390722R00319